D1006504

REA AND THE BLOOD OF THE NECTAR

REA AND THE BLOOD OF THE NECTAR

THE CHRONICLES OF ASTRANTHIA

PAYAL DOSHI

ILLUSTRATIONS BY BEVERLY JOHNSON

 mango & marigold press

For more information, please contact:
Mango & Marigold Press
hello@mangoandmarigoldpress.com

Library of Congress Control Number: 2020916711

CPSIA Code: PRV0221A

ISBN-13:978-1-64543-763-5

Printed in the United States

To Mom, Dad, and Norah

CONTENTS

CHAPTER 1

NO ONE CARES ABOUT BIRTHDAY PARTIES

Rea wiggled through her bathroom window and landed on the floor with a thud. She'd been spying on Rohan after school, trying to glean details about a game of cricket he had organized. A game to celebrate his birthday, but not hers. His own *twin* sister's.

Rea slammed the window shut.

It creaked hoarsely on its hinges and a trickle of water dripped down the yolk-colored walls, the blue tarp covering the roof doing little to prevent the leakage.

"It's the best we can do for now," Amma had said when Rea complained that muddy water had splashed on her head while she'd been brushing her teeth. Ignoring the incessant drip, drip, drip, Rea dusted the mud off her school uniform and shook out her shoulder-length hair. She'd been hiding in the bushes snooping on Rohan's friends, and several leaves had gotten stuck into her thick, wavy curls. As she brushed them out, Rea was thankful she hadn't come through the front door and risked her grandmother seeing her like this—there would've been a loud gasp and too many questions, which she was *not* in the mood for.

Rea grabbed a towel and wiped the sweat off her face. Anger fizzed within her, ready to burst like soda from a can someone had shaken. She couldn't believe Rohan didn't want to include her in his, no, *their* birthday. It used to be different, back before Rohan met his new friends and decided he was too cool for her.

The front door clicked open, interrupting Rea's reverie.

Rohan was home.

Most days, Rohan got home after she did, playing cricket in the street with his friends or grabbing a bite of chili-onion fries on the road, while she left school immediately, preferring to avoid any unnecessary social interaction. However, today, because of her expert (and time-consuming) sleuthing, they both ended up arriving home at the same time.

Rea washed the dirt off her hands with soap, rehearsed what she was going to say and casually stepped into the living room, which doubled as her and Rohan's bedroom. A soapy drama blared from the TV and Rohan, already sprawled on their frayed mattress, not having bothered to take his dirty shoes off, was reading an article on volcanoes from an old *National Geographic* magazine an inch from his nose. A plate of fried banana chips rested on his stomach. He chewed so loudly a cow would've been annoyed. On a normal day, she'd have walked right past him, but today she went over and cleared her throat.

He glanced at her; his eyes were hazel like their mother's.

"It's our birthday tomorrow," she said. "Got any plans?"

"Nope."

"Really? Nothing with your friends?"

Only because Rea had eavesdropped on two of his friends earlier did she know the truth: the cricket match was tonight, at midnight—the hour they turned twelve.

Rohan shook his head, licking the black pepper seasoning spotting the corner of his lips.

Rea narrowed her eyes. So, that's how he was going to play it. They might be twins, but they were nothing alike. Truth was, she hated having a twin. Everything had to be constantly shared or compared against as if they were two halves of a whole instead of two *very* separate, *very* individual beings.

Why don't you get grades like Rohan? Amma would ask.

Because sometimes I can't focus on what the teacher's saying, she wanted to say.

Rohan loves to read, why don't you?

Because I love puzzles instead. Give me one with a thousand pieces, or a mystery or quandary you can't solve, and I'll sniff out every clue the way I sniffed out Rohan's secret birthday plans. Rea seethed quietly to herself.

Rohan makes friends easily; you should learn from him.

Wasn't it easier for boys to make friends? All they had to do was play cricket and come up with silly pranks while she had to deal with the mean girls of her grade. That was *much* harder.

Rohan this and *Rohan* that. Rea wished he didn't exist. But he did. And he was lying to her.

"So, do you want to celebrate it together?" she asked. "It's not like Amma's going to throw us a party."

Rohan peered over his magazine. "Since when do you want to hang out with me? Besides, we're turning twelve, not two. No one cares about birthday parties. They're lame." He returned to his reading.

Rea felt anger building in her chest. Of course he didn't have the guts to tell her that he hadn't invited her for the match.

"Parties are lame, huh?" she crossed her arms. "What about celebrating with a cricke—"

The front door opened and Amma walked in. The pallu of her saree slipped off her shoulders as she bent to unclasp her sandals. She had returned from her job as a cook for a rich businessman.

"Rea, aren't you ready yet?" Amma scolded as soon as she saw her. "We leave in five minutes."

Ugh. The plantations!

Amma gave Rohan a kiss on the cheek as she hustled into the room she shared with Bajai, Rea and Rohan's grandmother.

"I can't come. I... er... have homework to do," Rea said from the doorway. Amma changed out of her saree and into her salwar kameez, which was better suited for picking tea leaves.

She came out of her room, her purse slung over her shoulder. "You can finish it when we get back."

"But I—I—Why do *I* have to work the slopes while Rohan gets to stay at home?" Rea's soot-black eyes bore into Amma's honeyed ones.

"HEY," cried Rohan. "Bajai has sprained her back and I have to be here in case she needs anything." He pointed to the kitchen where their grandmother stood by the stove. She was draped in a pale grey saree, humming happily to herself as she fried dollops of curried vegetables rolled in chickpea flour. The oil hissed and sizzled, and her tightly wound bun gleamed silver like the utensils around her.

Rea tried to swallow her resentment. Bajai had probably pulled a muscle. Although, it didn't stop her from cooking all day or obsessing about keeping the house dust-free.

"This is India," Rea told her time and time again. "There's dust hiding beneath dust!"

Bajai would stop for a moment, her grass broom held upright like a scepter. "Rea, these things are important. One can tell that a family is cultured when no film of dust sticks to their fingertip."

Rea sighed. There was no way she could get angry at her grandmother. Bajai was Bajai—she said the weirdest things and Rea loved her to bits, more than she did her mother and *certainly* more than Rohan.

"Hurry along," said Amma. "Everything with you has to be dramatic."

Rea scowled as she changed out of her school uniform. The only silver lining was Amma had pulled her and Rohan out of school for the next few days. At first, she thought it was for a surprise birthday trip! Then Rohan was told to take care of Bajai while she was made to go to the plantations.

It made no sense. Amma was a strict follower of the rules and had forbidden Rea from working the slopes on the sly for extra money (even though they needed it with Amma working two jobs), but today she was making her do exactly that. If the plantation supervisor caught Rea picking tea leaves, Amma would be in serious trouble. Only those over eighteen could work on the plantations. An almost-twelve-year-old, certainly not.

The more Rea thought about it, the less surprised she became. Amma had recently lost her third job as the Mishra family's cleaning lady, and with the festival of Diwali ten days away, they needed the money to buy sweets and dry fruits to give to the neighbors.

A twenty-minute walk later, Amma pushed open the gate to the Tombu Tea Estate. It creaked as it swung shut behind them. The sun, oppressive and scorching, shone overhead, soaking the hills of Darjeeling in liquid gold. As far as the eye could see, rows of tea shrubs unfurled like carpets, rolling high and low to reveal mist-covered valleys and the snow-clad peaks of the Himalayan mountains.

Rea dragged herself up the slopes. Her shoes itched. They were given to her when the Mishra family's youngest daughter had outgrown them. Overuse had nearly scratched out the logo on the side and the shoes were a size too large. Instead of giving them away, Amma forced Rea to wear them with two pairs of socks, and it made her feet sweat buckets in this terrible heat.

Hiding between the tea rows, Rea spotted others like her pretending to play while furtively helping their tea-picking mothers to get a higher day's pay. She hated that girls were the ones expected to help on the slopes while the boys never had to. At home, too, Rohan, got to play in his free time, which was always more than hers. If he was asked to help, he'd weasel out of it, saying he had too much homework to do. Amma never questioned him about it. Even Bajai would fall for his lies. "He's such a clever boy, our 'man of the house,'" she'd say, as she covered his cheeks with kisses and said that Rohan looked just like their grandfather, who neither Rea nor Rohan had ever seen.

Man of the house, pff. He barely lifted a finger.

Although, there was one thing Rohan had done that Rea cherished. He had taught her how to play cricket. When they were younger, they spent entire afternoons playing the game. That's how she discovered her talent for bowling. Oh, the rush of rolling a ball between her fingers, deciding whether to bowl with spin or pace!

Now, her blood bubbled thinking about how he had lied to her, pretending his birthday plans didn't exist. Sure, they barely spoke to each other; he preferred the company of his friends while she preferred to be by herself, but every year they celebrated their birthday together—it was the one thing that hadn't changed between them. Knowing Amma couldn't afford to buy them presents, they went to the bazaar and spent the few rupees they had collected on ice lollies, Ferris wheel rides, or platefuls of roadside momos and chili-onion fries.

Except this year, everything had changed. Amma turned doubly aloof and anxious, Bajai seemed old and a lot more forgetful, and Rohan had grown four inches, discovered girls liked him, and lost interest in finding out more about their Baba.

Rea wandered down the slopes until she found a shady spot. She sat beside a tea row, fiddling with the hem of her skirt. Lately, she'd been feeling like she was standing still while everyone was passing her by.

A pair of baby sparrows chased each other, their peanut-colored wings flapping to get airborne. Rea remembered how as kids, she and Rohan would play detective and go through Amma and Bajai's things to find clues about Baba. When they found nothing and she got upset, Rohan would challenge her to a match of who could spit the greatest number of berry seeds into a cup. Whoever won got to pick the cartoon show they would watch later that evening. When Rohan would miss Baba, they would dry balls of cow-dung into stones, and hiding in the bushes, fling them at passers-by. If one of them got caught, the other one would laugh so hard their bellies would ache.

"Maybe I ought to show up and bust his match," Rea said to a curved tea leaf. Not having anyone to talk to, she often confided in the tea shrubs. She had grown up playing amongst them, and thought of them as friends. She knew their scent, their taste, and the time it took a new tea leaf to grow and blossom until it was picked.

"Wouldn't the look on his face be priceless?" she asked the tea leaf. "Especially in front of his stupid friends."

Suddenly, an idea formed in Rea's head. She jumped to her feet, excited to get her plan started. *The first thing to do*, she thought, *is to pick a partner in crime.* She didn't want to show up alone. Besides, two girls breaking up a game of cricket was way more effective than one. Rea sorted hurriedly through names of girls she knew. But by the time her feet carried her to the bottom of the slopes, only one name came to mind: Leela.

Rea rolled her eyes. There *had* to be someone else.

"REAAAA?"

Amma's voice tore through the valley. She was frantically searching for her, her eyes darting left and right. The dust-blue dupatta of her salwar kameez fluttered in the wind, scattering knots of tea leaves from the basket hanging down her back. Their earthy perfume floated into the air, adding a dash of spice to the sweltering afternoon.

"WHERE ARE YOU?"

Rea grabbed a handful of tea leaves and ran up the steep slope.

"Didn't I tell you to pluck where I can see you?" Sweat dripped down the sides of Amma's face. It was October and the receding monsoons had left the skies swollen and humid.

"I was right there!" Rea pointed to a vague spot.

"I can't have you running off to wherever it pleases you. Not today. And what's this?" Amma waved a tea bud across Rea's face. The bud was hidden within four tiny leaves.

"How many times must I tell you? Pluck buds with two leaves. This is fine-picking season remember, not coarse-picking. If you don't pick correctly, we won't get paid."

The supervisor, a man in brown pants and a vomit-colored shirt with large sweat stains, was shouting at a newly hired plucker for the same reason. Rea wanted to tell Amma she didn't care and that she was welcome for helping her on a day when she had an extremely important plan to carry out.

"I bet Rohan is busy reading his stupid magazine and has no clue where Bajai is," snapped Rea.

"Why must you be mean to your brother all the time?" said Amma.

"I am NOT! He gets away with doing the easy things like being at home and looking after Bajai. And *you* always let him."

Rea's gaze turned icy. The blaze of the sun beat against her skin. "I want to go home."

"You! Is there a problem?" yelled the supervisor.

Amma quickly shook her head as Rea ducked behind a tea shrub.

"Get up. He's gone," she whispered after a minute. "Now get plucking and no more loafing around."

Rea stretched her neck to see how much further they had to go, and her heart sank. With so many rows to pluck, she was going to be here until the end of the day. Between then and dinnertime, she would have to leave the plantations, reach its foothills, cross Chowk Raasta, and get to her village where she hoped she could convince someone to join her for the midnight cricket match. That would've been hard enough if she had a best friend to lean on... And if Rea was honest with herself, she didn't really have a best friend, or even a group of friendly acquaintances to call on.

Girls her age were either obsessing over boys or grades— neither of which she cared much about. What she cared about was why Amma hadn't eaten the night before or who her Baba was or why a classmate was staring at her funny. The only girl who Rea had spent any time with was Leela. She lived three houses down and had a giant family. It wasn't that Rea didn't like her, but she found her exhausting at times. Leela was a free spirit—optimistic when times weren't good, excited to try new things, and too eager to hang out. It could be really draining and Rea had found herself backing away from Leela more and more this year.

Instinctively, Rea fingered the locket around her neck. Not long ago, she had stolen it from Amma's nearly empty jewelry box. Its silver edges had dulled with age and the intricate engravings of flowers on its sides had oxidized turning black.

Rea unclasped it and gazed at the charcoal sketch inside. It was the only picture she had of her Baba. He had died when Rohan and she were babies, and whenever she asked what had happened to him, Amma and Bajai evaded her questions. But once, in a rare moment, Bajai let slip that Baba used to call Amma 'his precious petal.' Times like these, when Rea felt alone, she turned to the dark strokes of her Baba's face. Through his eyes, she felt his embrace and imagined him smiling at her.

"Stop daydreaming," Amma hissed.

Rea hid the locket under her collar and gave Amma a dirty look. The supervisor blew his whistle. Another hour had passed.

"Amma, I'm tired." Rea huffed out a breath and let her shoulders drop. Most of it was an act, but the muscles in her arms were beginning to tense. "I want to go home."

"Stop complaining."

"This isn't fair. I saw Bajai in the morning. Her back looked fine to me. I don't care what you say, the next time I'm going to—"

Amma grabbed her. "Not another word, you hear me?"

Rea stared at her in surprise. Red squiggles had filled the whites of Amma's eyes and her breath grew short. The tea-picking women called out, asking if everything was okay, their bright clothes flapping in the wind like tropical birds. Amma broke out of her trance and she let go of Rea. Her gaze shifted to her hands and her fingers trembled.

"Amma, are you all right?" Rea asked.

"I'm fine. My only problem is a lazy daughter who does not

care enough about her family." She bent over the tea shrubs once more. "Keep plucking," she said.

At that moment, Rea hated her.

CHAPTER 2

ELEVEN PAKORAS

The whistle rang in three short bursts, signaling the end of the workday. It was half past five in the evening, and Rea's chance to recruit someone for her plan had long gone.

She and Amma huddled forward, making their way to the supervisor's office. They waited in line while the plantation women grumbled about the weather and the rise in vegetable prices, biding the time until their pickings were examined and weighed. Amma peered over the rest of the tea-pickers and frowned.

"Why isn't the line moving today?" she complained, checking her watch for the tenth time.

"It's *always* this slow," Rea said, irritated.

It wasn't like they were expected to be anywhere. Besides, if anyone should be complaining, shouldn't it be her?

UGH.

Everything annoyed Rea right now. Amma's twitchiness, her upcoming birthday, the chattering women, the stench of tea and the stupid mosquito buzzing in her ear. With a smack, she crushed the bug. Blood blotted her palm, and she brusquely wiped it on her skirt.

Amma slid the basket of tea leaves off her back.

"We should get a bonus today. I'm certain we've exceeded our picking goal for the day." She glanced at the sun. "If only we can get to the front of the line quicker. I wonder what's taking so long?" She tapped the tea-picker in front of her, asking what the hold-up was. The woman, chewing on a betel leaf, shrugged.

"Well, I stink," said Rea.

Without waiting for a reply, she skipped out of the line and ran to the public toilets. A strong whiff of urine greeted her as she walked up to the mirror, reeking of leaves, sweat and cow dung. Her skin had turned into the color of brewed tea and her black hair was bleached coppery brown from the sun. Rea made a face, seeing the frizz and knots in her curls. She scrubbed her face with spurts of water coming from the tap and by the time she was done, Amma was waiting by the door.

"Let's go," she said. "I'm late."

"*You're* late?" Rea reddened. "For what?"

Amma turned on her heels and started for home. She was walking so fast that Rea had to jog down the winding trails to keep up with her. One misstep and off she'd go, rolling head over heels down to the bottom of the hill. *Not that Amma cares,* Rea thought, sourly. Finally, they reached the main road and Rea was about to confront her when a cab driver narrowly missed plowing them over. The driver cursed loudly and whizzed his taxi past a truck carrying poles of steel.

It was rush hour in Chowk Raasta, a place where three roads met to form a junction, and it was drowning in a cacophony of whirring engines, whistling policemen and people yelling at traffic. Cars, bullock carts, scooters and jeeps waited in snaking lines. Horns shrilled, and clouds of exhaust fumes hovered. Hawkers selling fruits, toy planes, umbrellas, sunshields, firecrackers and freshly roasted peanuts in paper cones knocked on windows, singing slogans to tired passengers in hopes of a sale. Rea took in the scent of roasted peanuts. Her mouth watered; she hadn't eaten in hours, and her stomach growled. Amma would never spend the money on such a treat. Scowling at her mother's back, Rea eyed the peanuts. How she had to resist the urge to grab a cone and make a run for it!

As they hustled through the chaos, Amma kept an eye on the sun inching below the Himalayas.

"Stop walking so fast," panted Rea, turning into the gully that led to their village. A few locals walked alongside them, tired and wilted at the end of the day.

"Once we get home, I want you to stay inside with Rohan and lock the door. Understood?"

"But we never lock the door." Rea couldn't imagine anyone in their right mind wanting to rob them. There were things so old in their house, she'd willingly give them to a thief. "Besides, I'm going to meet Leela."

"No, you're not."

"I *am*."

Amma grabbed Rea's hand and marched towards their house. Brightly colored lanterns hung from their neighbors' doors and fairy lights twinkled, casting hued shadows over the darkening road. The village had begun adorning herself for Diwali.

"Stop!" Rea cried, yanking her hand away. "What am I supposed to do at home? Bajai will be watching her TV shows. Rohan will be reading his book. What do I do? Stare at the walls?"

Amma grabbed Rea again, more gently this time. "You can do whatever you want next week. I won't say a word, okay? But tonight, I need you to promise me that you'll stay home."

A sad desperation filled Amma's face and Rea meekly lowered her head. Together, they walked a few steps to a huddle of colorful rectangular houses. The town of Meruk was nestled over four thousand feet high in the hills of Darjeeling, but Rea's village didn't have an official name. Some referred to it as Tombu because of the Tombu Tea Estate that employed most of its inhabitants, while others simply pointed in its general direction.

Amma stopped before their house. She turned to face Rea, her expression inscrutable.

"Stay inside and lock the door."

"Where are you going?" Rea pestered.

"I have to work."

"Where?"

"Stop hassling me, Rea. Go inside."

"No. Tell me or I won't move from here no matter what you do." Rea buried her shoes into the ground, her final attempt at not surrendering.

"I have—" Amma glanced at the failing light. "I have to go.

The Mishras need me to clean their house. I'll be back in two hours. Now, *go*."

Rea wanted to remind Amma that she no longer had a job at the Mishras, but she knew better than to push her mother when the vein above her temple pulsed. Leaving Amma standing there, she slumped up their front steps.

The Chettri home stood out from the other houses because of its pomegranate-pink walls and the blue tarp that covered its roof. Even before entering the house, Rea could smell it. When Bajai was not sweeping, she was in the kitchen cooking, and the smell of food perpetually lingered. In winter, the walls turned cold, making it cooler inside the house than outside. To keep warm, they'd light a fire next to a patch of green Bajai called her garden. Although Rea had to admit, Bajai grew and tended to the most beautiful flowers.

Rea opened the door and stepped inside. She looked back over her shoulder at Amma. Her mother was standing in the street, watching her. Their eyes met, and she made an impatient gesture for Rea to close the door.

Rea rolled her eyes and shut the door, forgetting to lock it, despite Amma's orders. The next second, she slipped off her shoes, ran to the front window, and peeped out. Amma was scurrying down the road. Rea's eyes narrowed as her mother hurried in the direction opposite the Mishras' house. Something didn't feel right. Actually, a lot didn't.

Rea turned and sat down on their old couch, her mind clicking and spinning as it catalogued the mystery of Amma. She looked over at Rohan, who was still sprawled on the mattress on the floor, watching TV—he hadn't moved since he got home from school.

"Baccha, you're home!" Bajai said from the kitchen. She was enveloped in a haze of cooking steam. "Where's Amma?"

"She had errands to run. She'll be back soon."

"Very well," said Bajai and walked over to the front door. She drew the latch, locking the door.

"Is everything okay?" asked Rea. They only ever drew the latch before going to bed at night. But now both Amma and Bajai suddenly wanted it locked during the day. It was strange.

"Of course, everything is fine. You two blossoms are the world to me. You know that, right?"

Rea smiled half-heartedly. Bajai was acting weird as well, but she needed to focus on where Amma was running off to. Before Rea could think of her next move, Bajai brought out a plate of fried pakoras and Rohan sprang up like a dog awoken by the scent of food. He reached out and grabbed one, his eyes glinting greedily as he popped it into his mouth.

"Is it good?" their grandmother asked, a sparkle in her eyes.

"It's amaaaazing," he said, taking the plate from her. Without offering Rea a single pakora, he ate all eleven of them and burped loudly. "Oh, Bajai." He patted his stomach. "I'm going to sleep like a bear in hibernation tonight. Not even a bulldozer will wake me up."

Bajai chuckled and Rea scoffed. She knew Rohan's lies better than anyone.

Rea glanced out the window again, but Amma was gone. It bothered her how her mother could lie to her face and leave. Why was it so easy for everyone to do that? Rohan, now Amma. Did they hate her so much that they didn't care if she found out? She was practically twelve, not a child who could be distracted with made-up stories.

Rea decided, right there, if she wanted them to stop treating her like she didn't matter, she was going to have to stand up for herself. Today was the day neither Amma nor Rohan were going to get away with fooling her. But, first, she was going to find out why Amma was lying, and then later tonight she was going to make Rohan answer for himself by showing up at the cricket match.

Satisfied with her plan, Rea walked over to her school bag and took out the first notebook she could find. It was her history notebook. *Oh, history, I wish I could say I felt bad about this,* she thought, as she ripped a piece of paper from the last page.

"Um, Bajai, I need to go to Leela's house to work on a school project."

Her grandmother looked at the clock. Rea could tell she was about to say no.

"Er... Amma said I could go."

"Amma said yes?"

Rea nodded quickly.

"I suppose schoolwork is important. But be home for dinner. I've made your favorite egg thukpa."

Rea caught a whiff of the brewing noodle soup and gave Bajai a quick kiss on the cheek. Before leaving, she wrote on the torn scrap of paper, 'Meet outside our houses at 11:45PM for Rohan and my birthday cricket match.'

"What's that?" asked Rohan, craning his neck to see the paper. His breath smelled of pakoras.

"None of your business," snapped Rea. She folded the paper in her hand, smugly pleased that her response had surprised him.

Rohan watched her slip on her shoes and walk towards the door.

"Did Amma really give you permission to go to Leela's house? She told me I couldn't go out tonight."

"Like that would stop you," said Rea. "Anyway, I'm going. Are you going to tell?"

Rohan eyed her closely and then shook his head. Rea turned without another word and slammed the door shut. Her bicycle was lying against the wall of their house. She grabbed it by its rusty handles and jumped on. She had much to accomplish.

Leela's house, which was much larger than hers and okra-green in color, was a beehive of activity—the men chatted loudly, pots and pans clanked in the kitchen, siblings and cousins chased each other, and contestants on a TV show belted out Bollywood songs. Rea cycled from one window to the next. This was what it was like to live in a joint family. To have sisters and brothers to play with. To have aunties and uncles to spoil you. To have a father and a grandfather...

Diwali, the Festival of Lights, brought the whole family together but Amma didn't partake in the celebrations except in the customary exchange of sweets. For years, Rea asked why no relatives called on the phone or sent cards or dropped by for tea, but Amma's mood would turn, saying Bajai and her children were all the family she needed.

At least Bajai took her and Rohan to the bazaar to buy fire-crackers and rangoli colors. When they got home, Bajai would draw a collage of flowers outside their door and Rea would fill it in with the colorful powders, placing diyas around the house afterwards.

As Rea waited for Leela to appear, it occurred to her that they hadn't been to the bazaar this year and she made a mental note to remind Bajai when she got home. Right then, Leela walked into the kitchen, ate a laddoo, and walked back into her bedroom.

Rea snapped out of her thoughts. Urgently, she tapped the bedroom window before she lost sight of her, and Leela, visibly surprised, hurried over, her orange spectacles slightly askew on her nose. Before she could say anything, Rea slipped the piece of paper under the sill and pedaled off down the lane in the direction Amma had gone.

CHAPTER 3

AMMA'S STRANGE SECRET

The streets blurred past Rea in waves of sound and color.

She entered Haat Bazaar, a market situated in the heart of the village, making it the fastest (and bumpiest) way to get through to most places in Meruk. Looking for Amma, Rea whipped her wheels left and right, maneuvering her bicycle amidst cobblers hollering to shine and repair shoes, women haggling with sellers around pyramids of fruits and vegetables, and groups of peddlers calling out glowing descriptions of their wares: clothes, jewelry, books, pirated movies, and anything else that could bring them money.

A breeze blew, carrying the perfume of dhupi trees. People standing by tea stalls sipped on their evening chai as stray dogs rummaged through gutters littered with candy wrappers, banana peels and half-eaten fruits.

But there was no sign of Amma.

Dejectedly, Rea rode towards the exit. Between slabs of hanging mutton and sandalwood artefacts, a streak of blue flashed and the loose end of a dupatta fluttered out of sight. She squeezed her brakes.

Amma was rushing towards the market's exit!

Rea swerved her bicycle around, staying hidden behind the backs of locals. As remnants of twilight melted over the Kanchenjunga, a few street lights flickered on and Amma slowed her pace. She turned, disappearing behind a fringe of bamboo trees and entered Pokhriabasti, the farmers' village.

What is Amma doing there?

Rea followed, blending into the crowd, and watched Amma as she made her way through the shed-like houses. She moved as if she knew exactly where she was going. *How often has she visited this village that she knows it so well?* Rea wondered. Maybe she had a friend at the plantations who was also a farmer's wife? But the idea of Amma having a friend seemed strange. Much like herself, she preferred her own company.

What if she was secretly meeting a man? Rea's heart flip-flopped. No, Amma wasn't interested in that kind of thing.

ARGH!

Rea had lost her again. She scanned through the scattering of women and finally there was Amma with her dupatta draped over her head. Puzzled, Rea rode after her. Some Indian women wore their sarees or dupattas in that manner as a sign of tradition and deference, but Amma never did that. Hidden beneath the dupatta's embroidered edges, Rea could barely glimpse her face…

Just then, Amma stopped. Her shadow fell long and dark over

a shabby house. It was the color of the forest. Dirt browns merged into maroon-greens and smoky-greys. Paint flaked, exposing splotches of cement, and weeds grew from where shingles had slipped from the roof.

Muttering a prayer, Amma extended a leaf from a nearby plant and touched it to each eyelid. It was a ritual she performed whenever she was worried or nervous. She did it before beginning a new job or leaving one or when the bills began to pile up. Sometimes, she did it after Rohan and Rea returned late from school. It was the only superstitious thing Rea had ever seen her do.

A large stone well stood a few meters from the house. Rea placed her bicycle against it and hid behind the well. The village felt familiar. Before she could put her finger on why, the door opened and Amma slipped inside. A bulb above the curtained window came on, and Rea was startled by the sight of objects nailed into the outside walls.

There must have been at least fifty of them. Each consisted of a lemon and three green chilies pierced together by a metal string. It was a talisman to ward off evil. People hung them over their front door or on the backs of their cars or scooters. But never were there so many in one place. With a jolt, Rea realized whose house this must be.

The shed-house belonged to Mishti Daadi, an old lady known for reading the future by staring at a person's face or palms, Rea couldn't remember which. Every now and again, stories about her floated through the town, saying she had predicted a full harvest, or spoke of winning lottery numbers or healed cattle with a miraculous potion. Some thought her to be a saint, others an old woman who swindled money from the desperate, but most dismissed her as a harmless old crank. Rea remembered one of the girls at school whispering about Mishti Daadi. She said the talismans hooked on the walls weren't hung by Mishti Daadi; they were nailed in by those afraid of her letting out evil spirits.

Rea wasn't the brightest student in school, but she had a fairly good sense of the way the world worked. Mishti Daadi's 'powers' were nothing more than a trick. Amma used to say, "This world is full of people who say what you want to hear just to take your money." Bajai said, "Such people prey on the fearful and hopeless."

It didn't surprise Rea that people like Mishti Daadi existed. She was old and had no one to take care of her. She did what she could to survive. And some people were dumb enough to believe anything you told them.

What stumped Rea was that Amma, who didn't believe in such hoaxes, was inside the house of a fortune teller. For the life of her, Rea couldn't figure out why she needed her fortune read. Amma had once said, "If someone had the power to change fate, I would be first in line."

It was twenty past seven. Amma had been inside for fifteen minutes. A few feet away, a group of kids were playing hopscotch and Rea asked if she could join them. She didn't mind young children. They were easy—all they cared about was playing without any chit-chat.

As she awaited her turn, Rea hoped Leela would show up for the cricket match. In her note, she'd implied that the cricket match was a birthday celebration for both her and Rohan. Technically, that wasn't a lie. She and Rohan *did* share a birthday. As for Leela's cricket playing skills, Rea didn't care if she could bowl or bat. She simply needed the backup.

"Do people your age frighten you?" a female voice said from behind Rea. It was gravelly like a sore throat. "Or does your intelligence match that of a six-year-old's?"

Rea's heart sank. She knew that voice. She turned to find a group of girls from school, including the most feared girl in her class: Tara.

Tara was the self-proclaimed "most popular" girl at school. She was tall and gangly, her mouth caked in a cheap plum-colored lipstick. She was notorious for bringing others down with her unkind words, and Rea was often the target of her jokes. Rea's cheeks burned with embarrassment. She turned her back on the girls and flung a stone into the chalk-drawn boxes. Playing hopscotch suddenly felt incredibly silly.

"I have to go," she said.

The children whined.

"I'm sorry. I smell cow dung."

It was literally the most childish retort she could've come up with. Rea turned to leave, but Tara blocked her.

"This is our village," she said. "You don't belong here, *plantation girl.*"

The rest of the girls placed themselves on either side of Tara, resembling Ravana and his ten heads. Rea tried to push her way through. She didn't want to fight if she didn't have to. But the girls blocked her path, making it impossible for her to leave.

Turning to face them, Rea tried to think of an insult that would get them to back away. "Don't you have some potatoes to peel or boys to chase?" she asked.

"They chase after *me*," Tara said, blowing air on her painted nails.

Rea cracked a smile. "Sure, they do."

"You think you're so smart, ha?"

"You're catching on. Congratulations."

"Keep talking like that and I'll pound you into mutton curry!" The gang moved closer.

"Ooh, I'm scared." Rea stepped back a little, hoping they wouldn't notice. There was barely a foot between them.

"You should be scared. Or that hag will tell your Amma that her daughter's future is in danger after running that mouth of hers."

Rea stared, speechless. How did Tara know Amma was in Mishti Daadi's house? She hadn't seen anyone notice her mother and with the dupatta over her head, she'd barely been able to spot her herself.

"Maybe the old witch will ask for a lock of your Amma's hair and fat from her inner thigh and cast a spell on her, so she can finally find a husband and stop being such a sour puss all the time!" one of the other girls said.

Rea balled her hand into a fist. She burned with shame. Angry, hurtful words crowded her head, but they turned into a knot inside her mouth. She tried to speak, but no words came out.

One of the other girls (Rea couldn't remember her name) stepped forward. "Nothing to say?" the girl snickered. "Clearly, Rohan's the one with the brains in the family!"

Just because Rohan did better than her at school didn't mean she was dumb. Rea lunged forward and swung her fist, aiming for the cackling girl's face. The girl dodged out of the way and Rea's hand barreled through the air, hitting Tara on her lipstick-coated mouth. Rea's punch landed hard. Blood spurted from Tara's lip, dripping all over her chin.

"Pagal keti! You're going to regret that!" Tara screamed and pushed her to the ground.

The girls surrounded Rea and started to kick her. She bit back her groans, keeping silent as the rough edges of their sandals cut into her skin. Fury flowed over Rea. She wished there was a way to hurt them for what they said, but there was only one of her and too many of them.

"Lost your will to fight, ha?" Tara wiped the trickling blood off her face. A streak of purple lipstick smudged across her cheek. "You make a lot of noise with that mouth of yours but when it comes down to it, you're a phoosky firecracker—nothing but smoke and fizzle."

Rea stood up slowly. She stared into the mean girl's eyes, and then spat at Tara's foot. It missed by an inch.

"Try that again and you're dead meat." Tara raised a fisted palm. Then she lowered it. "Think about this, Rea Chettri: If we were to beat you up and leave, who would come to your rescue?"

Rea's heart beat fiercely.

"No one. Or did you forget you have no friends? You think you're better than us, but the truth is, *nobody* wants to be your friend." She stared Rea down, letting her words sink in. "I don't even think your brother would come."

Tara's sneer curled into a smile.

"Oh, did I tell you?" She turned to the girls. "He said I could borrow those books he loves to read whenever I want!"

Hearing them gush over Rohan made Rea want to puke.

"Oy, what's happening?" a farmer called out. He noticed Rea's bleeding legs and Tara's split lip and shook his head. "Chalo, it's getting late."

He waved his arms about, herding them like cattle. Tara threw Rea a scathing look and walked away. The man asked Rea if she was okay and she nodded. After he had passed by, she limped towards the stone well. Tara was right, she thought. If she were beaten up and couldn't walk, who would she call?

Rea stared at the countless stones lying on the mud road. What did it matter that Amma was secretly getting her future read or that Rohan hadn't invited her to his birthday game? This was her life. Nobody wanted to be a part of it. She reached to pick up her bicycle which had slipped to the ground—

Click.

The door opened and Amma stepped out.

In a second, Rea forgot her newfound acceptance of her life and ducked behind the well. Through the faint light of the living room, she saw Mishti Daadi, an old woman with wiry, white hair that fell to her thighs. Despite the distance, the red bindi pasted on her crinkly forehead ogled like an evil eye.

Amma bent to touch Mishti Daadi's feet in reverence and the old lady stroked her head. Rea shuddered, imagining her papery-thin touch. They exchanged a few words and Amma turned to leave.

Rea waited until Amma disappeared down the road before

mounting her bicycle. Speeding down one of the back roads, she headed for home.

CHAPTER 4

THE MATCH AT MIDNIGHT

The house groaned in the chill of the night.

After Amma had left Mishti Daadi's house, she came home, had her dinner, and forced Rea and Rohan into bed early. Luckily Rea had made it back in time to change into her pajamas before Amma noticed her bruises and questioned her.

It was well past Rea's bedtime and she could barely sleep a wink, not that she wanted to. She lay in bed, keeping warm under the blanket, most of which was taken up by Rohan. He tossed and turned.

At eleven thirty, the alarm, a black and white cat carrying a trombone, blared and Rohan quickly turned it off. He glanced at Rea. She shut her eyes and breathed evenly, hoping to trick him into thinking she was sleeping. He was convinced. Trying to move quietly, he got off the mattress, retrieved his bat and ball, put on his shoes, and slipped out of the house. When the front door clicked shut, Rea threw on a pair of leggings and a t-shirt and followed him.

A bald moon outlined the road with its milky touch. Leela was waiting behind a chestnut tree between their houses. Despite it being the middle of the night, her hair was combed into two neat braids. Rea hadn't bothered to look in the mirror. Now she wondered if her hair was sticking out at weird angles the way it usually did when she woke up.

Rea waved to Leela and placed a finger on her lips. If anyone heard them, their Ammas would be alerted and they'd be *Dead* with a capital D. Setting off together, they trailed Rohan at a safe distance. Every time he turned, Rea slipped behind a tree or stood stock-still. Leela, giddy with excitement to be included, copied her without questioning why they were hiding from Rohan, which was a relief to Rea. Soon, boys of all ages and sizes appeared from dark houses and joined the silent march. Rea felt a thrill deep in her bones.

Twenty minutes later, the party assembled at Scenic Point, a flat gravelly scrap of land that overlooked panoramic views of the tea plantations and the majestic Himalayas. But at this hour of the night, the view dropped into a shadowy abyss. Young lovers sat close, hidden under shawls or dupattas. A grove of trees surrounded the area, secluding it from the village and creating the perfect boundary line for the game. The moon dominated the sky and starlight shone—a twinkling across a coat of black—and nearby streetlamps provided backup.

Rohan glanced over his shoulder. Rea grabbed Leela and hid

behind a marigold bush.

"What's wrong?" Leela asked, confused.

Rea shushed her, waiting for the boys to finish setting up. In no time, they had outlined the batting pitch, built makeshift stumps with branches while using twigs for bails, and kept extra balls aside in case any got lost. They used tennis balls instead of the red-leather cricket balls as they didn't hurt as much if someone got hit. When they were done, Rohan, the captain, (*obviously*) dug out a coin from his pocket and tossed it into the air. Before it landed, Rea emerged from the shadows.

"We want to join, too," she declared.

There was a moment of pin-drop silence. Then a ruckus broke out. The boys cursed Rohan for inviting the girls and the younger ones stuck out their tongues, making faces.

"W-we weren't invited?" Leela's carrot-colored spectacles slipped down her nose.

Rohan marched towards them.

"What are you doing here?" He glared at Rea.

"We've come to play," she said, squaring her shoulders and readying for a fight.

"NO! You weren't invited. In fact, how did you even know about the match?"

"Well, those two—" Rea pointed at the boys she had eavesdropped on, "couldn't stop talking about it at school so I found out. Anyway, we're here now. Are you up for the challenge?"

"Please go home."

"Let's leave…" Leela said, tugging Rea's arm. Her eyes darted nervously between Rohan and the riled-up boys.

"I'd listen to her if I were you," said Rohan.

Rea's blood boiled. This was her *brother*. If no one else was going to be on her side, shouldn't she at least be able to depend on him?

"Guess I'll have to tell Amma what you're up to then."

Rea smiled as Rohan's face fell. He knew she would actually do it.

"Ugh, Rea," Rohan grimaced. "Why do you have to ruin my birthday?"

"It's mine too, in case you forgot."

A flicker of guilt passed his eyes, but he stayed quiet.

"Suit yourself. Can't say I won't enjoy Amma's reaction when she finds out what you're up to."

Rea walked away and Leela hurried after her.

"FINE! You can play," he said, and a shower of insults exploded from the boys. "It's her birth—you know what, she'll get us into trouble. We don't have a choice…"

The boys groaned, and Rea grinned, jogging back towards them. Seeing that the coin was going to be tossed again, Leela ran and stood beside Rea. Rohan's team won the toss and chose to bowl first.

"Both teams will play one innings each of ten overs with six balls per over," the umpire said.

"And each team gets one girl so both teams bear an equal disadvantage," Rohan said spitefully, and the others unanimously agreed.

Rea mentally cursed him, but soothed herself knowing they would soon be eating their words. When the teams were made, the umpire, the son of a milkman, whistled sharply and the match began. Within minutes, the rift between the boys and girls was forgotten. Both teams rooted for their players and booed their competition. Rea didn't consider herself to be a great batter so she sat on the sidelines with the rest of her teammates while two of their ace batters were on the batting pitch. Forty minutes later, the first innings ended and Rea's team had scored well.

Finally, the second innings began and the teams swapped places with Rea's team taking the field to bowl. Rohan and another batter from his team walked out to bat.

Rea took them by surprise with her bowling skills. She'd shake things up by throwing a spin ball right after three fast-paced balls. The batsman would get flummoxed and one by one the wickets started to fall. Her team burst into hoots, high-fiving and chest bumping her.

Leela held her own, too. She was the first one to whack Rea's ball for a six and they watched open-mouthed as the lemon-yellow ball soared through the sky, glinting in the moonlight and getting lost in the trees. Leela shrieked with joy.

An hour later, the match was down to its last over, the final six balls. The score was close. Rea's team was leading by six runs. Her captain called for a timeout and the fielders and wicket-keeper ran over, forming a circle around him.

"They need seven runs to win. We can do this, boys!" The captain was tall and athletic, his skin the color of almonds. "But I'm going to need a bowler who won't cost us any runs. One easy ball and the game is theirs."

Everyone nodded.

"Rea, you've been our best bowler today. This is your responsibility now."

Pride surged within Rea. She had earned her place in the team! Her teammates cheered, slapping her on the back as she took the ball from her captain's hands.

"I won't let you down."

As she walked towards the pitch, Rohan adjusted his batting stance. All she had to do was either get him out or make sure she didn't give away any runs. Rea spat on the ball the way bowlers did on TV, and taking her aim, she threw a medium-paced ball. Rohan swung hard but too early to make contact, and the wicket-keeper behind him caught the ball. He grunted like an animal, kicking in his heels. Rea bowled the next ball, faster this time. It hurtled towards him and as he swung at it, the ball nicked the corner of his bat, dribbling off to the side. Two fielders dove for the ball and missed the catch, but Rohan couldn't risk taking a run.

Applause broke out from Rea's team while the other team sat silent. Rohan took his stance again, chest heaving, and bat hovering mid-air. Rea let loose another fast-paced ball.

CLANK!

"Four!" screamed Rohan's team.

"Catch it!" yelled Rea's team.

"No ball!" shouted the umpire.

The ball shot through the air. Rohan's team cheered so loudly that birds awoke, chittering sharply. Rea's heart sank. She had bowled a no-ball by overstepping the bowling crease and Rohan hit it for a four. That gave his team five runs *and* an extra ball to play. All they needed was one run to tie the match and two to win, and there were four more balls to go.

Pangs of desperation hit Rea. Her teammates patted her, telling her to stay calm, to keep it simple. She couldn't afford another stupid mistake or the game would be Rohan's. For the next three balls, she altered with the pace and delivery. Unable to anticipate what she was going to throw next, Rohan couldn't make contact with the ball.

Neither of the teams made a sound. The match was too close. It was down to the final ball of the game. Rohan's eyes locked onto Rea's. He was expecting her to bowl a fast-paced ball. She could feel it in her gut.

As she ran the ten paces to the bowling line, Rea aimed the ball at his leg. When she let it go, the ball bounced in a slow, neat spin. Rohan leaped forward and swung hard.

The ball slipped under his bat and the middle stump flew out of the ground, the twig-bails twirling in the air like confetti. The umpire raised his arm above his head with his forefinger up in the air, signaling Rohan was out. Rea's team jumped, screaming and whistling as Rea stood still. They had won the match!

Her teammates hugged Rea and carried her on their shoulders. The night air danced around her. The stars dazzled like crystals. When the boys lowered her, Rohan and his teammates slumped towards their belongings, packing up to go home.

"I'm sure you'll do better next time," Rea said, tossing Rohan a ball. He hesitated for a fraction, but his reflexes kicked in as the ball reached him, and he caught it.

"See, getting better already!"

Rohan turned away. He picked up his bat and tennis ball and headed down the road.

"Hey," she called out. "Happy birthday!"

Rohan's shoulders tightened, but he didn't turn around. Giggling, Rea turned to her new friends. The events of the day fizzled from her mind and she even congratulated Leela on her impressive batting skills. Leela beamed and joined in the cheers, louder than some of the boys. Rea had no idea how long they spent recounting every ball bowled and hit, but by the time she got home she was so tired, she fell asleep the moment her head touched the pillow.

CHAPTER 5

A CRIMSON PIECE OF PAPER

"**R**OHAN!" Rea gasped as her eyes shot open. She sat up on the mattress, her heart racing and her neck wet with sweat. Then she sighed with relief. It was just a nightmare. She tried to remember the details but they slipped away. She glanced to her side, but Rohan wasn't there.

Rea got up needing to use the bathroom. It was still dark out. The time on the wall clock read 4:20 in the morning. The door to the bathroom was closed, and Rea assumed Rohan was inside.

"Hurry up, I need to pee," she said.

There was no reply.

Rea rapped on the bathroom door, crossing and uncrossing her legs.

"Rohan, GET OUT!"

She banged the door harder, and it swung open. The bathroom was vacant. Rea relieved herself and then walked back into the living room. She must have missed the lump of his form, asleep next to her, but when she pulled aside the blanket, the bed was empty. Rea tip-toed across the living room and peeked out the front door. Wearing no shoes or chappals, she walked the roads leading from her house. In one of the gullies, she stepped on a foot. A homeless man stirred in his sleep and Rea leaped aside.

Shadows creeped over her. Everywhere she looked, she met a dark, chilly silence. Rea rushed back. Three oak trees from her house, she spotted Rohan's bat and ball strewn to the side.

Of course! He had to be sleeping in Amma's room like he did whenever they fought. With a sigh and a shake of her head, Rea picked up her brother's cricket gear and headed home. She was relieved, but also irritated at having to carry his mess. Groggy with sleep, she slipped on something on the front steps, and grabbed the door handle to arrest her fall. She looked down at the culprit, a crimson piece of paper with her muddy footprint on it. Rea picked it up. Pasted on it was a hideous scrawl of letters.

'TiME tO sAy GoOdbYE.'

Rea wasn't sure what it meant, but she didn't like the sound of it. Suddenly she wasn't so sure Rohan was in Amma's room. She dumped the bat and ball on the sofa and rushed into Amma and Bajai's bedroom. Amma sat up right away, and switched on the bedside lamp. A quick glance across the floor confirmed Rohan wasn't there.

"Rohan isn't home, and I found this outside the door," Rea said, handing over the cryptic note.

Amma read the piece of paper. With a cry of fear, she sprang from the bed and ran through the kitchen, bathroom and living room calling his name. She threw open the front door and ran into the darkness.

"ROHAN!" she screamed.

The night was velvety thick. The sky was full of stars, and Rea could smell the scent of trees on the intermittent breeze. An owl hooted in the distance.

"Rea? Kunjan?" Bajai's wrinkled voice called from inside and she turned on a flashlight to see what the commotion was about.

Rea snatched the flashlight from her hands. Circling the house, she flashed it behind cans of paint, their bicycles, and the clothesline with a drying bedsheet. She kicked aside the mess of pipes, fallen roof shingles, and a pile of logwood.

"This isn't funny, Rohan," she shouted. "Where are you?"

Her calls traveled to the moon and back, but there was no reply.

"Reeli, come inside," Bajai said. "Come inside where it's safe."

Rea flicked the shaft of light onto the village road. Maybe if she walked back to Scenic Point, she might find him. She stepped onto the road when Bajai's voice sounded behind her, sharp and tense.

"Don't take another step." Bajai had slipped out of the light of the doorway and into the darkness. Rea couldn't see her, but she felt her fingers curl tightly around her arm. "You are not going anywhere. Come back inside. Now." Bajai's unflinching eyes, chilling as the night, ordered Rea to stop fighting her.

Shocked, and a little scared, Rea let her grandmother pull her back inside. The moment they entered the house, Rea heard her mother weeping in the bedroom. Rea ran to her.

With tears falling down her cheeks, Amma had opened their shared family closet and was shuffling through Rohan's clothes. Leaving it in a mess, she grabbed his school uniform out of the laundry basket and went through all the pockets. Finding nothing, she unzipped his school bag and emptied its contents onto the floor. Textbooks, a pencil box, the stub of an eraser, a half-eaten chocolate bar, and the tiffin box he had forgotten to remove came tumbling out. She stared at the scattered objects. Shivers engulfed her body and the school bag fell from her hands.

Rea watched, mesmerized, and confused. Why was Amma behaving like Rohan was gone forever? It had only been a few hours. He was out there somewhere, sleeping in a field, or at a friend's house...

In the living room, Bajai thumbed her necklace like prayer beads. Rea went over and held her hand.

"I'm sure he's okay," she said. Bajai looked at her and nodded with a shaky smile.

"H-How did this happen?" Amma said, facing Bajai. Her face was swollen and streaked with tears. She held the door as if it were the only thing keeping her from falling. "We did everything. They were with us the whole time. Rea with me, Rohan with you."

Rea glanced at the bat and ball on the sofa. That wasn't entirely true, she thought, guiltily. She and Rohan were not with them for the few hours they were at Scenic Point.

Oh, the cricket match! That's it!

Rohan must have gone to a friend's house after losing the game! He was quite the sore loser, especially when it came to cricket. Then, Rea's heart dropped. If he didn't show up soon, she would have to tell Amma and Bajai they had snuck out at night after they had pretended to go to sleep. *Stupid, stupid Rohan.*

"Um... maybe his friends know where he is?" said Rea.

"Why would they know where he is? He was asleep when I went to bed," said Amma.

"I don't know... maybe his friends called him, and he went to see them?" replied Rea. If she could get away with a small, white lie instead of telling Amma the truth, she was going to try her luck.

"What friends? Did you see anyone? Where did they take Rohan?" Amma's eyes narrowed in suspicion and she hurried towards Rea. There was a crazy look in her eyes, and Rea stepped back.

"I don't know! I didn't see anything! You're acting as if Rohan has run away or something so I'm just suggesting that maybe his friends know where he is."

Amma rushed to the telephone. She opened the drawer and grabbed the telephone diary. Scanning through the names, she began making call after call to Rohan's friends' houses. A few didn't answer, and the ones who did didn't know where he was. Not knowing what to do, Rea closed her eyes. The charcoal sketch of her father appeared.

Baba, Amma will ground me for life if she finds out what we did. I swear on the moon I'll never fight with Rohan again. And even if I do, I promise to let him win. Please, please, bring him home.

When she opened her eyes, Amma was sitting still, the diary left open on her lap. The circling wail of a siren somewhere in their village shattered the muteness in their house.

"Can I see the paper?" Bajai asked. Her outstretched hand trembled and Amma handed her the blood-red note.

A look of fear came over her and Bajai crumpled her handkerchief close to her chest. Tears filled her eyes and she wiped them before one fell.

"Kunjan…" she ventured, as though she was afraid of Amma's reaction. "Should we involve the… police? Rohan might still be out there. They could find him."

"Wait, the *police*?" Rea shouted out. If they were going to call the police, she was going to have to tell them the truth. "I-I don't think that's necessary, right Amma?"

"They can't help us," Amma said to Bajai, and Rea flopped onto the sofa with relief (and surprise that her mother had actually agreed with her.) "This is beyond what they can do, you know that. And they'll never believe us. This is all—" Amma stopped. She stared at the walls, her lips quivering in defeat.

"This is all what?" asked Rea, exasperated. "Are you both not telling me something?" This was exactly like when she asked them questions about Baba. The secret exchange of glances. The veiled way in which they answered the questions, if they did at all. Mostly, the way they ignored her. "Why wouldn't the police be able to help? Do you know something?"

They both said nothing.

"Say something!" Rea cried out. "Rohan's going to come back! Why are you behaving like he won't? Let's go look for him if you think something's wrong."

Rea marched to the door, but Amma's face hardened the way

it did when she wanted to evade a question. Rea turned to Bajai for an explanation, but she stared at her thick-veined fingers.

"Are you sure you didn't see anything?" Amma asked Rea. She stared at her with a look so fierce, Rea was sure she could see through her lies and into her soul.

Rea hesitated.

Once Rohan came home, he was going to have to tell Amma what really happened and then *she'd* be caught red-handed for lying. No matter how bad her punishment would be, she was better off enduring Amma's wrath than crowning Rohan as the good-little-truth-teller.

Amma had looked away but the harshness of her gaze lingered on Rea. If anything had actually happened to Rohan, Amma would never forgive her for lying.

"A-Actually," Rea said with a gulp, "at midnight, Rohan went to play cricket with his friends. I went too. He hadn't invited me even though it was our birthday—"

"You left the house in the middle of the night?" gasped Amma, and Bajai's hand flew to her chest. "Where did you go? Where was Rohan? Why weren't you both together?"

"We went to Scenic Point. After the match ended, he left before I did..."

"You let him walk back alone?" Amma's voice rose, her breathing loud.

Let him? It's not like he had asked. And hadn't he, too, left her to walk home alone? Amma didn't know she had Leela for company.

"He left because he was upset that I won," Rea said,

matter-of-factly.

"All alone? Alone at night. Alone in the dark. No one would know. No one would see him. It would be so easy..." muttered Amma.

Same here. I walked back in the dark too. No one could see me, either.

Amma's eyes darted around the room and she looked at Bajai, trying to say something.

"Think Rea, *think*," she said angrily. "Was he sleeping when you got back?"

Bajai touched Rea's arm gently. "Baccha... try and remember anything you can. What road did he take? Are you sure he was going home? Did he say anything about where he might be going...?"

Rea's anger rose. "I don't know! I only saw him leave Scenic Point. But I did find his bat and ball close to the gutter by the house."

"But he wasn't there, was he?" Amma said, her voice low.

Rea shook her head. Amma covered her mouth and cried with her whole body. Bajai held her close.

"He's been taken!" Amma cried. "I failed him. We failed him. And now it's too late."

Taken? Too late for what? Rea shook her head. This *had* to be some stupid game Rohan and his friends were playing. As creepy as the note was, it was made with awkwardly cut letters, badly glued to the paper. Amma needed to calm down. This was not as bad as she was making it out to be.

"Why would anyone want to take Rohan?" asked Rea. "He's

a plantation-boy. It's not like we have any money to offer for his return. It makes no sense."

Amma and Bajai glanced at each other. Their silence felt a lifetime. Rea dropped her head, giving up trying to make sense of their paranoia and their secrets.

"Everything isn't always as it seems," Amma said, her gaze unwavering. She had stopped crying, but her words had daggers around them. "Life is more complicated than that."

"Then explain it to me," pleaded Rea. But Amma turned to Bajai and collapsed into her arms. Rea squeezed her eyes in frustration. Amma was acting as if Rohan had died. If only she knew he was the mastermind who had lied to everyone and organized the cricket match. Her perfect son, not being so perfect after all.

Suddenly, Rea's throat clenched. Her breath came in wheezes and a cloud of pain bloomed in her chest. She felt herself falling from a great height and the locket around her neck burned. Realizing what was happening, she scrambled into the kitchen. Every once in a while, when an extreme emotion or physical reaction affected Rohan, its effect rippled onto her and she could feel it too, no matter how far they were from each other. The same thing happened to Rohan. It was a twin thing.

Rea dropped to her knees, gasping for breath. Was someone choking him? Was he not at a friend's house? Did someone really take him? The sensation hit her again and she fell, prone on the floor.

Wherever Rohan was, something bad, *very bad*, was happening to him.

The moon lingers, a freckled marble in the infinite grey. Clouds float, stretched like wads of cotton. Rea's hair flails in the ferocious wind.

A blurry object, yellow as a school bus, swerves towards her. It stops and a door opens. She steps inside. It has no beginning and no end; just a long, sun-colored tube. And it's empty. The person she's looking for isn't there.

The object careens through the viscous morning. It roars as it turns left then right, then right then left. Scrawny branches poke through its windows. Broken twigs litter its insides. Abruptly, it screeches to a stop and her body hurtles through the front.

A mist hangs like powdered chalk. Its lithe tendrils swallow the air. She wades through a bog, her shoes and socks clogged in muck. A fetid smell rises.

In the distance, a shaft of light shines, silvery and grey. Rectangular stones, white like ghosts, loom ahead. The talon-shaped moon glows brighter as the morning grows darker. The gravestone plinths get closer. They stand at awkward angles. Everything is coated in midnight blue. All except one plinth. It sparkles a luminescent white.

Rea falls to her knees. Clouds of air form at her nose and mouth. With the palm of her hand, she wipes away the dirt. Chiseled in stone are five words.

FIND ME OR I DIE.

She screams.

CHAPTER 6

WOOD ROT & WITHERED FLOWERS

"I need a favor," said Rea.

It was late Saturday afternoon. Two days had passed with no sign of Rohan.

"Of course," said Leela, her expression a mixture of sadness and sympathy. It was the same look everyone in the village gave Rea now. Rohan's disappearance was all anyone could talk about.

"Do you—" began Rea but Leela shushed her, and pointed.

Rea understood immediately; Leela's family, including her parents, three cousins, two sisters and grandparents were listening through the open door. Leela and Rea walked a few steps away.

"You were saying?"

"You've heard of Mishti Daadi, right? The fortune teller who lives in Pokhriabasti?"

Leela chewed on a fingernail. "Uh-huh..."

"I want to meet her... but I don't want to go alone, and I need um... a..." Rea paused. She wasn't sure if she could call Leela a friend. It didn't feel right. "I—I was hoping you would come with me. I know they say only crazies go to her, but I really want to see her."

"My aunty went to see her when her daughter couldn't find a husband."

"Oh, that's great," said Rea. "So, will you come with me?"

Leela hesitated, looking uncomfortable. "The thing is, I don't like going to fortune tellers, tarot card readers, crystal ball lookers, or clairvoyants. They scare me. I'm happy not knowing about all the bad things that are going to happen in my future. Ignorance is bliss, you know?"

Rea was taken aback. That was exactly how she felt. Her life was hard enough, and she preferred not to find out about the crappy things in store for her. She wondered for a moment what had happened in Leela's life for her to be worried about her future. She always seemed so happy; Rea had assumed her life was pretty good.

"You don't have to get your fortune read. Only I will so I can find out about Rohan. I—I just need the moral support..."

Deep down, Rea knew if Mishti Daadi predicted the worst— that Rohan was really missing—she didn't want to be alone when she heard it.

Leela looked like she needed more convincing.

"I'll give you all the sweets I get for Diwali and do your homework for a week," beseeched Rea.

"Oh, no no! Friends don't have to bribe each other. It's not that I don't want to help you. I really do but..." Leela looked at her feet. "My aunty died a few weeks after meeting Mishti Daadi. In my heart, I know Mishti Daadi didn't have anything to do with it, but my Amma is convinced her black magic killed my aunty. Although it doesn't make sense, the thought of dabbling in witchy stuff gives me the creeps," Leela said with a shiver, as if she could catch bad luck by simply saying the words.

"It's okay, I understand," said Rea. "And I'm sorry about your aunty. Losing someone you love is the worst."

Rea mounted her bicycle and pedaled away. She should have known better than to expect someone to help her. How she wished Baba was here with her. She would've run into his arms and he would have fixed everything.

"Wait, I wasn't done!" Leela ran behind her. Rea braked and turned.

"After my aunty and cousin went to see Mishti Daadi, my cousin found a husband, and a really good-looking one too! So…" Leela looked at Rea, but Rea wasn't sure what she was trying to say.

"Let's go see her," said Leela. "I hate that Rohan's missing and what are friends for if you can't count on them, right?"

Rea cringed internally. Leela considered her a friend even though she didn't feel the same way. A sliver of guilt crept into her but at the same time, Rea couldn't believe Leela had changed her mind.

"So, when do you want to go?" asked Leela.

"Now!" Rea said, excitedly.

"Now? Uh okay, on one condition. We'll cut through Sanobar to get to Mishti Daadi's house. It's also the quickest route."

"You mean, Sanobar, the *forest*?" Rea gulped. She hated dark and dank spaces.

Leela nodded. "If anyone from my family, and there's a lot of us, sees me go to Mishti Daadi's house, my Amma will start keeping tabs on me." Leela shook her head. "I cannot have that. I *need* my freedom."

"All right," said Rea. *Beggars can't be choosers*, she thought. Besides, she had to be home before dinnertime, which was soon anyway. "We'll go through Sanobar. And... hey, thanks."

"Oh stop. Friends don't need to thank each other."

That word again. Thrice now. The word felt hollow to Rea. Like a chocolate she had received in school during a classmate's birthday. It was big and in the shape of a bunny and she was so excited to eat it, but when she took a bite, the inside was empty. There was no yummy, gooey filling, no nutty surprise, only a chocolate shell of a bunny. That's what a friend was—a pretty word to say, but in reality, there was nothing there. Rea hoped by ignoring the word Leela would stop saying it, just like how Amma ignored her questions about Baba until finally she gave up asking.

"I've been seeing posters of Rohan all over Tombu," said Leela.

"Me too," said Rea. "It feels like we're looking for a lost cat."

"Don't think like that. At this point, any and every effort is useful. I'm sure someone will find him."

"That's what Bajai says. You know, she and Amma have been having these conversations about Rohan; I can hear them whispering, but they stop talking every time I enter the room."

"What are they saying about him?"

"Yesterday, Amma cried out something like, 'She's never going to send him back!' At least that's what it sounded like through the closed door. It could easily have been, 'He's never going to come back!' But I can't help but wonder if they know more than they're telling me?"

Leela stopped. "Really?"

"I don't know," shrugged Rea. "I tried asking her about it and she looked at me like I was speaking Sanskrit. And then she and Bajai began arguing about it being too late. I mean today's only the third day. That's not too long, is it? Or do you think they're right?"

"Oh gosh, don't say such things." Leela hurriedly made some hand gesture and pushed Rea to touch a tree.

A funny sensation spread within Rea. It was nice to talk to someone about what was happening in their house. And Leela didn't seem to judge her; she just listened like her tea shrubs did, and was always there when she asked for help. Before she knew it, Rea began confiding in Leela about her nightmare. Rea schooched her bicycle along, recounting her dream, and Leela walked beside her, listening with wide eyes.

"Do you think it means anything?" asked Leela.

"I think so. It keeps looping in my mind. I can barely sleep. It sounds silly, but it's the only thing which gives me hope."

"Like there's more to the story?"

Rea nodded. "Not that it matters, but Amma won't even listen to me long enough to hear about the dream, let alone help me figure out what it means, and I don't want Bajai worrying any more than she already is. I can tell she's trying her best to keep it together for Amma and me, saying Rohan will be back and to keep faith. But, sometimes it's like I'm invisible. I don't think either of them has noticed I've barely slept these last two nights."

"I know what you mean," said Leela.

"How could you possibly know?" snapped Rea. "Your house is full of family. You always have someone to talk to."

Leela affected a chuckle but not in a funny way. "It amuses me how people tend to think that. The truth is sometimes you can feel the loneliest in a room crowded with people."

Rea stopped and faced Leela, wondering how that was possible. Leela paled a shade.

"Last month, I ran away for three days to see if anyone would notice. I hitchhiked all the way to Kolkata, and no one realized I was gone. There's so many of us in the house, Amma and Baba had no idea. Rohan's lucky to have you looking for him."

Rea parted her lips to reply, but she was at a loss for words. She hadn't noticed Leela's absence either.

"I'm sorry," she finally said. "I thought having a big family would be nice."

"When you're one of nineteen siblings and cousins, not so much. Half the time, Amma forgets my name," Leela laughed, but she seemed a little sad at the same time.

"Isn't the forest dangerous?" Rea asked, riding down a kaccha road peppered with abandoned shanties.

"I don't think so," answered Leela. "But if you're scared, we don't have to go."

"Of course I'm not scared. It's just some trees."

The truth was, Rea had stayed clear of Sanobar forest her whole life, and didn't think that entering a wooded area in the early hours of the evening was the wisest idea. On the other hand, going back the route Amma had taken would've taken longer, and she couldn't risk getting home late.

"We'll be fine," said Rea, adding a fake bravado to her voice. "There's still some light out."

Leela pushed down the pedals and sped ahead, her face tilted towards the wind. "This is the first time I've ever done this!"

"Wait, you haven't been to the forest either?" Rea called out, but Leela had disappeared around the bend.

As they rode up the hilly terrain, squiggly plants on the side of the road grew into bursts of ferns, lichens, and capacious walnut trees. The air grew cooler, and the road became narrower and slippery with the mists of the woods. When they turned the corner, the gravelly path disappeared, and a wall of Himalayan pines towered before them. Rea skimmed the ground with her toes to reduce her speed. She felt dizzy just looking at the soaring tree trunks.

The air inside Sanobar was thick with the smell of wood rot and withered flowers. Branches creaked in the distance. Unseen wings fluttered above, and dried leaves cracked like a bed of eggshells. Rea and Leela got off their bicycles and walked with them. They treaded carefully, taking care to skip over gnarled roots popping out of the ground and noodles of trickling water.

"One of my uncles said if you walk through Sanobar in a straight line you come out at Pokhriabasti," Leela said, bending under a low hanging branch.

Rea hoped the uncle was right. The evening light had turned everything into a mossy shade of green and from somewhere within the forest an owl hooted. Rea scanned the lattice of leaves.

"Shouldn't it be s-sleeping?"

"It's probably an early riser," Leela said and they quickened their pace, pushing their bikes in as straight a line as possible. "By the way, how did you think of Mishti Daadi? I'd completely forgotten about her."

Rea's arms itched from the mosquitoes and she scratched her skin. "The evening before Rohan disappeared, Amma went to see her."

Leela's eyes went wide and Rea instantly regretted opening her mouth. "Forget I said anything."

"No, no, I won't tell anyone. It's just that your Amma doesn't seem like the type to visit a fortune teller."

"Exactly, she isn't. She was acting strange that day, stranger than usual, so I followed her and ended up at Mishti Daadi's house."

"How exciting!"

Rea shot her a look.

"I mean, not exciting. It is weird. Do you know why she met her?"

"No. That's why, with Amma secretly meeting her, Rohan going missing, and the nightmare I keep having, I feel like I *have* to see her. Maybe she can tell me what's going on or where Rohan is or help me make sense of all this."

To Rea, it felt like pieces of a puzzle. None of the edges matched yet, but if she searched hard enough, she was sure she would find the missing pieces to see the complete picture. Such strange occurrences in her otherwise-boring life *had* to mean something, right?

"If there's anyone who might have some answers, it's her," said Leela.

Rea lowered her gaze. "Amma blames me for what's happened. I blame myself too, but with every passing day it's clear she hates me for letting Rohan walk home alone after the game… so if I can fix things, maybe she'll…" Rea's voice trailed away. She wanted to say, 'she'll forgive me and love me again.'

"She just wants him back and is taking it out on you. Parents do that sometimes."

"I guess. But shouldn't she worry about me, too? She didn't even ask where I was going today or with whom."

"Hey, do you have any money?"

"Huh? Oh, shoot." Rea dug into her pockets and found a crumpled ten-rupee note. "Now what do I do? Mishti Daadi won't even let me see her face for ten bucks."

How stupid had she been to forget a means of payment. Leela stuffed her hand into her jeans and retrieved a fifty-rupee note.

"We'll plead with Mishti Daadi to read your palms for sixty rupees and promise to bring more if we need to," she said.

"Oh, thank you! I'll pay you back as soon as I can."

A pitter-patter sounded against the leaves on the trees and a second later, a light rain fell. Rea and Leela hurried forward. The trees had turned larger and denser and as Rea tried to edge past an obscenely thick tree, Leela gasped.

A waterfall of sky-high ropes dangled in front of her. On closer inspection, they were roots, not ropes.

"A banyan," whispered Leela, taking in the enormous tree. "In one of my favorite fantasy novels, an ogre disguises himself as a banyan tree and uses the banyan's roots as his dreadlocks!"

It was the first time Rea had seen a banyan. They were common in other parts of India, but she didn't know they grew in Darjeeling.

"This is so cool." Leela marveled at it as though she had come upon a dinosaur fossil. "Did you know the banyan is India's most sacred tree?"

Rea shook her head. Scores of mud-colored roots hung from the branches and surrounded the mammoth trunk. Venturing ahead, she stroked the roots, feeling their coarse, leathery texture under her fingertips.

"My hand!" Rea screamed. A root from the clump she was holding had slithered out of her grip and was coiling around her wrist.

Leela spun around.

"What's the matter?" She gaped at Rea, waiting for her to give an explanation.

Rea stared at her hand and at the roots hanging limply in it. *Did I imagine that?* She rubbed her wrist and a spot of blood oozed.

"We need to get out of here," she said.

A flash of lightning hit the trees and the branches crackled.

"*Now.*"

CHAPTER 7

BACCARA VINTERA VERAFARA

P anting, Rea and Leela emerged from the forest and found themselves on the road to Pokhriabasti. The village wasn't a large settlement and after a few quick turns, they arrived at Mishti Daadi's house.

Rea looked over her shoulder, hoping she wouldn't see Tara and her gang. Thankfully, they weren't there. The kids she had played hopscotch with were playing football with a ball made of plastic bags and twine. They shrieked every time it flew towards the pots of periwinkles lined up in front of the houses, afraid of breaking them and getting yelled at by the owners. Rea remembered how she had burst into ecstatic shouts when Rohan's team lost, and she looked away.

The lemon-and-chili talismans on Mishti Daadi's walls swayed in the breeze and Rea knocked on the door. A string of ivy had crawled up the wall and over the moldy eyehole. Minutes passed. She listened for the sound of footsteps, but none came. Rea knocked again, and jumped as the door swung open.

Rea and Leela looked at each other, and stepped forward into the house.

"Hello?" Rea called. "Mishti Daadi?"

The house was dark. Silhouettes of unseen objects loomed large, battling for space in the murkiness. Leela tripped on something and stumbled slightly.

"Smell that?" Rea tapped her nose. It was an agarbatti, an incense stick burning with the sweet, woody scent of sandalwood.

THUD!

The door slammed shut behind them and Leela and Rea spun around in the darkness. They started to run toward the exit when dim lights flickered on. The girls stopped and looked around in surprise. A sofa upholstered in floral prints sat in the living room covered in a mound of cushions. Paintings of flowers and idyllic landscapes adorned the buttercream walls and amoeba-shaped water stains peeked from underneath them. To the side was a wooden table with four rattan chairs; one seat had a cushion missing.

"Welcome, dearies."

Mishti Daadi waddled towards them in a pale-yellow saree and an immense red bindi. Wrinkled skin clung to her face and hung in folds along her neck. A chunky silver necklace rested on her mottled chest and her earlobes were stretched long with a pair of jhumkas, their silvery hues worn to black. Flashing a smile, she beckoned them to sit. Rea picked the chair without the cushion, but she hardly noticed.

"Welcome to my humble abode," Mishti Daadi said. "How

may I be of assistance?"

"Can we please have s-some water?"

"Of course, Leela dearie. Make yourselves at home. Rea, would you like some bandages?" A knobby finger pointed at her.

"B-Bandages?" Rea rushed to cover the scratches on her arms from the mosquito bites in Sanobar. "N—no, I'm fine. Thank you."

"Very well."

"Oh god," Leela said, the moment she was out of sight. "I feel like throwing up a little."

"Why? I thought you knew her."

"I know *of* her. And how does she know our names?"

Rea's heart forgot to beat for a moment. Had Amma told her about them? Or had she known through her powers of foresight that they were coming to see her? Both possibilities freaked her out a little.

"I'm sure you dearies are hungry after your journey here."

Mishti Daadi reappeared, carrying a tray with two glasses, a jug of water and a plate of jam biscuits. She set it on the table. Rea gave her shaky smile while Leela gulped down her water and grabbed three biscuits.

"So, dearies, what can an old lady do for you?" Her bleary eyes rolled onto Rea. They had the appearance of rotten grapes.

"I... um... was told you can read palms and reveal answers."

"And you have some important questions?"

Rea nodded.

"Well, you've come to the right place! I do pride myself in being a bit of a thaumaturgist," she grinned, the gaps in her teeth showing.

"A bit of a what?" asked Leela, a glop of jam hanging from the corner of her mouth.

Mishti Daadi ignored her. "But first, I must get my things," she said and left the room again.

Rea and Leela looked at each other nervously. A loud clanging sounded, and Mishti Daadi returned, lugging a heavy sack. Leela jumped off her chair to help.

"Not to worry, dearie. I'll manage."

Mishti Daadi dug her hands into the toast-colored sack and delicately removed its contents. Holding each piece to eye level, she admired them as if recollecting a memory, and proceeded to arrange them until the table was covered with all kinds of thingamabobs. There were relics, dusty scrolls, bundles of sandalwood sticks, sprigs of tulsi leaves, knotted balls of raven-colored petals, broken pieces of bone, sparkling stones, a dozen decanters filled with potions, and several other objects Rea couldn't make sense of.

"Er... Mishti Daadi? How much will this cost? I only have sixty rupees."

Mishti Daadi's face softened. "You don't have to worry, dearie. If I answer your questions satisfactorily, you can give me whatever your heart desires. I want to help, not steal from the desperate and frightened as some might think."

A blush creeped over Rea. She was guilty of thinking something very much like that about fortune tellers in the past.

"Silence now. We begin the augury."

Mishti Daadi tapped her fingers on her forehead and placed Rea's arms on the table. She lifted the lid of a crystal carafe and drizzled a sapphire-hued liquid over Rea's palms.

"To expunge the murkiness," she explained.

The liquid was thick on Rea's skin and a chill entered every pore of her body. She felt like an empty receptacle, clean and open. Satisfied with the 'cleansing,' Mishti Daadi plucked two of the darkest petals from the flower balls and laid them on Rea's palms. They looked like scraps of a moonless night resting on a pillow of snow. Rea glanced at the cuckoo clock hanging opposite her. She had an hour before she needed to head home. Mishti Daadi closed her eyes and tossed her head backwards.

"*Baccara sintera verafara.*"

An incantation in a peculiar tongue poured from her lips and the air around Rea tightened. With her eyes still sealed, Mishti Daadi picked a pair of shiny stones and swapped their positions in time with her chanting. In the swiftness of her movements, the light reflecting off their surfaces sent dazzling sparkles across the room. Her invocation grew louder, and a force pressed down on Rea's palms. The petals levitated. Rea watched with wide eyes. Leela's jaw dropped.

White hair unraveled from Mishti Daadi's bun and her bony hands with bulging spider veins shook with great intensity. Rea desperately fought the urge to scream, the burden on her palms unbearable. She yelled for Mishti Daadi to stop, but the old woman did not seem to hear. Mishti Daadi's eyes rolled to the back of her head. The chairs, the table, and all its contents shuddered violently, reaching a deafening crescendo. The lights died and Leela screamed.

Rea moaned, her mind blanking out. "Mi—Mish—ti Daa—

di pl... sto... p... p..."

The lights spluttered back on, starkly bright. Everything came to a spine-chilling standstill.

Rea's face lolled to the side. The horrible pressure on her palms had disappeared. Mishti Daadi's eyes were wide open as if pinned to her eyebrows. Her irises were deathly black and in their center was a white dot.

"Speak, dearie, of what you desire to seek," she said in a honeyed but distant tone.

A calm washed over Rea. Mishti Daadi's voice was silken and sweet. All Rea wanted was to close her eyes and sleep. She tried to focus on the shiny stones to stay awake, but everything—the walls, lights, furniture, paintings, Mishti Daadi and Leela—dissolved into oblivion.

Men tipped their feathery hats. Women blew kisses at her. Pink, yellow, green, blue, orange, purple! Peplums of petals in every color twirled around their waists. She laughed. Children played. The sun beamed yellow as yolk. Wherever she passed, flowers of every hue burst open from the tips of grass. They flapped their petals to say hello. It was paradise.

CHAPTER 8

RIDDLES! RIDDLES! RIDDLES!

"Rea? REAA!"

Rea looked left and right in a dreamy stupor.

"Look HERE!"

The voice came again, loud and warbled. It was familiar, but a million worlds away. Rea smiled blissfully and faded deeper into her reverie.

"WAKE UP!" the voice shrieked.

Rea forced her eyes open. Leela's face bore down on her, her nails buried into Rea's arms. Rea blinked several times. The room gradually coalesced. Leela let out a lungful of air and flopped onto her chair.

"Speak, dearie, of what ails your heart."

Mishti Daadi's words tickled Rea's chin for an answer and Rea searched her mind for the questions she had come to ask, but the vision of that colorful, happy place kept pulling her back.

After straining every muscle, she remembered.

"Where is Rohan?" she asked.

Mishti Daadi smacked her lips together, as if she were tasting the question on her tongue. Her eyelids blinked once, twice, three times, while Rea and Leela stared at her. Finally, she spoke.

> "Where day is night,
> And night is day.
> He sits and crawls
> Within copezium walls."

"He's alive! I knew it!" Rea sprang from her chair. But the answer confused her, and she returned to her seat. A root of dread inched up her spine.

"Is he all right?"

> "Alive and kicking,

Rea wanted to jump up with joy. She squeezed Mishti Daadi's hand so tightly, it almost broke their connection.

> ...Screaming and shouting."

"Wait a second, why is Rohan screaming and shouting? Is he safe?" Rea asked.

Mishti Daadi stayed silent, her white pupils still. Rea shook the woman's wrinkled palms, anxious for an answer.

"Mishti Daadi, answer the question. Is Rohan safe and unhurt?"

> "Harm comes to those who fear,
> when weakness and innocence are near.

> He who you ask for
> rebels the most.
> Of strength and courage, he does boast."

Of strength and courage, he does boast. Way to go, Rohan!

Rea looked over at Leela. There was no way they were going to remember these answers. Unless… "Psst!" she said to Leela, "Write this down."

Leela was staring at them with her mouth agape when Rea's words broke her out of her shock. She looked around and grabbed the notepad beside Mishti Daadi's home telephone and found a pen lurking under its first page. With a loud rip, she tore it out. Rea inched to the edge of her seat.

"Where can I find Rohan?" asked Rea.

> "Where day is night,
> And night is day.
> He sits and crawls
> Within copezium walls."

It was the same answer Mishti Daadi had given before. Rea and Leela looked at each other, momentarily discouraged. This wasn't enough to go on. They needed more.

"O-kay, but *how* do I find him?" asked Rea.

All of a sudden, Rea felt a poke, sharp as a thorn and oily as a tentacle, against her brain.

"Ow," she said and narrowed her eyes at Mishti Daadi, looking for a sign that she was working some kind of magic against them, but the old woman's face was expressionless. Her trance appeared intact and then her lips moved as she answered Rea's question.

"The answer lies in you.
Hidden within your mind, a clue.
Follow the beating heart,
In a journey to play your part."

Rea sat, bewildered. These weren't answers; they were riddles. Usually, she loved solving them, but these made no sense.

"What else do you see, Mishti Daadi?" she asked. At least the brain-prodding had stopped.

"I see
only what
you ask
of me."

Arghhh.

"All right, who is this horrible, horrendous person that has taken Rohan away?" Rea asked.

Mishti Daadi gazed into nothingness, as if no question had been spoken.

Rea gritted her teeth and steadied her voice.

"Who has kidnapped Rohan?"

It was the first time she had said the word aloud. *Kidnapped.* She shivered. It didn't feel good to say it and she worried she had somehow made it real by saying the word. Mishti Daadi's eyes wandered around the room and Rea followed them, creepy as they looked, until they halted and faced her.

"Fair and tall,
Ruler of all!"

Rea wanted to punch something. She was getting close to discovering where Rohan was but Mishti Daadi's rhymes were infuriating her. Right then, Mishti Daadi's eyelids drooped and her head dipped to the side.

"No, no, no. Please hold on. I only have a few questions left."

Rea stared into those milky abysses, willing them to stay open. Mishti Daadi's grip slowly strengthened and her head returned to position. There was no time to waste. Questions about Rohan were leading nowhere.

"I've been having a nightmare since Rohan went missing," said Rea. "Is it trying to tell me something? Is it a clue?"

The prodding on her brain returned, like an itch inside her mind.

> "As certain as fate
> The mind's eye lives.
> Slip past the sleeping lies
> To where hidden truths hide."

"What hidden truths?" she asked as slow breaths came and went from Mishti Daadi's lips.

> "S-Suns as bright bu-burning orbs glow,
> Unwavering, t-they watch and kn-know."

Mishti Daadi's breathing grew to large heaves and she struggled to keep going. Rea slid her fingers out of her grip.

"It's all right, Mishti Daadi. You can let go now—"

Mishti Daadi grabbed Rea's hands.

> "They gu-ide and you shall fo-follow.

I–Into a s-s-sylvan h-heart's h-ho-llow."

Mishti Daadi coughed violently. Her unnatural black irises vanished and their rotten-grape glaze returned. The levitating petals dropped gracefully onto Rea's palms and Mishti Daadi sighed. She looked entirely scrunched up.

"Apologies, dearie. The augury consumes a great deal of energy. I tend to forget I'm not as young as I used to be."

Mutely, Leela offered her Rea's untouched glass of water and Mishti Daadi slurped it down.

"There's no need to look so frightened. Don't you worry, I've got plenty more left in me." She wrinkled her already wrinkled face with a smile. "I hope you got the answers you were looking for."

"Well… in a way," said Rea. "You said Ro—wait, don't you remember?"

Mishti Daadi shook her head. "I have no memory of the prophecies once the augury is over. It's nature's way of balancing knowledge. It would be unwise for someone with the ability," she pointed to herself, "to be privy to another's destiny. The sacred gift must not be misused." Her curved forefinger moved like a windshield wiper.

"I suppose you want to go next." Mishti Daadi motioned to Leela. "Although, I do require a few moments to recover…"

"Goodness no. It was Rea who wanted to do it. Just Rea."

"Very well," said Mishti Daadi, seeming visibly relieved. "Have some biscuits to bring the color back into those lovely cheeks."

Leela eagerly reached for one. "Mishti Daadi, how do you

know our names?"

Rea turned in surprise and Mishti Daadi grew forlorn.

"It's a small town. When I pass through Tombu, I often see the two of you playing. Back when you were five or six years old, you were so close. Running around, chasing each other over monkey bars and slides."

Rea was pretty sure she hadn't known Leela when they were that young, but there was a more pressing question waiting on the tip of her tongue.

"Um... a few days ago, my Amma came to see you. What did she want to know?"

"Your Amma?" Wrinkles crowded Mishti Daadi's eyes.

"Tallish, hazel eyes? Kunjan Chettri?" said Rea.

"Why yes, she had on a blue dupatta."

"YES!"

"I'm afraid I don't discuss my patrons with anybody, dearie. As I've said before, I have no memory of what transpires during a divination, but I do know your Amma is a strong and wise woman. You needn't worry about her."

Rea gave a tight smile. The universe was clearly conspiring against giving her any answers.

"Mishti Daadi, why do you live alone?" Leela asked. "Don't you have a family?"

The cuckoo from the cuckoo clock swung out of its tiny door, chirruping in song, and Rea almost flew out of her chair. They should have left five minutes ago! She was dangerously close to missing dinner and Amma might have stopped caring about her, but Bajai would be livid.

"It's a long story, dearie. Maybe for another time."

Rea breathed a sigh of relief. She thanked Mishti Daadi for the augury, and tugged Leela's arm, trying to get her out of there before she asked the old woman more questions and made them even later. Getting the message, Leela reached into her pocket and pulled out the money. She held it out, but Mishti Daadi waved her hand away.

"I can't take money from children. Especially since I suspect your Ammas are unaware you are here."

Leela and Rea looked guiltily at each other and Mishti Daadi chuckled.

"Your company has been payment enough. Will you dearies come see me again?"

"We will!" said Leela.

Rea threw her a look, but Mishti Daadi's face lit up.

"We promise," Leela assured her and gave the old woman a hug.

"We have to leave now," Rea said, hurrying towards the door. "Thank you for your help."

Mishti Daadi lumbered behind them.

"The pleasure was mine, dearies. Now, ride home carefully," she smiled widely, her yellowed teeth on full display.

The gravestone glistens. The moon hangs low. Its pockmarks follow her as she wades through the bog. A few feet from the tombstone, Rea closes her eyes. She takes slow, careful steps. She must not see the words. On her sixth step, she spins around with her back towards the plinth.

She opens her eyes.

The bog, the shrubbery, the trees are blurry. They remind her of smudged watercolors she used to paint as a child. Dotted around this picture are countless sunflower-yellow spots, flickering incessantly. She hasn't seen them before. The spots grow. Hundreds of owls appear perched on every branch of every tree. Their dark feathers blend into the night, leaving only their glowing eyes to be seen. One stares at her.

Hoots and screeches fill the sky. The owls fly from tree to tree, branch to branch, crisscrossing each other. They swoop down low. Rea covers her eyes, fearing they'll be pecked out, and she stumbles onto the grave. Her eyes land on the carved words.

HELP ME. OR I DIE.

She screams.

Chapter 9

Pnigalion

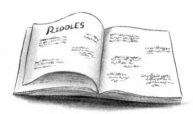

The waters of Senchal Lake shimmered in the afternoon light. White swans glided by. Rea sat on the water's edge, under the shade of a dhupi tree, as tourists mounted horses for a jaunt around the lake, or stepped into shikaras for a romantic boat ride around the rose gardens. Rea had walked the three miles to the lake, hoping the fresh air would clear her mind.

It had been four days, and hope was withering fast.

"It's time you accept your brother isn't coming home," Amma had said that morning as she flattened a crease on Rohan's t-shirt and laid it on a pile of folded clothes. She looked like a sack of skin fighting to stand up.

"You must learn to live with it like Bajai and I are trying to. First your father, then your brother. What sins have I committed to deserve such sadness?" She turned to Rea as if she had the answer. "Now all I have left is you."

As she remembered the words, Rea blinked away tears. She knew her mother didn't mean to hurt her, but she also knew she would never be enough. Rohan's spirit would haunt Amma's heart forever, leaving a hole that would never be filled.

Adding to the turmoil was Rea's nightmare. Even while awake, she could feel the mud sludge on her legs, the eeriness around her, the biting wind. She could see the shining tombstone, and those terrifying words.

This morning, she had finally confided everything about the dream to Bajai, hoping her grandmother would be able to offer her some comfort.

Bajai had listened carefully to the dream. When Rea was done, she said, "The mind is a mysterious place, Reeli. In its vast and many corners are hidden pieces of knowledge. When we sleep, they float up in the form of dreams. They can be wild, have a mind of their own, and lead us places. They can carry messages or warnings. If they recur, one must heed them."

Bajai handed Rea a diary they kept in their telephone drawer. Its pages were yellowed and blank.

"Write down each detail," she instructed. "And tonight, you must follow the nightmare. I fear it has not ended."

"There's more?" groaned Rea.

"I believe so, and you need a good night's rest to unravel this pnigalion."

"Nigh—what?"

But Bajai had disappeared into her room.

Sitting at the lake, Rea scribbled notes into the diary, analyzing the nightmare from every angle. Neither had she been able to 'follow it' nor had it screamed, 'I'm the message or warning you've been looking for!' If anything, the only message it gave her was that her puzzle-solving skills were disastrously failing her.

Frustrated, Rea picked up a rock and threw it into the lake. She watched as the ripples disturbed the calm waters. One of the nearby swans gave her a dirty look and she stuck out her tongue at the bird, but it didn't make her feel any better.

The one thing Rea was supposed to be good at was puzzles. If there was any way to use this nonsensical trickery to find Rohan, she needed her puzzle-solving powers. But her brain refused to pick up all the loose ends. It was horrible, the feeling that if she could figure out how everything fit together, she could reach him.

Rea stared at her loopy handwriting for a solid ten minutes, trying to force her brain to see the connection. Giving up, she turned towards her school bag, and fished out the torn piece of paper with Mishti Daadi's riddles and read the first one.

Where can I find Rohan?
'Where day is night,
And night is day.
He sits and crawls
Within copezium walls.'

What are copezium walls? Rea thumbed through Rohan's pocket dictionary. There was no such word. She circled it with tiny question marks and searched for 'sylvan.'

Of, pertaining to, or inhabiting forest or forest regions.

The shorter, relatively simpler riddles of Rohan being 'alive and kicking' and of the kidnapper being 'fair and tall, ruler of all,' meant Rohan was out there and a person—she wrote, 'powerful like a tea estate owner or a rich tourist'—might have kidnapped him. What confused her were the last two prophecies.

How do I find Rohan?
'The answer lies in you,
Hidden within your mind, a
clue.
Follow the beating heart,
In a journey to play your part.'

What hidden truths?
Suns as bright burning orbs
glow,
Unwavering, they watch and
know.
It guides and you shall follow,
Into a sylvan^(forest) heart's
hollow.'

With a red pen, she underlined 'hidden within your mind, a clue,' and 'beating heart.' What possible clue lay in her mind that had something to do with a beating heart? Rea drummed her fingers. Rohan had a beating heart. Maybe he was the clue somehow?

Continuing, she underlined 'orbs' and 'burning,' and an image of a bright, flaming sun popped into her head. But the word 'sun' was already mentioned so she changed her approach and played with analogies, jotting down things which were spherical and yellow or orange in color.

sunflowers
oranges
pumpkins
mangoes
turmeric

marigolds

tennis balls

Rea imagined them on fire and scratched them all out. She decided to come back to this clue later. That was one of her tricks to solving puzzles—if she hit a wall, she had to take a step back and try something else. Otherwise, she would get too discouraged and want to give up entirely.

Rea moved onto the last two lines.

'It guides and you shall follow,

Into a sylvan heart's hollow.'

Her hand stilled over the words, 'heart's hollow.' She turned to the last line and rewrote it as 'Forest heart's hollow' while adding in parenthesis 'a hollow heart in a forest.' A heart in the forest… Could it be Rohan's heart? But his heart wasn't hollow.

"Ugh," groaned Rea. She dug her face into her knees and mouthed the prophecies aloud, hoping for something to click.

"What are you doing?"

Rea stopped her recitation and looked up. Leela was standing over her, her orange glasses sitting crooked on her nose.

"You came!" Rea exclaimed.

"Of course! I went to the principal's office complaining of a terrible stomach ache. I told her I had momos from the street yesterday and if I was made to wait for someone to come get me, my stomach would empty itself right there in her office. She told me to run home and here I am!"

Rea grinned. Leela's knack for sneaking out of things sure came in handy. She handed her the diary and Leela read the updated nightmare.

"Speaking of your nightmare," her eyes shone with excitement, "I was researching at the library today and came across this phenomenon called 'sweven.' It's an Old English word for a dream or vision one gets in their sleep. Rea, it's a real thing! Bajai and Mishti Daadi are right. I had my doubts at first, but these things actually exist. There have been recorded accounts of people, mostly women, who have suffered through traumatic events, getting visions which are messages in the form of coded secrets."

"Really?" said Rea.

Leela nodded, looking thrilled. "It's such a slick sounding word too! *Swee-vin.*"

Rea mentally gave an eye-roll. For all her adventurousness, Leela was quite a word-nerd.

"And who's sending these messages into my dreams?" she asked.

Leela pointed at her, as if acknowledging that it was a good question. "Some think they are signs from the universe, while others say it's a type of survival mechanism created by one's own mind. Either way, these swevens can carry messages or signs."

"So, I'm not on a wild goose chase with this nightmare-message thing and it could *actually* reveal something important?"

Leela nodded. "We just have to find out what it is."

"Believe me, I've been trying," said Rea. "And to top it all off, we have to make sense of these prophecies. Rohan's alive and I need to keep him that way. So, think. I've come up with nothing."

"Here's what we'll do." Leela pushed her glasses up her nose. "Let's tabulate everything. That will make it easier to study them."

Tabulate? Rea's annoyance flared. *That's not how you solve riddles.* Her first instinct was to snatch the diary from Leela's hands and tell her to forget it. She was better off on her own. But Leela had already plopped down beside her, and was titling a new page with 'The Mystery of Rohan's Disappearance.'

Rea watched as Leela divided the page into three small columns and two large columns. Rea's irritation grew. Writing down every detail and laying it out in such an elaborate manner was a giant waste of time.

She was about to grab the diary away when she began to see the puzzle in a whole new light. Usually, her mind worked like the game of Tetris, where the pieces or clues fell to the bottom while switching positions to fit the shapes below. (She had played it once when Amma had taken her to the house of a family she cleaned for years ago, and the son had needed a second player to compete with.) But as Leela filled in the boxes, the puzzle morphed into a Rubik's Cube like the one they had in their school library. A square box that you had to keep twisting until the matching colors lined up.

Hmm... using a different method may not be such a bad idea, thought Rea. Besides, her usual methods had gotten her nowhere.

Perusing through Rea's notes, Leela wrote today's date, 'Monday, October 20th, and added the definition of 'sylvan' under *Facts*. Under *Assumptions*, she entered Rea's analysis on all things 'orbs' and 'burning,' the potential identity of the kidnapper, and Rohan as the possible beating heart or living being who could guide her.

DAY	DATE	FACTS	ASSUMPTIONS
Monday	Oct 20th	Sylvan = Of, pertaining to, or inhabiting forest or forest regions.	Orbs/things burning = sunflowers, oranges, pumpkins, mangoes, turmeric, marigolds, tennis balls
			Potential kidnapper = tea estate owner or a rich tourist
			Rohan could be the beating heart/living being to guide Rea

"Why are you looking at me like that?" asked Leela.

"Like what?" replied Rea. Even though she was giving Leela's approach a go, the extreme neatness and efficient tabulation was bothering her. Rea glanced at her own notes and saw a method one might call a little less structured—full of scribbles, strike-throughs, underlines, and messy word bubbles.

Rea held back her rising exasperation and in a calm manner said, "Under *Facts,* you should add that 'Rohan disappeared on October 16th between two-thirty and four-thirty in the morning.' That's when I found his bat and the note. Ever since that night, I've had the same dream with a few variations and based on what I've learned from Bajai, Mishti Daadi, and you, it might be a message in code. Let's add that, too."

"If you're saying, 'might be,' then it's not a fact yet," stated

Leela. "I'm putting the last part under *Assumptions* since we have yet to establish if your nightmare is indeed a sweven."

Rea narrowed her eyes. She didn't stop Leela from writing things down, but this whole process was starting to feel out of her control. And she didn't like it. But if she blew up at Leela, she would be alone again. And despite everything, she didn't want that.

"After giving it a lot of thought, the only place I think Rohan can logically be in is a foreign country," she told Leela, "A place with a different time zone, like where tourists come from. It would explain the first half of the riddle, 'Where is Rohan?' which says, "Where day is night and night is day.'"

"Oh, that makes sense!" said Leela. She dove back into the diary, writing it down. When she looked up, Rea was staring at her.

"Are you listening to what I'm saying? We're assuming Rohan is in another country so far away, it's daytime there when it's night here. That's crazy."

"I don't think it's crazy at all," said Leela. "All mysteries start with improbable situations. You, a person who loves to solve puzzles, should know that. And no matter how far-fetched, we need to consider it. That's the only way we'll find Rohan."

Leela returned to her neatly documented page, but Rea's gaze lingered on Leela. Her annoyance with her diffused a little. Leela always found something useful and encouraging to say when she felt all out of hope, or made a crazy suggestion like going to visit a scary fortune-teller or assuming Rohan was in a foreign country. Having Leela support her wild ideas without insulting them or tossing them aside actually gave Rea a sliver of confidence and hope that they would find Rohan by the end of all this. And here she was, ready to jump at Leela's throat at any second. Rea vowed to stomp out her annoyance.

"All right then," Rea said, "according to Mishti Daadi, Rohan 'boasts of strength and courage,' which means he's alive and putting up a good fight... Why are you making that face?"

Leela blinked nervously. "Um... should I enter that under *Facts* or *Assumptions*?"

"Obviously under *Facts*. If we put everything under *Assumptions*, what are we even doing? Besides, if he isn't alive... what's the point?" Rea said quietly.

"Of course he's alive," Leela said gently. "I was only asking for the purpose of tabulation," she said, and hurriedly recorded it in the *Facts* column.

Rea cleared her throat, trying to shake off the emotions rising in her chest. "As I was saying, Rohan seems to be putting up a good fight, which means the kidnapper might not be as strong as we feared. I followed Rohan's trail of footsteps from Scenic Point and lost it beyond the post office. Except for bullock carts or mules, no scooters or cars go there because the fields begin, and the ground is too soft from irrigation. So that means that wherever Rohan was taken, it was either by foot or cattle cart. And that, finally, is a fact," she said. "Although... with that kind of snail's speed transportation the kidnapper couldn't have taken him too far. Unless there's a large clearing where a helicopter or plane can land and fly Rohan to a faraway country..."

"Please, there are only mustard and paddy fields on the other side of the post office," said Leela. "We've lived here all our lives. Have you ever heard of a clearing area? No. And don't you think the farmers would have informed the police if they saw a helicopter or plane land?"

"Well, weren't you the one who said, 'all mysteries start with improbable situations'?"

"Improbable, yes. Not impossible!"

"Fine," relented Rea, secretly relieved Leela had squashed her assumption. "Well then, he couldn't have gotten too far. What place is close enough to Darjeeling *and* has a different time zone?"

"Maybe we're taking this 'time zone' thing too literally. I'm underlining it, so we know it's a doubt we need to clear up later. For now, let's assume he isn't being held very far away." Leela turned to the final two prophecies and read the one on how to find Rohan.

"Nothing about this riddle makes sense, not to mention it's the most important one," Rea said in frustration. "I mean, who's the beating heart—is it Rohan again?—what journey am I supposed to take, and where is this clue? You can turn me inside out and I can guarantee you won't find anything hiding within me."

Rea hurled another stone into the lake and watched the water swallow it as Leela added separate columns for *Questions* and *Inferences* and wrote within them. Then, peeking from above her glasses, she asked, "This line, 'hidden within your mind, a clue...' couldn't it be your nightmare a.k.a. the sweven?"

Rea was about to reject her suggestion, when suddenly, the colors of the Rubik's Cube matched! Knitting her eyebrows, Leela chewed on the pen, and Rea looked at her in awe. Leela had cracked open the puzzle and had no idea she had even done it. A sliver of jealousy passed through Rea, but she ignored it. She was finally going to rescue Rohan!

"You're right!" said Rea, startling Leela. "In both prophecies, 'how do I find Rohan?' and 'what are the hidden truths?' I have to *follow* something. I didn't realize they were connected until just now. The nightmare is the hidden clue! And the journey I'm meant to take 'to play my part' is code for the journey I need to take to follow the 'beating heart' in my nightmare!"

"Find the beating heart, follow it, and you'll find Rohan!" exclaimed Leela.

"Exactly."

"And, and... since you're in your dream, *you* could be the beating heart!" The words rushed out of Leela's mouth, and Rea threw her arms around her in excitement.

But then something occurred to her, and she dropped the hug, stepping away from Leela with a scowl. "Wait, though. If I'm the beating heart, how can I follow myself?"

"Oh," frowned Leela. "Is it so hard for other beating hearts to be there? I mean seriously, it would make this so much simpler."

Rea stared at the table Leela had created. Slowly, the boxes lifted, floating around like Tetris shapes, and fell into place. Her eyes came alive.

"There *are* others," she cried. "And it all makes sense!"

"It does?" Leela asked, flummoxed.

"The owls! They're in my sweven! See." Rea pointed to her diary entry. "In my last nightmare, there were owls flying every-where. Hundreds of them. They've got to be the beating hearts and their eyes, ohhh—they're a bright, burning orange!"

"That's what 'suns as bright burning orbs glow' must mean. Eyes bright like round, burning suns!" Leela squealed and flung the book in the air. She caught it and scribbled in block letters in the bottom-corner box.

"And guess what?" Rea grabbed Leela's arms. "I even know which owl to follow."

"You do? Ohmygodohmygodohmygod! I don't care if it's three in the morning, you have to wake me up the second you find out what the sweven reveals to you."

"I will!" said Rea. Excitement burst through her veins.

"But we still don't know who has taken Rohan," said Leela, her happiness vanishing. "Or why."

Fingers of fear squeezed Rea's heart. She had been so wrapped up in the puzzle, she had almost forgotten about the kidnapper.

"You know what? Baby steps," Leela said hurriedly, seeing the agony on her friend's face. "We solved one clue, and now you know how to follow the nightmare to reveal its meaning. One by one we'll find out everything and it will lead us to the person who has done this."

Rea held onto Leela's confidence and nodded.

Late that night, the receding rains fell. Through a crack in the window, a damp coolness licked Rea. She drew her blanket up to her ears and turned to her side. A tress of silver curls shone in the moonlight next to her. Rea smiled, comforted to have Bajai by her side. She had insisted on sleeping on the mattress so Rea wouldn't be alone at night. Before Rea closed her eyes again, she glanced at the moon. An owl soared across it with its wings spread wide.

Rea dove under her blanket and squeezed her eyes shut, willing herself to sleep.

"I'm coming to you," she whispered.

Rea stands beside the silvery plinth. Countless pairs of golden eyes blink at her. The night is a wicked black. The wind whistles wildly. Shivering, she warms her palms under her armpits and inspects the twinkling canvas. With her back facing the plinth, she sees the owl.

The one that never blinks.

From its sky-high perch, it is watching, waiting for her. Beckoning her. The bird, unblinking, spreads its majestic wings and takes to the heavens. Rea runs after it, sprinting through fields of grass as tall as her.

She isn't fast enough. The owl gains distance.

"Wait for me," she screams.

The owl is a faint white dot.

Angry and nervous, Rea pushes her legs as fast as she can. Stalks slice her skin and the mist returns. Its dirty white fingers slither around her, blotting the sky and the long-gone owl. Not giving up, she arrives at a wall of trees. Deep, dark and dense. The trees mark the ending, and also the beginning.

She steps within.

Standing tall, spreading thick and wide, and stained in blood, is the answer she has been desperate for.

CHAPTER 10

BEYOND THE BANYAN

Rea woke up and ran to the telephone drawer. Carefully, she brought out the diary and updated the *Inferences* column with the information her nightmare had revealed to her: the place where she would find Rohan. Rea stared at her scribbled words for a moment and then rushed out the door.

Her breath fogged Leela's bedroom window. She picked a handful of pebbles from the ground and flung them one by one through the gap that let in the draft. Leela sleepily brushed the stones away. Only when the fifth one hit her did she realize what was happening.

The night was quiet. Moths flapped their zithery wings around the streetlights.

"You decoded the sweven?" Leela asked, running towards Rea while slipping on her shoes. She hadn't been outside a minute and her nose was already bubble-gum pink.

Rea switched on her flashlight. "I know where Rohan is, and we've got to leave now."

Leela and Rea grabbed their bicycles and rode into the darkness, the yellow beam of light bouncing ahead of them.

"So, tell me, where is he?"

"Sanobar," said Rea, keeping her eyes focused on the barely lit road.

"The *forest*?" It was Leela's turn to be surprised.

A chilly wind whistled. Rea pushed down on her pedals and within a quick fifteen minutes, they reached the entrance of the wooded copse. Its trees, sharp as spears, impaled the silent sky.

"Wait a second, we're going straight in?" asked Leela, her eyes wide, and Rea turned with a look that said, 'What else did you have in mind?'

"I mean, what's the plan? Are we going to meet Mishti Daadi?"

The moon, hanging like a lantern, spilled its light over the edge of the trees.

"We're going to the banyan," said Rea and the nightmare flashed before her eyes.

The owl disappearing into the thicket. The close-knit trees. The enormous roots. The pair of burning eyes. The stain splattered on the skin of the trunk.

"It's where the owl led me, and it was covered in blood."

"*B-blood?*" Leela clasped her handlebars. Sweat covered her temples.

Rea steeled herself. She'd been foolish to assume Leela would come along. This wasn't the same thing as solving riddles by a pretty lake or going to visit a fortune teller. It was past midnight and they were alone with no idea of where they were going or what lay beyond the banyan.

"If you don't want to come, I understand…"

Rea put her foot on the pedal and rode into the forest. She didn't want to look at Leela. Or have Leela look at her. She wanted Leela to come. Without her this journey would have already been much, much harder. Leela was smart, scrappy, and despite her mind being full of nerdy information, she was pretty good company.

But there was no time to feel rejected or lonely, Rea reminded herself. Life had taught her to toughen her heart years ago. If she were to reach inside and feel it, her heart was harder than a cricket ball. She was used to being a lone, solitary soul and as she drew strength from the thought, the leaves beside her crunched like a crispy papadum.

"Of course, I'm coming!" said Leela, riding after her. "At least take this before you go any further." She handed Rea a sharp-edged stone and kept one for herself. "Mark the trees so we can track our way out. It's darker than a well in here."

Rea's gaze flitted towards the sinister silhouettes of trees and then landed on Leela. A smile rose from within her but stopped before it touched her lips. Leela was being supportive and dependable—two things Rea was still not used to experiencing. Leela hadn't once questioned whether she was a hundred percent certain the banyan was the right place her nightmare had led her to. If she was in Leela's shoes, her first instinct would have been to doubt. But Leela had faith in her. So much faith.

Rea so badly wanted to reciprocate the feeling, but suspicion needled her. What if Leela suddenly changed her mind and left her stranded like Amma and Rohan had? No, she was better off not letting anyone inside her heart. Rea turned away with a quick thanks and took the stone, and together, they rode their bicycles deeper into Sanobar.

The forest, quiet on the outside, was alive with a deafening fritinancy on the inside, as if a dozen crickets were twittering straight into their ears. Rea's heart pounded. Cutting a trail through the wild foliage, she hoped her gut was right. That she would find Rohan here. Unable to see much, she kept her eyes fixed on the beam-lit path. Damp leaves, wet like tongues, licked her face and she shook away the shudders scurrying up her spine.

"Um, Leela," she said.

"Yes?"

"We're riding in circles." The flashlight illuminated a ring of trees marked with X's.

"Oh no," Leela said, desperately looking for a way out.

"Follow me." Rea flashed the torch-beam from side to side and tested out different paths. Leela rode after her through a web of wrong turns and strewn forest debris. During one such turn, Leela misjudged the width of a fallen tree trunk and tumbled over it. She fell straight onto Rea, who hit the ground arms first.

"I'm so sorry," Leela cried out. "Are you okay?"

Rea picked herself up. "I'm fine."

Mud, stones, and leaves stuck to bleeding cuts on her hands and palms. Wiping them on her pajamas, she searched for the fallen flashlight.

"There's the banyan!" exclaimed Leela, gesturing at the beam shining over a veil of bristly roots.

Abandoning her bicycle, Rea grabbed the flashlight and ran towards the tree. Circling its trunk, she looked for the blood stain and any sign of Rohan. Leela, leaving her bicycle beside Rea's, inspected the ground using a branch to sift through animal droppings and withered leaves. They looked high and low, but there was no splatter of blood, only the occasional claw-mark from a bird, and a few dead roots. Halfway around the trunk, amid a set of paw prints, Rea found a large rectangular imprint.

"Check this out," she said and Leela huddled over to look at it. "What an odd mark."

Finding no explanation, they continued with their search. At a certain spot, Leela was concentrating so hard on studying the forest floor, she pushed a clump of roots out of her face.

"LEELAAAAAA!" Rea screeched. She had caught the roots millimeters from her face and now they were worming up her arm.

Leela grabbed the roots, but they wriggled out of her grasp, growing quick and strong. Rea struggled desperately. The flashlight slipped from her fingers, throwing light in the opposite direction, and the tree's roots, hanging down from its branches, wound their way around her body, pinning her arms to her sides. Her cuts bled, and she was lifted off the ground.

Leela lunged after Rea. "COME BACK!"

"Forget about me and find Rohan!" Rea yelled back, craning her neck to keep the roots from strangling her.

"ARE YOU CRAZY?"

Gathering her strength, Leela held onto Rea's legs. In seconds, the roots looped around her as if she was an appendage of Rea's they had forgotten about, and bound together, they dangled like ragdolls, screaming at the top of their voices. The cavernous hollow of the canopy opened its hungry mouth and a gut-wrenching jerk catapulted them into it. Instantly, all went black. Rea felt the roots slithering away from her body and as the last of Sanobar forest and the great banyan disappeared out of sight, a pair of fiery-orange eyes blinked down at her.

Rea and Leela shot through a tube. Darkness engulfed them in its throttling grip and Rea's insides trembled, rising close to her mouth. She was falling so fast she couldn't scream or blink when abruptly, the darkness vanished, and a flare of sunlight blinded her. Rea threw her hands up to cover her eyes as swaddles of root-twines snapped around her and she had the fleeting memory of being tossed into the air and falling into her Baba's arms. Leela, looking paler than the inside of a lychee, appeared by her side, cradled too in roots. They were out of the tree, and descending to the ground. The roots slipped away, and they landed on their feet.

"Breathe," Rea whispered above the beating of her heart.

A saffron sun blazed in the sky and Leela jumped as she spotted a patch of roots hanging beside her. They hung from a banyan just like the one they had been sucked into.

The banyan remained, but the forest around them was gone. Rea and Leela found themselves standing at the edge of a prairie. Clouds drifted across a lavender-blue sky. A giant dragonfly as large as Rea's arm buzzed past them.

"D-Did we travel from one b-banyan tree to an-another?"

she asked Rea.

"I think s-so." Rea couldn't fathom what had happened. She stared at the purple sky in shock. After a moment, she turned to Leela. "Are you okay?"

Leela nodded. "But where are we?"

Suddenly a small voice said, "Hullo? Is somebody there?"

Rea and Leela bolted behind the tree, sticking to each other like two bands of Velcro even though the trunk was wide enough to hide them both. Rea inched forward to peek at who was approaching, and her gaze fell on the grass. Flowers of every hue blossomed out of the blades as though rainbows had splashed onto them. The flower petals shimmered in the sunlight.

A vague memory nudged her, and she turned to Leela, but Leela was staring at a little girl wearing a tent-like frock made entirely of yellow and green leaves.

"You shouldn't be here." The girl blinked her long lashes. "It's forbidden."

Catching sight of something on the street, she scampered off and Leela let out her breath.

"Jumping horsefeathers!" gasped a lady dressed in egg-blue and smoke-orange flower-petals sprinkled with spots of fuschia. The girl clung to her legs. "Step away from the royal port at once!"

The woman thundered towards them, dropping her basket of vegetables to the side, and shooed them away from the banyan. "Must you lassies defy all rules and etiquette? And to dress in such odd fashions." She tutted at them and shook her head.

Conscious of their pajamas, Rea and Leela bumped into each other in their haste to escape the unwanted spotlight. They hurried toward a nearby road. At once, they were swallowed into a throng of people jostling their way along the thoroughfare: cobblers weaving ferns into sandals, artists painting on flat pieces of rock, people selling fruits and vegetables and someone selling—did Rea hear that right—*enchantment tonics?*

A scruffy boy wearing a cardboard sign with the words 'Boife's Bozan Boutique,' sang past her, "Book your bozan, book your bozan! We train 'em good! Getcha bozan from us today!" and disappeared behind rows of shops stacked with copper utensils, carriage wheels, and bags of seeds showcasing the weirdest flowers. A few stalls down, a woman with fierce black eyes was braiding ivy into another woman's hair. A woven fabric made of stems and dried flowers draped her body and she smiled at Rea, offering to braid her hair for half the usual price.

"Stop staring," Leela said and diverted Rea's attention to avoid a group of teenage girls walking past them with amused looks. One of them was wearing a dress of white and purple petals, which flared upwards from her knees like an upside-down lily, while the others sported outfits of maple leaves and thickly stamened flowers. They pointed at Rea and Leela's pajamas and burst into giggles.

Leela pulled Rea to the side of the road.

"Why are they laughing at us?" she asked in a whisper. "And why is everyone wearing leaves and petals instead of regular clothes?"

"I don't know but we have to find out," said Rea.

"Are you seriously going to go up to those girls and ask them why they're wearing what they're wearing?"

"No, idiot," Rea snapped, "I'm going to ask them what this place is."

But before Rea could approach the girls, a boy slid up to their side. He was about their age, and half a foot taller. He was wearing brown leaves for shorts, a long-sleeved tunic, a pair of green oversized leaves tacked together in the middle, and a leather belt with three pouches loosely fitted around his waist. He stared at them for a moment, and then hurried away. Rea and Leela exchanged nervous glances. They watched the boy from the corner of their eyes to see if he was coming back, but he had slipped into the crowd.

Rea and Leela scurried forward, keeping their faces straight and their feet moving quickly. Suddenly, the boy popped up in front of them and Rea lurched backwards. His darting eyes and unsure expression made him seem nervous, but nonetheless he put on a wide-toothed smile and flapped open one side of his jacket. Necklaces, bracelets, bangles, and earrings clinked from tiny loops.

"Would you, um, princesses like some fine jewelry?" A rush of ash brown hair fell over his cinnamon eyes.

"Thanks," said Rea, walking faster. "We're not interested."

"Ah, but princess, don't you see how these lovely earrings draw out your beautiful eyes? Two ponds of mesmerizing copezium!"

There was a slight shiver in his voice as he jiggled a silver and black earring in front of Rea's face. Leela did a double take and mouthed a word, but Rea didn't understand her. Instead, her ears turned hot and a blush filled her cheeks. The boy thought her eyes were beautiful. Rea turned her gaze away and quickened her pace.

"Hey, what did you say?" said Leela and the boy stopped dead in his tracks. His eyes shifted as though he wanted to run away.

"What's the matter?" asked Rea, turning around. Leela was staring at the boy's face, waiting for him to answer.

"You said copezium, didn't you?" pushed Leela. "I heard it," she said, looking at Rea with her eyes wide.

The boy looked so upset, Rea thought he might cry.

"Apologies, Princesses. Do believe me!" he said. "It was merely a slip-up. A terrible habit I have. I always forget the things I'm not supposed to say and then I say them. It won't happen again. I swear it on the moon!"

Rea remembered how the blood had rushed to her face when he called her eyes beautiful. She ought to have caught the word copezium instead. Mortified, Rea crushed the memory into smithereens. Thankfully, Leela had heard it.

The boy was talking frantically. "I know the Queen prohibits us from talking about copezium," he went on. "It's an extremely dangerous metal that she uses when she wields her Shadow Magic. Oh, I did it again!" His face filled fear. "I didn't mean to say... Shadow Magic," he uttered the last words very slowly and in a whisper. "It's my nerves. I haven't met a princess before, much less two, and never did I dream of speaking to them."

Rea and Leela looked at each other as realization dawned. They had discovered a big piece in the where-is-Rohan puzzle!

"I'm sorry," said Leela, awkwardly leaning to pat the boy's arm but then deciding against it. "I didn't mean to frighten you. I was taken by surprise, that's all."

"Princess, you are infinitely generous!" the boy said, practically singing with relief. "The metal, although sinister, is magnificent in its beauty with its dark color and glimmer. I was only using it as a compliment and not in any way trying to insult the Queen."

"We understand. Don't worry about it," said Rea, starting to walk again. There was no time for idle chit-chat. Rohan was here and they needed to find him!

"Very well then," the boy said, and flapped open the other side of his jacket to reveal another set of trinkets. "You may choose whatever jewel you like."

"If you don't mind, we really need to be on our way," said Rea.

"And where might that be?"

The girls looked at each other. That was a good question. Where were they going? A red cobble-stoned path stretched ahead until it wound out of sight. On either side, flowers as large as tractor wheels blossomed and wilted right before their eyes.

"Say, aren't princesses forbidden to venture out of the castle grounds without guards? I don't reckon I see any around," he said, casting an uneasy glance around them.

"That's because we're *not* princesses," said Leela.

"And yet you portaled through the Doda Alda Mara. I saw you land." His voice turned to a whisper.

"Portaled? Wait, you know about the banyan?" The boy suddenly interested Rea. "Can you tell us more?"

The boy took a step behind and buttoned up his jacket. "I see what this is," he swallowed. "This is the first time you've snuck out of the castle and now you don't know your way back."

"No, you have us mistaken. Can you please just tell us where we are?" implored Rea.

"Bouncing bozans! You're going to be in terrible trouble! The

Queen will be in a fit of rage. Never before did we live with such secrecy surrounding the royal family. Oh, where are my manners?" he gasped like a fish out of water and Rea noticed his hands were trembling. "Princesses, I'm Xeranther, barrow boy by morning, jewelry connoisseur by afternoon, and tour guide any time during the day."

He bowed extravagantly and Leela slid Rea a look that said, 'something is very wrong here.' But the boy gave Rea an idea.

"Nice to meet you, Xeranther. Can you excuse us for a second?"

She steered Leela a few paces away. "Play along. He thinks we're princesses who have stepped out of some castle for the first time. It's the perfect excuse to ask him whatever we want without sounding suspicious."

"Are you serious?" Leela's gaze ping-ponged between Rea and Xeranther. "He thinks we're princesses, and he's talking about traveling through the banyan as if it were the most common thing in the world. Rea, we came here through a tree and for all we know we're going to be stuck here forever."

"But the nightmare led me to the banyan, and we travelled between two of them! How can we leave without finding out more? I'm sure we can get home through the tree again."

Leela looked at her in disbelief. Inwardly though, Rea agreed with her—they couldn't be sure that the tree would take them home again. She glanced at the boy and his leaf-clothes and thought about the strange market. Images of the roots, the banyan's dark mouth, and the fall through space seized her. What if they couldn't go back? What if they really were stuck here forever? What if the roots had actually choked and killed them and now they were in the world of the dead? What if she never saw Amma and Bajai again? What if... Rea gasped. The thought hit her like a blow to the stomach.

"Leela," her voice quivered, "I'm as freaked out as you are but think about Rohan. We must have landed in this place for a reason. Maybe he did too. Wherever he is, this is what he must be feeling: lost, scared and alone. How can we leave without knowing for sure he isn't here?"

Leela looked around her, her face small and anxious. "But—um…" Rea watched as Leela's mind reasoned through the situation. After a moment, her shoulders squared and she nodded. "You're right," she said, resolutely. "We can't give up on him."

A sensation, soft as a bud and surprising as sunlight twinkling through a storm, spread through Rea's chest. She threw her arms around Leela, giving her the biggest hug she'd ever given anyone.

"I'm so happy you're here," she said.

Leela gave her a bear hug in return. "Me too." Then facing the boy, she said, "You caught us in our lie. We are princesses, and this is our first time out of the castle. Will you show us around?"

Xeranther gave them a look of mistrust. "Most certainly not. If I don't report you to the Imperial Guard this instant, my head will boil in a cauldron."

"I don't think anyone saw us come through the portal except you," said Rea. "In fact, a woman at the market got so angry we were standing beside the tree, she told us to leave. If you don't tell anyone, nobody will know, and you won't be in trouble."

Xeranther took a step forward, convinced for a moment. But

then he seemed to think better of it, and retreated again.

"If you help us, we'll buy some of your jewelry," ventured Leela.

"Buy my trinkets, huh?" He scratched the back of his neck. "Well, my assistance will come at a price higher than 'some' jewelry." He lowered his voice trying to sound imposing, but it cracked at the end and came off as a loud squeak. Embarrassed, he coughed and straightened his posture to look taller.

"We'll buy everything that's on one side of your jacket," Rea pointed to his left sleeve.

Xeranther's eyes doubled in size and he grinned as if he couldn't believe his luck. "It shall be my honor, Princesses! Consider me your guide." A flash of pity crossed his face. "I can only imagine your desire to enjoy your one day away from the castle."

Rea and Leela agreed as solemnly as they could.

"By the way, you can call her Rea and me Leela and for our safety it's probably better you don't call us princesses."

"Quite right. It's clever to use such peculiar names. So, Prin—I mean, Ree-aa and Lee-laa, where would you like to go?"

"First, can you tell us more about the portal?" said Rea.

"You don't know about it?"

The girls shook their heads.

"Nothing at all?"

They shook their heads again.

"I cannot believe the Queen keeps it from you. It is your birthright, after all. Well, it is one way to keep you from leaving, I suppose," he muttered, and mumbled a few other things about selfish royals under his breath.

Rea cleared her throat.

"Ah, yes, the portal," he said. "Any person in whom the blood of the nectar flows, which is to say all members of the royal family and few members of the common folk, can portal between worlds through the Doda Alda Mara. Me, like most common folk, cannot."

"Between worlds?" gulped Leela. Her face went from pale to colorless. "You mean we're in a different *world*?"

Xeranther scrunched his brows, looking skeptical.

"Er... what she means is what's the name of this place?" Rea corrected hastily.

"You aren't even told that?" he said.

"No, no, of course we are," Rea covered up. "We simply want to confirm if what we've been taught is true."

She hoped the angst she had picked up on this Queen lady would work in her favor. Fortunately, Xeranther offered a nod of understanding.

"We are in the realm of Delphinus," he said. "And this is the Kingdom of Astranthia."

CHAPTER 11

WHERE DAY IS NIGHT AND NIGHT IS DAY

"**A**stranthia."

The word rolled in Rea's mouth and for the first time she took in the landscape.

Giant dragonflies buzzed in a prairie teeming with wildflowers as pink mountains flanked its sides. Their slopes, delicate and blush-toned, sparkled with drops of sunshine. Trees swayed. Their leaves flapped like butterfly wings, displaying mesmerizing designs within them. The longer Rea stared, the faster the patterns swirled.

A calm stole over her.

"'Where day is night and night is day,'" she murmured, recalling the prophecy and the vision she had had during Mishti Daadi's divination.

Every nerve in her body tingled. The vision was where she'd seen the flowers growing from the tips of grass. This was *that* place! Rea checked her watch. The second and minute hand remained still at 1:11AM.

"What time is it?" she asked and Xeranther cocked his head to the sky.

"It's the second hour past the hour of the sun."

"Second hour past the hour of—oh, oh—you mean, it's two o'clock!" Rea contained herself from jumping up and down. She and Leela had deduced Rohan was in a place not too far away but with a different time zone. It was nighttime in Darjeeling and daytime in Astranthia, and they were only a portal ride away!

"Have you heard of a boy named Rohan? Rohan Chettri?" Rea asked Xeranther eagerly.

"Ro-hun... Chey-tree?" The boy shook his head.

"Shoot, we should have brought along a picture," Rea said to Leela. "He's about a few inches taller, hazel eyes, curly hair?"

Leela tugged on a ring of Rea's curls to help him understand.

"I'm afraid I don't know anyone with such a name or description."

"Can we ask around? We need to find him," said Rea. She felt her senses coming alive—all this was more proof that Rohan was here.

"Why?" Xeranther asked, openly curious. "Is he your betrothed?"

"What? No!" retorted Rea, her ears burning red, as Leela dragged her to the side.

"Are you sure we can trust him? We don't know anything about this realm."

"Leela, this is the place I saw when I blacked out at Mishti Daadi's."

"The place you called whimsical and weird?"

"Yes! The flowers that pop out of the grass, I saw them in the vision. And then there's the prophecy, 'Where day is night and night is day.'"

Leela flung her hands to her mouth to mute a squeal. "Also, Xeranther knows what copezium is! Oh my gosh, Rea, we solved one riddle!"

Rea nodded excitedly and Leela ran to Xeranther. "Rohan's umm... a... a servant boy at the castle and our very good friend," she said. "We haven't seen him in days, and we miss hanging out with him and are worried something bad might have happened, so we snuck out to look for him and—"

"Basically, we need to find him," Rea said, cutting short Leela's ramble.

"Astranthia is a vast land, but in the able hands of Xeranther you must worry not." He puffed out his scrawny chest. "With a name as remarkable as Roo-hun Chey-tree, he should not be hard to locate. If he's been around, someone will remember."

Rea and Leela high fived each other and turned to do the same with Xeranther. He looked uncomfortably between them and hesitantly raised his hand. The girls laughed, smacking their palms against his. Xeranther chuckled and led the way, providing a running commentary on the sights and scenes they passed.

"What are those?" Leela pointed towards bulbous structures that looked like gigantic onions scattered over the grassland.

"They are buds. They are our homes. I bet you have grander buds on the castle grounds."

"Uh... of course," said Rea, staring at the bud-houses. They were an enclosure of panels shaped in the form of petals folded over each other to create a wide bottom and a pointy top.

"If you climb onto a high branch, the petals coming together at the crown resemble a tansylion bud. It's quite lovely," said Xeranther.

"Do you live here?" asked Leela.

"Pickle my pudding! No, no." He looked comically surprised.

Rea related to that look. She had used it many times when tourists asked if her father owned the Tombu Tea Estate, wondering why else a girl as young as her would be spending her time wandering through the plantations. She, too, would hurriedly say no, chuckling at the absurdity of that idea. Rea was imagining the type of bud Xeranther lived in when he unexpectedly snatched her arm and pulled her to the side.

"Look out for clumps," he said, and quickly let go as if her skin were hot metal. Rea gave him a side-eye but he avoided eye contact. "I shouldn't have touched...er... and grabbed your hand like that. It's against protocol. I... I apologize."

Rea realized the protocol he was referring to might have something to do with a-commoner-not-touching-a-royal protocol.

"Oh, that's okay," she said. "You can hold my hand." And then she heard herself. "I mean... not that I'm asking you to! Only if you wanted to then it would be okay." Leela looked at her with big eyes and a smirk ready to erupt into giggles. "WHAT I MEAN IS, you won't get into trouble if you happen to grab my arm in the event of pulling me away from doing something stupid like walking into someone or something. That's what I'm trying to say," she said, running out of breath (what was she even saying?) and wanting to die of embarrassment on the spot. Then something moved.

Puzzled, Rea looked at the ground as a tuft of grass shook itself awake. Grunting angrily, it revealed its hooded, lime-green eyes, and gave them a dirty look. Tiny legs quickly appeared underneath it and the creature scurried into the bushes, the tuft of grass sticking to its back like camouflage.

"To think you almost stepped on him!" Xeranther burst into laughter. "Don't worry, clumps are harmless. Just grouchy. If you get bitten by one, their bite can put you in a bad mood for hours. You might cry, shout, or turn glum. After a while, all is well again."

"That's so adorable," said Leela, her expression melting into mush. "Do you keep them as pets?"

"You'd want that as a pet?" Rea asked, shocked. "I was scared half to death watching *grass* come to life. Didn't you hear what its bite can do?"

"Oh, he's such a cute, angry little thing. I've always wanted a pet, but I'm not allowed to have one."

Leela grew morose watching the clump hop away. As they continued along their way, several buds lowered their ivory-petal doors. At different heights, they formed verandas, balconies, and porches with elegant bamboo railings. A man sat in one of them reading a parchment, and a few buds down, a trio of children scampered out to play. From a window, their mother shouted warnings to keep clear of her flower beds.

"At night," said Xeranther, "the doors are drawn and the buds glow with lantern-light like drops of golden dew."

"Why is everything shaped like a flower?" asked Rea. She was tempted to stay put until night-time to watch these houses glow.

"It's our way of paying homage to the sacred Som, of course."

Leela slipped Rea a look and Rea dipped her head defeatedly. With all the things they needed to learn about, an explanation about the sacred Som was the last thing on her list.

"Um, Xeranther?" She tapped his shoulder. "Can we ask around for Rohan?"

"Apologies, Princess," he said and then bit his lip realizing his gaffe. "Yes, Rea, we must. Forgive me, I got carried away."

For the next two hours, Rea, Leela, and Xeranther visited budhoods painted in vibrant colors. They passed empty streets and busy roads. There were no cars, traffic jams, or blaring horns. Rea asked men and women on horses or in horse-drawn carriages if they had seen or heard of a boy named Rohan, and Leela did the same with people walking by. Xeranther knocked on buds and spoke to their inhabitants. No one had the slightest clue who Rohan was.

When their throats grew hoarse, the three companions rested their tired legs on a bench.

"The Whispering Walls!" Xeranther cried out suddenly. Rea and Leela looked at him, confused.

"Truly, what do they teach you in that castle??" He shook his head. "Legend has it that ever since the realm of Astranthia blossomed into existence, the Whispering Walls have lived. It's a ramshackle bud cast in magic with walls full of secrets." He leaned closer. "Other people's secrets. Secrets confessed, secrets spilled, secrets with their fat chewed out."

Leela let out an enraptured 'oh' and Rea nearly choked on her guffaw.

"Really, you believe this nonsense?" she whispered and Leela eagerly nodded.

"The only catch is that the walls whisper all the secrets at once. Only a few have been able to decipher the information they had been seeking. But no one knows how they did it."

"What are we waiting for?" Leela jumped to her feet. "Let's go find out."

"Hang on," said Rea. "This sounds like a silly tale."

Xeranther looked hurt. "Legends are not silly. They are truths of times past, woven into stories. You may not believe them, but that does not make them untrue. Through legends, ancient wisdom lives. Without them, we would fade into oblivion. As Poppy says, 'You'd be wise to regard them.'"

Or I'd be wise to dis*regard them and continue searching for Rohan*, Rea thought. She had half a mind to leave rather than entertain their ridiculous notions. At this rate, she had a better chance of finding Rohan on her own. *Pff, walls that whisper.* This place was whimsical but not out of a fantasy book.

"Look, I don't mean to offend you," she said to Xeranther. "But I don't have time to waste talking to walls that whisper."

She heard a buzzing in her ear and swatted at what she assumed was a large fly.

"How rude," came a voice, tinny and angry.

Rea whipped her head around. Floating in front of her was

a fairy-like being the size of Rea's palm. A lustrous white dress in the shape of a tulip draped her willowy body and snowy hair fell below her shoulders. On her feet twinkled the tiniest of white shoes.

"Oh my g-god. I'm so sorry. I thought you were a—a—what are—?" Rea tripped over her words.

"Flula!" Xeranther slapped his forehead. "I promised to help the princesses and forgot we were to meet."

"Princesses?" She glided towards the girls. "My, my, isn't this a day of rare sightings."

Rea threw Xeranther an uneasy look.

"Oh, Floo is my friend. You can trust her. She won't tell a soul."

Flula clapped her paisley-shaped wings together, casting a shower of rainbow-colored glitter. Her eyes shimmered purple and her lips turned into a mischievous smile.

Rea squeezed her eyes shut. When she opened them, the fairy was still there. Never had Rea cared for fairy tales or 'girly' books and here she was talking to a flying fairy. There were many strange things she had witnessed today. This by far was the strangest of all.

The fairy tugged on Xeranther's hair. "Introduce me!"

"Rea and Leela, meet Flula, a Pillywiggin pari."

Flula twirled in the air and landed on a plant with scarlet and turquoise flowers. Instantly, her body turned red and Rea blinked several times to find her. Enjoying the show she was putting on, Flula hopped from blossom to blossom, turning from blue to red and red to blue. By the time Xeranther finished filling her in on

Rea and Leela's hunt for a lost servant boy, she had returned to her normal self. Speckles of glitter fell to the ground around her.

"You poor petals. Have you no idea where he might be? Lost things have a terrible habit of staying hidden."

"No... we don't know where Rohan is," Rea answered and glanced at Leela who was staring at Flula in shock.

"I'm taking them to the Whispering Walls," said Xeranther. "They might hear something about the boy there."

"What a sweet-scented idea. I have to go by the Whispers as it is." She turned to the girls with a scowl on her face. "I'm a foliage reporter, you see, and my winter reports are due and I'm nowhere close to being done."

"So, it's true?" Leela burst forth. "Paries live in forests and it's their job to protect the plants and trees."

Flula nodded in amusement. "Us Pillywiggin paries, are in charge of reporting on the spread of invasive species, the health of flora and the rate of blossom withering and blooming as well as tending to the change-of-season foliage. This time from autumn to winter. That's why I'm on prairie duty today."

"Unbelievable." Leela fan-girled, bouncing on her toes. "I've read so much about fairies and paries, I can't believe I'm actually talking to one!"

"Oh, that's sweet as nectar! Humans, especially Astranthian ones, rarely appreciate all the good work we pari-folk do," she chuckled, looking at Xeranther. Then she swiveled towards Rea's dumbfounded face. "I know what you're thinking. I should have finished my reports, but you won't believe what I heard through the ivystem!" She somersaulted in the air and gold specks shimmied out of her. "There's been a Ceffyldwer spotting!

"A Ceffyldwer?" Xeranther gasped like he'd heard something terrible. "The last one was seen during the Shadow Wars, a thousand years ago."

"Times are a-changing," Flula said.

Xeranther grew serious. "Indeed, they are," he said.

Flula sailed ahead, glowing like a firefly. Luckily, the sight of three children hurrying after a pari didn't seem to raise any eyebrows. In fact, people dodged out of the way and some even tipped their hats with a grin. A short while later, they cut through the prairie, which had begun to grow wild. The blossoms on the grass—flowergrass, as Rea learned they were called—swayed in their direction.

"Do you think it's getting late?" she asked Leela and glanced at the weakening sun. It had certainly been a few hours since they had portaled and they didn't have long before the sun rose in Meruk and Amma found her missing.

"Need to get back to the castle, eh?" said Xeranther.

"No, to the portal," Rea said.

"Once I receive my payment, I shall take you right back," he teased, jingling his trinkets.

Rea cringed, remembering her lie about buying his jewelry. Never mind that she had no money on her, rupees would be worthless in this land anyway. She needed to come up with a plan to get out of paying him. A sneaking suspicion told her Leela would not be happy about duping him. *Oh well, I'll deal with it after Xeranther is done helping us.*

"Aren't there other portals closer to the Whispering Walls?" asked Leela. "That way we can get back home—er—I mean to the castle, faster."

As much as Leela was mesmerized by this land, Rea could tell she feared spending a minute longer than she had to in a place where they could be stuck forever. She had the same fear, too. Astranthia was no Kolkata—there were no trains, buses, or taxis to give them a ride home. Just a terrifying, unpredictable magical tree.

"We don't know of any other portals except the Doda Alda Mara and the one inside the castle you portaled from," said Xeranther. "If there's anyone who would know of others, it's you princesses."

"Right, of course," said Rea. He believed she and Leela had portaled from the castle. "How far are these talking walls from here? If we can't make it to the castle in time, we'll come back tomorrow."

"Will there be guards with you?"

"Um... no..."

Xeranther turned to Flula, who pursed her lips as if to say, 'Don't look at me.'

"Princesses, I understand it is difficult to live with the Queen, but if you sneak out of the castle tomorrow, I cannot risk helping you again. As an Astranthian, I am sworn to protect those who bleed the sacred nectar and it is my duty to report those lost and without the protection of guards. As a matter of fact, to save my head, I must hand you both to the first guards we see once we return from the Whispering Walls."

"You will do no such thing," declared Rea. "All we ask is for you to take us back to the portal. If you're not willing to help us, we'll figure it out ourselves."

Leela drew Rea to the side.

"Rea, we need them. We have no idea how to get back. Let's tell them everything. We're tangled in too many lies, and I don't want to be handed to the guards or get Xeranther and Flula in trouble. Besides, there's a good chance they'll help us if they know we're not princesses and have no connection to this Queen."

Rea bit the inside of her cheek. "But the truth is such a long story and who knows what's happening to Rohan right now? Mishti Daadi said he's 'alive and kicking, screaming and shouting,' and that he's rebelling against someone. The prophecy said, 'Of strength and courage, he does boast.' How long would your courage last if you were in his place? Please Leela, we'll waste whatever little time we have left to save him."

"We're already wasting time..."

Frustration mounted in Rea's chest. Leela wasn't wrong, but that didn't make this any easier. Rohan was out there, suffering, and she had no idea how long it would take to find him. But Rea had no better ideas. And she was all out of choices. *Argh!* Rea walked back to Xeranther and Flula. "There's something we need to tell you."

Standing in a huddle, she told them the truth about their identities, the story of Rohan's disappearance, the nightmare, the banyan, and the creepy roots that brought them to Astranthia—a place nobody back home knew existed.

"Leaping leprechauns, you two are Earthlings! Elder Pari, our Mother Leader, spoke of meeting Earthlings centuries ago. And now, here I am flying in front of two!" The flecks of violet in Flula's eyes shimmered and she fluttered so close, Rea suppressed the urge to swat her away.

"No one's called us that but yes, we're Earthlings," she said.

"If you truly are Earthlings from this other world, how did you portal through the Doda Alda Mara? Only those of royal or nectral Astranthian blood can," questioned Xeranther.

"All I know is the moment I held the roots, they grew over me and we were pulled into the tree and thrown out the other end, landing here," said Rea.

Xeranther paused a beat and his eyes turned wild. "I was stupid to have trusted you. You've tricked me!"

He stabbed the air with a fallen twig and Rea could see his legs were shaking. Flula raised her arms to calm him, but in vain.

"Please believe us, Xeranther—" began Leela.

"Stay away from me. I know this is one of the Queen's tests. No matter that you look like, girls, I will fight you! I say, reveal yourselves at once!"

With his spare hand, he rummaged through the pouches on his belt and pulled out a marble-sized bottle filled with a brownish-teal liquid. He dashed some on the twig and it vibrated, sprouting limbs. Leela blanched.

"Will you please stop?" Rea snatched the growing twig from his trembling hands and flung it to the side. She had no idea where she got the courage to touch the creepy twig-creature-thing, but she had spent enough time talking and chatting and not looking for Rohan. The twig deflated like a balloon and Flula doubled over with giggles.

"Trixter potions are side-splitting! They get me every time."

"Look at us!" Rea raised her voice and Flula hushed. "Look at what we're wearing. We know nothing about Astranthia. We have different names, and this is the first time we've seen a pari or a walking piece of grass or a spontaneously growing twig. We're more afraid than you can imagine. If you don't believe us, we'll portal to Earth with you and show you where we live. You'll see posters of my brother everywhere; you'll see he's missing."

"Ordinary Astranthians can't travel through the portal, but maybe people from Earth can?" Leela suggested, staying clear of the flattened twig.

"I bet that's it," said Flula. "And who cares for silly rules anyway? They're meant to be forgotten! Xee, let's help these girls."

Xeranther didn't answer Flula. He looked back and forth between Leela and Rea with suspicion and disgust. His once-friendly eyes had turned cold and hard. Rea could tell he wasn't going to help.

Suddenly, it was all too much. Tears welled up in her eyes. "Please," she said, her voice cracking. "My brother has been kidnapped and it's my fault. My family blames me for losing him. We've spent days looking for him and we finally found this portal. I was so excited. I thought we were getting closer. But we don't know anything about this place. Without your help, we'll never find him. Please, help us."

Embarrassed by her outburst, Rea looked at the ground,

hastily wiping away her tears. For the first time since he had disappeared, Rea acknowledged to herself that Rohan might never come back. Things might not have been perfect between them, but he was still her brother. Her twin. Her other half. She didn't care if Rohan never invited her to anything again—she couldn't bear the thought of losing him. And if he didn't come back, she knew Amma would stop caring about her altogether.

"We're begging you," said Leela, standing arm in arm with Rea. Tears filmed her eyes too.

With a downcast glance, Xeranther handed them each a leaf for a tissue. "I'll help you, but under one condition."

All of a sudden, a blood-curdling squawk filled the sky. With a sound of alarm, Xeranther pushed Rea and Leela under the cover of an enormous, spiral-veined frond. Only when Flula nodded that it was safe did he allow them to crawl out.

"The Queen's spies are everywhere." He glanced at the eagle-like bird flying in the distance. It was larger than any bird Rea had seen. "My condition is you don't tell a soul you are Earthlings. It won't be safe for either of us."

"We won't," said Rea, her heart sighing with relief.

"We promise," added Leela.

"Tomorrow, I will bring clothes to make you look more Astranthian. For now, let's make speed to the Whispering Walls."

CHAPTER 12

THE WHISPERING WALLS

A gigantic, mold-ridden bud sat on a dirt road emanating a buzzing hum. Susurrating voices rose and fell from its walls, and as they got closer, it turned into a cacophony of a thousand whispers. Xeranther led them inside without hesitating. Leela followed nervously and Rea's skin prickled as she trailed behind them.

Once inside, the bud was musty and cool, and the whispers dulled into background static. Flula flitted along the bud's inner walls, lighting cobweb-covered lanterns placed within alcoves. She lit them by touching each wick with the tip of her finger and within moments, the bud flickered in hues of amber and shadow. The light revealed its aged facade, peeling and mottled in places. Rea pictured people sitting close to the walls, letting go of their secrets.

"What do we do now?" she asked. The hollowness of the bud

echoed her words.

"Ask your question," Xeranther said, sitting down beside her.

Rea crouched close to the wall. "Have you heard of Rohan Chettri?" she whispered.

The drum of voices lifted and dropped, and Rea only heard gibberish. Judging by the quizzical looks held by the others, they hadn't picked up anything either.

"Is Rohan Chettri in Astranthia?" Leela asked, more loudly.

Flula sailed to various points on the wall, pressing her ears against it. Rea did the same, but all she caught between the swell of voices was a random word—collyfuzzle, was it?

Rea tried again. "Do you know if a boy named Rohan Chettri has been kidnapped from Earth?"

The whispers ebbed and intensified, pounding the wall like a headache. Flula hit her fist against it, producing a faint knock. "Help her, secret keeper! I demand you tell her what she has traveled all this way to know," she said.

The voices went on, fighting and scratching over each other. They escalated like chants from a hundred lips and Rea, still kneeling near the wall, wanted to scream for silence.

"I'm sorry," Xeranther said, kneeling beside her. "I hoped you would learn something."

Rea rested her face against the bud, defeated. They had portaled between worlds for nothing. A tear slid down her cheek and fell onto the edge of the wall.

Suddenly, the voices were silent.

Everyone exchanged glances except Rea, who was too deep in her misery to notice the change. She brushed away another tear and Leela grabbed her tear-streaked hand.

"Ask the question again and place your hand on the wall," she said.

Rea caught the twinkle in her eye and did as she was told.

"Rohan lies locked—" a raspy voice began, loud, lucid, and clear. Rea's heart leapt with hope. But before the voice could finish its sentence, the march of whispers rose and stomped out the rest of the sentence.

"Flaming flintstools!" Xeranther exclaimed. "How did you do that?"

"I think it's the tears," Leela said, her eyes round like chikoos.

Rea wiped another wet spot on her cheek and placed her damp palm on the wall. The bud went mute.

"Oh greatness," Xeranther bellowed and broke into a song.

"Come one, come two, come three, come all
Bequeath onto me your prayer calls
Those far and few on sincere pew
Leave behind a salt of dew
Now hear, now here
The whispers veer
As one does fall
Into one's ear
Sincere, and
In a drawl
A secret
from
the
Whispering Walls."

He finished his song, and looked at the girls.

"It's a rhyme every child in Astranthia grows up listening to. As children, we would come here, hoping to find out other people's secrets for fun. We'd leave behind dew drops or water from seas and rivers. Nothing ever happened, so we'd piece together the words we caught and make up our own secrets. Can we try your way again?"

Rea nodded. She repeated her question and touched the wall with her tear-wet hand.

"Rohan lies locked..." the voice said again before trailing off.

"It worked!" Rea yelled, and the bud swam in soft, golden light.

"Oh!" Flula shouted joyfully. She twirled, pari dust falling around her like glitter. Flula's body glowed brightly, and Rea felt a sudden warmth in her chest.

"When a pari is truly happy, her inner happiness flows out for all to partake in," Xeranther said, smiling at Flula.

Rea pushed back her tears, touched that a stranger cared so much. She went over to Flula and sat beside her.

"I have an idea," she said.

Rea repeated the question and counted to three before placing her tear. Since the voices stopped for only a moment, she had to pick the right time to hear the rest of the sentence.

"—locked in the Cellars of Doom," came the crackly voice.

Everyone's eyes lit up and she continued, waiting six seconds this time.

"—For the Night of Nilaya," the walls said.

Next, she waited nine counts.

No whispers came. Rea tried four more times. The secret about Rohan had ended.

"Rohan lies locked in the Cellars of Doom for the Night of Nilaya," Leela recounted once they were back outside. The sunlight was waning; the day was almost over.

"Where are these Cellars and what is the Night of Nilaya?" asked Rea.

"The Night of Nilaya is the most important ceremony for every living soul in Astranthia. It's the night the Som, our sacred flower and giver of life, rises to replenish the realm," explained Flula.

"Um... okay. When is it?"

"Four days from today."

"And what about the Cellars?"

The sky, a luminous purple, turned a shade darker and a cloud of worry passed over Xeranther.

"The Cellars of Doom are the most treacherous prisons in all the land," he said.

"You mean Rohan was brought to another world to be locked in its most dangerous prison like a criminal?" Leela asked, astounded.

"That's what the secret said," Xeranther replied grimly. "The Cellars exist somewhere underneath the castle. They're called the Cellars of Doom because each cellar is cast with a spell. They say that once you are locked inside, death is the only escape."

"The cells are guarded by spriggans," quivered Flula. "They can light you on fire with a single breath."

"How do you know so much about these prisons?" asked Rea.

"Maybe it's all just rumors." She couldn't believe Rohan was stuck in such a terrible place.

Xeranther lowered his head and Flula's glow dimmed as she landed on his shoulder.

"My Par was thrown in the Cellars because he gave a portion of haukernut harvest to a beggar woman without taking her coins. Under the Queen's reign, rations have to be bought no matter the price and no matter how poor we may be. Giving priced goods for free is a punishable offence under the new Covenants."

"The Queen detests any show of kindness," Flula added, softer than a whisper. "If she were our ruler, the pari-folk would have kicked her out of power." She kicked the air to mimic her words.

"If only it were that easy," grumbled Xeranther.

"What do you mean *if* she were your ruler?" asked Leela.

"The Queen's rule extends only to humans in Astranthia. Not pari-folk. We live by our own rules and don't meddle in their affairs. It's the only way we can live together in harmony."

Rea was beginning to understand the strange ways of this realm, but she needed to know more about the Cellars.

"What happened to your father?" she asked.

Xeranther's face hardened.

"It was the middle of winter. My Par found an old lady clothed in rags lying faint by the side of the road. She was sickly and hungry with barely a coin to spare, not nearly enough to buy food. So, he smuggled a few haukernuts and berries out of our landlord's orchard to feed her. When the Court of Coin inspected the ledgers, my Par confessed and explained why he did it. The

Queen would hear none of his reasons. She berated him for having a weak soul and imprisoned him, making him an example to all. Our family begged the landlord to appeal to the Queen, but he would do nothing. 'Rules have no exceptions,' he said. My Par had worked for him for twenty-three years. On the day of his hanging, he yelled about the torture he had endured at the hands of the spriggans and the bewitching prison cells. His words haunt me still."

"And… what happened to the old woman?" asked Leela. Her face looked like she didn't want to know the answer.

Xeranther's voice cracked with anger. "She was a ruse sent to test the obedience of the common folk. She wasn't even a real person. The Queen had created her using her evil Shadow Magic."

"Oh…" shuddered Leela. "I'm so sorry, Xeranther. What a horrible thing."

"I'm really sorry about your father but Rohan doesn't know the rules of this place. How could he have broken them?" Rea said impatiently. "I mean we're from Earth! There's no reason for him to be locked in these Cellars."

Leela gave Rea a look, but Rea wasn't sure what it meant. She had said she was sorry for what happened to Xeranther's father. What else was she supposed to do? They needed to focus on Rohan. He was the one who needed help now.

"There's a chance the secret of the Whispers isn't true," Xeranther said, his expression somber. "Although, you'd be a fool to think the Queen needs a reason to hurt people. She rules by her own fancy. Since she became our ruler, we live in fear that anything we do could be pronounced treasonous. A stray word can cost someone their life, their livelihood, and their family. Par's story is not the only one like it. Everyone in Astranthia has lost someone to the Queen's law. Yet, we live on and do nothing." His jaw clenched.

"Then help us to get to the Cellars. I won't have Rohan imprisoned for a second longer," said Rea.

Xeranther shook his head. "Not only is it nearly impossible to get to the castle but it's also extremely dangerous. It isn't wise at all."

"I don't care if it is wise or not," she snapped. "I finally know where my brother is, and you think I'm going to give up on him now?"

"The castle is surrounded by a venomous lake. Only those invited by the Queen can travel across it. Others have died trying. Do you want to die?" Xeranther's mouth tightened.

"What about you, Flula? Can't you fly over it?" Leela asked, trying to find a solution.

"My Earthling blossom, I can fly over the waters but there's nothing I can do about the dangers which reside under it. Those who want to enter the castle must traverse the lake themselves."

"But we can't just leave him there." Leela's eyes welled up.

"And we won't," Rea said. She turned to Xeranther with fire in her eyes. "If you could go back in time and rescue your father, wouldn't you do it? Or would you be too afraid to die?"

A piercing shriek tore the skies and Xeranther shrank under the cover of a tree. The others looked up as well, expecting to see the large eagle flying above. They breathed a sigh of relief when they saw a small robin-like bird and nothing more.

"That's it," Xeranther said, throwing up his hands. "I'm done living in fear. I'm done doing nothing when people get killed for no fault of their own."

"So, you'll help us?" Leela asked, hopefully.

Xeranther hesitated. "I'll take you as far as the lake."

Leela enveloped him in a hug. Blushing, he clumsily patted her. Flula glowed a bright pearly white.

"Tomorrow, Floo and I will make arrangements for crossing the lake. We will meet you at the market. Make sure your landing is inconspicuous, else you'll be handed right to the guards."

Rea held his gaze.

"Thank you so much," she said softly.

The journey to the banyan was quick and uneventful. After spying soldiers of the Imperial Guard patrolling the streets, Xeranther took them along a guard-free back road. When they reached the market, he and Flula created a diversion while the banyan roots swooped Rea and Leela into the canopy.

The moment they landed in Sanobar, the hands on Rea's watch jumped from 1:11AM to 5:57AM. The glow of dawn brimmed above the treetops. As they mounted their bicycles and followed the marked trees out of the forest, Rea hoped no one at home had noticed she'd been missing through the night.

CHAPTER 13

RAVISHING AND RUTHLESS

A motif of tendrils carved in gold filigree ornamented the lulewood door. It gave the impression of needing burly hands to open it, but as Queen Razya waved her fingers over the lock, the tendrils snapped backwards, and the door clicked open.

She entered her private quarters, a space where no one else was allowed, not even her chambermaids. What if they poisoned her bath or murdered her in her sleep or strangled her with a curtain rope? With everything she had gone through, she wasn't going to let them win that easily. For twelve years, she drew her own baths, dressed herself, and tidied her rooms. The cooks had to sample her meals lest they were poisoned.

Razya strode down the crimson-carpeted vestibule. Her gown, awash in shades of aquamarine, was made from Astranthia's finest silk. A frothy swirl of ruffles silhouetted her body, showing off her tall, svelte figure as a cloud of luminous red taffeta swam around her ruby-studded sandals. She appeared wrapped in a wave while gliding in a pool of blood: her exact instructions to the dressmaker. Her father's crown of branch, leaf, and petal, once crafted in gold, sat on her head forged in copezium, the metal of the occult, glinting a brilliant, glossy black. Razya slipped her hand into her dress pocket and checked for the pouch. Feeling the supple lump beside her thigh, she relaxed.

Then she chided herself.

These days, paranoia seemed to rule her every thought. It wasn't as if the pouch could be stolen when no one was allowed to step any closer than the distance of a fully drawn sword. It was unbecoming for a Queen to give into such insecurities, but the hostility of the past weeks had made her doubly watchful. Her plans were far from over.

With a flick of her wrist, she unlocked the door to her bedchamber. The air inside was stale, lingering with the scent of myntroot perfume. Similar to the corridor, the room had its natural light blocked with red velvet drapes. Candles in sconces offered the only source of light. After the room's completion, she had the architect and builders beheaded so none but herself had walked within these walls.

It wasn't the layout of the chamber she wanted to keep secret—the layout was similar to bedrooms in other castles: A grandiose suite containing a bedroom and a boudoir, a queen-size bed with a lace canopy, a bathroom furnished in porcelain and quartz, and an adjoining sitting area overlooking a labyrinth of iridescent scarlia blossoms many stories below—it was what she did in there, the enchantments she performed, she didn't want anyone knowing about. The last time she had been caught, she had to take cruel but necessary action. And now it seemed, fate was rearing its ugly head towards her to exact its revenge.

Razya extracted the pouch from her gown. She was anxious to know if Oleandra had any news on the location of the sacred Som's missing petal. She grimaced. Asking Oleandra for help twisted her insides into a gnarled root. She felt nothing short of disgust for that woman, if she could even call her that. Had she completed her training in Shadow Magic, her own powers might have been strong enough to trace the petal. But she had been hasty, and now it was too late...

Suddenly, Razya noticed something terrible in the ornate leaf-shaped mirror. Her mouth dropped open as she stared at a wrinkle near the corner of her eye. The fold of skin caused a wave of nausea and the mounds of her bosom rose and fell. Razya had worked hard to preserve her beauty. It failed her once and she vowed never to let it happen again. To calm her nerves, she admired the strings of baroque pearls cascading from her ears. They complemented her necklace—an intricate lattice of diamonds and pearls. She ran her fingers over its exquisite pattern.

"I am Queen Razya of Astranthia. Ravishing and ruthless."

As she ironed out the wrinkle with a spell, the events of the day assaulted her. Wasn't it ironic that the ministers of her Court had supported her decision to kidnap the boy when they feared their lives were in danger, but now that he was captured and their lives were safe, they had the audacity to question her authority? Not to mention spreading rumors of true ascension. Why, Minister of Trade Homburg Grime, the gap-toothed landlord whose livelihood she had revived by casting fertility spells on his milkweed fields to guarantee a full harvest, hardly wasted a moment before assailing her with his words.

"You may have got the boy, Your Extreme Greatness, but the Asurai warn of dark times to bloom once again in history," he had leered with a greedy glint in his eye.

Razya kept a straight face. The Asurai were the League of Alchemists and Scholars of Nectral Mystique. More like the league of scholars who spent their boring lives studying the magical abilities of the nectar and who tried every trick in the book to stop her from wielding her 'tainted' Shadow Magic. And failed each time, Razya reminisced with a grin.

"Anything else?" she asked.

Quivering behind a smile, the minister said, "They foretell one nobler will emerge to avenge the throne."

The fool thought *he* was nobler than her. How desperately she had wanted to chop his head off. But she couldn't order something that severe days before the ceremony. The ministers and the Asurai had gathered more allies on their side than she had, and they would surely challenge the order. No, she couldn't risk appearing impulsive, especially after the recent matter she had learned of only a week ago: The sacred Som was missing another petal.

Twice before, the sacred flower had sacrificed a petal, turning it to ashes. Once during the Great Revolution and the other during the gruesome Shadow Wars. This time, however, a petal had gone *missing*. Vanished, it seemed, and lost. Waiting, as the portents claimed, to reveal itself once the wrongful action was righted.

A chill cut through Razya's heart.

All those years ago, she had felt the weakening of the nectar—the magic which flows through Astranthia like blood flows through veins, keeping the land alive—wondering what was causing it to wilt. Not once did she think it was because of what *she* had done.

Razya rested her head against the back of her chair. She thought back to simpler times when she was first crowned Queen: sitting on the grand throne, shivering with excitement, ruling the land she was meant to rule. Unlike her father, she didn't care to be beloved. She wanted power—power over every Astranthian—and her time had finally come.

For twelve glorious years, her schemes worked marvelously. When landlords and farmers fretted over dry fields and poor harvests (an effect of the weakening nectar), she created enchantment potions to boost the fertility of their fields. The wretched souls hungered for them like a cackle of ravenous chimera. The Shadow Magic they once reviled, they now worshipped! Stamped with the royal seal, the potions were sold to merchants and tradesmen, who in turn sold them to farmers and landowners. Their pockets turned empty, but the villagers lived on the promise that the potions would bring to life their fledging fields and fill the starving bellies of their families. The royal coffers grew rich and her subjects were indebted to her with their lives.

That was how one ruled, mused Razya.

Now, the future of her reign hung in the balance. If the petal was not discovered before the Night of Nilaya, her hand in the weakening of the nectar would be exposed, and no amount of magic would save her. The people of Astranthia would lay their eyes on the missing *third* petal and see for themselves the price they'd been paying for her actions. They would realize why their lands produced fewer harvests, why pounding rains drowned their crops, and why rampant wildfires burnt their homes. She'd be stripped of her title and humiliated.

Since the day Oleandra told her about the third missing petal, with blatant joy no less, Razya hadn't slept. If word got out, every Astranthian as well as her power-hungry ministers would run amok in the quest for the lost petal—for whoever held it could claim entitlement to the throne. She paced her room night after night, trying to devise a plan to find the petal, and then, as if ordained by the heavens, the answer presented itself.

From the pouch, Razya brought out her most treasured flower: the kissed-by-death rose. Cousin of the scarlet bloom, the kissed-by-death rose smelled just as sweet but was infinitely more beautiful; its petals were the luminescent black color of three-eyed crows.

She plucked the roses and dipped them into a solution of foxboar's blood and crushed bat wings, and mixed into it a drop of her blood along with one of Oleandra's. A flame flickered on her fingertip and she lit the concoction. The rims of the petals ignited with fire and they lifted skywards. Glittering in black and burning in gold, they arranged themselves into the shape of a face—two petals for eyes, one for a nose, and two for lips.

"Miss me already?" the flaming lips of petals scoffed in Oleandra Ophrys's voice.

"I am your Queen and I will summon you every hour if I so desire," snarled Razya and the fiery lips settled into a sneer. "So, have you located the petal?"

"No."

"We are *FOUR* days from the ceremony."

"Indeed," the petal-face said, matter-of-factly.

"YOU HAVE TO OBEY MY ORDERS, OLEANDRA!"

"Frankly, I would rather have Astranthia see the end of her days than have you continue as Queen."

"How dare you? Look for the petal AT ONCE OR—"

"Or what? You'll destroy me like you do anyone who disobeys you?" The petal-eyes assumed a look of mock fright. "Oh, I forgot you can't. If you do, you shall never know where the petal lies and there goes your chance of continuing as Queen." The lips formed a smirk. "That's the thing about curses, dear Queen. They come back to haunt you."

Razya bit back the insult she wanted to hurl at Oleandra. "I have the boy and I will kill him if you don't start looking."

"After what you did to me, I don't care what you do to anybody else."

"He was MINE!"

The petals turned somber. "If only he lived to tell the tale…"

Anger seared through Razya. She wanted to destroy something, anything. A current of nectar, sizzling like electricity, sputtered from her fingertips.

"Anyway," the petal-face said, ignoring Razya's rage, "the flowergrass have told me about the arrival of a young girl looking for her lost brother."

Razya stared at the smiling face of flames. "How did she get here?"

"Through the Doda Alda Mara of course."

Razya blinked, holding back her excitement.

"Well, I thought you'd appreciate that piece of information. Now, if that is all, farewell until ceremony day!" The petals laughed and dropped to the floor.

A loud pecking came from outside the veiled windows and Razya snapped her fingers. A Sirion covered in purple-grey feathers appeared within her chamber. It had the face of a human with the beak of an eagle and was twice the size of a man. On its feet were sharpened claws.

"Urdaag," Razya said, shooting an invisible ray of magic. The Sirion screeched in pain. "Next time be more prompt with your information. I already know about the girl. Now go, keep a shadow on her."

Urdaag flew away, and Razya looked pensively at the petals strewn across the floor. Her lips curved into a smile. News of the girl's arrival impressed her. She hadn't expected her to find her way so soon. She was intelligent.

Foolhardy as well, she chuckled. The poor girl had no idea what was coming.

CHAPTER 14

A MALEVOLENT HISS

After the fourth knock, Mishti Daadi opened the door. She looked harried, her saree lined with creases as though it had lain crumpled on the floor. Seeing Rea, her face lit up.

"My dearie, what a delightful surprise."

"I really need your help again," said Rea, her head spinning with questions.

"Certainly, dearie. Come inside. Where's your friend?"

"She's at home taking a nap."

The truth was Leela was snoring louder than a drowsy goat after their escapades in Astranthia last night. Rea was exhausted too, but she had no time to waste. Rohan was trapped, and she needed to get him out. Plus, she wanted to prove Amma wrong—Rohan's fate didn't have to be like Baba's. They weren't going to lose him, too.

Mishti Daadi patted Rea's cheek and pointed at the table

where she performed the augury. "We shall try our best, won't we?"

Rea gave a small nod. She had snuck into bed before Amma and Bajai had woken up in the morning. She'd been extra quiet even though she knew how exhausted Amma had been these last few days. Between juggling her jobs and mourning Rohan, she seemed to sleep more deeply than ever, waking up in a fog. She had taken to drinking an herbal concoction of milk, honey and fennel seeds that one of the neighborhood aunties had given her to help her sleep at night. As for Bajai, she always slept like the dead, sleeping right through the milkman's incessant doorbell ringing every morning.

Once Amma left for the tea plantations this morning, Rea made up an excuse of catching up on schoolwork she had missed and told Bajai she'd be at Leela's house. Bajai looked suspicious, but Rea lied again and told her that Amma had given her permission. Bajai tried saying no but eventually allowed her to go, giving Rea her old cell phone in case there was an emergency.

Mishti Daadi laid out the broken pieces of bone, dusty relics, glittering stones, sparkling potions, and bizarre thingamabobs. She took her place on her chair and Rea prepared herself for the unbearable pressure that was soon to crush upon her. Something told her the vision of Astranthia would not return. She opened her diary to a list of questions and switched on the voice recorder on Bajai's cell phone. The red light blinked. It startled Mishti Daadi.

"Um... since Leela isn't here, I thought I could record the prophecies... is that okay?" said Rea, embarrassed not to have asked before.

Mishti Daadi cast a wary glance at the phone. "I suppose it's all right."

She rubbed the blue liquid on Rea's palms to 'expunge the murkiness' and then closing her eyes, said, "Baccara sintera verafara."

Rea was right. Once the energy of foresight seeped into Mishti Daadi, no reverie came to lure her. She had already lived out the vision's premonitions in Astranthia. With a flick, the lights in the room went from dim to glaring yellow and Mishti Daadi opened her chalk-white eyes. Rea peeked into her diary and read her first question aloud.

"Why has the Queen of Astranthia captured my brother, Rohan Chettri?"

All the words were there. Nothing could be misinterpreted. Slowly, Mishti Daadi began to chant:

> "Blue and precious, a sapphire hibiscus,
> On a cobalt moon, it comes to bloom.
> A lonesome bud, in need of blood,
> Of noble birth and gallant worth.
> In him it runs, the chosen one,
> The blood to offer for none to suffer."

Rea almost understood the verse. There was something about a hibiscus, a moon and someone's blood. Her heart skipped a beat. Could this 'blood' be Rohan's blood? Flula's words about a flower rising during the Night of Nilaya entered her mind. Was that flower the hibiscus, and the moon, the ceremonial night? She'd have to clarify all of it later. For now she needed to move on.

"How do I get to the Queen of Astranthia's castle?" Rea asked.

Mishti Daadi's head bobbed like it was charting a route in her mind. When she was done, a rhyme fluttered out of her mouth.

> "Past the forest widowed of leaves
> Into the hills towards the sea,
> A towering castle you'll come to see
> On the water's edge of serpent lilies."

Shoot. Xeranther and Flula had warned her about the sea. Or was it a lake? And what were serpent lilies? Rea remembered how terrified they were by that water and threw in an impromptu question.

"Are these waters dangerous?"

> "A malevolent hiss,
> A lightless abyss,
> A sudden move,
> Oh.
> It's Death's kiss."

Death's kiss? Xeranther said crossing the lake meant she could die but she hadn't believed him.

"Um... how do I cross these waters?"

Mishti Daadi gazed into nothingness with a decidedly evil grin, and Rea had to remind herself that the lady in front of her wasn't the Mishti Daadi she knew, just a possessed oracle. As if to agree, the lamp to the right flickered and half of Mishti Daadi's face fell in shadow. The eerie white dot in the center of her eyes roved up and down.

> "When the time is right, you must recite,
> O winged fury, hither do hurry
> To you I plead, O mighty steed
> With your coat of night
> and myrtle eyes,
> Sail me to the shore,
> O Ceffyldwer."

Ceffyldwer! Hadn't Flula said one had been spotted? All at once, the impossibility of what she was attempting to do pressed upon Rea. She had to cross a deadly sea with the help of a Ceffyldwer—whatever that was—enter the castle of a queen who had captured Rohan, free him from the Cellars of Doom before the Queen took his blood, and escape together without getting caught—or dying. Rea looked into those disturbing eyes and asked the question she was most afraid of.

"Will I reach the castle alive?"

Heavy pouches hung under Mishti Daadi's glaucous eyes.

> "Try you must and try you will,
> Success to you won't come until."

"Will I find Rohan?"

> "Try you must and try you will,
> Success to you won't come until."

Rea kicked the leg of the table. *Mishti Daadi didn't like*

answering questions regarding the outcome of my fate, thought Rea. A sharp pull tugged at Rea's fingers and Mishti Daadi began shivering. Rea let go of her hands.

"Thank you, Mishti Daadi. That will be all."

A cloudy sky blanketed Rea's walk home. She replayed the recording, trying to understand it, but her mind drifted to Rohan. What must he be going through? She couldn't imagine being kidnapped and imprisoned. Locked in those Cellars, he would be feeling so alone, not knowing if anyone was coming to help him.

Except for the constant feeling of dread in the pit of her stomach, her twin connection with Rohan hadn't given her any indication of what was happening to him. She willed it with all her might to tell him she was going to save him.

Rea pushed back her tears.

It wasn't too long ago when they had begun to drift apart. It was as if one day they had stopped being children and got busy with their own lives. Rohan began spending more time with his friends, and she began to retreat into herself, wanting to know more about Baba, their past, and the secrets Amma and Bajai so often kept. Rea vividly recalled the day she was walking towards the school quadrangle during recess when a group of boys whacked her tiffin box out of her hands. Turmeric-spiced rice flakes scattered over the ground and they ran away, laughing. Rohan, who was with his friends, charged after the boys.

"Stop pretending to care and stay away from me," she

screamed in front of everyone, mad at him for thinking her weak enough to need his help.

His face turned grim. Maybe that was when it had happened. She had shut him out. He had left her alone in their battle for answers and she hadn't been ready to forgive him then. Now, she couldn't stop thinking about how different things might have been if she had been more forgiving.

CHAPTER 15

A PERIWHITTLE'S WHILE

As the last of the roots slunk away from the Doda Alda Mara, Rea and Leela made a dash for the market road.

"The second time was worse." Leela held her stomach, looking nauseated.

Rea felt a little floaty in her head, too. They slowed down, blending into the crowd of shoppers. This time she noticed the knickknacks and curios of cobalt hued moons and sparkling blue flowers (oddly enough, with only three petals) twinkling and glimmering in shops. She thought of the prophecy about the flower, the moon, and maybe Rohan's blood, and touched her locket. Her fingers turned cold with fear. Astranthia was preparing for the Night of Nilaya.

"Not enough rain? Not enough sun? Ain't no need to fret no more!" a potion-seller hollered, clanking bottles of bubbling liquids in front of Rea and Leela's faces. "Forty coins to triple your harvests!"

Skedaddling away from him, Rea spotted Xeranther sitting on a low stone wall chewing on a stalk of grass. She signaled to him, and he jumped to the ground, pointing at a shrub whose berries burst each time someone touched them. A little boy, standing beside it, was licking his blue and yellow juice-splattered fingers when his father yelled at him to keep away from the berries.

Rea and Leela ran towards the bush and found clothes in a burlap sack hidden behind it. They quickly slipped them on.

"Mine's a couple of sizes too big," said Leela, pinching her outfit at the waist. The fabric ballooned around her.

"At least we won't stand out as much when we get to the castle," Rea said, wearing a dull rose-colored tunic made of lotus petals over her pajama top.

Leela looked down at her oversized husk-shaped dress. It seemed well-worn and had the hue of a dusty leaf. She snapped off two stem-shoots from a plant beside her and tied one around her waist and the other around Rea's. "See, all we need is a stem-belt!"

Rea distractedly agreed and stepped out of the shrubbery.

"I hoped my Mar's old clothes would fit," Xeranther grinned. "Now you can pass for Astranthians."

"These are great!" Leela said, flouncing in her dress.

"Yes, thanks," Rea added, less enthusiastically. "So, are the arrangements made?"

Xeranther's expression turned serious. "Hardly anyone was willing to offer their boat to cross the serpent waters. There's a good chance their boat would not return and by 'good chance' I mean, they are practically assured they would never lay sight on their boat again."

"Are you saying you *couldn't* arrange for one?" asked Rea.

"No, no, I have. One boatman finally agreed after I begged him. And... the best part is..." A look of mischief darted across his face. "It's a *stolen* boat used to transport crossbows, longswords, lances and spears to the castle. After our talk yesterday, I inquired around and discovered folks had been committing small acts of revolt against the Queen. The man who offered the boat needed it to be destroyed. He and his men had seized it before it got to the castle where the weapons were to be forged with magic..."

"And they wanted to do away with the boat so it can't be traced to them," exclaimed Leela.

"Exactly."

"Let's get to the boat then!" Rea said excitedly, dodging a kid licking a blue moon popsicle with stars of sugar revolving around it. The blood in her veins was pumping faster than an express train. She didn't want to waste another minute.

Xeranther grabbed hold of her arm to stop her. "I don't have the boat yet. The men are unloading and hiding the weaponry as we speak. They've agreed to transfer the boat into my possession only under the shade of night—"

"But it's noon. The hour of your sun," fumed Rea, twisting away from his grasp. "I can't believe we've portaled for nothing!"

"Well, it wasn't as if I could send a message to you," Xeranther said, looking chastened. "Anyway, I think it's best you meet someone before you leave for the castle."

"Who?" Rea asked angrily.

"My grandpar."

A gust of wind blew, creating eddies of dust and leaves. Xeranther raised his hand to shade his eyes. They were on a different path than yesterday, this one flanked by small fields, arid and barren, baking under the sun.

"You need to understand what a grave endeavor you are taking on," he said. "Having a boat to cross the serpent lake is one part, perhaps the smallest of parts. People have died crossing the waters even with the strongest boats. What you are attempting to do is far riskier than you believe; death is nearly guaranteed."

"Well," Rea said with a confident nod of her head, "I've been advised by an informed source to call on the Ceffyldwer. It will assure my crossing without dying."

"Call on the Ceffyldwer?" repeated Xeranther.

Rea and Leela nodded, and Xeranther laughed so hard, he held onto a tree to stop him from buckling over. Rea stared at him in quiet fury, and he tried his best to control himself.

"I'm sorry," he said, biting back his smile. "Ceffyldwers are elusive creatures. They do their own bidding and obey no commands. No one I know has ever seen one. And you can't just summon it. It has to choose you."

"Didn't Flula mention someone spotting one yesterday?" Leela asked.

Xeranther rolled his eyes. "Paries do love a good sap of gossip. They relish being the bearers of news even if it is utter codswallop." Unable to hold it in, he snorted in laughter again. "Call on the Ceffyldwer! That's the funniest thing I've ever heard. You best come up with another plan."

"That *is* the best plan to cross the sea," said Rea.

"It's a lake," he corrected. "An extremely large one and the castle is in its center like an island surrounded by a gigantic moat."

"Are you saying *no one* visits the Queen?" Rea asked impatiently.

"People do visit—"

"How do they get there? If this Ceffyldwer plan isn't going to work, let's do what the others do to get to the castle."

"Maybe we could sneak into one of their boats," Leela suggested.

"You don't understand. Nobody can simply trot into the castle. I've told you before, only guests who are invited by the Queen are allowed entry. For them, a boat with two Salient Keepers is sent. If the meeting goes well, they return to shore safely. If it doesn't, they get no ride back. They're thrown to the lilies... and trust me, you don't want to be lily-food."

"There has to be another way," said Rea.

Xeranther let out a long sigh.

"That's why you need to meet Poppy. He's the only person I know who has tried to cross the lake, failed, and lived to tell the tale."

Xeranther's budhood swarmed with bustle. The buds stood so close together that one could see right into the neighbor's windows. Their exteriors were splotchy and mottled, some covered entirely in moss or creepers, others blackened by chimney-soot or a recent fire. Folks milled about in worn and unwashed clothes while dogs (Rea was greatly amazed to find regular looking animals) ambled about, sniffing the dirty streets for food. Unlike the pristine buds they had passed on their way there, these buds had no gardens or pretty fences. The ground was squishy from puddles and the smell of garbage lingered.

As they made their way through the budhood, strings of vines stretched across the tops of buds. A few had clothes hanging on them, but most were draped with coils of flowers. Xeranther said the vines' velvety leaves glowed in the dark, lighting up the budhood after sundown in preparation for the Night of Nilaya. Rea was reminded of the fairy lights strung around lamp posts and trees during Diwali. Unsurprisingly, she felt more at ease in this budhood than she had anywhere else in Astranthia so far.

Xeranther banged the door of a bud, brown as nutmeg. "It's me!" he shouted. The door swung open, revealing a woman with eyes that looked just like his.

"My, my, with all this banging, you'll bring the bud down around our ears," she said. She looked at Rea and Leela and pointed at Xeranther with her thumb. "Always in a hurry, this one. Didn't stay inside his Mar's belly for the full term either. Out he wanted to come and out he—"

"MAR!" Xeranther said, pink to his ears and she covered her mouth to hold back her chortles.

"And who are these lovely lassies?" She waved a kitchen cloth in the air. Her cherry colored hair stirred in the breeze.

"They're my friends. They want to speak to Poppy."

Xeranther's mother stepped aside and let them into the house.

"Xee, these younglings be wearing the same kinds of clothes I used to have on in my younger years. Didn't I tell you, your Mar was quite the lass in her days?" She seemed to have no clue the clothes were hers.

Rea instantly took to Xeranther's mother. She reminded Rea of her schoolmates' Ammas back home—always kind, laughing and happy to welcome new people into their home.

As Rea entered Xeranther's house, the air tasted of pickle and guavas and as they got closer to the fireplace, it warmed to coziness.

"Poppy has been driving me up the trees today," Xeranther's mother was saying. "You three are just what he needs. I've put on a pot of blossoms to boil. Where's Floo?"

"Busy with foliage duty," Xeranther said, and turning to the girls, whispered, "She'll join us later."

Sitting on a rocking chair beside a fire was a man as old as time. He held a book over a thick blanket and his head lolled in sleep.

"Poppy can doze off anywhere at any moment. It's one of his many talents," winked Xeranther.

"Hey Poppy!" he said loudly. "I want you to meet my friends. They have some questions for you."

The old man was deep in sleep. Xeranther plucked a leaf from a potted plant and tickled his grandfather in the ear. Poppy awoke with a start.

"Terrible boy! Trying to send me off to an early grave, eh?"

"You're not going anywhere! Poppy, this is Rea and Leela."

Poppy squinted as he hunched lower to better hear their

names. Then in a gesture Rea had recently seen Bajai use when she couldn't hear clearly, he dismissed their unclear names with a wave of his hand, and kept the conversation going.

"What do you younglings seek an old man's company for?" The skin crinkled over his bones.

"They want to know how you tried to cross the serpent sea," Xeranther said, bringing out wooden chairs with seats in the shape of clovers.

"Inquiring minds, I see. So few these days... Might I ask why such a dark subject interests you?"

Xeranther gave Rea a look that told her *not* to tell the truth.

"Er... we like solving puzzles," she replied. "The lake is deadly and rumored impossible to cross but we believe there has to be a way to get to the other side."

"Without dying, that is," added Leela. "Our parents don't encourage us to know too much about it."

Poppy frowned. "They be right. What you're asking to know is not for the fainthearted. The realms, these days, be a hard place to live. But knowledge is all we need to survive. Isn't that right, boy?"

"Yes, Poppy. Knowledge can be your truest friend if you choose to befriend it," Xeranther said and from the corner of his lips, added, "That's Poppy's favorite saying, which obviously, he has made up himself."

"And seek it we must," bellowed Poppy, the book almost slipping off his lap. "Now, let's begin with what you already know."

Riveted, Leela moved closer.

"Every born Astranthian knows the rules of our latest ruler,

Queen Razya. One never goes to her unbidden. Either you find a way to be invited or you cross the serpent sea and risk death." Poppy leaned forward and widened his eyes for effect.

"Got Poppy off to telling you one of his stories, eh?" Xeranther's mother said, carrying a teapot and cups. A creature, a foot and a half tall with large pointy ears, a tail, and furry hands and legs stood beside her, holding a tray with bowls of water. His bulbous nose, thick with nose hairs, bobbled above his lips and a rush of cotton-like hair stuck out from under his hat. Seeming extremely shy, he nudged the water bowl towards Leela.

"Drink up, lassie. He isn't going to bite," laughed Xeranther's mother.

Leela took a sip and the creature, barefoot and dressed in a drab tunic, beamed, showing off his pitted teeth. In spite of his whiskers, he looked more human than mouse-like.

"Berber, what are you gandering at! Fetch me those snaries and biscuits," Poppy said, and the creature hurried over, his hairy feet thumping across the floor.

"If Poppy be telling you a story, you lassies better warn your Mar you'll be stuck here a periwhittle's while," Xeranther's mother said with a twinkle in her eye.

Poppy grunted, and Rea smiled unsurely as she helped herself to the cup of blossoms—flower petals floating in a cup of perfumed, rose-tinted water.

"A periwhittle flower blooms for a whole year before it begins to wilt," Xeranther whispered. "She means you might be here for a long time."

"Ooh," said Rea and Leela said in unison.

"Mind yourself with the biscuits, Par. Too much jelly isn't going to do you good. Lassies, you're in luck. These are my special raspjelly biscuits which this rowdy lad and his Poppy love to gobble up in one crooningbird flit. Now, don't be shy. We need to fatten those skinny bellies!"

"Bah, woman, you and your biscuits. What these girls are hungry for is knowledge! I dare say, that's the most delicious biscuit in all the realms. Am I not right, younglings?"

"Don't let Poppy be bullying you as he does me. He's a silly old goat who loves his stories."

"You spoil me good and put a fat of laziness on these old bones. A bit of story brings to life this foggy mind and puts a jig or two in my step. Now when has a jig hurt anyone, eh?"

"Mar, we don't have time for chatting," cried Xeranther.

"All right, all right," his mother said.

"Here now, lend me your hand, will you? Younglings, I be needing to tinkle," Poppy said (as Xeranther dropped his head in embarrassment).

Rea and Leela swallowed their smiles.

"Do you need help?" asked Leela

"You're a sweet lass," said Xeranther's mother. "But I'll help him. Poppy may be old, but his bones be strong."

Poppy chucked and pushed aside the blanket over his lap, revealing his legs. Rea tried not to stare. Poppy's left leg was amputated below the knee. He had a peg of wood where his leg should be. With a laborious grunt, he lifted himself off the chair, his bony arms quivering under his weight.

"These be battle scars. Looks worse than it feels," he whispered in a tight voice. He held his leg as if it ached, and Rea could tell it hurt him badly.

"There, there," Xeranther's mother said, carefully leading him out of the room. The creature followed her shy as a kitten.

"Don't tell me you don't have them on Earth, either?" said Xeranther.

"What is he?" asked Rea.

"Berber is a bud-bozan. Bozans serve a house and its inhabitants. They're fiercely loyal creatures. Close relations of brownies and more distantly related to boggarts who folk from other lands often confuse them with."

Rea glanced at Leela who looked like she had understood the difference as easily as if Xeranther was talking about cats and dogs. In the past, it might have annoyed her that Leela understood things more easily than she did. But now, she knew Leela would happily explain it to her if she asked.

Then, out of the blue, Rea remembered the boy in the market advertising etiquette training for bozans. Rea thought of Amma cooking and cleaning in other peoples' homes.

"Do they want to do this? Or are they forced into it?" she asked.

"It's what they were born to do. They live to serve human families and hate it when we go away. If a bozan isn't tied to a home or a family, it perishes. Which is why, most times, generations of bozans live with generations of one family. Just like our Berber. He's ninth generation."

Leela looked longingly into the kitchen.

"You want to adopt him, don't you?" asked Rea. Leela's eyes

lit up and Xeranther started laughing.

"Don't mind my daughter," Poppy said, returning from the bathroom. He wobbled back to his chair. "Stories are gateways that open your mind to think differently and question what people have stopped questioning. My Felza was once as bright and curious as you lassies. Then her big old heart went and fell in love, and now all her world revolves around this wildling." He ruffled Xeranther's hair.

"Not the hair, Pops!"

Rea felt a twinge of envy watching Xeranther with his grandfather. She glanced at Leela, wondering if she too longed for that kind of relationship with her family... but Leela seemed more interested in the biscuits on the plate. *Of course.*

CHAPTER 16

FEAR NEVER STOPPED A FOOL

"**N**ow, where were we?" Poppy picked the gnarled branch he used as a walking stick and limped towards the window. "Aye, the serpent sea. One must start at the beginning to understand a subject's full worth."

The three of them nodded attentively like students in a classroom.

"Not long ago, when Astranthia was ruled by King Zulgar, there be no serpent sea. Peasants and noblemen visited daily to tell the king of their troubles. King Zulgar, like any man, could not solve every problem, but he never closed his doors to common folk. The castle in my time was called the People's Castle. Nowadays, not so much."

"What happened to him?" asked Rea.

"The inevitable—heartache and death. It be his daughter who rules. Queen Razya, wielder of Shadow Magic. You dare not meddle with her or you can get cursed or imprisoned or killed. That be her way. We be knowing it well."

A sadness came over him and Rea could tell he was thinking about Xeranther's father. Her gaze slid over to Xeranther to see if he was all right. But Xeranther's gaze remained pinned on Poppy, not a flutter of emotion to be seen.

"Early in the Queen's reign, before this wildling was born," continued Poppy, "the constant stream of commoners and their flood of troubles vexed her good. So, the Queen darkened the waters to create the serpent sea. Folk could no longer enter the castle when it suited them, unless she wanted them to visit her."

"But the sea is a lake, isn't it?" said Leela.

"Quite right, youngling. But the Sea of Serpent Lilies has a more sinister ring to it, doesn't it?" Poppy shrugged. "Aye, so it stuck."

"What's so dangerous about these lilies?" inquired Rea.

"The lilies be venomous snakes."

"SNAKES?" gasped Leela. "I thought that was just a name. You mean there are actual serpents?"

"Aye." Poppy winced, squeezing the leg that absorbed his weight. "The Queen is no ordinary Astranthian ruler. She loves to watch her subjects squirm, especially those who defy her. With Shadow Magic, she created four types of lilies. One's venom renders the bitten unconscious for months, sometimes years, the other's causes an irrational fear of water due to which one inevitably falls into it only to be chomped to pieces, and the third's coagulates the bitten's blood, causing death within hours. The last type of lily, of course, is a simple water lily. One that causes no pain, unconsciousness, or death. It's the one that entices many a fool like myself to cross the sea with the hope they can outwit the Queen and reach the castle without dying. For us men, once sea-faring folk, it be a challenge to see which of us could do it. Fools, we be! But fear never stopped a fool, now did it?"

A look of thrill filled his face.

"In all these years, folk fewer than the fingers on my hand have made it to the other side. Some came close but died in the end. There was once a man who sailed across the lake, battled the serpents and won! He were mere inches away from the shore when he stopped rowing to take a look at the castle. In that motionless second, the serpents besieged his boat and he was eaten alive. More than thousands like him have perished trying and the rest be scared stiff to tempt fate." Poppy returned to his chair and stretched his leg out in front of him.

"So, you're saying it's impossible to cross the lake alive..." Rea was disheartened. She had thought the whole point of the story was that there was a way around the lake.

"Never did I say impossible! Every problem must have a solution. Didn't I say a few unknown souls have crossed to the other side?"

"Then how do we—I mean anyone who wants to—do it?"

The creases in Poppy's cheeks deepened with a smile. "The answer lies in the knowledge itself. The lake is created by magic. And magic fights magic! I believe there can be two ways to cross the lake. You can be a royal, born with the same nectar that runs through the blood of the Queen, or you can find the right type of magic to conquer the magic of the lake."

"What if you call the Ceffyldwer?" Rea asked over him. "It has magic, doesn't it?"

Poppy rubbed his scruffy stubble. "How did you think of that, youngling'?"

"Just a wild guess…"

"Some of them who made it were rumored to have summoned the Ceffyldwer. Magic fights magic! Alas, a rare few know how to summon one."

"What if you do know how to summon it?" Rea could barely mask her excitement.

Poppy gave a big bear laugh. "Then summon it you must."

"If only it was that easy to know the Ceffyldwer's call," said Xeranther. "Aren't there countless variations of it?"

"Aye, there be. And the magical beast won't come for any who know its call. The Ceffyldwer appears for those rare few with the truest of intentions. Our legends call them chariots of angels. But summoning the beast isn't something you take lightly. First you have to survive the lake. That be how I lost my leg. If my mates hadn't chopped it off, my blood would have thickened all over my body and I'd be good for dead."

Engrossed, Leela picked at her fingernail. "What about the Queen's family? Can they safely get across?"

"One doesn't know anymore seeing as the Queen has done away with her family. Distant relations fear her and prefer to remain distant. There was a time when the royal family were gracious hosts to their cousins and relatives. Now, the Queen keeps to herself as far as we know."

Poppy paused, lost in thought.

"King Zulgar believed the use of magic caused tyranny," he continued after a moment. "During his rule, its use was kept to a minimum, lending a feeling of equality betwixt the royal family and the common folk. Magic of the nectar was practiced only for the good of the people and in the most exceptional of circumstances. But the Queen rules for tyranny and for the division of classes. Dare I say, she is succeeding. Common folk fear her Shadow Magic. We are not equals. We stand far beneath her eyes."

"What about portaling in and out of the castle?" asked Rea. "Xeranther mentioned there's a portal within the castle grounds. Couldn't it be used to travel to and fro?"

"Portals allow transport betwixt realms, not within Astranthia. Lad, you should be knowing that." He thwacked the top of Xeranther's head with his stick.

"Ow," he cried, and Poppy's smirk evaporated.

"The time is upon us now for our history to be rewritten. We will be waiting to see what the Queen has in store for the Night of Nilaya. Whose blood powerful with the magic of the nectar will she sacrifice on the sacred Som? Will she wield her Shadow Magic? The only thing we know is on the night of the full blue moon she cannot hide behind the gloom of her castle walls. She will have to present herself in front of us all. And we await the day. If she cannot replenish the sacred flower, her claim to the throne will be lost and she will be banished for all of time! Her only chance is to conjure up the royal children. Bah, it be impossible!" His face puffed pink.

Rea's nerves tightened into a knot. Rohan was captured by

the Queen. Did that mean *he* was one of the royal children she needed to conjure? Was that why his blood was required? And... if that was true, was she a royal too?

Rea glanced at Leela and thought of their life in Tombu. Old clothes, coarse hair, small houses, no money, and skin that never looked as clean as the rich no matter how hard they scrubbed it. It was absurd to think she could be a princess.

"Are you done churning their innocent minds with your imperious rants, Poppy?" Xeranther's mother teased. She handed Poppy a cold drink. "Look at the lassies, you've scared them silly. Poppy's stories go round your head and get tucked behind your ear until you don't know where they begin and where they end. Come along now Par, it's time to go to the fields."

Poppy eased his weight on his daughter as Berber hovered with a pair of worn gloves. "Say Felza, is that pudding I smell on you?"

Xeranther's mother laughed. "He may not hear so well, but his stomach is in tip-top shape."

"All right my new friends, I must get to work before the land-lord cracks the whip on me. And she be right, don't go worrying about the serpent sea. Lucky for us, you don't have to cross it. Now, best be keeping those curious minds curious."

"Thank you so much, Mr... er—"

"Friends of my lad are my friends too. Call me Poppy."

"Thank you, Poppy," Rea said, and a fuzzy feeling spread within her.

Rea couldn't stop thinking about what Poppy had said. If getting to the castle was such a dangerous mission, she had to do it alone. It was her quest, and no one should have to pay the price for it except herself.

"I don't care if it's dangerous, I'm coming with you," said Leela, when Rea expressed her feelings on the matter. "I thought we were a team."

"We are. But I don't want you to feel pressured into doing it... What if something goes wrong?"

"This is important." Leela stood her ground. "Rohan is important and I'm not going to let you do this alone."

Powder-blue blossoms from nearby trees turned in their direction, infusing the air with a fruity fragrance. Rea struggled to find the words she wanted. Her heart, used to being empty, was filled with gratitude. Leela cared for her so much that she was willing to risk her life for her.

"You are a really good friend, you know that?" she said, calling Leela her friend for the first time and realizing for the first time what it felt like to have a friend. "I'm so glad you're here with me."

Leela threw her arms around Rea's neck.

"You know, I've always wanted to be your friend," she said, nudging a pebble, "but I thought you didn't like me."

Guilt creeped over Rea. She was ashamed of herself. After spending time with Leela, she had come to appreciate her knack for seeing the sunnier side of things. It wasn't annoying anymore. If anything, it was comforting. Amma and Rohan may have turned their backs on her, but maybe it didn't mean everybody else would... And what if Tara, the mean girl from Mishti

Daadi's village was right? The reason she didn't have any friends was because she was the mean one, only wanting to see everyone's faults, and never opening her heart up to anyone.

"Um," interrupted Xeranther. "Just to be clear I won't be joining you on the lake. I—er—don't want to risk—dying."

"I understand," said Rea, knowing he, too, was going out of his way to help her. "You've done so much already. I couldn't ask for a better Astranthian guide or friend."

Xeranther blushed, looking at his feet. "There are a few hours left until sundown. Will you be staying or portaling to Earth?"

"I can stay, if you don't have to get back," said Leela. "No one will realize I'm gone. Besides, Amma will think I'm at the library working on school stuff. I've been playing that up these past few days."

Rea considered what would be best. Although Amma hadn't once asked where she was going or if she had slept or eaten, Rea knew her mother wouldn't let her leave the house for an overnight mission without an explanation. But if she was gone when everyone woke up, she was pretty sure no one would notice her absence until well into the evening. Once they noticed, she wasn't sure if Amma would care that much that she was missing. Amma had never favored her anyway, and with Rohan gone, Rea had begun to feel like a burden to her. Bajai would be worried, but she'd forgive her after she came back home. Or maybe even Bajai would forget about her altogether.

"I'm not going anywhere until we rescue Rohan," Rea said decidedly.

Xeranther nodded and led the way. Since they had a few

hours to kill, they chose to walk to the lake. The sun, a flaming mango-orange, brushed the landscape in hues of sepia. Xeranther's mood darkened as the sun began to set. He implored them a dozen times to abandon their plans to cross the serpent sea. When they remained adamant, he reverted to long silences or monosyllabic replies.

"I have to meet with the boatmen later tonight to finalize the arrangements," he said. "It's best I do it alone."

Rea and Leela didn't argue. They walked on, the path turning narrow and rocky. Xeranther walked ahead as Leela and Rea followed behind.

"Have you thought of why Rohan might be brought here? I mean this kind of stuff usually only happens in books or movies..." asked Leela, walking closer to Rea.

Rea lied and shook her head. She wasn't ready to tell her about the possibility of Rohan being one of the royal children until she was absolutely sure. Her conscience pricked her. She wasn't being a good friend at all. Rea swallowed her guilt. It tasted bitter like medicine.

"What about your Amma and Bajai? Do they know he's in Astranthia?" asked Leela.

"Oh, no. Amma thinks Rohan's gone forever. From the moment we realized he was missing, she said it was too late as if she'd done anything to find him. And Bajai has shriveled up like a prune. She keeps asking about the nightmare, but I haven't said any more than I did before. It's not like she can help us, and I don't want her thinking I've lost my mind talking about portals and paries and evil queens. What about you? Won't your Amma and Baba be worried if we're here a few days?"

Leela looked at her and laughed. "It would be a miracle if they notice I'm not there. Anyway, I would much rather be here. Charting my own life path."

Rea grinned, glad that Leela had chosen to stay. "You know, I haven't been able to shake off the feeling that Amma knows more than she's saying... or rather, not saying," she confessed. "It feels like too much of a coincidence that Rohan went missing the day she met Mishti Daadi."

"What do you mean?" asked Leela.

"I think Amma knew something bad was going to happen and that's why she went to see her."

Leela went wide-eyed.

"After we get Rohan back, I'm going to find out what it is. It might have something to do with Baba..." *Maybe he's trapped here too*, she wanted to say.

"Parents can be a real pain sometimes," said Leela, letting an ordinary butterfly land on her palm.

Rea glanced at Leela, hesitating for a moment. "Before, you said you wanted to be my friend... why me?" she asked, not adding the 'since I wasn't particularly nice to you' part.

Leela shrugged. "You're different, like me. The kids at school call me 'nerdy' and 'too eager' and you, well, you don't care about what they think. I admire that because I do care, and it sucks sometimes. And I've seen you stand up for yourself when some of the girls are mean to you and that's awesome."

Rea's cheeks went red. No one had ever seen her this way before. Or said they actually admired something about her. She beamed at Leela. "You're awesome too. Everyone else is just stupid."

Leela winked. "You also didn't have any friends, so I thought, hey, there's something we have in common!"

Rea was prepared to feel offended by those words, but she laughed. "You know what, that's a pretty good reason!"

They chuckled as Xeranther turned, giving them a side-eye as though they were crazy to be making jokes at a time like this and they both stopped giggling.

"Hey Xee, don't you go to school?" Leela asked and Rea did a double take, hearing her call him 'Xee' like they were best friends.

Xeranther turned grimmer. "I used to, but after Par was taken away, Poppy was forced to work the fields. He could only work half the hours with his age and wooden leg. So, I left school to sell trinkets and do odd jobs."

"Oh," said Leela and she begged Rea with her eyes to change the subject.

A dragonfly with arm-long wings swooshed towards them and swirled over a host of bushes, creating a deafening buzz. It swallowed a fat, finger-sized bee and nodded towards them to say hello. Rea jumped back a good few steps and glanced at Leela who had turned still as a statue with an expression of shock etched on her face. Xeranther casually tipped his head at the insect and said, "Hello."

"Obviously there's magic in Astranthia," Rea said after awkwardly returning the dragonfly's greeting. "But no one uses wands or casts spells. Yet flowers bloom and wilt before our eyes, walls whisper secrets and paries help change the seasons."

"Well, it's not that confusing," said Xeranther. "Astranthia's nectar runs within her. Through her soil, air, and water. It's why her 'magic' manifests in spectacular forms of nature—in flowers, animals and all the pari-folk. There are so many manifestations, I haven't seen them all. And they keep changing. Though most have become commonplace for us, when we come across a new manifestation, it's like discovering a treasure." His eyes glittered.

"And the Queen's magic is different?"

"Aye. As an Astranthian royal, the blood of the nectar flows within her but the magic she conjures is utterly unnatural. It's made from stolen and elusive matter, which is evil in nature and the opposite of nectral magic, which is good and nurturing. Shadow Magic draws its power from sucking the light out of nectral magic. Only the magically powerful can wield it."

Leela shook off a shiver.

"What about potions and enchantments?" asked Rea.

"They're made from the Queen's Shadow Magic and are sold to help create larger harvests, deeper rivers, greener pastures—things the nectar once took care of. With these potions, the Queen has poured greed into the people and now everyone wants more than what the land can provide."

Xeranther grew glum again until his eyes fell on a tall plant with bamboo-like shoots. He snapped off three of its shoots and crunched down on the bulbous part with his teeth.

"You should try these lollisuckles." He sucked on the shoot like it was a straw in a milkshake. "They're delicious!"

Thick juice oozed down his chin, and Rea and Leela took one each. The shoot brimmed with a syrupy liquid tasting of sugarcane and honey.

"This is yummmilicious," said Leela and she broke off a few more for them to drink. Rea slurped hers down in seconds.

"There's a third kind of magic," said Xeranther. "Underground magic or trixter magic. Expert brewers, fermenters and alchemists—ordinary folk who study the use and philosophy of magic—experiment with the mildest form of nectral magic, which is the best they can conjure, to create amazing trixters that make objects do a host of tricks." He wiggled his belt-pouch to show off the last remaining drops of his 'make a branch grow' potion. It twinkled in the light.

"Once I give Mar the money she needs from the sales of my trinkets, I save the coins I have to spare, if there are any, to visit Hex Hollow, a night market where merchants, vendors and brewers of trixter magic come to sell their latest inventions. See, ordinary folk aren't meant to conjure magic—most of us aren't able to anyway—and although the trixters are harmless, you cannot be caught buying them. The Queen bans their creation and sale, so the market keeps moving, setting up shop in secret places."

"That's so exciting. I wish we could see one," gushed Leela.

"Well, you will." He grinned. "It's where I'm meeting the boatmen tonight."

CHAPTER 17

A TEAR IN THE NIGHT AIR

Walking in Astranthia at night was an experience. Flowers with iridescent petals glowed, infusing the air with scent and song, some humming soft lullabies, others a peppy, flute-like tune. Paries skittered. Buds swam in lantern light, dotting the landscape like bonfires. Some, in the wealthy budhoods, even glowed in hues of rainbow light. The celestial realm, translucent during the day, shone brilliantly against the liquid black sky. Its silvery light shimmered over the road for miles.

"We're here," Xeranther said, stopping beside a canopy of neon-colored blossoms sighing and rustling in a contended daze.

Rea saw flowers floating high above them. They seemed embedded into the sky, without a trunk or a branch to hold them there. The wind picked up, and the sky-flowers swayed. For a second, branches, darker than coal, glinted beneath the flowers, and Leela reached to touch one.

"Don't!" yelled Xeranther. "The Nightshade isn't a tree. He just looks like one. And his flowers bite."

Leela's hand stopped mid-air and Xeranther gave a sigh of relief. "Don't you have the Nightshade in your land?" he asked, confused at Rea and Leela's shocked faces.

"The only plant I can think of that bites is a Venus flytrap and it doesn't look anything like this. Besides, its leaves do the biting and eating. And if there is a tree like the Nightshade in our world, its flowers don't bite, right?" Leela turned to Rea.

"To the best of my knowledge," replied Rea.

She had taken for granted that a tree was just a tree, that no flower would ever bite, that grass would never turn into an animal, and a twig would not morph into a weapon. She eyed the frightening but alluring Nightshade, which was showing off its ruby, jade, sapphire, and pearl flowers. Despite looking like a tree, it commanded respect and Rea stepped back so as to not intrude its personal space.

Xeranther turned to the hole in the trunk, barely visible under the sheen of starlight. "Overseer of the Hollow of Hex, may we be granted entry?"

The tree-creature sashayed its fluorescent flowered branches and blew a gentle breeze. The blossoms broke out of their branches, waiting in the wind.

"The passphrase?" emerged a gurgled voice, coarse as bark and deep as a rolling wave, and Rea and Leela inched closer together.

After a quick glance down the road to make sure no one was watching, Xeranther murmured:

"Catch a witch to make her twitch,
Bewitch a witch to make her itch!"

Xeranther waited until the blossoms flew ahead and he ran behind them. A little ways away, the flowers halted in the air. Standing under the twinkling blossoms, Xeranther peered into space, his eyeballs moving up and down, left and right, as if searching for something.

All of a sudden, in the air before him, a thin line appeared. Gradually, it widened into a tear. The tear was made of light and if Rea hadn't been paying attention, she might have thought it was the golden-white trail of a glowing firefly.

Xeranther stepped closer. Pinching its edges, he stretched it open. Rea watched spellbound as he kept going until the tear was as long and wide as him. Giving her and Leela a nudge, he stepped into it and behind the cloak of night. When all three of them were through, the seam stitched close and Rea and Leela's mouths fell open. They had walked through a hidden doorway, and into a secret bazaar.

Tents hovered above the ground, reverberating with music. Looking up, skirts flared, hats soared, and the bottoms of shoes tapped away on the floor of the night sky. Cerulean moons and sapphire flowers floated about, bursting into sparkles. Merchandise followed sellers wherever they went, food and drinks chased after people much to everyone's delight and giggles, and the strangest inventions and fashions were being showcased along with contraptions that would have Rea and Leela scratching their heads for days.

Pari glow streaked through the air like mini-rainbows, and each time a sale was made (which was very often), a display of fireworks went off. Under a tree, wispy like cotton-candy, a boy sat turning leaves into snowflakes. People, pari-folk and all sorts of whimsical creatures (flying toad-like ladybugs, a cow-monkey dressed in jewels reciting poetry, a half woman-half giraffe operating a rolling Ferris wheel ride) milled about, and Rea and Leela, not fathoming what their eyes were beholding, blindly followed Xeranther through the maze of alleyways and gullies.

"Wait here," he instructed when they reached an intersection of sorts. "I'll be back soon."

Within seconds, vendors accosted Rea and Leela, selling enchantments that could make one walk on water, fly, or grow taller. There were hexes to freeze one's parents, or grow a wart on an enemy's face (the effects of which could last from two hours to two days). Rea had to hold Leela back when a lady levitating in the corner of the street enticed patrons by spritzing an array of concoctions on her face. One turned her lips, eyes, cheeks, and hair a sparkling maroon. The other turned the maroons into swirling shades of orange! The shoppers tried the trixters and fished out a series of copper and silver marble-like coins. *Whoosh! Whoosh! Whoosh!* Firecrackers exploded in the sky.

"I want that swirly orange stuff," exclaimed Leela.

"Look at that!" Rea pointed at a creature resembling an ogre, who was dabbing a creamy ointment on his leg. In a matter of seconds, part of his leg disappeared and in minutes, it reappeared. Rea clapped her hands in glee.

"I can't believe you've decided to cross the lake," cried Flula, materializing out of nowhere.

"Floo, you came!" Leela said.

"Xee, told me to meet you here. Oh, you petals are flying into a trap and... I... I can't even think about it." Infinitesimally tiny tears slipped over her cheeks.

Hex Hollow had made Rea forget her troubles for a while, but after seeing Flula, the dazzle of the market faded, and reality came rushing back.

"He's my brother... I won't leave him imprisoned in the castle," she said.

"I know, but it's all so terrible."

All of them were silent for a moment, thinking of what was to come. They watched as a man wrapped in sheepskin pants and an arrangement of dahlia-like flowers for a shirt jumped into a puddle in front of them. Mud and water splashed over him. He turned in a circle, showing off the mess, and then held up what Rea thought was a coin. He tossed it in the air, where it burst into a fountain of rain. The rain drove steadily down on the man, like his own personal storm. The mud and damp were whisked away, and the man was clean and dry in seconds. As incredible as the magic trick was, it no longer amazed Rea. She turned towards Leela and Flula and saw the long looks on their faces, too. Their time to enjoy the market had come to an end.

"Good, you're all here," Xeranther said, materializing out of the crowd. His manner was brusque.

"Everything go smoothly?" asked Rea.

"Yes, the boat should be there when we arrive."

Rea sighed, relaxing her shoulders a bit. She had been worried something might go wrong with the boat. Without it, she would have had no way of crossing the lake and reaching the castle—and then she'd have to portal back to Earth without Rohan. Now that all the arrangements were in place, she hid the relieved smile that nearly creeped across her face. If Xeranther saw it, he would not take it well. His anxiousness was already contagious. Leela had turned quiet and nervous. Flula's wings flitted without a sound, and a tense silence descended over them.

Annoyed, Rea trailed behind to stop their mood from denting her confidence. She was the one who should be allowed to wallow in fear. After all, wasn't it her brother's life hanging in the balance? Shouldn't they be encouraging her and raising her spirits instead of being so glum? As if she wasn't battling enough, it was now on *her* to cheer them up.

"Maybe Xee is worried about himself and his family?" the little voice behind her ribcage prodded. "He's revolting against the Queen for you, the Queen they fear so much."

Rea ignored her conscience. Then, in a snarkier tone, it asked, "Would *you* put everything on the line for someone you barely knew, like how Leela and Xeranther are for you?"

Argh, cursed Rea. Her conscience was right. She blamed Leela for awakening it by being such a good friend and suddenly, she felt awful. She realized how much Xeranther was doing for her when he could easily have refused. Rea walked briskly to the front of the group, and matched his steps with her own.

"I know you're risking your life to help me, and I want you to know that . . . I—I promise to make it up to you somehow."

Meandering past groups of laughing teenagers trying their

newly bought trixters, they finally reached the spot of the tear. Xeranther glanced at her. "Just make it back alive, okay?" he said in a quiet voice. "That will be payment enough."

The words smacked Rea hard in the chest. Her heart ached in a way she hadn't felt before. Not sure what to say, she nodded. Xeranther murmured the passphrase in reverse, bringing them out of Hex Hollow and back to the rocky path. The tear in the night air sealed shut.

"How far are we from the lake?" asked Leela.

"About a lege."

"Lege?" repeated Rea. She remembered, with a strange prickle down her spine, how Bajai always mispronounced 'league' as 'lege.' No matter how often Rea corrected her, she never learned. Another wave of guilt passed over Rea. She wished Bajai knew where she was.

"Say half of an hour," he clarified, and Rea couldn't decide what was worse: being at the lake that might kill her soon, or spending the next thirty long minutes thinking about how she was potentially going to die.

"Will there be other travelers, too?" she asked.

"No. We're going to the most isolated part of the lake. It's where Floo and I will be safest. If anyone sees us helping you, we'll get our heads done in."

"Or our w-wings," chirped Flula.

Rea's heart sagged with the weight of fear they were carrying because of her. She shivered, drawing her petal-sleeves close to her body. The cold night air had developed a sharp freshness to it, like a peppermint burst open. With each breath, it burned the insides of her nose with a chilly sting.

"Um guys...? WHERE'S LEELA?"

Xeranther swiveled around. When he didn't see Leela, he turned to Rea shouting, "Close your eyes!" and ran back the way they had come. Flula bolted into the trees looking for Leela.

I'm not going to close my eyes! thought Rea in panic. But as she searched for Leela, her calls got lost in her throat as though she had forgotten who she was looking for. Instead, her eyes fixated on dozens of orbs, glowing mist-blue, coal-red, fire-yellow, and weed-green. They floated towards her, appearing out of thin air. They moved slowly at first, and then darted from spot to spot like fireflies playing connect-the-dots. Rea chased after them, first the red ones, then the green, now the yellow!

"BLINK!" Flula shouted in her ears.

Rea blinked and sneezed. The daze cleared and the orbs snuffed out like candle flames. "What just happened?"

From behind a knot of trees, Xeranther brought out a con-fused-looking Leela and Rea ran towards her.

"Are you okay?"

"Um, I think so." Leela rubbed her eyes. "I think I hallucinated."

"Oh, it was our fault," cried Flula. "We should have warned you about the pari-golis."

"Do you feel better now?" Xeranther asked and Rea and Leela nodded, partially sure.

"We must get going then. When you spot the pesky pari-go-lis, you know you've entered Pariland—pari territory."

"It's where we paries live," Flula said, twirling with pride.

As if on cue, the ground glowed in ribbons of fallen glitter and clusters of paries within gold-tinted bubbles floated into view. Rea spotted a cricket-sized pari folding his wings behind his back and stepping into a dew drop without popping it. Pushing his arms out, he stretched the drop until he fit within it, and giving the dew-bubble a good shake, he spread open his wings and the bubble took flight.

"They're water sprites," said Flula as they wandered past a leaf as large as a donkey glittering in pari shimmer. "A mere drop of rain can be fatal for them, and the heat can burn them if they aren't careful."

The sprites were tinier than Floo, practically half her size. A group of them flew by, and Leela watched them go, her eyes mesmerized. In the distance, waterfalls crashed against the rocks.

"Those of us on foliage duty have no choice," continued Flula, ducking under vines strung across the trees like thick wires. "We're experts at dodging rain or snow or harsh beams of sunlight. I was first in my foliage-report-training class! Water and moor sprites are delicate pari and need dew-bubbles to protect themselves from getting injured by natural elements."

Rea and Leela nodded, entranced by the dreamlike landscape. Tiny nest-like houses appeared within the trees decorated with flowers, leaves, and glowing mushroom caps. Paries of all types flitted in and out, shimmering in every color.

"Anyway, pari-golis aren't dangerous," defended Flula. "It's just a bit of mischief, really."

"Easy for you to say, seeing as pari-folk created them and you're immune to their effect," said Xeranther.

"There now, we're allowed some innocent fun."

"Innocent?" he grimaced. "When you stare at the pari-golis for a moment too long," he explained to Rea and Leela, "they latch onto your gaze and lure you places. If you don't blink, you could get lost following them like you both did, giving the paries much to snicker about."

"All right, all right, you must be careful," Flula said and doubled over in laughter. She flew ahead, facing the girls, the pari mischief alive in her face.

"Sometimes, I toss a few pari-golis at Xee and watch him wobble around like a googly-eyed sod until I shoo them away. He gets a sneezing fit—and oh my, Xee's sneezes are some of the loudest I have ever heard," she teased.

Xeranther turned a shade darker. Rea and Leela smiled at each other, trying not to laugh. Releasing her own fit of giggles, Flula flew ahead of them like a shooting star leaving behind a shimmering trail. By the time, the last speckles of her pari dust melted, they had arrived at the shore of the lake.

CHAPTER 18

THE SEA OF SERPENT LILIES

A rowboat moored to a rock bobbed lightly in the water. It was painted a school-bus yellow. The same yellow as in her nightmare, Rea realized with a chill. Against its side rested two paddles.

Rea walked to the edge of the lake. It was enormous, at least twenty times the size of Senchal Lake. It may as well have been a sea. Dewy mist rose from the water like wisps of smoke. Without a word, Xeranther nudged the boat into the lake. Dark ripples licked its sides.

"Good luck," he said, barely looking at them. "Don't forget what Poppy said about a motionless second—keep the boat moving at all times. Don't stop paddling at any cost. The castle is in the center of the lake. You can't miss it."

Rea nodded her head. "We won't forget," she said, holding his gaze.

Without warning, Leela threw her arms around Xeranther and wrapped him in a hug. "Thank you, Xee," she said.

Stunned for a moment, he eventually lifted his arms and hugged her back.

Leela turned towards Flula, ready to say goodbye. The little pari shook her head. "No. Don't say goodbye. I'm coming with you as far as I can."

"Are you sure?" Xeranther asked. "It's close to the edge of pari territory. You can't go too far into the lake."

"I'm sure," Flula said bravely. "I know where the boundary is."

Rea gave Flula a gentle hug between her fingers. "Thank you," she said.

"I will see you both soon," Xeranther said, his eyes turning to rest on Rea once more. Solemnly, the two girls walked down toward the lake.

The night's darkness expanded around them, and the moon, rotund as an ostrich's egg, spilled its light onto the inky waters. Rea and Leela stepped into the boat, taking their place on the wooden beams—Rea in the front and Leela at the back. Xeranther untied the rope from the rock and gave the boat a push. Flula flitted overhead, following along. Rea watched as Xeranther grew smaller on the shore, his troubled expression growing harder to see as they drifted out into the lake.

At first, Rea and Leela paddled slowly and awkwardly. It seemed to take ages for them to learn how to paddle in sync.

Eventually they figured it out and rowing together the boat moved swiftly through the smooth waters.

"No one said paddling was going to be so hard," said Leela. "It's barely been ten minutes and my arms feel like they're going to fall off."

"Hush," whispered Flula from high above. "You'll wake them!"

"But where are they?" Rea had expected to find the lilies all around. "I don't feel any resistance under my paddle either."

"Same," said Leela, and she dipped her hand into the water.

"What are you doing?" cried Flula.

"Checking to see if the lilies are submerged. It happens sometimes to lotuses back home."

Flula's glitter turned dark. "You don't have to go looking for them. They *will* find you. Now keep your hands inside the boat. Both of you."

They rowed deeper into the lake. As they found their rhythm, Rea and Leela paddled with greater ease. Pari-golis twinkled far away along the shore, the water shimmering with their reflections. It would have been beautiful if it weren't so eerie.

"Glibbety gibbots..." quivered Flula. "I see them."

The mist lifted, and a profusion of moon-white lilies surfaced above the water.

"Uh oh," uttered Leela, as the boat cut through mats of flat, rubbery leaves.

Rea breathed in their soft floral scent.

"LOOK!" she said.

A hazy outline of a castle appeared in the distance, shrouded in moonshine. Rea couldn't believe it. Before her very eyes was the Queen's castle and somewhere inside it was Rohan. Flula's glow dimmed in fear, and Rea and Leela paddled with all their might. But as time passed, they were no closer to the castle than before.

"Let's slow down a bit," Rea said, settling her paddle on her knees and leaning against the side of the boat. Her arms felt like they were weighed down with sandbags.

"DON'T STOP ROWING!" yelled Flula.

"We're not, we're not! We just took a nano-second break," said Rea, paddling immediately.

"Ew, what's that?" Leela asked, pointing.

A fetid smell curled up from the lake and one by one the lilies darkened with decay.

"Let's not panic," said Rea. "They're only li—"

"AHHHHHH," shrieked Leela.

A creature as long as her leg, fanned with petals, coiled around the shaft of her paddle. As Leela tried to shake it free, the creature's tongue, forked like a snake, shot out of its mouth toward her. The boat wobbled precariously.

"Get off, get off!" Rea screamed, jabbing the clinging flower-snake with her paddle. The creature retreated and slipped back into the water. "Are you all right?" she asked Leela, continuing to paddle urgently.

"I—I think so..." said Leela. Sweat covered her face and she held onto the side of the boat, shivering.

Terror hooked its claws into Rea. If anything happened to Leela, it would be her fault. Just like losing Rohan was.

"I'll do the rowing," she said. "You try and stay calm—"

Right then, Flula screeched. In their shock, they had stopped paddling and the lake belched like an undersea monster.

Rotting lilies from every direction sprang out of the water. Their sinewy stems had transformed into slithering bodies, and their petals with razor-sharp teeth crowned their reptilian faces. Locking onto their prey with their bloodless eyes, they shot through the water, their flat, slimy leaves twisting into fins.

"Xeranther was right. We're going to DIE," cried Leela, her teeth chattering.

"KEEP MOVING," shouted Flula, and Rea whipped the water with her paddle, creating waves to keep the lilies from coming too close.

"REA, THE POEM! Call the Ceffyl-whatever NOW!" Leela shouted at the top of her lungs.

The serpent-lilies bared their fangs. Acid-venom dripped from the tips of their teeth, and the smell of rot permeated the air. Rea tried to recite the poem in Mishti Daadi's prophecy, but the words failed her. Each time she started to say a line, a lily leaped out of the water, snapping its serrated teeth and missing her by a hair's breadth.

"Look away from them!" said Leela. "Now concentrate!"

Rea shut her eyes and focused on each line. Bit by bit, the words came back to her. Half a dozen tries later, she recited the whole poem.

> "O winged fury, hither do hurry
> To you I plead, O mighty steed
> With your coat of night

and myrtle eyes,
Sail me to the shore,
O Ceffyldwer."

Nothing happened. Rea didn't know what she was expecting. She recited the poem again and Leela joined in. A sturdy tug reverberated from under the boat and alight with excitement, Rea turned.

"LEELA!" she yelled.

Serpent-lilies, excreting sticky secretions, were slinking up the edges of the boat. Taking turns, she and Leela thwacked them, but the serpents inched higher, smacking the paddles with their sharp tails. Every few seconds, Flula cried warnings as more lilies slid up the boat or soared out of the water. Rea was completely drenched. The boat had veered considerably away from the castle, and before Rea could think of what to do next, Leela sprang out of her seat.

Two serpent-lilies had snuck inside the boat, right between her and Leela's legs. Rea tried to kick the creatures back into the water, but they pounced, snapping their jaws. Leela smacked them with her paddle while Rea rowed with a vengeance, kicking at the heads of more lilies as they slithered their way in.

In the midst of everything, an idea came to Rea. An incredible, fabulous, probably impossible idea.

"Floo!" she yelled. "Bring as many pari-golis as you can. HURRY!"

In a burst of energy, Flula darted across the water towards the woods. Rea didn't know whether her trick would work, but they had nothing to lose at this point.

Turning back to the lilies, Rea continued to recite the poem.

She and Leela took turns paddling. At last, it seemed they were starting to tire out the lilies. One by one, they fell over the side of the boat and into the midnight water. Just when things seemed to be getting better, a lily sprung out of nowhere and coiled itself around Leela's leg!

Rea threw down her paddle and grabbed the serpent with both her hands. Peeling it off of her friend, Rea hurled it far into the lake, and as the serpent-lily arced through the air, she spotted a piece of Leela's petal-skirt snagged on one of its fangs.

Heart pounding, she glanced at Leela, who was frozen with fear. Their feverish movements had generated enough velocity to keep the boat moving on its own (at least for a moment).

Leela turned pale as the moon. "We're as good as dead," she said, staring at the relentless lilies.

Desperately, Rea tried to come up with more ideas. *This is like a puzzle*, she thought. *Just another puzzle to be solved with the tools we have.*

As she wracked her brain for a way out, serpent-lilies gorged on the soggiest parts of the boat. Others shot out of the water to get a bite of human flesh. A pack of lilies seized Leela's paddle with their teeth, snapping it in two. Leela swung around in terror, slicing Rea's arm with the broken edge of her paddle. Blood poured out of Rea like a river and her wound throbbed as if it had a heart of its own. White spots clouded her vision and she cried out in pain.

Leela gaped at Rea's wound. "What have I done? I'm so sorry, I'm so sorry!"

"It's okay. Keep paddling," Rea said with a wince as her paddle slipped from her hands. Leela grabbed it and began paddling like crazy, creating a fury of splashing water, which made the boat go round in circles.

Rea tried not to pass out. She stared at the blood flowing down her arm. Trying to numb the pain, she shook her arm over the water.

Leela's eyes went wide with disbelief. "Look! The lilies are swimming away!"

As droplets of her blood dripped into the lake, Rea watched in amazement as the serpent-lilies darted away from her blood like it was poison. As long as she bled into the water, the lilies circled at a safe distance. Rea was excited and relieved; she couldn't believe her blood was scaring these fierce animals away.

"How—?" she started to ask, but before she could finish her question, she heard a familiar voice in the distance. Flula was flying toward them along with hundreds of her pari friends—each glistening in colored shimmer. In their hands, they held a cluster of pari-golis.

Rea locked eyes with Flula and gave her the go ahead.

"On my command, FIRE!" shouted Flula.

The paries flung the pari-golis over the lake and the white eyes of the hissing lilies fastened onto the dancing dots. In seconds, the nefarious serpents went limp, floating in a daze.

The paries twittered with joy. Leela stopped paddling for a minute, mesmerized by the pari-golis, until Rea reminded her to blink. Taking advantage of the paries' distraction, Rea recited the Ceffyldwer call. The two girls paddled as fast as they could, hoping to make as much progress as possible before the pari-golis' spell wore off.

"I can't go any farther!" Flula called from behind them. "Keep paddling and stay safe. Good luck, my petals!"

"Thank you, Flula!" called Leela as they paddled with all the energy they had left.

The castle appeared through the mist for a moment, and Rea's heart jumped with joy.

But their good luck didn't last. The pari-golis only distracted the lilies for a few minutes. Rea's bleeding slowed down, and the blood in the water thinned. All too soon, a cluster of serpent-lilies rose to the surface beside the boat. They snaked and slithered over each other, inches away. In their devil eyes and spitting tongues, Rea saw her death. Brutal and cruel. Desperately, Rea stuck out her arm again and shook it, but merely one drop of blood fell over the serpent-lilies' heads.

The moment the droplet touched one of the lilies, its skin sizzled and its eyes bulged. The serpent-lily twisted its root-like body out of the water and screeched in agony.

"Watch out!" cried Leela.

The writhing creature leaped for Rea's face but before it could reach her, its body swelled like a balloon. Then, like a firecracker, it burst, guts, blood and flesh flying everywhere.

"You did it! You did it!" Leela yelled.

"Did I?" Rea asked, dazed. "How? With my blood?"

Unexpectedly, Poppy's words on how to survive the lake came to her.

...*You can be a royal, born with the same nectar that runs through the blood of the Queen, or you can find the right type of magic to conquer the magic of the lake...*

Could she really be of royal blood with the same nectar as the Queen's? Or did her blood have another type of magic that matched the magic of the lake?

Leela grunted heavily, interrupting Rea's thoughts. She was trying hard to keep the boat moving.

"Let me help," said Rea.

"No, I'll paddle. You call for the Ceffyldwer and fight the monsters."

"All right. Recite with me, then."

As Rea and Leela chanted the poem, the lilies rose. Their faces glistened, and their fangs dripped with hunger. Rea and Leela flung the remaining paddle into the water, giving them something other than the boat to chomp on. In seconds, there was nothing left of it. Watching the snapping jaws come closer, Rea and Leela crawled into each other's arms, crying and reciting the poem.

The boat cracked. The water rushed in.

Rea looked at Leela.

She had failed her. She had failed everyone.

CHAPTER 19

THE MOST ORDINARY OF DOORS

"**K**ick your feet," shouted Rea, as the serpent-lilies circled them, their slimy, scaly skin glistening in the moonlight. The little remaining blood from her wound bled into the water, keeping the lilies away.

"Help!" cried Leela, splashing to stay afloat and gulping in mouthfuls of water. She didn't know how to swim. Rea dove underwater and grabbed her by the waist, trying to pull her toward the surface.

Water stung Rea's eyes.

Kick!

She moved upward.

Kick again!

The water entered Rea's nose and ears. She used every ounce of strength to swim back to the surface and coughed out cold, mossy liquid as she searched for the castle. She had to save Leela no matter what. Kicking with whatever energy she had left, Rea pulled Leela through the choppy waters. If she could get her to the shore, she didn't care what happened to herself. Rea kicked again, her arms and legs aching with exhaustion.

Suddenly, a bolt of lightning splintered across the sky, blinding her. Seconds later, thunder roared.

Then the night shook.

Rea looked up.

A beast, black as a bat, with fire-golden eyes, flew through the clouds, flapping its massive, gold-feather-tipped wings. With a mountainous splash, it nosedived into the lake and rose up through the water with Rea and Leela on its mammoth back. Leela clung to Rea and Rea clung onto the creature's horns, holding on for dear life. As they soared above the deadly waters, Rea saw Flula flying into the woods and disappearing into the trees. Rea was glad that she had escaped to safety.

With a quick and smooth descent, the Ceffyldwer landed onto the sandy shores of the Queen's castle and Rea and Leela slid off his back. Rea looked up at the giant stone structure, dark and foreboding, and at the equally terrifying creature who had saved them. She didn't know where to begin. Both took her breath away to the extent that not a single coherent word formed in her head or mouth.

The Ceffyldwer was a blend of horse, bird, and antelope. Unfurling his wings, he shook off the water in a downpour of rain. His feathery tips glittered like drops of honey catching the moonlight.

"He's beautiful, isn't he?" Leela ran her fingers over his long, slender neck.

Two spots of blood oozed from her left calf.

"Are you feeling okay?" Rea asked, searching for signs of coagulating blood.

Leela gazed at the Ceffyldwer as he nuzzled her leg.

"Thank you for saving us," she said.

His spiral horns extended high above his head and his striped wall-like flank rippled in gold whenever he moved or flexed. Rea nervously approached the winged beast. His muscles relaxed under her touch and for some reason—perhaps that he had saved their lives—she forgot her fears and wrapped her arms around him.

The Ceffyldwer turned to Rea's bloodied arm and Rea felt her heartbeats evening out. The warm breath of the animal and the care with which he looked at her comforted her. Dipping his head, he ripped off the edge of Rea's petal-tunic and placed the fabric on her bleeding wound. Wordlessly, Rea tied it around her arm.

"Thank you," she whispered.

The Ceffyldwer turned his head and nuzzled her. An unexpected emotion surged through Rea and a single sentence appeared in her mind as if she had thought it herself.

Thubian is my name.

She leaped backwards, gawking at the Ceffyldwer.

Are you in my head?

Thubian nodded.

You can understand me?

Aye. Your love for your brother and your determination to save your friend in the face of death makes you a worthy Ceffyl-rider. I am proud to be bonded to you.

A smile formed around his thoughts, warm and affectionate.

Leela's going to be mad with excitement when I tell her I can talk to you!

Thubian whinnied a laugh. *Your friend's soul shines of starlight. A true friend, indeed.*

Rea glowed with his praise for Leela. She knew more than anyone how much Leela deserved it.

How does your arm feel? asked Thubian.

Only then did Rea realize that her arm had stopped hurting. She removed the fabric she had tied on it and saw that her wound had healed. Barely a scratch remained.

Did you heal me? she asked him.

Thubian nodded.

Can you heal Leela too?

My powers are sworn to protect you, rider. I can heal your physical wounds but not the wounds of your soul. Alas, my powers cannot heal your friend. They are of no use to anyone except you.

Thubian turned to Leela, who was caressing him like he was a lost puppy. Enjoying the attention, he gave her the back of his ear to scratch. Rea smiled and turned away from them, walking towards the castle.

It was nothing like she had imagined. There was no mansion with high spires, large gates and fluttering flags, no manicured gardens like those surrounding old Indian palaces, nor an army of guards to hide from. It was large—very large—but that's where the similarities ended.

Leela came up beside her.

"This isn't what I expected at all," she said in a tired voice. Rea nodded.

The castle, surrounded by sand and lapping waves, did not have a clearly defined shape. Crimson creepers grew over its tall and narrow windows and the undulating façade looked swollen and sunken in places. Under dregs of moonmist, Rea counted twenty-three windows fitted with stained glass of beastly flowers trapped in a whorl of tendrils. Beneath them were bone-colored balconies of the most peculiar design.

"They look like eyes staring at us," she said, pointing at the balcony walls, which had two circular holes in them. Within their gaps were soldered twisted rods of the same bone-colored material which Rea assumed were placed to prevent someone from falling through.

"That can't be the only way in," Leela said, eyeing the most out-of-place component of the whimsical structure—the door.

It was the most ordinary of doors. Small, brown, and plain. And it had a horseshoe for a knocker. Rea looked for another, less obvious entrance. She hadn't thought it through, but she vaguely imagined sneaking into the castle through a chimney chute or in a barrel full of potatoes. Not once did she think she'd walk in straight through a door.

Leela shook off a shiver and Rea glanced at the roof, looking for another way inside. There weren't any chimneys they could squeeze into, but there was an owl perched on a turret, staring at her. She couldn't say for sure, but it looked very much like one she had followed in her nightmare. They locked eyes and it didn't fly away this time. It seemed Rea had reached her destination.

"There's no other way in," Leela said, her breath heavy. "This place is all wall and ivy."

"Then we'll have to use the door," Rea said with a confidence she didn't feel. She turned to Thubian. "Will you wait until we return?" she asked.

Chewing on a branch, he regarded Rea and the castle and bowed his head. A look of understanding passed between them and he stepped into the shadows, blending into the night. Somehow, Rea knew all she had to do was call for him when they needed to leave, and he would appear.

"All right, let's get Rohan and get out of here," she said, knocking on the door.

Within a minute, a man no taller than her chest appeared. His eyes shifted between them and then skirted around their sides. "Who bees you?"

"We are here to see the Queen," said Rea.

"You bees travelling alone?" His bushy eyebrows flew to his forehead.

Rea slunk a glance at Thubian, who was camouflaged so completely she couldn't tell where he was. "Yes."

The dwarf's beady eyes rolled over their drenched clothes. "What—er—how bees you arriving at the castle?"

One of his eyebrows landed back over his eye and the other crooked higher. A smothered light from inside the hallway fell on the gilded insignia of a tree emblazoned within the symbol of a sun embroidered on his robes.

"Does it matter?" said Rea. "We're here now and we want to speak to the Queen."

The dwarf kept looking around as if expecting to see someone.

"Very well," he said. "Since you bees crossing the lake without—er—incident, you bees granted an audience with Her Extreme Greatness. What bees your business with the Queen?"

Leela covered her mouth and fell into a coughing fit.

"Leela?"

"I'm fine, I'm fine." She breathed rapidly. Putting effort to make her words audible, she said, "The Queen has something my friend wants returned to her."

The dwarf's doughy face frowned. "What bees your names?"

"I'm Rea and she is Leela."

"Permission bees granted to Ree-aaa and Leee-laa to enter the castle of Her Extreme Greatness, Queen Razya of the House of Flur. I bees Torgar, First Order of the Salient Keepers," he announced, tapping his chest with his fist.

Rea stared at the dwarf. She had already forgotten his title and name when Leela exchanged a glance with her and followed him through the door. A narrow passage, dingy with the smell of dampness, welcomed them. Rea expected a corridor resplendent with crystal chandeliers and jewel-framed portraits of the royal family. Instead, stout candles in cages hung from the ceiling, making their shadows leap in the flames.

"It's a castle, not a palace. Built for battle rather than beauty," Leela whispered, reading Rea's thoughts. Rea shot her a wary glance.

If the corridor wasn't creepy enough, its walls were decorated with three dimensional flowers, some twice as large as their faces while others as tiny as pimples, each the shade of a decomposing fruit. They were thick and oily, somewhere between solid and liquid. And they moved. Stems overlapped each other, leaves suffocated under one another, and thorns stabbed into the other's flesh. Rea elbowed Leela to look and she muffled her gasp.

"We bees turning here," the dwarf said, halting beside a bolted door. He pulled out a set of rusty keys from his robe.

A pair of guards in full armor stood on either side of the door. One held a sword perpendicular to the ground and the other clenched a battle axe. They wore metal masks over their faces and while the dwarf huffed to get the key to work, Rea stared at their weapons. Like the flowers, they shrank and stretched before her eyes, the opposing blades of the axe fusing together and swelling into a solid ball with spikes. Rea let out an inadvertent gasp. She flicked a look at the guard and spied an evil smirk from the slit in his mask.

Before the other guard's sword shapeshifted, the dwarf pushed the door open in a dispersion of dust and Rea and Leela hurried down a flight of crudely placed stone steps. The ceiling was so low they had to bend to avoid hitting it. After reaching the landing, they ascended another, shorter, flight of stairs. Entering a third corridor, they went up and down more stairs, all of which were dank and cold. The hairs on Rea's neck rose. How many passages existed within these underground tunnels from hell?

"Um sir, how much further?" Rea asked, her legs weak with exhaustion.

They had entered the seventh or eighth gutter-dark corridor. Leela's pace slowed too and Rea held her hand to keep her from trailing behind. The dwarf didn't answer. The corridor stank of pungent fumes and shuddered with sounds of hammering. Through a gap in a slightly ajar door, Rea glimpsed a roomful of soot-covered dwarves hunched over long worktables and oily candles. A guard in the doorway noticed her looking. He hissed at her and slammed the door shut in her face. Finally, at the end of what seemed like the millionth passage, the dwarf ushered them into a circular room flanked by twelve doors.

"Bees waiting here," he instructed. Giving a nod to one of the guards to keep watch on the girls, he shuffled back out.

"We made it," said Rea.

Leela licked her parched lips. "If I wasn't feeling queasy, I'd be jumping with excitement. I'm sorry—"

Rea shook her head. "You're sorry? Leela, I'm the one who is sorry. We could have... If the Ceffyldwer hadn't shown up... Gosh, I was stupid and selfish and foolish—"

"Stop. You're doing this for Rohan. There's nothing foolish or selfish about it. And I'm fine. I'm just recovering from the boat wobbling and freakish serpent-lilies." Leela gave a feeble smile. "I'm glad we're out of that suffocating maze of corridors and stairs," she added, leaning against the wall.

Rea agreed and gazed in awe at the cavernous room. Beams of wood curved across it like a tree spreading its branches. Marble statues frozen in pain, agony, and screams jutted above the twelve doors and a potpourri of flowers with prickly centers, thick stems, and lustrous black leaves crowded the walls.

"These flowers..." Rea cringed at the exuberance and ghastliness of one withered-yellow, macabre-red, and burnt-blue floret.

"They look... *infected.*"

Leela leaned closer.

Whisssssssh!

A chandelier hidden in darkness lit up, sizzling like a small fire. It hung wide and low with rows of skulls and bones interlaced in an intricate design.

"Don't the dead make for charming decorations?"

The voice was sharp as a knife and luxurious as a sheet of satin.

The dwarf hurried into the room, panting. "Presenting Her Extreme Greatness, Queen Razya of the House of Flur, Ruler of the great and bountiful realm of Astranthia!" He bowed with extravagance, the curved end of his hat touching the tips of his shoes.

The Queen stood in the center of the chamber and Rea stared unabashedly. Her opulent gown flared in the shape of an orchid and as she walked, the flouncing petals shimmered in hues of burgundy and silver. A cloak of feathers of deep aubergine draped her back and resting on her head was a crown of entangled branches, leaves and petals, glistening in black. Her face was perfectly angular with a dainty nose, crimson lips, and teeth as straight as a row of ashoka trees. Her eyebrows, a knitted row of thorns, were curved to perfection and her eyes, a vivid green, glowed as if they were ablaze.

"I see the girls are deaf."

"Um..." Rea muttered, her voice stuck in her throat.

"I shan't be here all day. Speak at once."

"Y-you've kidnapped my brother and I demand his release!" she announced as loudly as her nerves allowed her.

"*Demand?*" The Queen raised her contoured thorn-brow and the dwarf squelched like he'd eaten a sour grape. "Alas, I loathe unfortunate manners."

She raised her forefinger and a flash of electric light screeched through the air. Leela was lifted off the ground and Rea screamed. She jumped to pull Leela down, but she was out of reach. Coughing and sputtering, Leela tried to rid the invisible bind around her neck, her face turning purple as the Queen's magic cut off her breath.

"I'm sorry, I take back my words!" Rea cried. "I beg you, please release my friend. Torture me, if you want to. Please let her go!" Rea trembled, and the Queen lowered Leela to the floor.

Leela stood up slowly. Rea could see her eyes were blurry, her face pasty. She reached out and held Leela, knowing she would fall without support. The dwarf scurried towards them with a lavishly carved stool and Rea lowered Leela onto it.

"Thank you," she murmured to the dwarf. He looked at her in surprise, as if no one had thanked him for anything in a long time. With a brisk nod, he turned and walked swiftly back to his station by the door.

Leela turned to her in gratitude. "Don't worry about me," she whispered. "Go get Rohan."

Rea walked towards the Queen nervously. "T-thank you for your mercy, Your Highness—"

"*GREATNESS!*" croaked the dwarf. "Your *Extreme* Greatness!"

"Oh, sorry!" Rea said. "Your Extreme Greatness, I've come to rescue my brother. I know he's imprisoned in the Cellars."

"Imprisoned?" The Queen's face turned cold.

"Um... yes... he is... um... isn't he—er—here in the castle?" Rea's resolve was shattering to pieces. The tirade of insults she had rehearsed countless times evaporated on her lips and she was a mumbling mess. What had she been thinking? The Queen would hand Rohan over because she told her to? Her tears threatened to spill.

"Indeed, he is," stated the Queen, surprising Rea. "But I shan't allow crude words such as 'kidnapped' and 'imprisoned' to be used when he was brought here to fulfil his duty."

Words failed Rea. *What duty is she talking about?*

The Queen lowered her chin and her cold, moss colored eyes pierced her. "Would you like to see him?"

Rea couldn't believe her ears.

"YES!" she answered, a little too loudly.

CHAPTER 20

THERE BEES DANGER

The Queen twirled her fingers and strings of rainbow-colored light flew from their sharpened tips, forming a diaphanous orb. Within it, images started to take shape.

A ribbon of steps plunging into the belly of the castle. Wisps of moonlight floating in its shadowy depths. Green-flamed candles lining a passage with time-worn walls. At its end, an arched stone entrance.

The image trembled like a nervous hand.

Skeletal prisoners on either side of the passage banged the iron bars of their jail cells, hooting and whistling. A woman with bedraggled hair and yellowed teeth shot out her hand to grab someone. She cackled as her chained legs slid across the floor.

Rea's heart beat wildly. *Are these the Cellars of Doom?*

A lizard-man with wing-shaped ears snarled at the prisoners, his skin shimmering a blackened-blue. The prisoners shrank away, crawling back to their corners. His fiery-red eyes with diamond pupils bore into them, his lids swiping across them like a sliding door. With a final look, the lizard-man turned and halted beside a jail cell. The cell was scant. A broken sink stood beside a cot woven in coarse, jute-like fibers. On it sat a boy, his face gaunt and his cheeks sunken. He wore loose rags the color of potatoes and on his feet were wooden clogs with chains around his ankles. He was reading a book embossed with the words 'The Covenants of Astranthia.' Shaking his head in anger, he flung the book against the wall. Rags were wrapped around his wrists, and rust-colored blood seeped through the cloth. Plates of untouched food lay in the corner.

It was Rohan.

Fear tore into Rea as desperation clung to the walls of her heart.

"Can I t-talk to him?" she pleaded.

"Interactions with prisoners are forbidden I'm afraid," the Queen said. "However, there is a condition you can fulfil to secure his release."

"Anything!" exclaimed Rea. "I'll do whatever it takes."

A sugary smile cut across the Queen's face and with a flamboyant twirl of her fingers, she peered into the orb again.

A beautiful hibiscus appeared. Its color was that of a deep ocean— blue, twinkling, and pure. Every vein in its petals, every groove in its stamen, every fuzz in its pollen could be seen with the clearest of detail. The flower, infused with magic, throbbed like a living heart. Then, just like that, two petals dissolved to dust while a third fell to the bottom.

"As you can see, the Som, our sacred flower, is bereft of three petals. Two perished in wars and the other hides somewhere in the realm. Only two petals remain. Find me the lost petal and I shall set your brother free."

The Queen's manner was calm as she issued her caveat. But her exquisite burgundy gown changed hue, staining the edges of her dress black.

Thinking she could retrieve the fallen petal from inside the orb, Rea reached into it to pick it up, but the image of the flower and the petal cracked like a bad TV connection, disappearing altogether for a moment before appearing again. It was an illusion, she realized. A trick of magic. The real flower and its missing petal were somewhere in Astranthia.

"C-Can't you use your magic?" she asked the Queen. The only place she knew how to get to in Astranthia was the market road, and that was because she had portaled straight onto it. "Couldn't it help you find the petal?"

Scorn stretched across the Queen's face and Rea's tongue flopped out of her mouth, swollen like a fat, slimy, overgrown slug. Leela mewled with whatever little energy she had left, and Rea choked.

"Nthaw thaoop thussh thheuuush thuuhmp!"

"I caution you against telling me what to do," the Queen said, her eyes narrowing to slits. Her cape fluttered under an invisible draft and its shivering feathers resembled a thousand scolding fingers.

Rea stumbled in fear, trying hysterically to stuff her tongue back into her mouth. Leela began to cry.

"The choice is simple," the Queen continued. "Fulfill the condition or never see your brother again."

Rea nodded profusely. At this point, she was willing to

do anything to stop her tongue from swelling any further. The tension eased out of the Queen's face and Rea's tongue shrunk back to normal size.

"I'll do it!" gasped Rea. She sucked on her tongue to ensure it was intact. "I'll find the petal! But please, please tell me where I should start looking for it."

"Well…"

The sacred flower within the orb morphed into an image of Xeranther and Flula walking down the market street.

"You've made some friends, haven't you?" the Queen said, her bejeweled fingers glinting under the light of the orb.

Rea's heart sank. Xeranther and Flula's lives were officially in danger. She glanced at Leela to ask her what to do, but she looked so drained, she could barely sit up straight. Rea thought about the piece of skirt stuck on the serpent-lily's fang and the spots of blood on Leela's leg. She was certain the lily had bitten her.

"And there is your nectar, of course," the Queen said.

"My n-nectar…?" Rea asked, her voice smaller than a mouse's squeak. She was trying to focus on the Queen's words while simultaneously making sure Leela was breathing.

"Yes, your *nectar*," she repeated. "Don't you know what that is?"

Rea was terrified the Queen would get upset if she didn't know what her nectar was and put a spell on another part of her body. Her tongue was back in working condition, but her heart hadn't recovered yet. Right now, it was thumping so fast, it was about to burst out of her chest.

Not knowing what to say, Rea kept silent. The Queen sighed

and the image in the orb changed once again. Rea peered into it.

Amma and Bajai were sitting on throne chairs. Bajai was dressed in a gown of crimson and teal leaves laced with pearls of dew drops. On her head she wore a crown similar to the Queen's, only smaller and golden. An outfit of blush-pink petals swathed Amma and a silver tiara of petal and leaf sat amidst her dark, rich curls. They were both younger. And smiling.

Rea stopped breathing. A thousand questions exploded in her mind, each detonating parts of her soul.

"Ah, I see they did it to you as well," the Queen smiled.

"D-id what?" Rea managed to say, the ground underneath her starting to tremble. She looked around, but everyone else's balance seemed fine.

"They lied to you. Kept secrets. Treated you like a child who has no mind of her own."

Rea couldn't bear to look the Queen in the eye, nor could she tear her eyes away from the image of Amma and Bajai dressed as royals.

"You and I have blossomed from the same seed, dear niece. Rules, secrets, lies—they stifle us." The Queen curled her long fingers around her slender neck to illustrate her words. "We can't be forced to live our life in accordance to someone else's whims. We make our *own* rules, mark our *own* way, get what *we* want..."

The reality of the truth numbed Rea. Pain, anger, and sadness quarreled within her, turning into a jumble of emotions too heavy for her heart to bear. Thoughts failed to guide her, and the Queen's words rolled away like a pack of marbles, scattering into the dark corners of her mind.

All except one word. It stayed put, glaring at her, rooting her in the present.

Niece.

Rea had had her suspicions ever since Poppy mentioned the royal children, but hearing it being confirmed as the truth shook her to her core. The ground, already trembling, cracked beneath her feet and Rea's soul teetered. She stared at Amma and Bajai in the orb. How could they hide something like that?

"Mother and Keona know how to keep a secret, or should I say, spin a lie," the Queen said, her voice full of contempt. "I see my words are causing you pain, but it is time someone drew you out of the darkness and into the light to hear the truth. I am your aunt, dear one. Your mother Keona's older sister. Daughter of your grandmother, the now deposed Queen Yuthika of the House of Flur. Being the first-born, it is your brother Raohan's duty to sacrifice his blood on the sacred flower to keep Astranthia's nectar flowing. Had I not brought him to perform his obligation, your mother and grandmother would have left Astranthia reeling with another lost petal, putting the lives of this land's inhabitants in greater peril. Don't be fooled, dear niece. They knew this day would come."

A viscous emotion, thick with betrayal, flowed through Rea. Amma had blamed her for what had happened to Rohan. She told Rea this was all her fault because they had played a harmless game on their birthday and had convinced her to take the blame for losing him. Even Bajai, who Rea believed to be on her side, had punished her by lying. How could they have treated her this way? Lied, blamed, and guilted her into believing it was her fault when it was theirs? Did they not care for her at all?

And honestly, did they even care for Rohan? Rea thought back to all the times they had pampered and praised him. Had they known, this whole time, that he would wind up here? Rea remembered how Amma acted like Rohan was never coming back the second they found out he was missing. She remembered Amma crying and saying he was taken, and how she didn't call the police because she knew they wouldn't be able to help them.

Rea's fingers rolled into a fist and she willed her knees to keep her standing.

Amma and Bajai had always known what had happened. Rea's head spun. If they knew Rohan was here, why hadn't they come to rescue him?

Breathe, she instructed herself. *Keep breathing.*

A strange kind of courage came over Rea. A courage pushing its way up from the despair wracking her gut.

She had come this far without any help from Amma or Bajai. She didn't need them, or their lies.

She had come here for her brother and she wasn't going to lose her chance at saving him because her mother and grandmother were too cowardly to face the truth and fight for him.

"If Rohan is a prince, why have you locked him in a prison?" Rea asked, raising her voice to sound brave. It still quivered and she hoped no one heard it.

Green fire burst from the Queen's fingertips and she doused it by closing her fist.

"Because I cannot trust Mother or Keona. In their greed, they might try to take him away, ruining the future of Astranthia.

They're caught up in their tiny lives and don't care for what will become of us, of the very land that birthed them, of the very people who worshipped them. They aren't like you and I, Raelia. They live for themselves, hurting those close to them, not caring that we are family or of one blood—the blood of the nectar, no less."

Rea hadn't missed that her real name was Raelia just as her mother's real name was Keona and not Kunjan and Rohan's name was Raohan while Bajai was Queen Yuthika of Astranthia. But what she still could not understand was this 'nectar' the Queen kept speaking about that seemed to hold such importance.

"What is the blood of the nectar?" she asked.

The Queen closed her eyes. When she opened them, she looked crestfallen.

"Raelia, Princess of Astranthia, you have the magic of the nectar flowing within your veins. It is the blood of our tribe; the brothers and sisters of the nectar, and you, young and untarnished by life, are blessed with its untamed powers." The Queen's voice was as tender as the song of a koel.

"As you well know, there is magic in Astranthia and the Som is our sacred flower. It is a flower both magical and extremely dangerous. In its center lies the elixir of nectar, the purest of magic, which keeps Astranthia alive and courses through the bloodline of our family. To seek its offering, the sacred flower, weak from exhausting the nectar, emerges to refill its elixir. It blooms on the Night of Nilaya—the night of the first full moon after the heir to the throne turns twelve."

The images in the orb gave shape to the Queen's words.

"On that night, the moon glows blue. At the stroke of twelve, a drop of the heir's blood, filled with the health and glory of youth, must be offered into the hollow of the Som's petals. If no drop of nectral blood is sacrificed, one of the petals will wither and Astranthia, already teetering on an unsolid foundation, will further burden the Som to keep the realm alive. Gradually, crops will die, creatures will perish, and men will fall prey to disease and ruin. If all the petals disappear, the magic of the land will vanish, and the realm will plunge into eternal darkness."

The image of Astranthia in the orb crumbled to ashes.

"You don't want the blood of the people on your hands, do you? I imagine neither does your brother, isn't that right...?" The Queen trailed off, studying Rea as if to determine if she might actually be that selfish.

Rea's nails sliced into her skin. She needed time to process what the Queen was saying. A *lot* of time.

"The Ceremony of the Night of Nilaya is in two days. You must return with the petal by then," the Queen said. "Remember, enemies of the crown are everywhere. I learned quickly not to trust anyone. Not even our own family. I admit my own efforts at locating the petal have failed—I was thwarted at every stage—but with the power of your youthful nectar, you are certain to find it."

"If you free Rohan, both of us can look for the petal. I promise we won't say a word to Amma or Bajai," implored Rea.

The Queen shook her head. "The severity of the mission isn't for the fainthearted and I need your motivations to stay strong. I give you my word your brother is safer in his cell than you will be in the wilds of Astranthia. Now, there isn't much time. Salient

Keepers, escort them out, the girl has a realm to save."

Rea caught a twitch in the Queen's voice. A slight tremble in an otherwise even-keeled tone. The Queen was scared. Her gaze bore into Rea as though she was handing over a torch she had been carrying, a torch burdened with duty, and now it was Rea's time to carry it towards the finish line. The Queen blinked, shaking Rea out of her thoughts, and with a snap of her fingers, she vanished and a second dwarf, identical to the first one, appeared in her place.

"I bees Dalric, Second Order of the Salient Keepers," the twin-dwarf said with a wide grin and wobble of his belly.

"You better bees leaving." Torgar waved Rea and Leela out the room. "Time bees running out!"

Leela stopped Rea and whispered in her ears.

"Can it wait?' asked Rea.

Leela vigorously shook her head.

"Hmm... Dol—um—sir?" said Rea.

"I bees Dalric, Second Order of—"

"Yes, yes, Dalric. Is there a bathroom? My friend needs to use it."

The dwarves looked at each other, befuddled. Rea lifted her little finger to say number one; it was the sign they used in school when they needed to be excused to use the bathroom. The dwarves looked more confused.

"Salient Keeper, I really need to go. If you don't show me the way, I'm going to pee right here!" Leela said.

"Oh!" said Torgar and led the way through a series of winding corridors. This time, they stopped beside a marble staircase.

Flowers and leaves of the same decaying material on the castle walls crawled around its balustrades and curved railing. To its right, a door engraved with the words 'Public Rooms' led to a chamber of bathrooms. Leaving Torgar and Dalric waiting outside, Leela rushed into one of the intricately inlaid stalls. Ornate mirrors filled the walls and the counters gleamed in stones of satin-white.

Rea waited for Leela inside the chamber when a shadow moved from underneath the furthest stall. Then another. Rea peeked under the gap of the door. There was no one. Again, two shadows, tall and elongated as they are in an early evening light, moved. Wary at first, she opened the door and sure as the stars in the sky, it wasn't a bathroom—it was a secret passage! Without looking back, Rea stepped into the passage. She wondered why it was hidden in a bathroom of all places. *Maybe that is precisely why*, she realized. *Who would think to check for a secret passageway in the public bathrooms?* The Queen was clever.

The corridor was padded in red velvet and steeped in the smell of incense. It came to an abrupt end with two curtains drawn to the middle. A string of blue-gold light shone through it.

"You think me a fool? I've always been a step ahead of you!"

Rea recognized the voice as the Queen's.

"Well, do you have the petal? Or do you believe the girl who has not an inkling of the power coursing in her blood is going to learn to unleash it in time and find it for you?" the speaker retorted with a touch of cunning. "If I were you, I wouldn't harvest my henbanes quite so soon. Failure is unbecoming on you, Razya."

Rea couldn't place the second voice. It was tender as a blossom, yet thorny with revenge. She parted the curtains slightly and a scream nearly flew out of her mouth. Hurriedly, she muffled the noise with her hand.

A woman's face made of fire-rimmed petals hung in the air. There wasn't a body or limbs attached to it nor was it a real face, simply an arrangement of petals laced in flames resembling two eyes, a nose, and a pair of lips. It was a floating face that talked. Rea swallowed her fear.

"The girl you speak of isn't going to find the petal and certainly not in time," the flaming face continued. "If I were you, I'd pray to the Som for a blossom-scented miracle because unfortunately for you, I'm the only one who knows where it lies. And these lips you cursed me with shall remain sealed forever." At that, the lips swelled with red-hot fire and a chuckle erupted, reeking in malice.

"That remains to be seen," the Queen said, unflinching in the heat of the raging flames. "There are two alternatives, Oleandra. Either I continue as Queen or Astranthia loses her will to live."

"I wouldn't worry about Astranthia," said the petal lips. "I'd worry about what will become of you when the people discover the price they've been paying for your actions. As for death, I will welcome it."

Rea heard Leela call out for her back in the bathroom, and she missed the Queen's reply. Rea knew she needed to head back, but she wanted to hear the rest of the conversation. She was certain the girl they were talking about was her.

"I pity the boy and the girl," said Oleandra. "Their souls have suffered greatly for people so young."

"Well, you can save them," said the Queen. "Tell me where

the petal lies, and their lives will be spared. After all, weren't you always the righteous one?"

The petal-face lifted her head. "You snuffed out the good and righteous in me all those years ago. Hate is what courses in my veins, and I will watch the boy and girl sacrifice their lives without a twitch of heartbreak. I would rather they die than you win."

Rea cowered from the words. Leela's voice came again and she let go of the curtains and ran to the bathrooms. But Leela was nowhere to be seen. Rea found the dwarves waiting for her in the hallway.

"Where is she?" she asked the dwarves.

"Your friend bees inside where you left her," said Torgar. "You must bees hurrying."

"Times bees a-ticking," giggled Dalric.

Rea darted back into the bathroom. Without bothering to knock, she pushed Leela's door open. It didn't budge. She pushed harder and the door began to give way. With a final heave, it flew open with a little blast.

Leela was sprawled on the floor. The serpent-lily bite on her leg had swollen, the wound inflamed and bulging with bubbles of yellow pus. Rea gagged. She grabbed Leela and half-carried and half-dragged her out into the hall.

"Please help! She's been poisoned by a serpent lily."

Torgar, small as he was, rushed into action. He signaled his brother to assist him and Dalric stopped snickering at once. The change in their expressions scared Rea.

"We need a doctor," she said.

"Shuuush! No one must bees hearing you," Dalric said, petrified.

"You bees following us," instructed Torgar as he and his brother lifted Leela above their heads, their feet moving quickly.

"She mustn't bees seen by guards or she bees sent to the sick chambers," he warned, hurrying down a new string of hallways. These were crowded with servants.

The working men and women looked grimmer than the walls. Pushing past them, the dwarves brought Rea and Leela out through the same plain door they had entered from, and Torgar hid Leela behind a hedge of bushes. He and his brother spoke hurriedly and Dalric disappeared into the shrubbery. Torgar kneeled beside Leela's leg. He prodded her wound. It had turned an ugly purple with a yellowish center. If Leela had been conscious, a touch would have made her scream, but she was still unconscious.

Torgar kept pushing the skin towards the center of the bite. Pus oozed from the wound. Rea turned her face away, feeling like she was going to throw up. She wanted to tell him to stop out of the fear that something might happen to Leela, when two white shards poked from under her skin.

"Are those teeth?" she asked.

"Aye," said Torgar, concentrating under the watery moonlight. "When serpent lilies bite, they bees leaving their teeth inside the victim. That bees their poison."

"How do they bite again?"

"New teeth bees filling their place. They bees growing them all their lives."

"H-how do you kill them?" Rea asked. *Besides spraying them with my blood*, she thought.

"As you bees doing any plant. By uprooting them."

A pinprick of blood gathered on Leela's skin. Then, another.

"Your friend bees lucky. If we hadn't bees finding the serpent's teeth, she would bees gone. Now, she will live." Torgar's shoulders eased as he sat cross-legged on the ground. Gently, he pulled the teeth from Leela's wound and, using a stone, crushed them until the two incisor fangs turned to powder.

"The main ingredient in the cure for a serpent lily's bite bees the poison of the teeth itself. Few bees knowing this."

Dalric came hobbling out of the shrubbery carrying a pile of leaves with a gooey, gum-like sap. Torgar rubbed the sap on Leela's wound like a balm and sprinkled the teeth-dust over it. With the remaining leaves, he created a bandage and tied a stem around it to keep it in place. Gradually, the tint of blue on Leela's body began to give way and a healthy color took its place. She awoke, her eyes fluttering open.

"You're okay!" shouted Rea. "You're okay, right?"

Torgar hushed her with a finger. A yell came from inside the castle and Dalric flew up in terror.

"The Queen bees summoning us!" he tottered. "If she bees seeing us helping you, our fate bees like the Prince."

Torgar signaled Leela to stand up. "Bees sure to rest," he said before scurrying off into the castle. Poking half his body out of the door, he spoke to Rea in a rushed whisper.

"There bees danger coming and you bees true royalty, Princess. In your blood bees power. Many in the realm bees born with it, rich and poor. But only those who bees awakening it, bees wielding the gift. It will lead you to the petal. Prince Raohan must bees saved."

"Wait!" panicked Rea. "How do I awaken it?"

"By awakening your true self."

Before Rea could ask how she was supposed to do that, he shut the door. Two days was barely enough time to awaken her true self. Besides, wasn't she her true self already? She knew who she was, there was no need for more discovery. Frustrated, Rea propped Leela against her arm and chanted the Ceffyldwer verse. In a quick blur, Thubian flew out of the stars and stood before them.

"You're a lifesaver, literally," Rea said, rubbing his nose.

You needn't recite the verse every time you need me. You are my rider. I shall come whenever you call my name.

Rea looked into his eyes and felt in her heart the bond which connected them. It was as deep and powerful as she had ever known.

Rea turned to Leela. "Are you strong enough to climb up?"

"I feel much better," Leela replied and turned to caress the gold-tinted beast.

"His name is Thubian," said Rea.

Leela swiveled to face her. "How—? No. You're kidding me. You can talk to him?!"

Rea grinned. "I'm his rider."

"Ohmygod, really?"

"He says your soul shines of starlight."

"Awww." Leela kissed him on his long snout. "You know in

every fantasy book I've read, rider and beast are chosen by destiny. It means you were fated to come to Astranthia."

The words seeped into Rea. How much of her life was chalked out just waiting for her to follow the markings?

"The dwarves saved your life. I put yours in danger," Rea said. She couldn't look Leela in the face. "I... I'll never do that again."

"Are you sure? Never say never," Leela chuckled and relief poured out of Rea.

"You're crazy."

"And you're a princess! With magic! AND a Ceffyl-rider! Ugh, you're so lucky!"

Rea looked at her, incredulously. "None of it makes sense, but let's get to Xee and Floo and hope they know how to find this petal."

Rea and Leela climbed onto Thubian's back and he took to the skies, carrying them towards where Xeranther and Flula had left them at the lake.

How was the encounter with the Queen, brave one? Did she offer you answers for the questions you seek about your brother?

The wind whipped Rea, threatening to push her off balance.

I found out that the Queen has Rohan and now I have to find the missing petal of the Som to free him. Do you know by any chance where the petal might be? Rea asked, hoping against hope that he did.

Alas, the magic of the Som transcends us all, Thubian said. *I'm unaware of where the petal rests.*

A chilly mist stung Rea's face as they flew over the lake. She could see the white bodies of the serpent lilies writhing under the water. A shiver ran over her and she felt Leela's grip tighten around her waist.

Do you know anything about awakening my nectar? The dwarves said something about how I must awaken it to find the petal, but doesn't my blood already have power? It destroyed a serpent lily.

There is far more to your power than destruction, brave one. There are things about your magic that you must learn for yourself. Nectral powers are rooted in the actions of the bearer: you were born with the potential for great power; your bravery and determination have allowed you to tap into some of your abilities, but there is more to awaken.

But how do I awaken all of it? Rea asked.

Thubian paused a moment. *I am afraid that is a path you must discover on your own. I have faith in you, fearless one. You will find your way to a full awakening.*

Rea struggled to quell her frustration. She was tired of people keeping things from her. First Amma and Bajai, now Thubian. Didn't they understand they were holding her back with their secrets? A voice in her mind reminded her that Thubian had helped her when no one else could. Perhaps she should give him the benefit of the doubt. But it was hard. She was feeling so defeated.

CHAPTER 21

HOGGISH HARPIES

Thubian dropped off Rea and Leela on the edge of Pariland and the lake. As she watched him fly into the clouds, Rea knew she should feel victorious. She and Leela were two of the rare few who had crossed the Sea of Serpent Lilies and survived. But her heart was heavy with the weight of what had happened at the castle. The Queen's words rang in her ears, and Rea couldn't help but think that her aunt was right. She couldn't trust anyone. Not even her family.

Deceit blackened Rea's consciousness. Obviously, she didn't like the Queen—she had refused to free Rohan—but the secrets Amma and Bajai had kept from her filled her with spots-clouding-your-vision anger. And these weren't white lies. They were massive, bone-chilling truths about her life.

"Do you know how much time I could've saved looking for Rohan? We could have rescued him by now had they not lied to me. Their grief and worry—what is it? An act? A show? Why didn't they go looking for him when they knew where he was and why he was taken? How could they sit there doing NOTHING?"

"Breathe." Leela patted Rea's shoulders.

They were walking through Pariland searching for Xeranther and Flula. It was far into the night, and most of the pari-folk were asleep. Only glitter from fallen pari dust lent a shimmer of light along the way.

Rea pushed past a large frond of flowers iridescent under the moonlight. A family of winged slugs flittered away, annoyed with the disturbance.

"I'm sorry," she said to them.

Her mind was trying to grapple with the truth she had learned from the Queen. She could see Amma lying to her, but Bajai... how could she have hurt her like this? She had trusted her. Of all the times she pestered Bajai for details about their past, asked why they had no extended family, or which town Baba came from, Bajai had kept mum. They were queens and princesses, for goodness sakes! Why hide that? Didn't they trust her and Rohan? Didn't they see how badly she had wanted to know about their life before Darjeeling and their life with Baba?

"You're alive!" Xeranther yelled from a tree. He swung down from a branch like a monkey and landed on the ground with a thump.

The girls turned with a jump.

"Yikes, Xee!" Leela slapped his arm. "You scared us!"

Flula came up beside Rea, showering her with silvery sparkles. "Our Earthling is a smart one. Calling the pari-golis on the serpent lilies—that was as clever as talking firetoads!"

"It was just a lucky idea. But we would have been lost without you, Floo," Rea said, returning Xeranther's high-five shyly.

"Come on, flinging your blood on the lilies was pretty badass," Leela said and enthusiastically enacted how Rea's blood had destroyed the serpent lilies.

Rea's ears burned. She had come so close to losing her. "Leela was... bitten by a serpent-lily," she said, shame filling her cheeks.

Xeranther cast a horrified glance and the color emptied from his face. "I'd warned you about the lake," he said. "Where are you bitten? How are you still standing? Come, we'll--"

"It's fine! I'm totally fine!" said Leela. "The dwarves from the castle healed me."

"Poppy said that was impossible. Hoggish harpies! Did you have to cut off—" Fright sprung from his eyes and Flula spat out black glitter.

"NOTHING was amputated," Leela said, holding out her hands to calm them both. "The dwarves used the serpent-fang as the antidote to the poison. See!" She showed them her healed leg and Flula fanned herself in relief.

"You are strong to have resisted the serpent venom," said Xeranther. "Poppy is going to lose his other leg when he finds out the secret to curing the bite is the fang itself."

"The dwarf said if he hadn't found the fang in her skin, she would not have made it..." Rea's chest tightened. The more she lingered on what might have happened, the more her resolve wavered—she would never have forgiven herself if Leela had died. Just the thought of it nauseated her.

"Stop worrying, you two!" Leela said. "Honestly, such a fuss over a little snake bite."

Rea admired Leela's courage. If the situation was reversed, would she have stuck around to help Leela find her brother? Rea felt the answer forming in her mind and she squashed it, vowing to be a better friend.

"The fang is known to dissolve in the blood and spread the venom like quicksilver. For those of true valor, like Poppy and Leela, it takes longer to work. For us common folk, we'd be done in minutes," said Xeranther.

"You should give yourself more credit," Rea said, facing him. "Revolting against your Queen, securing a stolen boat to cross the serpent waters, fighting for justice by helping us save my brother—I'd say all that requires a heck of a lot of valor to pull off."

Xeranther waved the compliment away with his hand as a smile lingered on his face.

"She's right!" said Leela and Xeranther flushed with pride.

"You did the impossible then and entered the castle?" he asked, his expression vacillating between shock and amazement.

"And on a Ceffyldwer, too!" exclaimed Flula.

"Fluting furbingles!" Xeranther's mouth fell open. "You really flew on a Ceffyldwer? Are you *certain* it was a Ceffyldwer and not a flying quillcow or a feathery mammoth?"

"Oh, we're sure," said Rea, briefly wondering about the existence of a flying cow.

"He's called Thubian," smiled Leela.

"He flew out of the skies at the moment Leela and I were

going to become serpent-food and brought us to the castle. Anyway, we're back now and I need your help in finding something that will save Rohan," Rea said.

She knew Xeranther was excited about her riding a Ceffyldwer, but the minutes were passing. She needed to start looking for the petal instead of updating him and Floo on every little detail. Besides, there was too much to tell—her true identity, her family history, her magical nectar, and the condition to save Rohan.

Xeranther slapped his thigh in delight. "Prancing ponies on a Pillywiggin pari! We've only ever heard of Ceffyl-riders in lore and legends. Now here you are, standing before us on the very limbs which rode astride a great Ceffyl!"

Rea pressed a smile on her face. "Anyway—"

"The warm flank, the velvet hairs, the curved antlers sharp enough to slice a man like butter," cooed Xeranther. "Oh, oh, will you give me a ride?"

"We're... um... still getting to know each other."

"Come on, tell us every detail. What was the castle like? Were there savage spriggans guarding it? Were there trolls created out of Shadow Magic? Did the guards have blood on their weapons? Splitting heavens, don't tell me you had to fight them? And the Queen? Did you see her? Speak to her? Oh, sweet nectar, you did, didn't you? Did she use Shadow Magic? Did she have an army of soldiers? And your brother! Was he in the Cellars? Did you get to talk to him?"

"STOP!" shouted Rea. "We'll tell you everything later. Didn't you hear what I said before? You need to help us find a lost petal. It's lying somewhere in Astranthia."

"Huh?" said Xeranther.

Leela glanced at Rea. She knew what that look meant, but she had no time to tell them everything.

"Well..." said Rea, trying to remain patient. "I learned a few things about myself in the castle and let's say the only way I can free Rohan is if I find this missing petal and deliver it to the Queen."

"Whatever you say, your *greatness*," Xeranther said sarcastically.

"*DON'T* call me that," snapped Rea and she looked around to see if anyone had heard.

"What's got into you? Did the Queen cast a spell on you to be rude?"

"I *said* I'll tell you later."

Xeranther's gaze turned icy. "You know, this fight isn't yours alone. It's mine too. If I am to rebel against the throne and seek vengeance for my Par and the people of Astranthia, I need to be more than someone who just helps you. I need to know what I'm up against."

"Rea... let's tell—" said Leela.

"No, I don't have time!"

"It's always about you, isn't it?" said Xeranther. "Help me find my brother. Help me cross the lake. Help me know more about Astranthia. I took you to the Whispering Walls. I took you to my family. I arranged for a boat when no one was ready to give me one. I did all that even though when we first met, you lied to me."

"Xeranther—" Leela started.

"No!" he said, holding up a hand. "You both lied. You said you were princesses. Now that I know you better, I can't believe

I fell for that."

"Well, do you really want to know who I am?" challenged Rea. Flula hovered close, her face a mirror of concern. "I'm a princess. *Your* princess. Princess Raelia of the House of Flower."

"It's the House of *FLUR*," Xeranther shot back. "HAH! Some princess you are!"

"Well, I *AM*. The Queen is my aunt and Rohan's the heir to the throne. That makes him a prince and me a princess. It's his blood she needs to give to the sacred flower, which is why he is locked in the castle. As a common Astranthian you are sworn to protect and serve Astranthian royalty. Well, guess what? That's *me*!" She cocked an eyebrow and lifted her chin the way the Queen had done, to give her an air of importance.

Leela cringed and Xeranther glanced in the direction of the castle. Rea remembered its grotesque tips, hazy amongst the smoky clouds.

"Are you really one of them?" he asked, guardedly.

Rea nodded, crossing her arms.

"Hadn't I told you? It's why you can portal." All the joy that had filled his voice when he first saw them was gone, replaced with distrust and fear. "Only those with the nectar like an Astranthian royal can."

"No wonder the banyan roots didn't grow on me," Leela said, smacking her forehead.

"Well, you were right," Rea said to Xeranther. "That's why you *have* to help me."

"I don't *have* to do anything. And especially not for someone who shares the same blood as the *Queen*," he retorted. Hurt, of the painful and angry kind, glistened in his eyes.

"You don't have a choice. It's... *AN ORDER!*"

Xeranther stopped inches from her face. "Well then, *ORDER* one of your royal minions to find this dead petal. I for one, don't give a clump's bottom about it! Come on, Floo, let's go."

Flula flitted between Rea and Xeranther and when he disappeared into the shadows, she darted after him.

"I should have listened to my good sense when I first met you and left you on the market road!" The echo of his voice, hot with rage, rang through the trees and melted into the fog-heavy morning.

"It's a *LOST* petal, not a *DEAD* one! And it's not from *ANY* flower, it's missing from the *SACRED*—"

"Um... they've gone. They can't hear you anymore," Leela said, and Rea shut her mouth.

"It's fine. We don't need their help," she declared, even though her heart sank, knowing Xeranther and Flula had left them to fend for themselves.

"Who needs Xee and Floo or Amma and Bajai? I mean my blood has *magic!*" Rea said with affected confidence.

"But you don't know how to use your magic except when you bleed. You can't possibly do that every time." Leela looked at her matter-of-factly. "We needed someone from this land to help us and Xeranther was our best chance."

"Shouldn't you be on my side instead of supporting Xeranther? You're my friend first!" scowled Rea. She didn't want to be angry with Leela, but just as things were starting to fall into place, they had already begun falling apart.

Leela's expression softened. "Of course I am, but that doesn't solve the problem we're in..."

"Well, aren't you the 'all problems have a solution' type of person?" Rea countered in irritation.

"I'm only saying it would've been a lot easier with Xee and Floo. We should have told them everything. After all, didn't Xee help us get to the castle and risk his life for us?" Leela asked, calm and composed as if she was trying to make a child understand.

"Didn't you hear what the Queen said? I have just *TWO* days to find the petal or else I won't see Rohan ever again—you know what? If you want, you can leave too. I don't have time to convince everyone to help me." Rea threw her hands up in exasperation and walked away.

"Did I say I wanted to leave? Geez!" Leela ran towards her, shaking her head. "Okay fine, let's think of different ways to awaken the magic in your blood, all right?"

Rea's anger cooled. She was glad Leela was back on her side again.

"I should've asked the Queen how she awakened her magic..." Rea said, dejectedly. "Wait, what about the books you've read about fairies, paries and magical beings... do they say anything about how to wield magic?"

Leela thought about it. "Well, most characters either go to schools of magic, have wands, or have devas like Brahma and Shiva bless them with a magical boon."

Rea didn't go to magic school. She didn't have a wand or know a single spell. And she certainly didn't think she'd been blessed by a deva. But both Torgar and the Queen said her blood had power.

Rea stared at her palms. Would the magical blood thrumming through her veins shoot out of her like Spiderman's web and lead her to the missing petal? She pointed at objects on the street, summoning the petal, fire, water, and light. Nothing shot out of her like it had from the Queen's fingertips. Perhaps that was Shadow Magic. And the magic of her blood was different...

As they made their way out of Pariland and onto the main road, sunrise broke from the canopies of trees. A detergent blue flecked the sky. *I ought to make myself bleed again*, thought Rea. It had worked to destroy the serpent-lilies. Maybe, if she sprinkled her blood on the soil, the sacred petal would grow into existence? *Or it would destroy the soil*, she thought with a frown.

"Let's stop here," said Rea. She looked at her arm, and considered squeezing the cut for a trickle of blood. But her arm was healing, and the idea of opening the wound made her feel a little sick. She spotted a bush with thorns by the side of the road. Maybe that would do?

Rea grabbed hold of a thorn in the bush and pricked her finger. A drop of blood bloomed on her skin and she placed it on the ground.

"Come on, petal. Appear!" she commanded.

Within seconds, in a patch of barren soil, pinkish green stems curled upwards and tiny buds stretched themselves awake, turning into a mélange of pink-blue blossoms.

"Oh my god, oh my god," yelped Leela. "You cloned the plant right next to it!"

Rea blinked. She literally had. But it wasn't the sacred blue hibiscus. "Um... Flower, do you know where I can find the lost petal of the Som?"

The plant didn't reply like the Whispering Walls had. She kneeled on the ground and talked loudly to it. When that didn't work, she tried communicating with it like she did with Thubian.

Rea dropped her head in frustration. As always when she felt angry or stressed, her mind cast out for someone to blame. *Amma and Bajai should have taught me how to wield my magic*, she thought sourly. Another instance where they had failed her. Rea kicked a tree.

"Ouch." Her toe throbbed and Leela came up and put a comforting hand on her shoulder. Even with Leela there, Rea had never felt so alone. She wished she could portal back to see Mishti Daadi. She was the only adult left that Rea could trust. But if they portaled back, they would lose too much time. Rea had to find another way.

Rea went from flower to flower. She rubbed their petals, thorns, leaves, stems and branches, asking for the missing petal. She pleaded with the flora until her throat hurt. She touched the leaves to her face like Amma did. She kissed stalks of grass and stopped at every plant, bush, tree, and blade of grass she could find, asking for the petal while picturing the sacred Som. As the last resort, she cried her tears on the plants, hoping it would work the way her tears revealed the secret about Rohan at the Whispering Walls. Leela watched helplessly.

"ARRGGGHH," shouted Rea to the skies. "WHAT AM I DOING WRONG?"

They were nearing a small budhood. Buttery sunlight poured over the road, but the cold morning air still stung their throats.

"I think we should go find Xee and Floo," Leela said and Rea shot her a look. "They might know how you can awaken your magic—"

"I'm not going to beg Xeranther to help me. He doesn't understand how important this is."

Leela sighed. "You need to understand that you need him more than he needs you. Besides, didn't he help us when he had every reason not to?"

"Well, I don't care!" stormed Rea. "He chose to help us."

"Yup, just like he chose to leave us."

Rea opened her mouth to retaliate, but she didn't have a comeback. Arguing with Leela felt like arguing with an older sister. Rea could see the sense in her words and yet she wanted to be stubborn and disregard it. But it was in vain. Leela's guilt trip (and good sense) was working, mostly because she had run out of ideas on how to get her nectar to work and find the petal. Maybe she could simply ask around for it? Although, if it were that easy, the Queen would've done it already. Xeranther was her best chance. *Arghhh.* She had wasted half the day failing to awaken her magic and who knew how long it would be before they found him. He could be anywhere! For all the magic in the realm, couldn't they use cell phones in Astranthia?

"Fine. Let's go look for him."

Leela raised an eyebrow.

"All right," Rea scowled. "I'll apologize."

They turned to leave, and a cloud of dust rose like a mountain in front of them. Men and women charged forth from the budhood, banging their weapons of logs, pitch forks, and axes.

Terrified, Rea and Leela ducked behind a cluster of shrubs.

"Renounce the throne! Renounce the throne! The Queen has failed!"

"She's plundered our earnings!"

"Ruined our crops!"

"Slaughtered our families!"

"Your time is up! No blood, no throne!"

The protestors roared, scaring the birds. They came in waves, thundering down the road, banging their weapons against the ground. Children held onto the torn hems of their parents' clothes and peered between the weapons, their faces similar to the ones Rea had grown up with: poor and dirty, looking like they hadn't smiled or eaten for days. Rea and Leela huddled closer. As the first set of men, women and children marched by, fifty more followed.

All of a sudden, hooves galloped down the streets and the ground shuddered as a flank of soldiers met the protestors.

Swords sliced the air and steel clinked like chimes. Leela grabbed onto Rea. Soldiers in black and gold uniforms ruthlessly brandished their swords, cutting open throats and torsos. The men and women's faces filled with fear. The gilded insignia of a tree emblazoned within the symbol of a sun—the same one Rea had seen on the dwarves' robes—splattered in red as soldiers on mighty steeds mercilessly trampled on the fallen who were piling up like mounds of flour sacks. They cared not for the men or women or children. Amidst the chaos, Rea saw Xeranther. He was waving a spear at a soldier, screaming at the top of his lungs!

"No mercy for the treasonous!" yelled the soldier as he slashed

Xeranther's leg with his sword and kicked him in the stomach. Xeranther cried out, curling into a ball. The soldier moved on to his next victim and Xeranther lay motionless. Rea and Leela screamed.

The captain of the soldiers raced into the mayhem astride a black horse with a braided mane and a golden-red saddle encrusted in jewels. He raised his hands, signaling his men to stop. Then he peered down at the cowering protestors. They were crying for mercy.

"Her Extreme Greatness has been kind enough to spare the degenerate lot of you," he bellowed. "If it were up to me, ungrateful specimens such as yourselves would get exactly what your comrades received. You shout your slogans of treason and what does the Queen do? She wishes to share with you a valuable piece of knowledge to pacify your anger."

His lips quivered with excitement as the soldiers parted to make way for a horse, white as a dove's feather, led by two blue-bodied, lizard-men like the one Rea had seen guarding Rohan's cell in the orb.

"ROHAN!" she cried out and the captain and his soldiers looked in her direction, their fingers curled around the hilt of their swords. Leela pulled her hands over Rea's mouth as she squirmed under her grip. Seeing no movement, the captain turned back to the protestors and Rohan, who was locked in a cage tied to the back of the horse. He was thin as bones and bound in chains.

"You will never have my blood!" he yelled, banging furiously on the bars of his cage.

The captain ignored him and turned to the protestors.

"The Imperial Guard presents to you the exiled son of Former Princess Keona, Betrayer of Her Extreme Greatness Queen Razya of the House of Flur. On the Night of Nilaya, the boy's blood will be sacrificed on the sacred Som and Her Extreme Greatness Queen Razya will continue her bountiful reign as the Queen of Astranthia. May she reign a thousand years!"

The soldiers clamored in agreement.

"REPEAT, you heathens!" the captain shouted, jerking the reins of his horse.

"M-may she r-reign a t-thousand years," the villagers chanted, their measly hopes for a better future left dead on the road with their friends.

"Consider this your final warning. Go to your budhoods and report the news. One more protest or word against the Queen and she shall not be as merciful. Now, out of the way!" The captain reared his horse and galloped away.

The protestors crawled towards the fallen bodies. Leela slowly released Rea and they stared at Rohan, retreating out of sight.

Turning to the side, Rea threw up.

CHAPTER 22

MAGIC IS A FICKLE THING

"RISE FOR HER EXTREME GREATNESS!"
announced the guard.

The doors flew open and the seven ministers of the Queen's
Court jumped to their feet, their voices hushed into a pin-drop
silence. They bowed and smiled at her nervously. It pleased
Razya to see how her last-minute switcheroo of assembling in
the Throne Room instead of the more intimate chamber of the
Court's Quarter had caused such unease.

In her early days as Queen, she had coated the walls of the
Throne Room with the Sinisterus Charm—an enchantment she
had invented, earning her the coveted spot as the favorite pupil
of the Sorcerer of Shadows—so that all who walked through the
chamber felt in their hearts the cold grip of fear.

Razya glided up the thirteen steps to her throne. Its bone-
like branches coiled and recoiled like the body of a serpent. She

raised her hand and the ministers took their seats at a long table facing the throne. A row of servants filed in with plates of meats, cheeses, and fruits, and laid the feast before them. When the last of the servants exited, guards with shapeshifting weapons took their place on either side of the doors.

"Mr. Lootin, what urgent matter has befallen us days before the Night of Nilaya that commands my personal attention?" Razya asked the Minister of Ceremony and Rites. Her nails, painted the same dark hue as her midnight-blue gown, clicked against the tendrilled arm of her throne.

"I-Indeed, my Queen. I—we—er—" he replied, muddling his words in the mess of papers he was shuffling in his hands.

"I have no patience for your stammering," thundered Razya, although in truth, it pleased her to see the Sinisterus Charm working its magic.

"Apologizes a hundredfold, my Queen. My papers are out of order and I... oh... there—!" He located the scroll of ash-leaf he'd been searching for, and adjusting his monocle, read from it.

"We have received news on the whereabouts of the sacred Som. It is to rise in the Leafless Forest. The flowergrass there have begun blossoming in full bloom."

Razya paused at the news. The sacred flower had chosen to appear at the first spot she had charred with Shadow Magic. Were the sacred forces playing a joke on her?

"Very well. Make speed with the ceremonial preparations. Heaven knows why that piece of information turned you into a blubbering fool."

"Your Extreme Greatness—um—there's one other piece of news."

Urdaag flew in from an open window and the sound of his wings drowned out Vurk Lootin's words. Unperturbed by the commotion he stirred, the Sirion folded his raven wings and perched beside the Queen. Lootin swallowed a gulp.

"The Asurai confirm the omen we've been fearing about the boy-prince."

"The boy is *NO LONGER* a prince!" shouted Razya. She flicked her wrist and shot a beam of magic, sharp as the touch of ice, into Lootin's side. He gasped, and doubled over in pain.

"Next time, I shall not hesitate to aim higher." She pointed at his heart as the tip of her outstretched finger sizzled with cold vapor.

"A-Apologies a hundredfold, my Queen. It was merely my duty to report the Asurai's readings," Lootin said, flopping onto his chair with a hand over his chest.

Razya seethed. Had they forgotten she despised any reference to her past? Hadn't each of her ministers sworn never to mention it? She had destroyed every painting, every memento that reminded her of her family's existence. Her nerves twisted. The boy she had caged was not a prince, just a necessary tool to further her rightful reign.

The Minister of Ceremony and Rites regained his composure and hesitantly continued, "The Asurai postulate that if the boy sacrifices his blood unwillingly, or if his blood has not been awoken with the power of the nectar, the sacred flower shall sacrifice yet another petal. It is imperative we do not let either of the two situations come to fruition. It will outrage the already enraged peasant folk and your life, your Extreme Greatness, will be monumentally at risk."

"And—and ours too," mewed one of the male ministers.

"But most importantly, the life of the realm will be at its end," Ainely Buci, Minister of Land and Water Preserves said. Her waist length hair, bone-white and smooth like a waterfall, fell over her shoulders. "If the boy unwillingly sacrifices unawoken blood, only a single petal will remain on our sacred flower, and Astranthia will enter the darkest of her ages."

A shudder passed through the ministers and Razya knew what they were thinking. Never had Astranthia's future been so dire. If they knew the whole truth, that the sacred Som bore *two*, not three petals, they would drag her off the throne. For all their faith in the Asurai, the scholars hadn't discovered that of the three remaining petals, one had disappeared, hidden somewhere in the realm. If the girl did not find the missing petal and the boy's nectar did not awaken in time, the Som would sacrifice its last two petals and in a matter of days, Astranthia and her every living inhabitant would perish.

Oleandra had prophesied the same things the ministers were reporting. If the petal was not located soon, Razya knew she would be in grave danger. The Queen needed a miracle. Her best laid plans were falling apart. The girl had indeed arrived as she had planned, but the girl hadn't fully awoken her nectar yet. If she didn't do it soon, it would be impossible for her to locate the petal.

And then, there was the boy. He would willingly sacrifice his blood, of that she had no doubt, but would the harsh conditions in which she had imprisoned him be enough to awaken his nectar? He had rejected every meal sent to him and that was a good sign of him upholding his principles and being selfless—a requirement to awaken the nectar—but would it be enough? On top of it all, the Sorcerer of Shadows had stopped replying to her nectral missives for help. Razya was on her own.

"If I may add…" Heinzel Beamleaf, Minister of the Court of Common Pleas by Persons and Magical Folk, interjected, disrupting the silence which had consumed the room. "What indeed will happen to the boy? I fear if he is killed, there will be riots from the peasants who are loyal to Princess Keona and her family. I shudder to think of it, but they will fight like they have nothing to lose."

"Yet if the boy remains imprisoned, we fear the consequences will be no different," stated Ainely Buci.

Razya's fingers turned claw-like, piercing the arm of her throne. How dare the ministers talk so insolently to her? Why wasn't the Sinisterus Charm working to cause fear in their hearts? Rage pulsed within Razya and a tendril snapped under her nails. The throne revolted in pain and Razya's heart turned a darker shade of black.

No, it cannot be.

She had invented the Sinisterus Charm. *She* had carefully crafted its words and intentions such that those of weak hearts and frail souls were infected with its spell, causing their fears and suspicions to magnify and swallow them. She had not realized, until this moment, that she was not above the Charm either, and as she sat in front of her Court today, she could spot the ministers who knew the power she wielded was not as strong as it once was.

Razya leaned against her throne, needing the extra support to quieten her nerves. The spell of her own Shadow Magic was intensifying her fears, throwing her into turmoil. She had to gather herself and not allow the Court to sense her fear.

Magic is a fickle thing, she thought, remembering the Sorcerer's words, *No matter its intention, good or evil, its allure is eternal, but its power is as real as an illusion.* The Sorcerer had warned her from making Shadow Magic her singular purpose of life, but she had ignored his words and sacrificed everything for it.

Razya raised her eyes to her Court. If the men were disgraceful, the women were worse. Jealousy dripped from their eyes for the power she commanded as Queen. And if that weren't enough, Disira Teague, Minister of Coin, another one untouched by the Sinisterus Charm, spoke up.

"If I may also add, the royal treasuries are running lower than ever. The infertility spells you had cast on the farmer's fields for tax defaults have caused poor harvests, leaving them no money for their livelihoods, let alone for taxes. At this rate, if we don't receive tax payments, the royal coffers will be empty by year's end."

Razya saw right through Disira's expression of feigned worry. "Very well, I will lift the infertility spells off their fields. The farmers have learnt their lessons and I doubt very much they will default on their taxes again."

Disira bowed slightly. "No doubt it will bring great joy and relief to the people, Your Extreme Greatness. However, the benefit of lifting the spells will only help next year's harvest. Our current problem of nearly-empty coffers continues to remain unsolved."

"Not to forget that the foliage reports have brought news of quicker withering of blossoms and many species of flora have been turning sick," Ainely Buci chimed in. "The elixir in them is worryingly low and they are slowly dying. I fear using magic against nature in the form of fertility and infertility spells has caused a revolt in its own way."

Razya ignored Ainely's jibe and turned to the Minister of Coin. "As we have discussed many times, Disira, if the farmers have no capacity to pay, we will give them more time. You should have issued statements about delaying the collection of taxes. I want the people to be happy on our auspicious night. *Not* outraged." Razya's gaze, inflamed with fury, travelled to Ekimmu Welt, the Minister of War. With a fist under his chin, he was intently reading the summons before him.

"Mr. Welt, how are the parades going?"

He glanced up.

"Better than expected, My Queen. The Imperial Guard has completed its village rounds. Every breathing soul in Astranthia is aware the boy is in your possession. If they were geared for revolt before, they have now been snuffed into submission. You will be pleased."

"Excellent," said Razya, genuinely relieved to hear some good news.

A look of concern flitted over the rest of her court, except over Dybuk El Strag, Minister of Crimes and Punishments. He was the only one digging into the feast before him. None of the other ministers had touched their plates. Did they fear the food was poisoned? A dark feeling warmed her. They were still afraid of her.

"Riots! Revolts! Such talk angers me!" She slammed her fist on the arm of her throne. She was their Queen. It was their duty to bring her the solutions, *not* the other way around. "The Imperial Guard has been successful in putting an end to the peasants' protests. Aren't the rest of you capable of handling your own ministries?"

She stared coldly at her court. They had brought her the 'people's problems' about the boy and the riots, when clearly it was what they hoped would happen. Was this how a coup took place? Royal advisors plotting and planning to fool their ruler, who would mistake their worries as concern for the reign and land?

"Tell me, what answers have you given the peasants who interfere in matters beyond their realm of understanding?" she asked.

"My Queen, it is hard to argue against the people when they talk about true ascension to the throne," said Homburg Grime, Minister of Trade, his chin bulging over his collar. "Perhaps you can take the boy under your wing and have us train him for the future... whenever you see fit that is. In this manner, the people will be pacified by your actions. It will restore faith in the blood-line of the nectar."

A fog, cold as frost, descended into the room and the ministers, terrified by the magicked change in air, drew their robes closer to their chests. Razya couldn't help herself. She was trying to keep her anger in check, but she was failing to do so. She knew why the ministers were vying for a twelve-year-old boy to be the future king. It wasn't about true ascension or the happiness of the peasants. It was because they could taste the power they would control at the hands of a child. *Bah, a child!* Not for the first time, Razya wished she had completed her training with the Sorcerer of Shadows and learned how to wield the full force of her power. Already, with her incarnations and enchantments, she had lost so much of it.

Razya willed herself to think happy, vengeful thoughts. The Sorcerer had warned her against skipping the nuances of the Magic of Outward Manifestations. As she looked at her shivering ministers, she thought of the girl returning with the petal and the boy tapping into his nectar. She saw the petal attach itself to the sacred flower and felt the glory of her reign surge through her body. Victory would soon be upon her. *That will shut them up for good.* A smile filled her face and the mist dissipated. The ministers gulped in large breaths of air.

"Homburg, you and the others have been quick to come up with a solution, but I must uproot your plans. The boy's fate has been decided. Be assured his blood, awoken with its youth-filled nectar, will be willingly sacrificed on the Night of the Blue Moon. So, rest your worry-riddled minds and gather your resources in preparation for the ceremony. It will be a fine night indeed."

CHAPTER 23

THE BLOOD OF THE NECTAR

Eddies of dust settled over the road. Bodies lay everywhere, some breathing, some not. Rea and Leela scrambled towards Xeranther.

"Xee! XEE!" Rea shook him. A low, laboring breathing came from his lips. Rea could tell he had lost a lot of blood.

"Say something," Leela said, her voice trembling with worry.

Rea opened his mouth and breathed into it, the way heroes did in Bollywood movies to save the heroine, but he still lay limp. His clothes were full of muck and his leg drenched in blood.

"Can you try using the magic in your blood?" asked Leela.

Rea checked her wound. It had healed completely, and she wondered if her blood from her thorn-pricked fingers would be enough to heal Xeranther.

Use your touch, Thubian whispered in her mind.

Rea immediately obeyed. Placing her palms on Xeranther's

cut, she closed her eyes. A rush, similar to that of adrenaline, surged within her, and a thrumming energy flowed out of her hands and into his wound. By instinct, Rea could feel his body growing stronger. When she opened her eyes, his blood had congealed, and he began to breathe normally. Rea turned to Leela in relief and they helped Xeranther to the side of the road where he could rest.

Then Rea rushed to the villagers. She held their wounds, healing them with nectral energy as Leela followed behind, covering the treated wounds with bandages of leaves. Rea couldn't resurrect the dead—she tried—but the injured, like Xeranther, gradually began to heal. The villagers, spellbound, watched her with reverence.

The hours ticked by. Healing the villagers was draining Rea's energy. Her eyes watered and she worked in a dizzy trance. She had tended to so many injured, she had lost count. Her body was bereft of strength, but she soldiered on. There were only a few wounded left.

Finally, Rea leaned over the last injured person. She had almost lost Leela, had treated Xeranther poorly, and Rohan... she had failed him by shutting him out because he had begun to care about other things in his life besides her and Baba. The truth was, in each situation, she had put herself first, caring little for the other person.

The injured man beneath her stirred, regaining consciousness as Leela tied his bandage. Rea sat beside him. Her body burned with a chill. She was thankful her nectar had helped to heal the wounded villagers. *I'll rest a moment*, she thought, *and then look for the petal again.* Rea closed her eyes and collapsed to the ground, sweating and shivering. She had helped every injured villager and there wasn't an ounce of energy left in her. Bile sloshed in her stomach and she retched weakly.

"I want you to take this in case s-something happens to m-me." She made Leela tear a bit of her dress and she pressed her thorn-pricked finger on it. Dots of blood oozed until they soaked through her fabric. "Place it over the banyan roots. Maybe it will let you portal back."

Leela bit down on her tears as the healed villagers pushed each other to get a glimpse of Rea. They stood on their toes and stretched their necks. They cried, kissing her hands and feet, and left her whatever coins they had in their pockets. Rea refused their money. She tried to say they didn't have to thank her, but her mind swirled in a fog. She glimpsed Leela bringing her a flowercup of water, and the world faded.

A bolt of lightning shot through her, and she jerked upwards, impaled on the bolt. The moon shone. A near-perfect sphere in the midnight sky.

Current sizzled in her veins and her nerves exploded. Shudders racked her body.

She was in such pain.
She melted into liquid.
She awoke in flames.
She became... elemental.

Slowly, the current ebbed. It flowed more gently, calming her senses, warming her body. A cushion of light ensconced her, and she was lowered onto a bed.

The bolt disappeared.

Rea woke up, confused. She was in a bed in someone's bud. A painting of a man hung on the wall, his features familiar except for the thick moustache. A garland of flowers was strung across the frame, the same way they commemorated the departed in India.

Rea sat up, and looked at her hands. Her fingertips tingled.

Your nectar has been fully awoken, fearless one.

She smiled, hearing the deep, gentle voice.

It has?

Your act of true selflessness has brought your full power to life. You served the injured without a thought for your quest or well-being. Combined with your bravery and determination, your compassion for others has awoken all three tenets of the blood of the nectar.

Rea was elated. Maybe her powers would finally work to find the petal!

But how do I wield it, Thubian? I've tried every way I can think of.

Your nectar had not been fully awoken then. Use your instinct. It will guide you. Bear heed. The nectar is a gift, and it can be tainted. Use it unwisely and the road turns shadowy.

I won't let you down, Rea said.

I am proud of you. Your heart is brave for one so young. But also, fragile. Protect it well. I might not always be of help. I can only be of assistance when you find yourself in a magical predicament. The same way I can avail of your help when I'm bound in a human predicament.

So, you can't help me when I'm stuck in a non-magical problem?

Alas, the magic of Astranthia is rooted in fairness, justice, and goodness. It wouldn't be fair, just, or good to use magic against an entity that has none and gain an unfair advantage. The trails of taint are slippery. Hurry on now. Time eclipses over your quest.

Rea stood up and a wave of wooziness hit her, and she sat back down. She stood up again slowly, and walked to the window. She parted the curtains. Night cloaked the sky. How long had she slept? She went to the door and down a set of spiral stairs.

Xeranther, his mother, Flula, and Leela were sitting around a leaf-shaped kitchen table. Rea's heart soared with happiness.

"Hey," she said, standing shyly at the edge of the doorway. Snores erupted from another room.

"You saved my XeeXee," Xeranther's mother ran towards her and grabbed her in an unwieldy hug. Her radish mane caught a ray of moonshine, turning a shimmery red. By the time, she released Rea from her grip, Berber appeared with bowls of steaming stew. For Flula, who was perched on the table, he placed a thimble of slivered berries dusted in sugar. Hunger struck Rea. The stew reminded her of Bajai's spicy noodle soup and she felt a stab of betrayal.

"I'm forever in your debt," said Xeranther, barely making eye contact.

"You're not," said Rea. "You would've done the same for me."

His wound had healed. Only a crusted line remained. Leela fidgeted with her fingers and stared at her food. She seemed more uncomfortable than either of them.

"These are unsafe times," said Xeranther's mother, reaching towards the potted plant in the corner. Rea watched as she touched each eyelid to one of the leaves, exactly as Amma did. A tear slipped down her cheek as she laid her hand on Xeranther's cut. "The Queen has reminded us of her true nature again. Lassie, we are blessed by your presence."

"S-same here," said Rea, slightly embarrassed.

"Mar, what do you know about the nectral powers of the royal family? Do you know how they wield it?" Xeranther asked.

Rea tried to catch Xeranther's eye, but he wouldn't let her.

"I don't know much about all the powers of the blood of the nectar, but I've always envied their ability to speak Vossolalia, the language of flowers. Through it, they can talk to flora and seek knowledge from them. It's how their bloodline grew to become the royal Astranthian family. Scores of centuries ago, the rulers, then of common blood, sought folk with nectral blood to use their gift to learn secrets about their enemies. Soon, those gifted with the nectar grew tired of the oppression and overthrew the empire, reclaiming it for their own. Ever since, their bloodline sits on the throne. Mostly, they've been fair and just rulers. Sadly, all good things come to an end," she said wistfully. "The bearers of nectar are the few selected ones whose duty it is to act as guardians to the great natural realms. They say if their blood is dropped on a seed, it can grow without soil or water. That is as much as I know. I've haven't been in the presence of royalty to know how they wield their nectar. Until tonight, that is."

"Thank you. This is very helpful," said Rea. "But I should be going. I don't think I have long to find the sacred petal."

"The ceremony is tomorrow night," said Flula, her face pinched with worry.

"We've got less than a day," added Leela.

Rea's heart dropped to her toes. A painful grunt came from the back room and Berber rushed out of the kitchen to help Poppy.

"I'm afraid he's having a rough night." Xeranther's mother gestured to her leg to indicate his pain. "Xee, your Par wouldn't want you to risk your life for him. If a-anything happens to y-you..."

Xeranther's face clouded and he turned away.

"But I know you won't listen when your mind is made up. You were always as strong-willed as he was. For better or worse," she smiled feebly. "Promise me you will stay together. There is courage in numbers and the courage of children is some of the strongest I've known." She gave them each a kiss on their cheeks and exchanged a knowing nod with Flula. Turning to Rea, she curtsied. "Good luck, your Greatness."

"Oh no, please don't call me that." Rea reddened with embarrassment. "I can't thank you enough for taking care of me... and for allowing Xeranther to come with us."

Xeranther's mother caressed her cheek and hurried towards Poppy's room.

The three of them stepped outside the bud with Flula flying beside them. Dawn peeked over the horizon.

"Leela told us everything," Xeranther said. "The sacred flower cannot afford to lose another petal. It has lost two already. To think it has lost three? It could lead to the end of the realm and our lives. If the petal can be found and reattached, we must do whatever it takes."

"Can we... um... talk first?" Rea said to him. The elephant in the room felt like a fire-breathing dragon.

"I'm sorry about how I acted before. I didn't mean to be selfish." She touched his hand and he made a move to shrug his arm away. She tried not to feel hurt.

"It's still just me, Xee. Earth, Darjeeling, that's my home. I have no connection to this place except that my brother is imprisoned here, and it's *because* of the royal blood in us. The same blood which runs in my Amma and Bajai, who have betrayed me, too. After everything you've done for me, I shouldn't have been so rude. I don't care if I'm a princess. I just want to free Rohan and... have everyone stop lying to me." Her breath snagged on the last sentence. Although she had uttered it to regain Xeranther's confidence, she found herself passionately feeling its depth. Those words were her truth.

Mumbling something, Xeranther kicked a pebble, sending it rolling into the bushes.

"What was that?" said Rea.

"I said, I'm sorry." He kicked another pebble.

"You have nothing to apologize for."

"Knowing you're a princess, I don't know, it made me feel weird. Even though you're nothing like the Queen, it stung to know you're related to someone who hurt my family."

"I'm so sorry, Xee. If I could change the truth, I would…"

"I thought we were alike, from the same background." He glanced at her and looked away. "It's stupid, I know."

Rea bent and flung a handful of mud on him. Stunned, he glared at her and then flung fistfuls of soil back at her and they both burst out laughing.

"Do you think a real princess would have nails as dirty as these?" she said, sticking out her hands.

Xeranther grinned, showing her his equally filthy nails.

"Enough silliness," admonished Flula. "If what you say is true, we need to find the petal. The fate of the pari-folk rests on it too."

Rea nodded and handed Xeranther a peony-like flower. Leela did the same.

"To friendship across worlds."

CHAPTER 24

THE LAND ON THE OTHER SIDE

The weight of Rea's guilt lifted as the sun rose in the sky. Her hand began to tingle. They were still standing in Xeranther's vegetable-patch of a garden. A light wind blew, and the grass swayed. She sensed the spark of current flowing in it.

"So... Guess what? My nectar has awoken," said Rea, her eyes alive with excitement.

Everyone did a double take.

"It has?" Flula's eyes grew to the size of pumpkin seeds.

Rea nodded. "Thubian said it's because I helped the villagers."

"H-He did?" Xeranther fanboyed hearing the Ceffyldwer's name.

"He said there are different stages of nectral power. Before, I could only do little things because it hadn't fully awoken yet. But after the act of selflessness, it has fully come alive."

"What're you waiting for? Show us!" exclaimed Leela.

"I haven't used it yet, but I think I know what to do."

Flowers dipped in shades of indigo and marigold swayed in the morning breeze. Rea caressed one, its petals soft under her skin. She closed her eyes and felt as if she was back with the tea shrubs in Darjeeling. Being among them had always brought her a sense of calm. As Rea breathed in the Astranthian plant with its scented leaves and velvety blossoms, the din of noises cleared. She could feel the spark of nectar flowing through the plant and she held onto it. But it sputtered, and then it was gone.

Rea took a deep breath. She concentrated on the inhalation and exhalation of air until the last smidgen of oxygen was consumed by her lungs. Slowly, the chaos in her mind ceased and the world turned mute. She felt warm and clear. Peace wafted upon a breeze and one by one, dots of worry drifted away from her and faded into the light. She felt empty. Whole. Like a circle.

In an instant, she fell.

Far into a void.

Until a heart other than her own thumped in her chest and she could feel the life of the plant pulsing through her veins. Their souls merged, the moment of conjunction electric.

Where does the missing petal of the sacred Som lie? she asked the plant.

Current burst through her body and an image of a tree flashed behind her eyes.

Rea opened one eye. Everything was the same. Nothing testified to the fact that an image had been sent to her by a *plant*. To anyone watching, she was a girl holding a flower in the early hours of the morning.

How do I get there?

Below her fingertips came vibrations. Rea held her calm, focusing on the deep soundlessness within her when the flower beamed image after image.

Petals of liquid lavender. An ancient stone structure. A babbling river.

Rea couldn't hear anything. She could only see. After a series of images, the communication stopped.

"It worked!" she cried. "The plant shot images into my mind!"

Hurriedly, she asked another question, one that she couldn't resist. It took her a few tries, but the slip into tranquility was easier.

"Why did Amma visit Mishti Daadi?"

The plant remained silent. There came no vibration or rumblings of messages. Maybe Astranthian flowers didn't know of the happenings on Earth... For now, her questions about Amma would have to wait.

"How did it work?" asked Leela, her eyes dancing with excitement.

"Like a camera snapping photos. Click, click, click!"

Xeranther and Flula looked puzzled but their elation trumped their confusion.

"What did the flower say?" he asked.

"It showed me images of a willow with a LOT of lavender flowers. It's by a river and an old arch-like thing," Rea breathlessly said.

"I know of one by River's Arc," said Flula. "Larkspur, my

water sprite friend, told me yesterday the willow there is soon to shed its blossoms."

"Excellent. Lead the way!"

Whistles of wind blew as Rea, Leela, and Xeranther followed Flula through a vibrant forest. Around them, the trees and plants had tripled in size, cramming over each other in their quest for sunlight. Their sharp, tapering leaves arched overhead, bending under the weight of chunky dewdrops. The willow, Flula said, was to appear along the Wildwater River but so far, the ground was bereft of even a puddle.

Rea retreated into the shadow of her thoughts. With every blink, she saw the bodies, heard the wails and felt the manic stare in Rohan's eyes. Paries within rainbow-tinted bubbles flew past them and she remembered how she and Rohan used to blow soap bubbles from rubber rings and chase after them.

"There," Flula pointed and raced towards a narrow brook making its way across the forest floor. "I see water sprites and the Wildwater."

"It gets bigger," Xeranther said, noticing Rea's doubtful look at the trickling waters.

Breaking into a run, they followed the fledgling river to a dilapidated arch consumed by creepers and tendrilled plants. It was the same stone structure the flower had beamed into Rea's mind. Behind it was an old willow.

Rea's hands tingled. The tree's branches drooped low with

flowers made of lavender-tinted water. At the end of each branch, the liquid blossoms faded to white. A whiff of wind unclasped a watery bloom and it fell to the ground. Instantly, it dried into a withered flower. Rea ran towards the dusting of white blossoms and placed her hand on the wizened tree trunk.

Where is the missing petal of the sacred Som?

The hum of the willow buzzed under her touch. Unlike the other flora, it spoke directly into her mind. The willow's words were ancient, weary and firm.

It is not for you to know. Humans are unworthy of this knowledge. With greed and violence, you have given up your right to the petal. I will say no more.

Rea's spirit splintered to pieces.

Why was I led to you if you won't tell me about the petal? she challenged the willow. The beating of her heart slackened to slow, heavy thuds.

Guardian of the nectar, offspring of the Som, I have borne life through my roots since the stars sprayed light over the advent of night. I have seen many a war and many a halcyon day. My sister and I have our reasons for our silence. The sacred petal departed its dwelling to remain missing. It wants not to be found and no tree nor leaf shall tell you where it lies.

"NO, NO, NO! I will *NOT* accept it," Rea cried, slapping the tree. She slid to the ground, sobbing like a child, not caring if anyone heard.

After the horror she had witnessed, how could she fail now? What use was talking to plants when they had nothing to say to her? With no petal, what did she have to trade Rohan's freedom with? Rea wiped her snotty palms across her cheeks. *Think, think, think,* she ordered herself. *Someone else* has *to know where this stupid petal is.*

Suddenly, she grabbed the willow.

O-Ole... Oleandra! Tell me where Oleandra lives.

Within seconds, the willow beamed a route into her mind. Oleandra was close—a few miles ahead. Taking a moment to match the route in her mind to the one in front of her, Rea darted ahead. The others followed her as she turned left and right and jumped across the river, which was steadily growing larger. She ran at full speed until a blast of sunlight blinded her and she teetered to a halt. She had reached the edge of a cliff.

"This cannot be." Xeranther stared agape at the sight ahead. He wiped his face, his sleeves smeared in mud-splattered sweat.

The roots of the trees lining the cliff had grown across the chasm, forming a bridge to the other side. It oscillated in the wind. At its end stood a hut high on stilts.

"That's Oleandra's house," Rea said, avoiding a look at the Wildwater frothing and churning at least five hundred feet below.

"Whose house?" asked Xeranther. He exchanged a look with Leela. "I thought we were looking for the petal."

"The petal does not want to be found, but Oleandra knows where it is. She's the face I saw talking to the Queen."

"The flower-fire-face-thing?" said Leela.

Rea nodded and holding onto her locket, took a wobbly first step onto the bridge. Nausea overcame her, and she grabbed the leathery railing. Flula charged forth. The fierce wind struck her and she squealed a tinny scream and flew straight into Xeranther's pocket.

"This is not good, this is not good," swore Xeranther, coming up behind her.

As they inched forward, the wind slapped them from every angle. Sprays of water wet their arms, faces, and clothes. Ever so slowly, they kept moving. After what seemed like a lifetime, Rea leaped off the bridge onto the other side. Leela followed, her pinched lips white. Xeranther whistled as he jumped to safety and Flula shot out of his pocket, pink and cold with joy.

"I've never been this far before. It's a foliage-reporter's dream!" she said, peppering the air with wet, golden flecks.

But there was no time to celebrate. They speedily made their way to the stilt-house and climbed up the ladder. A wreath of flowers hung on the door. Beside it, a painting of a blue full moon and a hibiscus shimmered in the damp sunlight. Rea sent a plea to all the gods of Earth and Astranthia to change Oleandra's mind about revealing the location of the petal and knocked on the bamboo door. Dollops of rainwater fell from the thatched roof.

The door opened, and Xeranther gasped aloud. A face of flaming petals floated in the air in front of them.

"Greetings," the face said.

Leela's knees buckled and Flula flew into Xeranther's pocket. But Rea's heart soared. She had found Oleandra.

"A Princess, an Earthling, a bud-dweller and a Pillywiggin pari. What a treat! Do come in."

The scent of petrichor, wet leather, and old paper greeted them. The room was bare of chairs or stools and the light flickering from the petal-face fell over piles of severely tattered books. The covers had grown moldy with the tropical weather, peeling like boiled potato skin. Wild and strangely beautiful blossoms littered the space and an assortment of perfumed weeds sprouted unabashedly from nooks and crannies along the walls and floor. From within the shadows came a flapping of wings, but none of them could see what made the sound. Rea, Leela and Xeranther found room in the little available space and sat cross-legged on the bamboo floor.

"I'm honored to have in my company our nectar's offspring." The petal-face bowed and hovered to the side to reveal the owner of the voice.

Out of the corner of her eye, Rea saw movement. She turned to see a figure sitting on the floor, enveloped in shadow. It wore a hooded cloak of autumn leaves. A swarm of sun-yellow butterflies flecked in violet covered its face such that only specks of shriveled skin lay exposed under the flutter of their wings. The eyes were a startling blue.

Rea's stomach roiled at the grotesque sight. Xeranther let out a mini-scream and hurriedly covered his mouth. The fluttering voice laughed, although not unkindly. Rea stared at the two faces in front of her and realized that the person sitting on the floor *was* Oleandra. She was using the floating face of fire-rimmed petals almost like a puppet.

"Fear not, I am used to seeing folk shocked out of their skin," she laughed, leaning out of the shadows. "So, what brings you so far inland to LOTOS?"

Her azure eyes watched as Rea, Leela, and Xeranther looked

at each other, confused.

"The Land On The Other Side," she explained, at ease in her dwelling of books and plants. "Where never-before-seen creatures roam wild! Now there, that's simply a hoax to scare children to sleep. You needn't look so afraid. I'm not as grotesque as I look."

Xeranther mumbled words of apology and both of Oleandra's faces smiled. Leela inhaled slow breaths to calm herself.

"We've come to learn about the location of the sacred flower's missing petal," said Rea. "I heard you tell the Queen you know where it is."

Before Oleandra could interrupt or say no, Rea carried on.

"I also know you don't care if my brother lives or dies, but you are my only chance. I've asked the flora and they pointed me to the willow, but the willow says the petal does not want to be found. I have one day left. Please, I'm begging you, help me, so I can save my brother."

CHAPTER 25

BLOODOATH

Oleandra stretched out on a cushion. Under her flowing leaf-cloak, she was a rather large woman. Rea tapped her foot against the floor, waiting for Oleandra to reply. Instead, with slow movements, she plucked a flower from a plant spilling with piglet-pink blossoms. Its petals undulated in a movement of dance, forming a petaled chalice, and Oleandra drank the sweet-smelling liquid that poured into it.

"I do apologize. If I don't have my hourly brew of capuli, my head pulses like it's been stung by a thousand beebats. Not a pleasant feeling." She cringed. When she was done with her tea, the blossom reattached itself to the plant. "The truth is, Princess, I'm happy you've come."

"You are?" asked Rea, surprised at Oleandra's sudden change of heart. Hadn't she told the Queen that she would rather have Rea and Rohan die than have her win?

Oleandra's hood of autumn leaves slipped, and a rush of bright blue curls fell across her shoulders. She shook them out.

"When the Queen declared she no longer required my assistance in bringing her the petal, I was alarmed. After hectoring me for days to disclose the petal's whereabouts, she revealed her plan of having *you* find it. Why would she do that, I wondered, when I'm the one who knows where the petal lies?"

Rea shifted in her spot.

"Ahh," exclaimed Oleandra. "I realized she had me fooled. Had us all fooled! See, I had the knowledge of the petal's location, but you had the motivation to get it."

"But the Queen didn't tell me about you," said Rea.

"Are you sure, little bud?"

Her butterfly face, azure mane, and haunting eyes turned wicked and the words wilted in Rea's mouth. She remembered the secret passage and the conversation between Oleandra and the Queen she had chanced upon. Could Oleandra be right? Was the encounter planned by the Queen and not an utter stroke of luck? Had she seen her go into the public rooms and then lured her to spy on their meeting?

"Oh, you see it too," Oleandra clapped her hands. "Isn't Razya's web of cunning a thing to be coveted? She was devious, even as a child." Oleandra twirled a vine of bristly leaves in her thick, creamy fingers. "Nevertheless, I questioned why she didn't simply tell you to come to me? Why the grand charade?"

Leela looked like she wanted to attempt an answer but Oleandra ignored her and continued.

"Perhaps, she thought I might not have looked favorably

upon you had I known she had sent you to me." The butterflies spread into a smile. "That left Razya with only one way to get the petal—you would have to find me yourself. A desperate girl wanting to save her brother might sway my convictions and get me to divulge the petal's location..."

"But you don't care about me or my brother," Rea countered bitterly.

"Indeed. The fate of the realm is vastly more important than two of its inhabitants. Delivering the petal to the Queen would be akin to handing my only weapon to my worst enemy, to our realm's worst enemy. I would never do that!" The petal-flames burned fiercely, and Rea simmered with rage. She should never have come here.

"Any who, I've changed my mind."

"You *have*?" Rea exclaimed and Oleandra's face contracted in pain.

"Ugh, this throbbing head. It does me no good." A fresh flower-cup refilled itself and the smell of daffodils filled the hut. "Care for some?"

The four of them declined and Oleandra took a long sip.

"Did you say you've c-changed your mind?" Rea wanted to make sure she had heard her correctly.

"Over the years, I cultivated the skill of Vossolalia, the gift you were born with, Princess, except mine is a great many times stronger. Through it, I gleaned information about you and your friend, Mr. Thistlewort."

Xeranther turned red, and Rea and Leela hid a giggle at the sound of his last name.

"Therefore, it is only fair I tell you a little about myself. I am Oleandra Ophrys and I've been helping a covert faction known as the Insurgency. They have been working to overthrow Razya and her posse of ministers while fighting for a person true and fair to reign our land... and I, as their ally, have a proposition for you. A barter if you like."

"In exchange for the location of the petal?" asked Rea.

"Aye."

"I accept!" She lurched forward, and some of the butterflies on Oleandra's face fluttered away in surprise.

"Step back," Oleandra shouted, and Rea meekly slid to her spot.

With the butterflies gone, a patch of charred skin marked with blisters lay exposed on her cheek. With a whisper, Oleandra summoned the butterflies back, and waited until they had settled. It took a minute for Rea to realize Oleandra's face was burnt and the butterflies she wore were a mask to cover it.

"Before I lay out the terms of our trade, you must understand that by agreeing to assist the Insurgency against the reign of the Queen, you are labelling yourselves as rebels and can be tried for treason if caught. The punishment at the hands of the crown will be severe," said Oleandra.

Rea glanced at Leela, Xeranther, and Flula. How could she put them in any more danger than she already had?

"It matters not that the Earthling is an alien in the realm of Astranthia and the pari belongs to the world of pari-folk. Your presence at this meeting embeds your involvement in our trade without exception."

Flula peeked from Xeranther's pocket, her glimmer flickering. "I-I will lose my place in Pariland if I betray the treaty of peace between the pari-folk and Astranthians. Ooh, Elder Pari will clip my wings and dry my glow if I'm part of your rebellion." Tears glittered in her eyes. "I-I want to help s-s-save your brother... oh, oh, but I mustn't, I can't—" she sobbed and flitted out of the hut.

Rea got to her feet to stop her from flying away, but Xeranther held her back.

"She'll wait outside until we are done," he whispered. A moustache of sweat had formed above his lip and he turned to Oleandra. "W-What, may I ask, has the Insurgency achieved so far?"

"Pertinent question, Mr. Thistlewort," Oleandra said and flicked her gaze towards Rea. "As an Astranthian princess, you should borrow a leaf from the barrow boy. Impulsiveness is deep-rooted in you as it is in your Aunt Razya. It won't serve you well. You are fortunate I am of clear heart and simple motive. In the future, agreeing to a condition before knowing its contents will promise an unkind outcome."

Rea felt embarrassed to her core. She apologized and Oleandra acknowledged her words like a teacher does an apology from a recalcitrant child.

"The Insurgency," Oleandra continued, "has been responsible for providing courage to the failing hearts of the people. They have become a voice, a beacon of hope, a fight for a better and just future. Over the past several months, I have been working with them, helping them to rally thousands of protestors and preparing Astranthians to revolt against the crown."

For the first time, Oleandra betrayed real emotion. "But yesterday, the Imperial Guard paraded your brother, the true heir, across the streets and villages, squashing the will of the people to a pulp."

Rea exchanged a worried look with Leela and Xeranther.

"With his blood, Razya's reign will continue. Hope has withered. Souls have shattered. The only weapon left is the location of the missing petal—a petal Astranthians don't know is missing, not even the Insurgency. Only I know its true location."

"But won't Rohan need to awaken his nectar before his blood is sacrificed on the sacred flower?" asked Rea. Since the sacred flower was to rise to replenish its nectar, it only made sense Rohan's nectar needed to be awoken.

"An astute observation, Princess," said Oleandra. "And a potential stumbling block for the Queen. The flora have been whispering that Rohan's nectar has not awakened."

Rea felt a rush of bitterness toward Amma and Bajai, who had left them unprepared once again. Without knowing anything about it, how was Rohan going to awaken his nectar? She was certain the Queen would punish him if he couldn't do it.

"The Queen has been a step ahead of us," Oleandra said, her voice turning grave. "The Som does not discriminate against pure, awoken nectral blood. It cares not if an heir sheds his blood on it or a pauper from the streets. It has been a time-honored tradition for the heir to fulfil this role, but it is not the nectar's requirement. If your brother fails to awaken his blood, the Queen will turn to you." The butterflies on Oleandra's face rested their fluttering wings, and for a moment, they looked at peace.

Defiance rose within Rea. "I'll never do it."

Finally, she had some power against the Queen.

"Alas, little bud, when the Queen threatens to kill your brother, you will walk to the sacred Som and willingly sacrifice your blood to save him. Trust that the Queen has prepared for every instance. It would be foolish to think otherwise."

Rea sat in her place, deflated. Olenadra was right—if the Queen threatened Rohan's life, she would give anything to save him.

"But—how did this happen? How did the Som lose another petal? And how come nobody knows about it?" Xeranther asked. The fear of what was to become of his beloved realm was evident on his face.

"The Som shed her third petal twelve years ago when Razya stole the throne from Queen Yuthika, the Princess's grandmother. I was informed of it by the flora only in the last few days."

Rea was still getting used to the idea of Bajai and Amma being royalty, let alone having their throne stolen. What had they done to hurt the Queen that she betrayed them so harshly?

"Covenant 4086 says: 'If the crown be wrongfully worn, the fate of deception shall befall the kingdom until such time as the faith of the realm be restored,'" recited Oleandra. "The general belief was that a rebellion would rise against the false power in the event of a wrongful ruler. But when the flora warned me of a lost petal, I realized the sacred flower had sacrificed another petal in retaliation to the wrongful claim to the crown, causing the realm to suffer until the petal is found and the wrong is righted."

"Has there ever been a wrongful ruler before?" asked Leela.

"Never in our history. The right have always triumphed eventually. We've suffered losses no doubt—wars claimed many lives and we carry the burden of losing two of the Som's five sacred petals. The first, sixteen hundred years ago, during the Great Revolution, when a drop of blood was not given in time and a petal turned to dust. The second, six hundred years later, during the Shadow Wars, when the Som sacrificed a petal to prevent a battle-tired Astranthia from burning to ashes. Now, the third petal is missing, vanished with no trace of ash or ember, and we can feel Astranthia's elixir receding. As our folklore says, one cannot cheat the moon or her flower for they see all."

Rea finally understood why Bajai used to ask her to make promises to the moon or say the wisdom of the moon saw the truth. It happened so often, she had made a habit of it and she wondered now how many references to Astranthia and its customs she had missed growing up.

"Our hope is for the people to burst forth with fury when they behold the third missing petal," declared Oleandra. "The people's revolution will topple the crown and the Queen shall fall."

"What if she doesn't?" asked Xeranther.

"That is where our barter comes in." The petals blazed in a surge of flames and Oleandra faced Rea. "I want you to assassinate the Queen."

The hut went silent.

"*A-Assass-inate?*" stuttered Leela.

"The *Queen?*" gasped Xeranther.

"Aye, I want her dead. The Insurgency wants her dead."

As much as Rea disliked the Queen, she had never thought about *killing* her.

"Why?" she asked. There had to be another alternative.

"The Queen and I have a past which warrants my seeking such revenge, but that is a personal matter. As for her insidious and cruel reign of Astranthia, death makes for a lesser punishment. You can vouch for that, can't you, Mr. Thistlewort?"

Xeranther looked down at the weeds and nodded. Clearly, Oleandra had known about his father.

"How would we d-do it?" mewed Leela.

"I failed to kill the Queen. Her guard is too strong. She has dwarves and soldiers who wield copezium weapons, chambermaids who are more scared than flies, and spriggans who are loyal beasts. And her magic, of course, is far greater than mine."

Oleandra's fiery face glided towards Rea. "The only way is a battle between the nectars. Pure against tainted. Good against evil. Yours against hers. It was a chance we didn't have until you set foot in the realm, royal one."

Rea held her breath. She had come to Astranthia to take matters into her own hands and find her brother. But the truth was she was a pawn in everyone's game. Ignorant daughter of Amma and Bajai. Petal-finder for the Queen. Queen-slayer for Oleandra and the Insurgency.

"When do you want it done?" she asked. If this was her path to rescue Rohan, she was going to take it.

"Tonight, on the Night of Nilaya, when the sacred flower rises before Astranthia."

Rea stuck out her hand to shake on it.

"What? Are you sure?" Xeranther asked in shock.

"I swore to do whatever it takes to save Rohan."

He pulled her aside. "You think you're capable of *killing the Queen?*"

"I don't know. All I know is she's going to tell us where the petal is and that's what matters right now."

Rea's eyes pleaded with him to let her do this. Knowing she could never go back to a normal life after agreeing to Oleandra's cruel condition, she needed his and Leela's support.

Xeranther sighed, and returned to his spot. "What happens if we—er—she—fails?"

"You become plant feed." Oleandra didn't bat a butterfly-winged-eyelid.

"M-me too?"

"That is the burden of a witness, Mr. Thistlewort."

The life dropped from Xeranther's face.

"No," Rea said, firmly. "I won't put them in danger again. I accept your terms, but you have to leave Xee and Leela out of it. Else, the deal is off."

"This isn't a negotiation, Princess. Either you accept the terms as they are, or you may continue without my aid. The choice is yours."

The clock was ticking, and Oleandra was her best shot at getting to the petal. Rea desperately wanted to accept the terms so she could free Rohan soon, but she wasn't going to be selfish anymore. She looked at Leela and Xeranther. They had done everything they could to help her, even put their lives on the line. It was time she stood up for them and acted as their friend.

"I'm sorry," she ultimately said. "I can't accept the barter. Finding the petal is my quest, not theirs. They have already done more than I could have hoped for." Rea stood up to leave but Xeranther stopped her.

"We accept," he said grimly, but in solidarity. "We're not letting you do this alone. I have my own reasons for justice, and I will assist you in any way I can."

"And I promised to help you get Rohan back," said Leela. "You're stuck with me till the end."

Rea didn't know what to say. Her heart trembled, thinking of the dangers they would face because of her, yet knowing they were going to be by her side made her feel so fortunate. For the first time, the burden of saving Rohan was not just hers to bear; she was sharing it with Xeranther and Leela. The load on her heart was lighter, but her resolve and courage stronger because they were in this together.

Rea felt within her the desire to avenge Xeranther's Par, to bring the Queen to justice not only for what she did to Rohan but also for all of Astranthia, especially Xeranther. And for Leela, she felt a rush of love—love for a sister, for a friend, the greatest kind in the world. From that moment, Rea knew she could never live without Leela. *This is what true friendship looks like*, she thought: a promise to always be there for one another.

Rea, Leela, and Xeranther held hands as Oleandra pulled a silver thimble from the air and pricked her thumb on a thorn. A drop of her blood fell into the vessel and she beckoned them to do the same.

"They really love sacrificing blood for everything, don't they?"

Leela muttered, as Oleandra drew blood from her, Rea, and Xeranther (whose "ouch" was quite audible).

"We are now tethered by a bloodoath—an unbreakable bond. Act against it and the price will be fatal. Praise to the nectar, evil will be purged!"

Rea faked a smile. "So... where is the petal?"

"In the Village of the Dead."

Rea glared at Oleandra for a full minute. "The Village of the—*Dead*?" She wanted to scream and shoo the butterflies from the woman's face.

"Isn't that what I said?"

"Dead as in dead, *dead*?"

"Is there another kind?" Oleandra reached for the potted plant.

"You didn't think to tell us *BEFORE* we signed in blood that we have to fight the *DEAD*?" Rea turned frantic. "I have LESS than a day left! How am I supposed to get a petal from DEAD PEOPLE?"

"Well, little bud, I—"

"DON'T 'LITTLE BUD' ME!"

Xeranther, hyperventilating himself, restrained Rea from lunging at Oleandra, who looked as calm as the moment they had walked in.

"My, that's a temper. Unsuitable for a princess. Befitting for a warrior! Now, I promised to disclose the location, not to hand you the petal. The Village of the Dead is where it lies and, oh, there will be a test. If you pass it, you will be granted access."

"A test? What kind of test?"

Oleandra shrugged. "I've never had to take it myself."

Rea seethed.

"Er... Is the village close?" Leela held Rea in case the answer threw her into a fit again.

"Well... I might have something which can get you to the village in a snap. All you do is take a sip, say where you want to go, and *poof* you'll get there."

"That would be great," said Leela.

"C-can we get some for the way back as well?" asked Xeranther.

Oleandra levelled a look at him.

"Very well," she said, dryly. "Could you summon your pari-friend? I require a sprinkle of pari dust."

Glittering motes jumped out of Flula as she re-entered the hut and Oleandra, assuming a meditative pose, hummed a chant. Fuzzy stamens, fruit fibers, rotting roots, raindrops, multiple-limbed insects, and other flora-fauna-related items flew in through the windows and into a beaker of bamboo and straw. A rush of air swished over Rea's cheeks, up her neck, and over her limbs, and a wavy strand of silver hair lifted from the side of her petal-skirt.

"Grey and wise with a smell of rolled up carpets. That can't be yours, can it, Princess?"

"That's Bajai's hair!"

The strand fell onto her dress, camouflaged again. A few more puffs later, a fleck of dry skin floated above Rea's arm. It, along with a short strand of Xeranther's hair, glided over to the hovering ingredients and dropped into the beaker one after the other.

"Floral and feisty with a force of purpose. That's you, Princess," grinned Oleandra. "Mm... salty and grimy with a taste of grit. That's your scent, Mr. Thistlewort."

Leela sneezed and a drop of nose-goo *swooshed* towards the bubbling concoction and fell into it with a sizzle.

"And what have we here? Treacly and minty with a clanging of spirit. My, Earthling, you sure live around a crowd of folk," Oleandra chuckled and summoned Flula, who shook and shimmied until the right amount of pari glitter mixed in the brew. When it was ready, Oleandra poured the concoction into four vials which they slung around their necks with a rope of twine.

"It's called wortel-motus. Root-travel. Part of millennia-old flora-magic."

"So, all we do is take a sip and say 'Village of the Dead' and it will get us there?" Rea asked.

"Aye," said Oleandra. She turned to Flula and said, "Pari, your glow is part of the brew. A smidgeon of the potion for you should do."

Rea held her hand out. "This is how we make a promise and give thanks on Earth. No blood required."

Oleandra hesitantly extended her arm and shook Rea's hand. "I rarely touch human-folk these days. It isn't as terrible as I remember," she laughed.

Halfway down the ladder, Rea ran back up.

"Did you know my mother and grandmother?"

Nostalgia flitted across Oleandra's eyes. "There was a time when I knew your entire family."

"My father, too?"

"Aye."

Rea wanted to know more, but Oleandra cut her short. "There shall be other times to visit the phantoms of your past, Princess. For now, you have work to do."

CHAPTER 26

THE VILLAGE OF THE DEAD

"On three," said Rea and they each held the vial to their lips. "One... two... *three!*"

The potion tasted bitter like turmeric water. It swished and sloshed in her stomach and when she felt the need to run to the bathroom, her face and arms and legs melted into a puddle and within seconds, she was a blob of jiggling jelly seeping through the soil.

Whooshing through a twisty-turn-y network of roots, she whizzed past rotting plants, bugs, earthworms, and a blur of under-the-ground paraphernalia until *phut! phut! phit! phut!* she, Leela, Xeranther, and Flula coalesced beside each other amidst a carcass of trees.

"That was the scariest and coolest ride I've ever been on," gushed Leela, patting herself to check if all of her had transported. "And I've been on a rollercoaster!"

"What enchanting words you use," Flula said. She stretched her wings, mouthing 'roll-er-cos-ter'.

Rea coughed out a mouthful of soil. She was glad to be back in solid form. All around, felled trunks cluttered the ground, some so large it appeared monsters had snapped them to pieces. Even for Astranthia, this place looked otherworldly.

"Sweet nectar," laughed Xeranther. He wiped the dirt off his clothes. "I'm going to ask Oleandra for a barrelful of this potion. Zipping from one corner to another, my pockets will be over-flowing with coins!"

Rea squinted through rays of murky light trickling through looming layers of nimbuses. Under their dark shadows, the trees resembled crooked hags.

"Why is it so dark?" she asked. "Isn't it supposed to be morning?"

Leela's enthusiasm of a minute ago disappeared. Low hanging clouds gathered close and the skies greyed. Flula's glow sputtered.

"We've reached the Village of the Dead. The light of the living has been snuffed o-out," she said, growing nervous. "I remember now. This is where souls go before they transition to their next life and where souls with... unfinished business reside."

"A village of souls..." said Xeranther and Rea glanced above. The rustling leaves sounded like squeals and the trees swayed as if there was something living in them.

"Oh." Flula glowed red. "Elder Pari warned us about banshees protecting this land."

"Banshees?" said Leela. "Aren't they heralders of d-death?"

"Yes," she replied in a small voice. "We are taught as foliage-reporters to stay clear of them, especially the wailing ones. Banshees feed on people's sadness and fly through the night looking for prey. When they find their victim, they let out a mourning scream so high-pitched, their victim's soul shatters, making them d-drown in their own blood."

Rea's nerves stiffened and Xeranther shuddered when a branch grazed his arm. As they traveled down the eldritch road, smoke hissed from the ground as ruins of an ancient temple appeared, forgotten and abandoned. Time passed, and they turned forlorn. Rea searched for dead people, banshees, or even a gate.

"Can we stop for a while?" Leela groggily peered through dregs of smog. "I feel tired."

Xeranther tottered with his eyes half-closed and Flula floated in a daze. Her glow had weakened, diffused to a flicker. Merely a shimmer or two sprinkled out of her. Rea felt sluggish too. The air lulled her like a lullaby. She leaned against a cypress, her eyes closing. The bark was comfortable and her troubles... what were they?

"No," she panicked. "I have to find the petal!"

Rea lunged to her feet and her eyes fell on bodies upon bodies of people glimmering in the shadows, sound asleep. She staggered to a halt. This was the Village of the *Dead*. No other living beings roamed its pathways and the ones who did—*the four of them*—were having their souls sucked into a deep slumber, maybe never to wake again.

Rea ran to Leela and Xeranther and slapped them on their cheeks. "Snap out of it! The village wants us to sleep and never leave."

Leela yawned lazily and Xeranther gave his eyes a good rub. Rea held Flula in her hands and blew on her face.

"*Aachooooo,*" she sneezed a flurry of glitter.

That's when they saw the bodies. Leela shrieked, accidently stepping on a sleeping woman's arm and Xeranther, breathing rapidly, emitted a string of incoherent Astranthian curses.

"We need to keep talking to stay awake, okay?" Rea instructed and she prayed for none of them to fall asleep. "Tell me, what else do we know about banshees?"

"I think owls mark their coming," Flula answered, fighting a yawn.

Rea thought about the owls in her nightmare and the owl on the Queen's castle.

"Banshees can also change forms," said Leela as she steered away from a corpulent man in embroidered robes. "Sometimes they appear as old women—"

"OWLS!" Xeranther yelled, pointing at a dozen fire-orange eyes blinking at them from hidden branches and the blood fell from Leela's face.

"O-Or as a y-young lady," she completed her sentence.

A beautiful woman with burning owl-eyes and luminous hair glided towards them wearing loose rags, ripped and frayed at the bottom. She was a banshee, a spirit of watery-white light and her gossamer robes shone through the willows of the night.

"Aliversss at the Village of the Dead!" Her voice, thin and singsong, flowed from two rows of needle-sharp teeth. "What do you ssseek?" she asked with a hint of fascination.

Xeranther nudged Rea and she mumbled, "Uh... we've come

to collect... the missing petal... of the sacred flower."

"Only soulsss of the dead and pure soulsss of Aliversss are allowed into our hallowed gatesss."The banshee crisscrossed from Leela to Xeranther to Rea and Flula safely tucked herself back into Xeranther's pocket. "Who daresss try?"

"I will," said Rea.

The banshee swung to the other side and signaled for her to cross. Rea took a step and the tips of a thousand needles jabbed into her. She fell on her knees.

"There's some kind of invisible barbed-wire fence," she moaned. Pinpricks of pain throbbed on her skin. Luckily, there was no sign of blood.

The banshee cackled. "An Aliver with an impure sssoul."

"What? NO!"

"A well of pain residesss in you, Aliver. There isss already much sadness in our village. You shan't be allowed."

"I don't care! I have to save my brother."

"Aliversss." The banshee swayed between Leela and Xeranther. "Who daresss try?"

"I'll go."

"Xee," exclaimed Rea. "Don't do it!" She ran after him, but it was too late. He stepped into the invisible boundary and was assaulted.

"Rocksss of anger reside in you. Ssstep away, Aliver."

Xeranther crawled back, apologizing.

"I guess, I'm next..."

"No, Leela, no," Rea screeched but Leela walked right through to the other side as if there was no invisible fence. Flula shimmered in delight and Rea and Xeranther gaped in shock.

"Aliver with a pure sssoul," crooned the banshee. "What do you ssseek?"

The banshee hovered in front of them, eyeing Leela as it awaited her answer. Leela's glasses slipped to the bottom of her nose. "I-I...er... seek the missing petal of the sacred S-Som."

"Our village isss a place where soulsss come to ressst," the banshee said as a field of frosted-blue flames appeared behind her. Scattered in their midst were gravestone plinths shoved haphazardly into the ground. "If you ssseek to unrest one of our soulsss, you must pay a price."

The blue-flamed souls wafted close and Leela pushed up her glasses.

"What k-kind of price?"

"I won't let you do this!" Rea shouted from behind the invisible barrier.

The banshee circled Leela. "The petal isss a part of a flower's sssoul. To ssseek it, you must part with a part of your sssoul."

"NOOOO," screamed Rea.

She ran ahead, and the stabs pierced her. Shouts came from everyone as she thrusted forward, first her arms, then her legs, pushing with all her might. She didn't care about the pain or the drain on her strength. If anyone was going to give up a part of their soul, it was her. Not her friend.

PHAT!

She reeled and fell face down. Her arms and legs moved jaggedly but a smile crept on her face. She had made it to the other side. Dots of blood appeared over her hands and legs and the banshee screeched like a wounded bird.

A soft, shaky smile appeared on Xeranther's lips and he turned to Flula who was covering her face with his pocket.

"Did you see that?" His eyes gleamed.

"Are you all right?" Leela helped Rea up. "That looked horribly painful..."

Rea nodded as the banshee circled around her.

"Aliver with a well of pain..."

Her heart beat fast.

"*And* an ocean of courage. Welcome to the Village of the Dead."

Rea beamed with joy.

The banshee swooped low and gave a horrifying smile. "A part of your sssoul for a part of the flower's sssoul."

"How do I—?"

"Hold it," said Xeranther, and the banshee swiveled to face him, the annoyance apparent on her face. Averting his gaze from her, he looked at the girls. "Before you give away a part of your soul, shouldn't you see if the petal exists?"

Realization slapped Rea in the face. She had been too impulsive, *again*. She turned to Xeranther, incredibly grateful.

"I want to see the petal before I give up anything," she stated, and the banshee flew precariously close.

"A memory or emotion. Pick your price."

"A memory or emotion?" repeated Rea.

"A *memory* or *emotion*?" Leela asked even louder.

The banshee remained silent, wasting no breath on repetition.

"Are you asking me to choose between giving up a memory

or an emotion?" asked Rea.

"If your price isss memory, a memory we choose will disss-appear from your mind. If it isss spoken about, you will feel itsss absence like the losss of sssomething torn from your sssoul."

Leela held Rea's hand.

"If your price isss emotion, an emotion we choose will dis-ssappear from your sssoul. You will no longer know what itsss presence feelsss like but ˋitsss absence will feel like a crushing emptiness into which nothing can be sssubstituted."

Memories of Rea tripping down the steps to her house, of her playing with Rohan, of her fighting with him, of Bajai kissing her to sleep, of her running through the tea plantations, of her sitting in school with no friends, of Amma aloof and overworked, of her, Leela, Xeranther, and Flula's friendship, of the betrayal from her family, of her fear of the Queen, of her sadness at not being a better sister, of her pain of never knowing her father, of her anger at being lied to—swirled in her head.

Feebly, she faced the banshee and the banshee began to sing. It was hypnotic. Rea caught a few words, "Hither comes, that forlorn soul," and the banshee lifted her hand to the skies.

A sapphire petal rested on her bloodless palm.

Xeranther and Flula let out a gasp.

The petal sparkled with a tinkling of tambourines and glim-mered with a beauty which overshadowed Flula when she was at her happiest. If there was ever a word to describe it, it was magical. And it lay before their eyes. Rea had to do all she could to resist grabbing the petal. Rohan would be free at last!

"Memory," she said. It was the first choice that came to mind and Leela's grip on her tightened. "Take whatever memory you want. I'm not afraid anymore."

"Wondrousss."

Rea didn't think her choice was wondrous. She had just chosen it.

The banshee dipped her head in acquiescence and the torment in Rea's soul subsided. She was ready. No memory of her past was worth more than Rohan's freedom. When the banshee stopped circling, Rea knew she had chosen the memory she would take from her.

What if the chosen memory was of Rohan? How would she rescue him? Rea realized, agonizingly, she didn't want to give up even the worst ones.

"The memory we ssseek isss of your father."

Rea's throat constricted.

"No, not Baba!" she cried, grabbing her locket. It burned so fiercely, she had to let it go.

Her mind churned. The memory of his face was draining from her soul faster than salt through a sieve. Every thought, every wish, every desire she had felt for him was being snatched away. Her insides revolted, not ready to give him up.

Then, the pain stopped. When she looked up, a shimmering, blue object rested in her palms.

"The petal! The sacred petal!" she screamed with joy. "It's in my hands!"

As fantastical as it looked, it felt like an earth-petal—soft, velvety and light. She could fold it, bend it, caress it.

"If what you ssseek isss obtained, you may return to your world, Aliver."

Rea ran back. "I passed the test!"

Flula's chin trembled and she turned the other way.

"What's the matter? I can free Rohan now. Aren't you happy?"

"Of course, we are," Xeranther said, placing his hand on her shoulder. "We're very happy." His voice faltered.

"Rea...your Baba... do you remember him?" Leela asked, her lips trembling.

Xeranther shot Leela a look.

"Baba? Who?" Rea knitted her brow in confusion. A strange feeling passed over her. It was cold and hollow with edges so sharp they scraped her insides. A deep, dark well with no way out. The emptiness wounded her. The more she tried to soothe it, the more it deepened. When it subsided, she raised her eyes to the petal.

"I better tuck it away safely," she said and put the petal carefully inside her pocket.

"You are a brave soul, Raelia of the House of Flur."

"Aw, thanks Floo," said Rea. She was confused as to why everyone was behaving weirdly. But she didn't care. She had found the petal and Rohan would be saved at last.

"Do you mind if we see the petal again?" Xeranther asked, the veneration in his voice palpable.

Rea cradled the petal in her palms, and they marveled at it, its glittering blue glow brightening up their faces.

CHAPTER 27

THE MOST TRUSTED AIDE

The meeting had ruffled Razya. For the first time in years, her rule over the kingdom had turned fragile. As had her nectar. She felt it leaking away, drop by drop. The only thing she had left was the power of the crown. With the crown on her head, she didn't need anyone. Its power soothed her. It fueled her desire to live.

Beauty was transient and love was meaningless; it had betrayed her brutally. Some say it's why she destroyed her family. The crown made her feel superior, important... worthwhile. Without it, she was no one, nothing.

Razya felt herself slipping, slipping towards the edge of a cliff. She was calling for help but no one turned. A tear slipped from her eye. She felt as she did when she was a young woman. Not good enough for Mother or Father. Not matching up to her sister's goodness. Not being loved by the man she would've left everything for.

Razya burned the tear before it slid off her cheek. As Queen, she had made sure her ministers were well looked after. The poor might have suffered,but her council got rich, their clothes grand, their properties large, and their bud-bozans greater in number. But they were turning against her, thinking the bleak chance of power was theirs to claim. Well, all except one.

"I've been waiting," she said. She was sitting in the castle's reading room, which she used for private consultations.

"Forgive me, my Queen. I couldn't risk raising doubt amongst the ministers. They need to believe I'm part of their circle."

Razya faced Ekimmu Welt, Minister of War, and her most trusted aide. Her eyes travelled over his towering stature dressed in robes of silk and horn which covered the crocodile scales on his skin. His shaved head glinted and his pale eyes glowed.

"You barely spoke in there. Didn't even touch your food. Did you think I would poison you?"

A muscle in his forearm flexed. "My Queen, I must play the part. I'm sure the goose-duck was as delicious as it looked."

So, it was true. The ministers believed they could be poisoned and standing so close to victory, didn't want to take a chance.

"Eki, the boy must be killed after the ceremony. I will not have it any other way. His presence in the kingdom is wearing me down. I feel it draining my powers."

"Consider it done, Your Extreme Greatness. I will arrange for the dwarves to carry out the orders when the time is ready."

"What about the revolts? The villagers have been quieted for now. What if they rise again? I can't simply turn them to cinder."

Ekimmu moved closer. "The Night of Nilaya has impassioned

the people but it will pass. Once you reclaim the throne, the boy will be forgotten. Things will return to the way they were. Don't forget the army you are building. The weapons you are forging. The dwarves have been loyal."

"When will the army be ready?"

Ekimmu held her look and she felt a strain at the back of her neck.

"We need more time."

She dropped her defenses, and confided in him about the missing petal. "If the girl fails to find it, I fear the people will know the petal disappeared because I took the throne..."

"Now, now, my queen. If the girl fails, feign surprise when the sacred flower rises with three missing petals. No soul will suspect a thing. When the boy's blood is sacrificed and the flower does not lose another petal, the people will sing your name. They will see you have saved them. We won't let them forget it."

His way with words eased her. Razya smiled. "You are right, Ekimmu. This is why you are my most trusted minister."

Knock!

Ekimmu stepped aside and Razya hid her twitching fingers under the folds of her gown.

"Enter," she said and Urdaag framed the door. "Is there news of the girl?"

The Sirion spoke in squawks and guttural sounds, and Ekimmu watched as pet and master communicated in a language of their own, perfectly understanding each other.

"Excellent," she said. "You have done well."

Urdaag's face swelled with the unexpected praise.

"The girl has found the petal by seeking Oleandra's aid. That silly fool, I knew she couldn't refuse a child's plea."

Ekimmu's face lightened. "That is wonderful."

He kept his words brief. Razya liked that. Shouting requests to enter the room, Torgar squeezed past Urdaag and hurriedly bowed before his Queen.

"What on Delphinus is the matter?" she said.

"Your Extreme Greatness," he wheezed loudly. "The boy bees threatening to poison hisself."

CHAPTER 28

SOUR BERRIES

R oiling nimbuses gained speed. Winds keened. Thunder clapped. Rea and the others found themselves on the edge of the woods, across the bridge from Oleandra's house. They looked at each other in relief. They had made it through.

Rea reached into her pocket and pulled out the petal, making sure it was still there. Suddenly, it vanished from her hands and reappeared a few meters away, twirling as if caught in the wind.

"Excellent work, little niece," the Queen said, stepping out of the shadows.

An eagle-like man-bird emerged from under a welter of branches and Rea stared in shock. How had she found them?

Without warning, the Queen swept past Rea and stood before the petal.

"WAIT," Rea cried. "You promised to release Rohan first."

The Queen ignored her. She slipped a nod to the man-bird

and said his name like an order, "Urdaag."

As the Sirion spread open his massive wings, Rea ran forward and grabbed the floating petal from under the Queen's gaze. She hurled a look at Xeranther and Leela.

"RUN," she yelled.

Flula, terrified at the sight of the Queen, darted into the trees. Xeranther and Leela sprinted towards Rea, and the three of them ran like the wind, making their way through the woods. They dodged trees and jumped over logs, pushing their legs as hard as they could.

Rea had never run so fast in her life. She had no idea where she was going or if the petal she had stuffed in her dress was crushed—all she knew was the Queen could not get her hands on it. She debated taking a sip of the potion, but she couldn't see Leela or Xeranther. What if they didn't drink their potion in time and the Queen got hold of them? No, she couldn't risk it. Rea ran as wildly as she could. Only once did she turn to see the Queen. She was right behind her, walking serenely as if taking an afternoon stroll.

With a flick of her aunt's wrist, Rea's legs and arms stiffened. No matter how hard she pushed or kicked, they didn't move. She shouted soundlessly, trapped inside a prison of air. Moving her eyes to the side, she saw Xeranther and Leela, both trapped in frozen bubbles like she was.

"If I may?" the Queen said and slipped her fingers into Rea's pocket. With the flourish of a magician pulling a rabbit from a hat, she brought out the petal. Her eyes glittered. "Oh, how I've longed to hold you," she whispered to it.

A smile snaked across her face. "Alas, nature daren't win against me either."

The spells around Rea, Xeranther, and Leela broke, and they toppled to the ground. Rea found herself staring at a giant claw, clenching into the dirt. She looked up in horror to see the Sirion staring down at her.

"Lock them in the Cellars," the Queen said to Urdaag and with a smirk, she disappeared in a puff of smoke.

"Spread out," Xeranther shouted, jumping to his feet. "He won't know who to catch first."

They ran in opposite directions and Urdaag hesitated for a moment. Then, he made a beeline for Rea.

"Drink the potion!" she yelled to the others, trying to outpace the giant bird-creature. But in one swoop, he hooked his talons into her petal dress and dragged her off the ground.

Leela ran toward her, but Rea held her hand to keep her away.

"Go, save Rohan!" she cried, knowing she couldn't escape the taloned grip.

Tormented, Leela rushed towards Xeranther and before Urdaag got to them, they drank the potion and melted into the ground. With a howling screech, Urdaag and Rea soared into the sky.

Rea was back in the hideous castle that Razya called home. Urdaag had dropped her like a carcass onto a narrow rampart where she was met by Dalric and a blue-skinned lizard spriggan, who had a crossbow in one hand and a spiked hammer in the other. Pretending he had never laid eyes on her or saved her friend's life before, the dwarf wordlessly led her down the rampart and into the belly of the castle, the very one she had seen in the Queen's orb. The corridors here coiled and bent under black metal arches and curved around teetering mezzanines. No railing or banister ran along its edges and Rea almost wobbled off balance.

"Bees careful." Dalric's face curdled in the ghastly-green light. "We bees entering the Cellars."

Rea wanted to remind him who she was, but her mind was heavy like molasses. A fusty smell weighed thick and she gagged, burying her nose in the crook of her arm.

"Wait here," he said, inserting a key into the lock.

Opening the jail cell, he pushed her inside. Rea stood still, numb and dazed, as Dalric secured heavy chains around her ankles and wrists. Without a word, he turned and locked the cell behind him. Green flames burned along the walls and the air was stuffy as an old winter coat. Rea stood there, listening to the quiet sounds of the Cellars.

Suddenly, brisk orders echoed in the corridor and harried footsteps followed.

"WHAT IS THE MEANING OF THIS?" The Queen stormed toward the cell diagonal to Rea's, her cloak swinging like a cape. Torgar scurried behind her. "Threatening to poison yourself, are you?"

"Finally," a voice replied. "I've been waiting for you to show your face in here."

Rea's breath caught in her throat. Pulling on her chains, she raced to the front of her cell. She knew the voice. It was dry, cracked, and a little grown up. She opened her mouth to call out his name when—

A shadow emerged from the back of the cell. When it came under the bleak light of the window, Rea saw him. He looked worse than when he'd been paraded on the streets.

"ROHAN!" she cried out, clutching the bars. "IT'S ME, REA!"

But it was as if her words had fallen on deaf ears. Rohan didn't acknowledge her. She waved her shackled arms, banging them against the metal bars to get his attention when the spriggan growled in her face.

"ROHAN, LOOK HERE," screamed Rea, not caring about the spriggan. He should have been able to hear her. They were not that far apart. What was going on? In despair, Rea realized why Rohan couldn't see or hear her. She glared at the Queen. *Shadow Magic*, there was no other explanation.

"He bees refusing to eat, Your Extreme Greatness," Torgar said. "Or d-drink."

"He bees expelling it out!" wept Dalric.

Rea glowered. The dwarves were just as two-faced as Razya.

The Queen flicked the cell door open and glided towards Rohan, her fingers shaped in a claw about to rip open his throat.

"Disobeying my orders is high treason, young man."

"Try your tricks, but I'm not giving in, *Auntie Razya*."

Auntie? Rohan had figured it out! Well, she shouldn't be surprised. In more ways than one, he was smarter than her. A prick of jealousy stubbed her. *NO*. That was the old her. She was going to be better than that.

"I've chosen to die before you steal my blood," declared Rohan.

Rea blanched at his words.

"See this book?" It was the one he had thrown in frustration when the Queen had conjured the orb for Rea to see him. "I take it that you keep the *Covenants of Astranthia* to remind the prisoners about the laws they have broken to warrant their capture. So I read the book from front to back and I know it is my blood you need for the ceremony on the Night of Nilaya. I realized it when your soldiers showcased me like a caged animal to the people of this land."

The Queen smirked. "I was beginning to think you were the dim-witted one in the family. Sitting here for days not realizing why you had been captured. Especially with these mumblers around."

Dalric's hands flew to his throat, thinking she was going to strike him, and his keys fell to the floor with a massive *clank!* Horrified, Torgar, seized them and hid them within his sleeve.

"If we are related and I'm the heir to the throne, that would mean I'm in line to be King and it should be my line of predecessors sitting on the throne. Yet neither my mother nor father are. Their names are written differently in the book, but it says my grandfather and father are dead. That is true of my family too. My grandfather passed before I was born, and my father died many years ago, but my grandmother and mother are alive, only they're in a different *world*. While here you are, reigning as Queen."

The Queen's lips uncoiled into a smile.

"I'm afraid you get no applause for your powers of deduction. The realm knows who you are and more importantly they know what *my powers* can do. You'd be wise to fear them, too."

Rea couldn't believe Rohan had figured all this out by reading *one* book while being *trapped* in a cell. The Queen's gaze turned wicked and lightening sparkled from her fingertips, forming a ball of white-blue electricity.

"You will NEVER have my blood," yelled Rohan and Rea shouted to warn him against testing the Queen's power, even though he couldn't hear her.

"Gather yourself, boy. If you must, rage against your mother and grandmother. They've lied to you about who you are, your true home, your inheritance. That's familial love for you. Personally, I was never a fan."

"I don't believe you. And even if they did, they would've done it to protect me." His eyes blazed.

Rea felt her ribs squeeze. She had fallen for the Queen's words and turned on Amma and Bajai in an instant. She felt a pang of guilt, but they had lied to her, hadn't they...?

"They knew I'd be coming for you and what did they do? Nothing!" laughed the Queen. The cell danced in electric light. "I shan't complain. It made kidnapping you rather easy."

Rohan bared his teeth.

"If you think I'm going to help you after what you've done to my family, you're mistaken. You stand here as the Queen of Astranthia, but you are in *my* hands—the hands of your kidnapped nephew, begging *him* to do your bidding."

Razya grimaced. The ball of electricity shot from her hands

and Rohan flew backwards. Ropes of current sizzled around his neck. Rea screamed, and the spriggan spat on her, demanding silence. The skin on her wrist split beneath her chains. Pain bloomed over her eyes.

"The Ceremony is tonight," hissed the Queen. "You can starve and parch yourself, but you will still be alive. It takes more than a few hours to perish. As for your threats, come up with something more believable than *poison*."

"If it's s-so unbelievable, w-why did y-you come to see m-me?" Rohan coughed as more jolts shot through him.

Narrowing his eyes, he slid a steely gaze towards the book.

"Last n-night, I came upon the c-case of Crowley Weedly, a serial seed stealer, n-notorious for stealing banned and p-poisonous seeds," he said. "No doubt you remember his p-punishment..."

The Queen's expression faltered. Rea could tell she was nervous for what Rohan was about to say.

"What about Weedly?" the Queen snapped, and the grip of electricity fizzled.

Rohan fell to the floor. He rubbed his throat, his body still jerking from the residual current.

"Well, his punishment was death by poison: the very poison from the berries of the seeds he had stolen—Moonfire berries. The book says, if you eat five, you'll die within a day."

A wild look entered his eyes, and he opened his palm. Five black-colored berries splashed in pink dots lay on it.

Rea stared in horror. *No, no, no. Don't do it, Rohan, PLEASE!*

Razya lunged for the berries, but Rohan thrust them into his mouth. Swallowing quickly, he stuck out his tongue to show her they were gone. The Queen screeched, and Rea wept.

Rohan had signed his death sentence.

"If you could help me..." he said, turning to the dwarves and they rushed to push his cot away from the wall.

A single stemmed sapling, green with leaves, growing from a hole in the floor came into view. Beside it was a shard of ceramic stone stained in blood. Rohan mimed hitting the spine of the book against the sanitation pot, which had a large chip in it the same shape as the shard.

The Queen seethed.

"It was an experiment to test my so-called 'powers,'" he said with a manic look in his eyes. "I dug a hole with that shard and then cut myself to see what feats of magic my blood could achieve. Pouring my blood into it, I thought of the Moonfire plant. I bled for hours. Right when I was about to faint, a tiny shoot wiggled from the floor. My heart lifted but my eyes closed. When I woke up, it had grown three inches. The more blood I shed on it, the more it grew. This morning, it grew berries. I thought you'd like to see them."

The Queen snarled and Torgar and Dalric whimpered in fear.

"The irony is, I sacrificed my blood after all. But this way, I get to stop your lies and deceit."

"Uproot that plant! NOW!" screamed the Queen.

The dwarves ran to pull out the plant, but a flash of red flew past them and incinerated the sanitation pot to ashes. A plume of smoke rose from where it once stood.

The Queen stared, aghast, and Rea nearly fell off balance. The ray of magic had shot out of Rohan's finger. Rea blinked, giddy with joy and disbelief. He had awoken his nectar and he could shoot energy from his hands! For the first time, she was proud of something he had that was way cooler than hers. Together, with their nectral powers, they could easily take down the Queen!

"You keep this vermin of a boy alive! You hear me?" The Queen grabbed the dwarves, bringing them to an inch of her face. Spittle formed in the corners of her mouth. "I want to crush the life out of him with my bare hands. I don't care if you have to drag him out unconscious. Keep him breathing. Or else you won't be."

She flung them aside like garbage and rattled Rohan like a child's toy. "You said I was in your hands, begging you to do my bidding. Well, how is this for begging: If you die before you sacrifice your blood on the flower, I will kill your precious little sister."

"My sister?" Rohan's voice laced with fear.

Rea wished she could break away from her cell and chains. Suddenly, she remembered Oleandra's potion around her neck. But when she looked down, there was only a locket with a sketch of an unfamiliar man.

"The poor dear came all this way looking for you and find you she did. Even ran a dangerous little errand for me in exchange for your freedom."

Rea watched the Queen's words hack into Rohan's heart.

"Rea… she came to find me?" His voice was filled with shock and tender surprise.

"Aye, she did. She almost died for you and now she rots in a cell like this." The Queen cackled and her laugh disgusted Rea. It reeked of hatred and revenge. "I was going to set her free after the Ceremony, but your disobedience will come at a price, nephew. And she will pay for it... like your father did when he tried to save you all."

Her voice was smoother than poison.

A brutal pain enveloped Rea. The same kind that hit her when Xeranther and Leela and spoke about someone called Baba. Rohan pushed aside the Queen and ran to the door of his cell.

"REA? REA? WHERE ARE YOU?" he screamed, desperately looking for her in the grimness of the Cellars. "If you can hear me, if you're really here, RUN! ESCAPE! GO BACK HOME! Send Amma here and you stay with Bajai, protect her, keep her safe."

Rea burst into tears. She was right there, a few meters away, but he couldn't see her. And neither could she bring Amma or Bajai to save them. Oh, what a mess she had made, shunning and blaming her family for everything in her life.

Rohan lowered himself to the floor, his shackled hands gripping the cell bars.

"And... Rea..." he said, tears falling from his eyes. "You were right to keep asking about Baba. I shouldn't have stopped caring. I'm sorry. I'm so sorry."

He spoke to the darkness between them.

"Every moment that I was stuck here, I worried you were kidnapped too. I begged and prayed for you to be safe, for Amma and Bajai to be safe. The only thing that kept me going was to fight and escape this prison so I could save all of you. And here you came to save me. Now, you're locked somewhere in this horrible place." Rohan shook with sobs. "But I'm going to find you, even if I just have a few hours left," he wiped his tears and stood up, the chains clanging like church bells. "I'm not giving up before finding you. If you can hear me, please don't give up either..."

Rohan broke down again. What cruel games the Queen had played, thought Rea, her heart numb with sadness. No wonder Amma and Bajai kept the truth hidden from her and Rohan. They had never wanted them to come here.

The Queen cast a disgusted look at Rohan and then flicked a gaze at Rea. Their eyes met for a second before she glided past them in disdain. The dwarves scurried behind her. The taste of the sour berries filled Rea's mouth. She could feel the beating of Rohan's heart slowing down.

CHAPTER 29

THE NIGHT OF NILAYA

Rea couldn't believe what Rohan had done. She called out to him several times, ignoring the threats of the spriggan guard. But her voice was only hers to hear. She slouched against the wall. It was over. Rohan was going to die. She probably was, too. And they definitely were not going to see Amma and Bajai again.

Rea's tears fell freely. Her magic was useless. All she could do was say 'Hi!' to a plant. Wow, amazing.

You have MAGIC. If you don't want it, give it to me! She heard Leela's voice in her head. Rea smiled, knowing it was something she might have said. She prayed Leela and Xeranther had safely escaped and that Leela had used the blood-soaked shirt to portal back to Earth.

There was nothing left to do in Astranthia.

Rea peered through the metal bars to see what Rohan was

doing, but he had retreated into the shadows of his cell. She stared at her chains, wishing she could go back in time. If she could, she wouldn't hold as much of a grudge against Amma and Bajai. Considering where she had ended up, they had good reason to hide the truth. She would've befriended Leela a lot sooner and been nicer to Rohan. She wouldn't have let him walk home alone that night, or any night. And she would've stopped pestering him about... um... wasn't there somebody or something she was mad at him for not caring about? Rea wracked her brain. There was. There definitely was. But what?

A scathing emptiness assailed her, and she curled onto the floor, her cheek pressing against a welter of tally marks and dates scratched in the ground by prisoners of the past who never escaped the cell.

This was it. Everything was over. Razya had won.

No.

Rea pulled herself up. She wasn't going to let her and Rohan become a scratch on the floor. There was still time left. There had to be a way out. Rohan had told her not to give up. She couldn't see him, but she was certain he was thinking of ways to escape his cell and come to her. Rea crawled the length and breadth of her cell, looking for a stone, a stick, a hidden panel—anything. The gaping pain in her heart had waned to an ache, but she found nothing she could use. All her cell had was a cot, a sink, a sanitation pot, and a window barred with rods. Rea pushed her cot under the window and stood on it.

A labyrinth of hedges covered in blossoms of the most entrancing indigoes and turquoise spanned before her. She was close enough to see that each leaf was bordered in vermillion as if it bled rich, luscious blood, and far enough to take in the entire maze. A breeze blew, and a wave of red-rimmed leaves danced. Freckles of water resting on the flowers caught the light, splintering into a million fragments. Rea had never witnessed a sight so alluring, so mystical.

Hoots and cackles rumbled through the corridor, and she turned, her heart pounding. Some poor soul must be getting imprisoned, she thought, and returned to the view. The labyrinth had turned into a desolate land. A red sun burned. The sky was colorless. Giant birds circled, howling cries of hunger.

Rea longed to be there. Anywhere but the Cellars.

Help me, Thubian.

Turn away from the illusion, brave one. It is there to tempt you, to remind you of what lies outside while you're trapped inside. It can m-make the prisoners go m-mad.

Their connection crackled.

You have to get Rohan and me out of here.

I am t-trying. I came because I sensed your distress, but the Q-Queen has fortified the walls with S-Shadow Magic. There are too many l-layers. It is h-hard to p-penetrate t-them.

Thubian? Can you hear me?

He was gone.

"Psst!" a voice whispered in a panic.

Rea almost screamed with glee seeing Leela and Xeranther outside her cell, and she jumped off the cot.

"We are... um... junior recruits for the—er—Order of the Salient Keepers. We are in training... and we've been o-ordered by Her Extreme Greatness to check on the prisoner before she is taken for the Ceremony," Xeranther fumbled, lying to the spriggan. "We have been asked to see if she is—er—fit for the task she is to perform for the—er—Her Extreme Great—"

The spriggan leaned low, rancid breath misting his face. Xeranther swallowed a gag.

"Hurry, take this and say Leafless Forest." Leela stealthily handed Rea a vial of wortel-motus through the cell bars. "Oleandra gave us some more."

Rea was amazed and grateful to Oleandra... until she remembered her bloodoath.

One problem at a time, she reminded herself.

"We have to give some to Rohan too," whispered Rea. "He's in that cell." She pointed and Leela stole a quick look.

"The cell's empty."

"What?"

"Rea, we don't have time. The ceremony begins soon. They must have taken him already."

There wasn't time to argue. The spriggan scratched his head and twisted his mouth angrily, snorting out a red-hot puff of fire. It was clear he was starting to see through Xeranther's rambling monologue.

"*NOW*," shouted Xeranther, and with a swig of the potion, *whoosh!* they melted into the prison floor.

A grand moon, glowing an ocean-blue, dominated the sky.

It was the Night of Nilaya. The night of the full blue moon.

Soldiers of the Imperial Guard banged their batons, ushering crowds of Astranthians into the Leafless Forest. True to its name, the forest bore not a leaf nor blossom. The trees were charred to the bone and the wind carried with it the smell of ash. Rea remembered the words in one of Mishti Daadi's prophecies, *'Past the forest widowed of leaves...'*

Spying a scrap of open space, Rea, Xeranther, and Leela charged ahead and squeezed through the throng until they had a clear view of where the ceremony was to take place. There was a podium with seven chairs on it. It overlooked an empty spot around which twelve rows of iridescent flowergrass swayed. From magical beasts to ordinary people and animals, every living creature had gathered to witness the arrival of the flower. Music blared, conches blew. Torches atop wooden poles blazed, casting yellow flares and sinister shadows.

A grimness hung in the air. Seated on the ground, Rea searched for Rohan. Nausea swept over her. She tried to settle it, but her energy was draining rapidly. Rohan was dying.

"You found her!" exclaimed Flula, sprinkling Rea with her glow. "And your brother?"

Rea's chin trembled. Just then, Thubian's voice rumbled through her mind.

Have courage, fearless one. The Q-Queen has cast a circle of Shadow Magic around the Leafless Forest. Its fortifications are strong, b-but I am trying to come to you. Be strong.

Rea swallowed her tears. Knowing that Thubian was coming gave her strength.

"Have you seen Mar, Poppy, and Berber?" asked Xeranther.

"No... but I'll look. Oh, sap! Elder Pari is here. I have to go."

Rea looked up. Male and female paries of every color began congregating on the branches of trees. Those dressed in gold and silver kept watch over the sacred spot, their glittering hues giving light to the enveloping darkness. Atop a branch bathed in leaves, Rea caught a flash of yellow. Then a glimmering purple.

"Oleandra is here," she said and Oleandra, high on her perch, acknowledged them with a nod.

"Oh no, the bloodoath," cried Leela. "I'd forgotten about it."

Rea hadn't.

"What am I going to do?" she asked, sweat dripping down her back. Without the petal, she had no leverage against the Queen, let alone any means of destroying her. Not to mention, she was going to be singlehandedly responsible for each of their deaths if she didn't fulfil the bloodoath.

"Focus on your brother for now and we will focus on the villagers. Let's worry about the bloodoath later," said Xeranther. "You're not alone, remember... we're in this together."

Rea's eyes welled.

THRUM. THRUM. THRUM.

The drums beat and one by one ministers in flamboyant garbs and faces puffed with anticipation took their seats on the podium. The seventh chair sat vacant.

A guard dressed in full regalia stepped forth.

"Presenting Her Extreme Greatness, Queen Razya of the House of Flur, Ruler of the great and bountiful realm of Astranthia!" he announced into a conch shell, sending echoes of his words across the forest.

A moment of silence followed, and then the air exploded with swirls of fire and raindrops. Floating above the forest floor, fire and water danced with the dazzle of diamonds and coalesced into the figure of the Queen. The flames cooled into a gown of crimson while the rising smoke settled into ruffles of black. Her crown, fanned by a headdress of ivory and thorn, glistened like a well-oiled weapon.

The audience and the Imperial Guard, enthralled, fell to their knees. A man, pale as bone, sheathed in robes of metallic silk with tribal tattoos on his knuckles and neck appeared behind the Queen. A chain in his hands clinked. Bound like an animal, Rohan appeared behind him, his head lolling to the side. The poison was taking effect, Rea thought in despair. Urdaag and the dwarves loomed beside him.

"We're going to get him out," Xeranther said, his eyes turning into slits. "I have an idea."

A minister dressed in a coat of cerulean orchids and a turban of ferns stood up.

"It is time," he said, looking down at a device through a monocle. His wrinkly lips twitched as he halted beside the Queen and waited awkwardly until she stepped aside and nodded for him to begin.

The minister chanted words in an ancient language. As he sprinkled water into the center of the flowergrass, a shower of stars descended from the sky and the people joined in prayer. Flowers, tiny as fireflies, bloomed from each twinkling star and twirled in the golden-blue light. Every other head in the forest was bent in reverence, but Rea couldn't take her eyes off Rohan. If the minister wasn't holding him up, he would be sprawled on the ground, barely alive.

When their prayer ended, a shaft of moonbeam aligned over the flowergrass, shimmering like a spotlight. The minister closed his eyes and raised his hands to the moon. Not a whiff of breath or flit of a pari's wing broke the silence.

Rea moved to get on her feet.

"Not yet," whispered Xeranther.

Under the moonshine, a prickly stem grew. Leaves popped from its sides and the plant rose higher. From its tip, unfurling like ribbons, opened two perfectly shaped hibiscus petals, glittering like jewels.

The front-rowers leaned forward to see the Som, and the murmurs spread. Astranthians accustomed to the loss of two petals gasped at the sight of a third missing petal.

"SILENCE," commanded the Queen. She opened her palm and the missing petal floated above. "Here is the third petal! I had to scour the realm to find it."

"LIAR!" Rea screamed, leaping out of Xeranther's grip. "It was me, Princess Raelia of the House of Flur, sister of Prince Raohan, the heir to the throne and granddaughter of the true reigning Queen Yuthika, who found it. Hand me my brother, or I will tell everyone why the flower lost its petal!"

The audience cried out and a breath of air slipped from the Queen's lips. She shot the guard a look so blistering, he could've exploded into smithereens.

"Seize her," she ordered, and the guard grabbed Rea, pinning her hands behind her back. Rea shook from side to side as the Queen's chameleon eyes fell on her angered subjects and on the open-mouthed faces of her court. She stiffened.

"It is true I employed the aid of my niece to bring me the petal. However, were it not for my powers of foresight, neither would I have known about the missing petal nor have it in my possession tonight."

The crowd hesitantly settled into silence.

"DON'T BELIEVE HER," shouted Rea. "It was because of *her*, because she stole the throne from my grandmother and mother, that the sacred flower sacrificed its petal!"

A current of magic shot from the Queen's hand and Rea crumpled in the guard's grip.

"It would behoove you to know," the Queen turned to her subjects, "that because of me, your lives are not in danger anymore. As for what I did twelve years ago, do I not have the very petal which chose to hurt us?"

"Your Extreme Greatness," intervened the minister holding Rohan. "You owe us no explanation." He stepped forward, jangling the chain to draw attention to Rohan who staggered ahead, delirious.

"As for the heir," the minister addressed the crowd, "he has poisoned himself with the deadly poison of five Moonfire berries, wanting to end his life before rejuvenating our sacred Som. Had our Queen not intervened, his selfish actions would have cost us the loss of one more petal and our lives would be eternally at risk."

"Minister Welt speaks the truth," exclaimed a minister, hairier than a mountain goat. "The Queen is our savior! Without her wisdom and swift action, the missing third petal would never have been found, while the boy would be dead before sacrificing his blood, causing a fourth petal to perish." The minister's face went rife with terror. "Who knows, how many moons our children would live to see with merely one petal on our beloved Som? Our plight would be abysmal. Our bellies would starve, our lands would burn, and our beautiful Astranthia would begin to rot."

"Aye!" said a third minister, and the Queen smiled as if she were a saint who had rescued them all.

Rea's mind reeled at how the ministers were twisting Rohan's actions. She was focusing her strength into freeing herself when a *BOOM* erupted, and beams of fiery-yellow light sprang through the air. She cowered in reflex as the crowd exploded in applause.

Rea peeked from the crook of her elbow. She couldn't believe what she was seeing.

It was Amma and Bajai!

CHAPTER 30

THE PEOPLE HAVE SPOKEN

Amma marched through the crowd, shooting rays of golden light, while Bajai followed close. The villagers kissed the ground they walked on and the wealthier Astranthians, confused by the commotion, leaned out of their seats for a better look. Recognizing their former Queen and her daughter, expressions of smug delight appeared on their faces, if only for a fleeting second.

The Queen glanced at Rea writhing in the guard's grip.

"A futile effort, little niece."

The Queen thought she had brought Amma and Bajai here.

"RELEASE MY CHILDREN," yelled Amma, halting behind the flowergrass. There was a power in her that Rea hadn't seen before. The soldiers spread out, ready to act on command.

"Well, hello, Keona, Mother. It's been a while," the Queen said with a chilling smile.

"I'm no longer the sister who loved you, Razya." Amma bared

her teeth like a wild animal. "I'm your darkest foe and you shall pay for this.'"

The Queen laughed. "Darkest foe, is it? How, then, do I have *your* children in my possession?"

Amma's golden nectar pulsed like a coin in the center of her palms.

"Razya..." implored Bajai, "It doesn't have to be this way..."

"It's *Your Extreme Greatness*, Mother," the Queen snarled.

"Look around you," shouted Amma, gesturing towards the crowd whistling and cheering at their arrival. "Twelve years later and your subjects continue to despise you. A mere glance at their true queens and their faces are alight with happiness. They are begging to be released from your miserable clutches."

The Queen's face contorted. "Is that how you want to play, little sister?"

A beam flew from her fingertips and sliced open the side of Amma's arm. Rea screamed, and the crowd shrank in horror.

"Hurt me as much as you want. You are not going to win tonight." Amma clutched her arm as blood pooled onto the ground.

"We are family, Razya," begged Bajai. "Don't do this again..."

The Queen's gaze turned sharper than a dagger's edge. "In no other realm does the crown belong to the heir who sires children first over the heir who is first-born. *Only* in Astranthia."

Amma's face hardened with severity. "That has been the Astranthian way."

"And yet, must it continue?"

"Tradition has been the cornerstone of our civilization. Generations upon generations have ruled Astranthia this way. Neither you nor I can change it on a whim. Just because it does not suit your ambition to lay claim to the throne, you have rejected our age-old custom. Life does not always go according to plan and one does not always get what one wants. But you make the best of what you have. It is a simple truth that you've never understood."

Amma stepped closer, not fearing the Queen or her guards. The authority in her voice added a charge to the air. Everyone listened, hanging on her every word.

"You blame me for having children before you and taking your place on the throne. But what did it get me? A dead husband and a curse from you that exiled our family from the land we called home, leaving my children homeless, fatherless, and penniless. Did I come raging after you to hurt you? No. Life isn't fair, Razya. When will you accept that?" Amma railed. Blood stained her white salwar.

"Look around you. Each of us, young and old, rich and poor, have suffered life's injustices. Yet we prevail, striving to do better, be better, *not* make others suffer for our unhappiness like you have. You were once a sister I longed to emulate. Smart, sincere, and beautiful. But when life acted against your wishes, you changed. Now look at what has become of you. You imprison and torture children who have never known of your existence, an existence I hid from them because I feared this day, this moment would come," Amma's voice quivered. "You betrayed our family to gain power, you treated your subjects with terror and trickery, and you hurt the Som to let go of its petal—a petal which wouldn't have been found were it not for my daughter. Tell us, what has all this hatred, vengeance, and cruelty gotten you, Razya?"

Animosity dripped from the Queen's face and she clapped her hands. "My, my, little sister. You have finally found your voice. I'm impressed. In these twelve years, none have had the courage to look me in the eye and utter such strong words. I can see you regard yourself as a wise and good woman, a woman who has made the best of her trying circumstances. Well, it is only fair then that I shed more light on your virtue and impeccable prudence."

The swirls of black on the Queen's gown flared with flames, matching the burning loathing in her eyes.

"In fact, it can be a game we play to make life more fair and give the people a chance to decide who they prefer as Queen— you or me?"

"Yes, let's see who they prefer," replied Amma. Her eyes flicked to Rea for a single moment. The look told her to run and save Rohan while she kept the Queen occupied in their war of words. Rohan had folded over his knees, and Rea kicked and stamped the guard's legs as hard as she could, struggling to free herself.

The Queen smirked. "Tell us, little sister, what were you doing the evening before you son's twelfth birthday, a day you knew I'd come for him?"

She left the statement hanging, and the nerve above Amma's eye twitched. Her gaze faltered, guilty, like she had been caught in a lie.

"Did you latch your door to protect him? Did you keep him safe at home and in bed? Did you stay awake to ensure nothing happened in the dead of night? Or did you visit the village fortune teller who was known to spin tales and steal money?"

The Queen waited for Amma's reply as Rea looked on with confusion. How did she know about Amma meeting Mishti Daadi?

"I take her silence as an admission of guilt," the Queen stated to the people. "See, I wonder, if my sister hadn't spent her energy pouring her pathetic heart out to an old fortune teller, would she have been alert enough to hear her son sneaking out of the house and perhaps stopped him from being alone on the gravest day of his life, a day she knew I would be coming for him?"

Amma's face went cold. "I don't have time for your sick mind games."

It slowly dawned on Rea why Amma had pulled them out from school that week; why she was forced to accompany her at the plantations, while Rohan had to be stuck at home with Bajai. Not knowing when the Queen would strike, her mother and grandmother had tried to keep her and Rohan by their side at all times during the day. Amma's only mistake was she hadn't considered they would sneak out at night...

A lot about Amma's behavior was starting to make sense to Rea—her aloofness, her pain, her silent suffering. Every day, she had been grappling with the betrayal of her sister. It still hurt Rea the way Amma's love for her had felt a little restrained, but she was beginning to understand why she didn't love her as freely as other mothers loved their children. Maybe Amma was afraid of the pain she would feel if she lost her and Rohan like she had when she lost her family and home.

"Frankly, I'm shocked it took you this long to show up,"

the Queen taunted Amma. "Then again, with your self-pitying personality, I shouldn't be surprised."

The right side of Amma's salwar kameez was soaking in blood and she struggled to keep her balance. Her breaths had turned heavy and Rea wasn't sure if that was because of the amount of blood she was losing or the truth of the Queen's words.

"What does that say about you, Keona, my good little sister? You knew what I was capable of and yet you couldn't save your children. It begs the question: are you fit to be a ruler if you can't even be a good mother? Why, I take it your own daughter doesn't trust you either." Amma flung a trembling gaze towards Rea and Rea looked at the ground, consumed with guilt. "Did you know she followed you when you scurried off to see the fortune teller?"

Bajai's hands flew to her lips and Amma's expression slackened.

"After that, it didn't take much for her to visit the charlatan herself. So full of curiosity about her Amma's secrets, she confided her own secrets—the kidnapping of her brother, the nightmare she'd been having. And what did the old hag do? Plant clues in her head to lead her to the portal! The very one I've hidden under your nose the entire time. I made it obvious too: A banyan. It's the only one in Darjeeling."

Amma closed her eyes and her tears flowed like rivers. Rea couldn't comprehend what was happening. How did the Queen know all of this? It was Mishti Daadi's powers of divination that led her to the banyan. Mishti Daadi's riddles and prophecies that brought her to Rohan. She had even given her the Ceffyldwer's call!

The Queen chuckled. "Aren't children wonderfully easy to manipulate?"

Her opulent gown transformed into a faded yellow saree and her striking face crinkled into folds of wrinkles. A big, red bindi grew on her forehead and her lustrous black hair turned stringy white.

"NO," Rea gasped, as the Queen cackled like an evil crone enjoying every minute of her exposé. "You *can't* be Mishti Daadi, you CAN'T! She helped me find Rohan, she *cared* for me." Dizzying spots of anger danced before Rea's eyes.

"Mind you, it wasn't easy shapeshifting into *this* every time the doorbell rang. Fools in Pokhriabasti rang it in jest and it leaked my powers each time I transmogrified," she said to Amma. "For years, I kept watch on your family, noticing what a neglected child your daughter had become. Overlooked and shunned by you. I pitied her. I knew what that felt like."

Bajai sobbed into her saree.

"But the day you appeared at my door, I realized the stars had aligned and the gods, cruel as they had been, finally approved of me."

Amma's body shook, her lips mouthing 'no, no, no' and she shrank into Bajai's arms. Rea tried to deny it, squash it, burn it, but there was no escaping the truth: The Queen had used her from the very beginning, and she had been so angry, so self-pitying, that she had fallen for it.

"I must admit, your daughter is a clever one. There's a lot of myself in her. The impulsiveness, the feistiness, the jealously, the cunning. Is that why you pushed her away, Keona? Afraid she was more like me than you?"

A crack formed in the walls Amma had built around her and a cry flew out of her mouth.

"STOP YOUR VILE LITANY OF ACCUSATIONS!"

But she didn't deny the Queen's words. Limp in the guard's grip, Rea stared at her mother. Did Amma really feel that way? Time after time, she had been told in Astranthia that she was impulsive and feisty like the Queen, that she thought with her emotions instead of a sound mind. Was she truly more like her aunt than her own mother?

"HOW DARE YOU SPEAK OF MY DAUGHTER IN THE SAME BREATH AS YOUR NAME? SHE IS *NOTHING* LIKE YOU!"

The words were a salve. The clutch around Rea's heart lessened although the relief came a moment too late. But it had come, she told herself. And for that she was infinitely grateful. Although she had turned on Amma repeatedly, blamed her, doubted her, questioned her capabilities of being a good mother, and then turned on Rohan, doubted him, blamed him, and questioned his capabilities of being a good brother, she had never thought to hurt them like the Queen had, and she had wanted to find Rohan with all her heart. Hopefully, Amma saw there was good in her and that she was not as horrible as the Queen...

The Queen grimaced. "Enough about you."

A pall of gloom fell over the Leafless Forest.

"Astranthians, as your ruler I will stop at nothing to secure your future. You can blame me if you want but it won't behoove you to dwell on the past. Our future was at stake and I did what

I needed to to protect it. When I learned about the missing petal, I led the girl here. With the untamed power of her nectar, I knew she was certain to find it. Now, ask yourselves, would you rather have a Queen who can save the fate of the realm or have one who can't protect her own children?"

"That's not true," said Bajai, her voice watery. "You tricked us, all of us. What you are doing is wrong. This is not going to give you happiness, Razya... Let us help heal you... All I ask—"

"Mother." The Queen raised her arm. She discarded her garb of Mishti Daadi and returned to her Queenly self. "Don't force my hand."

Sparks of electricity crackled from her nails and she took aim at Rea.

"N-N-No," cried Bajai. "Take w-whatever you w-want. Just give us the children."

"I will take nothing that isn't rightfully mine by destiny and power. My people," she said, casting her serpent-green eyes over the crowd, "if you desire the return of your former queen, all you must do is stand up. Stand up and choose her, and I will step aside, honoring your wishes as the inhabitants of our realm."

The people of Astranthia, terrified as they were, looked at Amma clutching her wounded arm with tears falling down her face and turned to Bajai, their once-queen, who was trembling in despair. They didn't have to give an answer. Even if they had picked the losing candidate, none had the courage to say so.

A smile slithered onto the Queen's face.

"The people have spoken."

Her gown, hot and burning, swirled with spitting curls of fire.

On her command, the Minister of Ceremony and Rites plucked a thorn from the stem of the Som and recited the holy words. He made his way towards Rohan, barely conscious in the arms of the minister who held his chains.

Amma charged at him. She let loose beams of nectar as a line of guards rushed into action, seizing her. When they came for Bajai, she cried helplessly and surrendered into the hands of the Imperial Guard she had once ruled over.

Rea wept with her whole heart.

Rohan glanced unsteadily at the approaching minister and offered his hand. The minister pricked his finger and a drop of Rohan's blood fell on the sacred Som.

CHAPTER 31

SWIRLS OF SHADOWS

A ripple of blinding light surged through the forest and the petal fused together with the sacred Som. The blast threw Rea and the guard backwards and the ministers and noble persons toppled over their chairs. Villagers curled into their knees. Soldiers held onto their weapons, trying in vain to remain upright, and flying high above, pari-folk cheered like euphoric fans.

Astranthia was replenished again.

Rea took advantage of the seconds everyone needed to recover and darted into the expanse of darkness. Her adrenaline soared. When no guards came chasing after her, she tiptoed towards the ceremonial circle. Xeranther was pocketing a fallen conch similar to the one the guard had used to announce the Queen's arrival and signaling to Leela, he climbed nimbly up a tree. A ring of golden-blue light was spreading towards the horizon and from between the silhouette of trees, Rea glimpsed the sacred flower.

Revitalized, it had begun its descent into the ground. Astranthia would live until the next heir turned twelve.

"BE IT KNOWN UNTO ALL THAT THE SACRED SOM HAS DECREED RAZYA ZULGAR OF THE HOUSE OF FLUR TO CONTINUE AS THE RULER OF ASTRAN-THIA! LONG AND BOUNTIFUL BE HER REIGN!" the guard announced over the din of people and pounding of drums.

"Beloved Astranthians," the Queen said, her arms wide.

Rohan's eyes rolled to the back of his head. Saliva frothed from the corner of his mouth and his body jerked in fits. Neither the minister nor the dwarves standing beside him moved a muscle.

Rea's eyes fixed on the stage as her body pulsed with pure nectral energy. Rage and despair coursed through her veins. Her fingers tingled. And a current shot up her spine. She could feel the blood of the nectar building in her chest like pressure before a storm.

"This ends now," she whispered and raised her hands.

Suddenly, the minister holding Rohan buckled to the ground. He twitched in pain as the Queen, mid-word, flew backwards like a bird swept up in a gale. The crowd gasped as they beheld Rea, beams of white-hot energy shooting from her palms, her nectral magic blinding. People cried and shrieked as she tossed aside the soldiers of the Imperial Guard like rag cloths. She closed her palms into a fist and the beams disappeared. When she opened them, silvery beams shot forth.

The captain and his soldiers charged at her. Their swords shapeshifted into spiked maces and arrows flew from all sides.

Amidst the commotion, Amma gave the guards the slip. She sprinted towards Rohan lying abandoned and motionless on the ground and shot Rea a glance to say, 'Escape! I've got him!' A wildness had taken over Amma and wielding her magic, she made quick work of the guards trying to stop her.

Escape was the last thing on Rea's mind. She prowled forth, her eyes on the hunt for one person. Beams of her magic swirled in the air, striking the dwarves, the captain, and the throwers of arrows. She forged ahead, venturing deeper into the forest.

Whole trees had fallen. Branches blazed. Smoke and fumes choked the air. Rea grabbed one of the flaming branches and a flash of electricity whizzed past.

She swiveled around.

Blood dripped from a cut across the Queen's cheek. Her hair had come undone, dirty with forest debris, and her gown was torn, smeared in ash. Her crown was nowhere to be seen. Rea threw down the branch and set loose two sizzling beams. She was aglow, burning with nectral magic.

The Queen ducked, firing sprays of nectar. The air turned sinister red. Rea leaped sideways, but the current pierced her, sending shocks through her body. Stumbling, she held onto a tree and it burst in flames. Mortified, she sprang to the side, gasping for breath.

"You think you can beat me? You are nothing but a tea picker from a small village in a foreign land," the Queen sneered.

"I'M AS ASTRANTHIAN AS YOU ARE. OR ARE YOU AFRAID OF WHAT I CAN DO?"

"Afraid of a child?"

Shafts of magic burst from the Queen's fingertips and Rea, prepared this time, dodged out of the way. Taking cover behind a fallen tree, she retaliated with beam after beam of her own nectar as if she was bowling in a cricket match. A fast-paced beam, a bouncer beam, a top-spinner beam! The Queen avoided all but one and fell.

Rea stepped into view. "We had a deal. You promised to release Rohan." She readied to take her aim, and the Queen vanished and materialized beside her ear.

"Get used to it, dearie. Promises mean little to our family."

Rea jumped out of her skin and the Queen cachinnated in loud chuckles.

"Betrayal is in our blood. It's a trait I've inherited just as you have. Haven't you been a betrayer, too? Lying, hiding, plotting, conniving, thinking of only yourself?"

The Queen cocked her head and Rea thought about wanting to upstage Rohan at the cricket match, to uncover Amma's secrets, to selfishly use Leela. And these she had plotted only in the last few days. Her breath quivered. She lowered her hand. Razya stepped forward, reaching for Rea.

"Don't be ashamed. It's because of these traits that you made it to Astranthia and found your brother. You did it with courage and with no help from your Amma or Bajai. See how far you have come. You discovered the banyan portal, you battled the serpent-lilies, you located the missing petal, you escaped the Cellars of Doom—you did things that no other human in the history of Astranthia has accomplished individually, never mind altogether. Your mind and grit are things worthy of praise..."

The Queen reached to touch Rea's face. The tips of her fingers grazed Rea's skin and Rea flushed pink, standing stock-still.

"You are destined for greater things, dear one. Don't play second fiddle to your brother or your family."

Rea remembered the times when Amma favored Rohan over her. It was subtle; a larger portion of food, a cleaner plate, a few more clothes, more money on books. It was the little things, the unconscious things Amma did for him that upset Rea because her mother didn't realize she was doing them. Loving Rohan and caring for his needs came more naturally to Amma than doing the same for her daughter.

"I don't intend to be a wedge between you and your family, contrary to what others might think," the Queen's voice softened, and she took Rea's hands in hers. "But I do want to prepare you for what will become of your future. Your Amma and Bajai will see to it that your brother will marry and sire children before you do. They will do this to solidify his claim to the throne—they did the same to me, favoring your Amma over me—for they always pick the children they believe they can control the most in the name of level-headedness."

She looked at Rea matter-of-factly and led her across the singed forest floor. Except for Leela, no one had told Rea she was good at anything and even though it was coming from the Queen, a part of her wanted to hear it. In her heart of hearts, she knew she had a potential she was just beginning to tap into. It surprised her that her aunt could see through her heart and into her soul more than Amma ever had.

"I have ruled for twelve years and I know what it takes," the

Queen said, facing Rea. Despite the dirt and the blood, a radiance emanated from her. "Join me, Raelia. Be my heir. I will train, groom, and nurture you. You have a thirst and a purpose within you that is required for this role, much more than your brother does. I'm not asking you to leave your family or to choose me over them. I'm asking you to imagine what kind of future you envision for yourself..."

Rea thought about their house in Darjeeling and their small, simple life, and then she thought of Astranthia and how quickly she had become part of it. There was a connection here, she could feel it. To rule this beautiful land, as a princess and maybe one day as a queen... Rea's hopes grew wings and soared high into the midnight sky.

"Your Extreme Greatness!" The minister who had conducted the ceremony ran into view, his turban falling askew. "There's been—OH!—" His gaze fell on Rea and he scurried towards her, unsheathing his sword. His opulent robes billowed in the wind.

Rea raised her arms to defend herself when the Queen hissed, "GET OUT OF HERE, LOOTIN."

The minister screeched to a halt in confusion. His gaze volleyed between Rea and the Queen. In that moment, the spell of Razya's words was broken. Rea shook her head, emptying out the deceitful temptation.

"I won't betray my family the way you did," she said, pinning her eyes on the Queen. "Your words made me feel important and for a minute I was tempted by them, but Amma is right. I'm nothing like you and even if I am treated the way you say I will be, I won't turn on my family. I will always choose them over you.

Even over myself."

In the distance, came the beating of drums.

"ASTRANTHIANS!" boomed Xeranther's voice and Rea could picture him shouting into the conch he had stolen. "THIS IS YOUR MOMENT OF REVOLUTION. JOIN ME IN AVENGING THOSE WE HAVE LOST AT THE HANDS OF A MISBEGOTTEN QUEEN. THE TIME HAS COME TO FIGHT! LET US RISE TOGETHER AND BRING BACK JUSTICE!"

His words reverberated throughout the forest. The minister hesitated for a moment and then ran towards the eruption of battle cries. The Queen turned venomous.

"I SHOULD HAVE DONE AWAY WITH ALL OF YOU WHEN I HAD THE CHANCE," she screeched, sending fireballs hurtling towards Rea.

Rea leaped, ducked, and rolled to the side. She was thankful for the minister's intrusion. It had snapped her out of the Queen's spell. She was ready now to fulfil her bloodoath.

In a stunning display, dark and light nectar clashed against each other, setting alight the night. The Queen sprang through the air, leaping ten feet high, firing bolts after bolts and Rea fought back, sustaining cuts, shocks, and throbbing lacerations. She dipped and bowed in reflex, trying to aim her attacks at the Queen's heart, but her nectar was depleting her energy and she had little time to do whatever she could to defeat the Queen.

Quickly, she snuck behind a tree and waited to gather her strength. The Queen's footsteps came closer, crackling the dry brushwood. Rea's muscles tightened. *She's going to burn me to toast!* With her heart thrashing against her lungs, she hurled a beam. The Queen barely flinched. Rea threw another. The Queen side-stepped it as if it were a puddle. Rea tried again but her magic sputtered.

A ray of scarlet nectar zipped past her head. Then, another. Then two, three, five, seven. The Queen was doling them out like candy at a birthday party, giving Rea no time to defend or attack. Cuts bled from her cheeks, arms, and legs, and just when she found a free second to shoot a beam, the tree she'd been hiding behind was sliced in half.

Shivering and exposed, Rea faced the Queen. The blue moon shone, and the air thrummed with the music of mutiny.

It was now or never. They raised their arms at the same time and beams shot to and fro. The Queen's power was stronger, and every time Rea shot out a beam, the Queen released two beams or a flaming fireball. She laughed heinously as Rea's arms struggled to stay aloft. Rea fought to keep going when in the glare of clashing magic, the Queen's lips trembled, and her eyes closed.

The Queen's powers are failing!

Rea's spirits soared and instinctively, she threw out every ounce of nectar she had towards the flora around her. Suddenly, roots, branches, tree-trunks, and the shrubbery rattled awake to her calls. Multiplying, they grew long and wide, twisting into a cage of bark, branch, root, and thorn. Rea controlled the cage with her nectar, and when she was ready, she let it drop. The Queen's eyes shot open. Thorns cut into her, roots suffocated her, and an especially gnarly branch wound around her neck. Rea dropped her hands in exhaustion as the spell-bound trees continued to do her bidding. It was time to fulfil her bloodoath.

"You were never going to win," the Queen croaked, as a ray of light enveloped in fumes spun from her finger.

It hit Rea squarely in the chest and she stumbled to the ground, spitting up blood when a second beam slammed into her. Rea screamed in pain. The cage broke apart and the Queen rose, her eyes white like Mishti Daadi's. Her lips moved and shadows from the cage of root, thorn, and branch peeled away. They stretched and swarmed over Rea, pinning her arms to her chest forcing her under their crushing weight. The Queen towered before her.

"You made the wrong choice, dear niece."

Rea gagged for breath. A memory of her and Rohan rushing towards their dinner table where Amma and Bajai were sitting with a plate of sugar-dusted chocolate biscuits and a pot of tea—its steaming aroma curling into the room—floated before her eyes. She remembered how hungry she had been and the excitement of those rare yummy treats. Rea smiled, comforted by the warmth of that memory, and then the shadows filled her mouth.

"Baccara sintera verafara," said the Queen.

The swirls of shadows smothered Rea as the last vestiges of breath strangled her chest. She lay on the cold forest floor. The moon swam. The stars dimmed. And everything dissolved to black.

CHAPTER 32

DESTINY AWAITS

T he morning light was bright. Rea brought her hand to cover her eyes. The pain was excruciating.

"Good morning." A pair of hazel eyes greeted her.

"ROHAN?"

"Oy, you're not supposed to make any sudden movements. Complete bed rest has been advised," he said, kneeling beside her.

Rea grabbed his arms and legs to make sure he was real and caring not for the pain she was in, dove her head straight into his chest.

"Ow! I didn't die before, but you'll crush me to death now," he laughed, returning her hug. The frothing saliva, the dead look in his eyes, the gauntness in his face had gone.

"You saved us," he said. "You saved me."

So, they had won!

Relief cascaded through Rea. With Rohan's help, she propped

herself up. A large bandage covered his wrist and she could smell the odors of ointment and herbal pastes slathered over her. Like a mummy, her arms, legs, and stomach were wrapped in cloth.

She looked around. Mounds of fire blazed across the forest and people scurried in and out of tents, carrying medicines, poultices and long, white sheets to cover the bodies.

Rea remembered the shadows. The Shadow Magic.

"How did we win? Where is the Queen?"

Rohan hesitated. "She—"

"She's awake!" A stampede of footsteps followed and Amma and Bajai threw their arms around Rea.

"How are you feeling?" Amma kissed her hands. Rea winced in pain, but she didn't complain.

"Like the Queen almost killed me," she replied with a dry smile.

Amma rocked her like a baby, the curve of her neck redolent of tea leaves. Despite the lies and hidden truths, Rea hugged her, breathing her in. It was an embrace she had longed for.

The sun cracked through the sky and the faces of Leela, Xeranther, and Flula beamed at her. Leela suffered a few scratches but Xeranther's body was streaked in cuts. His hair was matted with blood and a bandage around his calf splotched red.

"Don't worry, I'll live," he grinned. "What about you?"

Rea shrugged. "Me too."

She looked at everyone. "Did I k-kill her?... Is she dead?"

"After I regained consciousness, Amma left to find you," Rohan said, turning to where a mass of trees lay felled, burnt and in flames.

"It wasn't difficult to see where you and Razya had battled. There was charred carnage everywhere," said Amma. "The flora led me to where Razya was hiding. I gathered that's where you must be too. But by the time I reached the place, you weren't there, and I glimpsed a cloaked figure helping Razya—I couldn't make out who. Then in a puff, they both disappeared, fleeing the scene." The agony in Amma's eyes spoke of the unfinished business she still had with her sister.

"Wait, the Queen *fled?*" said Rea. After all she had done!

"Far away from here, I hope," said Bajai, bringing a leaf-chalice of water to Rea's lips. "If my nectar was not as old as I, I would have been of... better use."

"Bajai, you and Amma were amazing. How... how did you know how to get here?"

"You were gone three days, Reeli. We were beside ourselves with worry. We thought Razya had taken you too..." Amma quivered.

"Then I remembered the diary I had given you," said Bajai. "It was in the telephone drawer. We read everything—your nightmares, the riddles, the owls, the banyan in Sanobar..."

Of course!

Rea was relieved she had done at least one thing right by taking Bajai's advice and writing her analyses and conclusions in the diary.

"When we found the banyan, we saw your bicycles there and realized you had portaled through the tree. After we landed here, we followed the crowds making their way to... the forest." Amma looked apologetically at Flula.

"It wasn't your fault, Your Greatness," Flula replied.

"The Leafless Forest used to be home to the pari-folk," explained Xeranther.

"Pareevan, or the forest of paries, was alive once, entangled in vines and cables of the most fragrant luleblooms and covered in leaves so grandiose, we'd have to light our wings to get around. Now, the soil is burnt through and not a spot of moss can grow out of it," said Flula. "But life goes on and we love our new home of Pariland."

Amma smiled tenderly at Flula's optimism and Rea took a sip of water. If the Queen was out there, she'd be coming for her...

"You are not alone, Reeli," Amma said, sensing her fears. She held her and Rohan's hands. "There'll be no secrets between us anymore."

"Promise?" said Rea.

"I do."

Xeranther and Berber got a fire going and Bajai, Amma, Rohan, Leela, Poppy, and Flula gathered around it. Xeranther's mother along with others bustled between teams of medics tying tourniquets and comforting the injured. The moon shone a verdant blue, though paler in the wintry morning.

"I should help," said Rea. "My blood healed Xee and the villagers."

"Bajai and I donated our blood and nectar," said Amma. "There's enough to heal the ones who can be saved."

She stroked Rea's hair and Rea turned to Rohan. "You shouldn't have poisoned yourself."

"I couldn't let her have the one thing she needed from me.

Not after what she did to our family... our Baba. She wanted to kill us, but he bore the brunt of her spell and... gave his life to save ours."

Bajai nodded somberly and Amma's eyes filled with tears. An unaccountable aching seared through Rea. Rohan spoke of this 'Baba' like she should know him, but she didn't. She wanted to know more about this man, but instead a quiet sadness bloomed in her heart.

"So, how did it all end?" she asked.

Amma drew a breath and rubbed her hands over the fire. "After I carried Rohan to safety, Leela rushed to help me. Rohan was trembling with chills. His body was hot, then cold. He was delirious, slipping in and out of consciousness. My nectar wasn't helping..." She stared into the flames.

"That's when Xee began rallying the crowd," said Leela. "You should have seen him."

Rea took another sip.

"I remember hearing the drums and then your voice. The Queen's face was a sight to see. The minister who did the ceremony, he was there, too. When he heard your voice, he ran. I've never seen anyone look so afraid."

Xeranther lowered his gaze. "I felt my Par beside me, and the words came pouring out. Before I knew it, the villagers had risen together like an angry beast and we charged at the soldiers, fighting with everything we had."

"Your Par will be proud, lad." Poppy wiped a tear from his eye. "You did us all proud."

Rohan turned to Poppy. "And I wouldn't be sitting here if it wasn't for you, sir."

"Why, I'd give my right hand and left leg for my Prince!"

"I can never thank you enough."

"My grandson is right. We are forever in your debt," said Bajai.

Leela caught Rea's confusion.

"When Floo found us, she took one look at Rohan and immediately called Poppy."

"I know a thing or two about deadly bites and poison. When I was told by the dwarves that the Prince had consumed five Moonfire berries, I put them straight to work. Floo brought me suckleseeds from across the prairie, Leela scourged for whittle leaves, your Mar fetched me some forest herbs, and your butterfly friend brought me the most elusive drops of dewgold. I mixed it up and forced it down the Prince's throat. He was up and about in no time!"

"The dwarves helped?" asked Rea. "And Oleandra too?"

Her heart stopped. The battle had ended, and she had forgotten one extremely important part. She had failed to fulfil the bloodoath and now Oleandra was going to kill them.

Oleandra's butterfly face flickered through the branches and she swooped down. Rea was prepared to beg when Oleandra spoke.

"You tried your hardest, Princess, and for that I cannot punish you. You have more power in you than I imagined. A power that matches Razya's. But a power that needs training. I shall extend you more time and I'm willing to offer my services to harness and hone your nectar. When your nectral powers are ready, your time to fulfil the oath will come. We fear there are greater forces at play eviler than Razya. Your destiny awaits you, little bud, and our pact holds." She turned to Xeranther. "Mr. Thistlewort, you've been a true ally. From now on forth, you are all my friends. I wish you well. Call upon me as you desire, and I shall appear. Until we meet again, farewell." With a nod, she took a sip of her potion and seeped into the ground.

"What pact is she talking about?" asked Amma.

Xeranther turned the other way and Flula turned white.

"Er—It's nothing," said Rea. "Oleandra told me where to find the petal and in return, she wanted me to... um... defeat the Queen. Anyway, I don't understand how we won or why the Queen had to run away?"

"That part's a little fuzzy," said Rohan.

"Some villagers said they saw a Ceffyldwer tear out of the sky and bring you out of the burning forest." Leela smiled.

"And I didn't see him, *again*," groaned Xeranther as if it was the worst thing that had happened to him today.

Thubian, you came.

Of course, brave one. I wouldn't have given up on you until my last breath.

How can I thank you? said Rea. *I hope you are all right.*

I am and I'm pleased you are too. You fought valiantly.

When I'm feeling better, we will celebrate. Xee can't wait to meet you.

Thubian neighed in laughter.

Where is the Queen? asked Rea.

She fled into the nether regions of the realm. It will be a time before we hear from her, if we do at all. Rest well, brave one.

Rea smirked, thinking of the 'nether regions of the realm', a place she was certain was as far away as it sounded.

"Once the Queen disappeared, the soldiers surrendered," said Flula, her glow a mellow mauve.

"Her evil man-bird disappeared too," added Leela.

"And I suppose the minister who brought out Rohan is gone too?"

Everyone nodded.

"Naturally, the rest of the Court rushed to offer us their sincerest apologies, citing their forced hand in servitude to Razya," Bajai said.

"No doubt they want to keep their cushy jobs under your grandmother's rule, now that she is Queen again." A smile appeared on Amma's face. "Feels like we've gone back in time."

"Are you really going to stay here and take your place as Queen?" Rea asked, looking at Bajai.

"I must, mustn't I?" Bajai grinned with a twinkle.

"What can I say, Astranthia be restored!" Poppy exclaimed, raising his mottled arms.

A cheer went around and Leela sighed. "Come tomorrow, life goes back to normal."

"Same," said Xeranther, fiddling with a stalk of grass. "I'll be back to selling my trinkets and wares."

"Well..." said Rohan. "If you'd like me to get kidnapped again so you can have another adventure, let me know. I'm sure I can try and arrange it."

"No, no. That's not what we meant!" Xeranther and Leela laughed.

"The only reign I've ever known was Queen Razya's, I mean, ex-Queen Razya's and I didn't like it." A flush spread to Xeranther's ears. "Never did I imagine sitting around a fire with the royal family, laughing with them."

"That's because you're not sitting with the royal family," Bajai said. She turned to Leela, Flula, and Xeranther. "You're sitting with family."

Xeranther beamed. Flula glowed pink, showering everyone with a healthy dose of pari dust and Leela smiled so wide she could have lit up Astranthia for miles.

Leaving Bajai, the reinstated Queen Yuthika of Astranthia, to remain at the castle and get its affairs back in order, Amma, Rea, Rohan, and Leela portaled to Earth. Meruk twinkled with diyas and fairy lights. Firecrackers sparkled on the streets and rockets exploded in the sky. Bollywood songs blared from loudspeakers.

"Today is Diwali," exclaimed Leela as they entered their neighborhood. There was a loud shriek in the distance, and Leela's Amma ran to greet them, enveloping Leela in a giant hug.

"Where have you been?" her Amma cried, tears running down her cheeks. "We were so, so worried, my baccha!" Leela grinned in shock and returned her mother's embrace.

Colorful lanterns twirled in the breeze and beautiful rangolis glittered in diya-light. Strangers greeted them with "Happy Diwali!" and when the residents of Tombu saw Rohan, they rejoiced.

"Our Ram has returned!" The aunties pinched his cheeks and popped a ladoo into his mouth. "You gave us such a fright."

Rea watched from the sidelines, her heart abloom with happiness. She was glad to see the neighborhood welcoming her brother home. One of the aunties caught sight of her. With a sound of joy, she pulled Rea into a hug. The other aunties pinched her cheeks, just as they had done with Rohan, and handed her a sparkler.

EPILOGUE

"**I** need time to get used to the idea of living in the castle I was imprisoned in," said Rohan. "It doesn't quite spell 'home' to me yet, you know."

It had been a month since they returned, and Amma told Rea and Rohan they could take their time in deciding whether they wanted to move to Astranthia, and said she'd be okay if they chose to live on Earth, too. Her main concern was for them to feel safe. As for their royal duties, Bajai had employed a tutor during their once-a-week visits to the castle and relayed that the arrangement, although resulting in slower progress, was working well. It was obvious, however, even to Rohan, who wasn't the greatest at picking up undertones, that Amma desperately wanted to return to Astranthia.

"I hear you," said Rea, dipping her roti into her bowl of dal. "I've actually begun to appreciate the dullness of going to school and doing homework without the burden of saving or destroying any member of our family."

Rohan agreed and Leela sighed.

"Astranthia was the most incredible experience of my life and I can't believe there exists another realm nobody knows about except us." She grew silent, playing with the peas in her pulao. "I miss it. I miss the rush I felt there. And I miss Xee and Floo the most."

Rea missed them too, but she didn't talk about it since Rohan was still recovering.

"Have you both decided what you're going to do?" asked Leela.

"There's so much to consider," said Rohan. "What about school? My cricket practices? It's been my dream to be a batsman in the Indian cricket team. But then again, I might be the future King of Astranthia."

Rea remembered the Queen's warning of Amma and Bajai choosing Rohan to be groomed as king and strangely, she felt okay if it turned out that way. Rohan would make a great king, she thought.

Leela stared at her plate. "I'm really going to miss you guys when you leave for good. I wish it didn't have to be a secret..." She looked from Rea to Rohan and shoved her spoon into her mound of rice.

"What about you?" Rohan asked Rea.

"I don't know. Our nectar training sessions begin with Oleandra soon and seeing her reminds me of the bloodoath. Amma and Bajai don't know about it yet and I'm going to have to tell them soon. The whole thing scares me... And frankly, I think I'm more Earthling than Astranthian. Although we're royalty there, the thought of leaving Darjeeling, Meruk, and even Tombu makes me sad. I like it here. Shocking, I know. But then there's Astranthia with its whimsy and magic and Xee and Floo and the buds and the pari-golis and oh, I just don't know..."

The clock struck eight thirty.

"Shoot. I better get home."

Right then Leela's Amma yelled for her and Leela scowled. "Of all the times I've run away, how did she realize I was gone *this* time? You know, she's given me a cell phone, so she can check up on me every time she doesn't see me for five minutes."

Rea and Rohan chuckled and Leela peeked into the kitchen to thank Amma for dinner.

Rea clasped Leela's hands. "Next week, tell your Amma you're coming with me and Rohan on a trip to Mumbai and we'll go to Astranthia for the weekend and hang with Xee and Floo."

Leela's face lit up. "And we'll show Rohan a clump or two!"

Rea giggled, imagining Rohan's reaction at seeing a walking piece of grass. She waited until Leela reached home and they waved goodnight. Turning to go back inside, something on the welcome mat poked her foot and she picked it up. It was a scrap of crimson paper.

"tHe sHAdoWS aRE cOmiNG," it read.

Rea turned pale. This wasn't over yet.

GLOSSARY

agarbatti [uh-gurh-but-tee] *noun*: Hindi word for incense sticks

Amma [Uh-maa] *noun*: an Indian word (one of many) for mother

Ashoka tree [uh-sho-ka tree] *noun*: The Ashoka tree grows in the Indian subcontinent. It is a tall, conical tree with deep green leaves, growing in dense clusters.

Baba *noun*: an Indian word (one of many) for father

baccha [baa-chha] *noun*: Hindi and Nepali word for child

Bajai [Ba-zai] *noun*: an informal Nepali word for grandmother. Darjeeling, which is in the state of West Bengal, India, is home to immigrants from Nepal, Sikkim, Tibet, Bhutan and even Europe.

bindi [bin-dee] *noun*: an ornamental dot worn by Hindu women in the middle of the forehead or between the eyebrows

chai *noun*: a type of Indian tea, made by boiling tea leaves with milk, sugar, and cardamom

chalo [chha-low] *intr. verb*: Hindi word (informal) for let's go

chappals [cha-pul] *noun*: a pair of sandals, usually of leather, worn in India

chikoos [chee-koos] *noun*: a brown fruit with a rough skin but sweet brown pulp inside. Each fruit may have 4 or 5 black seeds. It is native to southern Mexico, Central America and the Caribbean, but is largely grown in India. It is also commonly known as sapota, sapodilla, naseberry, nispero.

dal [daal] *noun*: a thick Indian lentil stew

deva [dey-va] *noun*: a Sanskrit word for heavenly, divine, or god in Hinduism. Deva is a masculine term; the feminine equivalent is devi.

dhupi [dhoo-pee] *noun*: common Nepali name for *Cryptomeria japonica* trees

Diwali [Dee-vah-lee] *noun*: a major Hindu festival held in late October or early November that heralds in the New Year as per the Hindu calendar and celebrates the triumph of good over evil as depicted in the Hindu epic *Ramayana*

diya [dee-yah] *noun*: a small oil lamp, usually made from clay

dupatta [du-pat-ta] *noun*: a long wide scarf draped across the shoulders over a salwar kameez

jhumkas [jhoom-kahs] *noun*: Hindi word for a pair of traditional chandelier earrings designed in the shape of a bell

joint family *noun*: a family (especially in India), consisting typically of three or more generations, living together as a single household. It is a large family where the grandparents, father, mother, uncle, aunty, and their children live unitedly under one roof.

kaccha [kuh-cha] *adjective*: Hindi word for a dirt road or an unpaved road

keti [kay-tee] *noun*: Nepali word for girl

koel [ko-el] *noun*: The Asian koel is a member of the cuckoo order of birds, the *Cuculiformes*. It is found in the Indian Subcontinent, China, and Southeast Asia. The Asian koel is a brood parasite that lays its eggs in the nests of crows and other hosts, who raise its young. It is usually held in high regard for its birdsong.

laddoo [lud-doo] *noun*: a ball-shaped sweet popular in the Indian subcontinent

momos *noun*: a type of steamed dumpling with some form of filling either meat or vegetarian. It is a traditional delicacy in Nepal, Tibet, as well as for the people of Northeast India and Darjeeling regions of India.

pagal [paa-gal] *adjective*: Nepali and Hindi word for crazy

pakora [puh-ko-ra] also pakoda [puh-ko-dah] *noun*: an Indian fried snack

pallu [puh-loo] *noun*: a Hindi word for the decorated end of a saree that hangs loose when worn

papadum [pa-puh-dum] *noun*: (also called papad) a thin, crisp, round flatbread from the Indian subcontinent eaten as an appetizer or an accompaniment to a meal. Made from flour, it can be either fried or cooked with dry heat (usually flipping it over an open flame)

phoosky [phoos-key] *adjective*: Hindi word for someone or something that disappoints or does not meet expectations; a damp squib

pulao [poo-la-o] *noun*: a steamed rice dish often with meat, shellfish, or vegetables in a seasoned broth

Ram [Raam] *noun*: the Prince of Ayodhya in the Hindu epic *Ramayana* in which he returns to his kingdom after being banished for fourteen years and after winning the battle of good against evil by rescuing his wife Sita, who is kidnapped by the ten-headed demon-king of Lanka

rangoli [rang-o-lee] *noun*: a traditional Indian art form using colored sand or powder to decorate a floor, courtyard, or other flat surface, especially during the festival of Diwali

Ravana [Raa-va-na] *noun*: the mythical ten-headed demon-king of Lanka in the Hindu epic *Ramayana* in which he kidnaps Prince Ram's wife Sita

receding monsoons/receding rains *noun*: (also known as the retreating monsoon) The monsoon season in India lasts from June to September. During September, when the monsoon is about to leave, the northeast winds gain strength and push out the southwest monsoon winds. This action of winds creates thunderstorms causing rainfall. This phenomenon is known as the receding rains or the retreating monsoon and generally takes place in the months of October and November.

roti [row-tee] *noun*: a flat bread, thinner and softer than a tortilla usually accompanied with Indian food

salwar kameez [sal-war kam-eez] *noun*: a pair of loose pajama-like pants, narrowing at the ankles, worn with a long loose tunic, typically up to the knees; chiefly worn by women from the Indian subcontinent

saree [sa-ree] *noun*: a garment consisting of a length of cotton or silk elaborately draped around the body, traditionally worn by women from India

shikara [she-kaa-ra] *noun*: a flat-bottomed boat

thukpa [thook-paa] *noun*: a Himalayan staple of hot noodle soup mixed with meat, eggs and vegetables

tiffin box *noun*: a compartmentalized lunch box used in India

tulsi [tul-see] *noun*: Hindi word for holy basil

ACKNOWLEDGMENTS

I want to begin by thanking my publisher, Sailaja Joshi, a true visionary and a champion of bringing diverse books into the world. The email you sent me in September 2019 asking to chat about my manuscript changed my life. The publishing process can be a tough and trying journey (as it certainly was for me) but it's been nothing short of extraordinary to be a part of your vision and to undertake this exciting journey with the whole team at Mango and Marigold Press. Thank you so much.

How do I even begin thanking my incredible, wonderful, wildly talented, and brilliant editor, Amy Maranville. As a writer in the querying and submission trenches, I dreamed of my book landing in an editor's inbox and having them fall in love with it. But even in those dreams, I didn't think I would be so lucky as to find someone who understood me as a writer, my characters, and the essence of the story I was telling as much as you did. I cannot thank you enough for seeing the potential in this book and trusting that with your guidance, I could make it the best version of itself. The book has blossomed under your care as I have grown as a writer. I'm blessed to have found a friend, a confidante and one of my biggest supporters in you, and the best part: working with you has been such a load of fun! I never imagined that the young girl who began this book ten years ago in Mumbai, India, would find the editor of her dreams across the seven seas. Thank you for your unwavering support, belief in me, and for not deleting most of my flowery prose and metaphors that you know I love so much!

They say you need a village to raise a child and I can say the same about writing a book. Without my village, this book would not exist. I'm eternally grateful to—

My amazing parents, Asha and Chetan Doshi, who unflinchingly and with excitement said, "Go follow your dreams!" when I asked if I could leave my job, stay at home and write a book. I would not have had the courage to start this journey without your support.

Mom, for all the times, you went to the library when I was a little girl and brought home creased copies of The Famous Five, The Secret Seven, Nancy Drew, and Anne of Green Gables, you inculcated in me my love for books which to this day remains my place of comfort and escape. We all know you are the most gifted storyteller in the family, and I'm so glad to have inherited a sliver of your gift. Our mother-daughter trip to Darjeeling for conducting research on the book is one of my most cherished memories. Dad, thank you for making me fall in love with the art of storytelling and with the power of a carefully chosen word when you told me if I learned five new words a day, I'd know 1825 new words a year! That made me buy a pocket dictionary which I kept in my bag (a dictionary I still own and carried well into my late twenties) so I always had a way to look up a word I didn't understand when I read in trains, taxis, cars and any place I had a free minute. Your way with words astounds me to this day.

To my insightful and incredible critique partners:

Sangeeta Ramakrishnan, my best friend (the truest of all BFFs) and book-reading-partner since we were twelve, what would I do without you? This book would have had some very limp characters if it wasn't for your straight-shooting, honest feedback. No matter the time of day or the number of things on your to-do list, all I have to do is demand that you read my draft and you do it without question. You've been my very first reader and the only one who has read every single draft. I couldn't ask for a better friend—you lift me up in every aspect of my life.

To Mary Anne Williams, who would have thought two writers from the opposite ends of the world would marry into the same family and become the closest of friends and writing buddies? Your insights from a western perspective and that of a mother (I wasn't one yet when I was finishing the book) have been a pivotal part of Rea's story. With all that you do as a writer and an amazing mom of four, thank you for always encouraging my dream.

To Ratik Jain, my very first kid reader who gave me a written review which I was most fearful of reading! Your lovely words meant the world to me and pushed me to strive harder when the road turned bumpy. You asked each time we met when the book would be published, and I'm thrilled I can finally give you a copy! To Jesse Williams, my second kid reader, who on vacation chose to read my book over playing with his brother and sisters in the snow. Thank you both so much.

To my sister, Pooja Doshi-Sharma, who continuously inspires

me with her boss-mama ways and is the idol I strive to be. To my in-laws, Kamal and Boman Moradian, who supported my dream through my toughest times. To Lakshmi Iyer, your razor sharp-intelligence, thoroughness, patience, 1AM discussions and take-no-nonsense attitude got me over the finish line. I thank you all infinitely.

To my teachers at The New School where I completed my MFA program, specifically Helen Schulman who was a wonderful mentor and inspiration, and my thesis advisor Sarah Ketchersid whose suggestion of making Rea win the cricket match instead of losing it was a turning point in the book. I hope that one day you get to read this book that you've had such an influence on. To my wonderful thesis partners, Samhita Ayyagari, Matthew Mallum and Courtney England—through all our writing days, there was never a dull moment! Your critiques on the not-so-good parts and the high-fives on the good-parts have indelibly shaped this book.

To Beverly Johnson, illustrator extraordinaire, who brought Rea to life more fiercely than I could have hoped for. Not to mention, the chapter illustrations and maps you created—they are simply amazing. To Megan Boshuyzen, who designed the cover (among several other book-related creations) and patiently accommodated my many, many suggestions and requests—you came through for me every single time. To Rachel Marchant, the first person I corresponded with at Mango and Marigold Press, who has been instrumental in every aspect of the book from the cover reveal to book launch. The book wouldn't be what it is without your efforts. To Marcie Taylor, my publicist and all-round coordinator of things, I'm thrilled to have you in my corner as we navigate through book promotions, marketing, and publicity. To Kate Perry, Nina Bhattacharya and Gaby Brabazon for their incredible insights, thought-provoking critiques, and words of encouragement. Thank you all.

To my grandfather, Suman Doshi or Pops as I loved to call him, who isn't here with us anymore, but who I remember every day. I was cleaning out my childhood room in my parents' house when I found a blue-lined ruled paper with brown age spots that I'd safely kept in a folder with pages from my very first draft. I had forgotten it was you who I trusted to read these nascent, un-polished words and I will forever cherish your note on that blue-line paper. It said, 'What a mysterious way to end chapter five! I think you have great talent. Congratulations and do phone me.' I love you, Pops. Thank you for always believing in me.

To the most important girl in my life, my daughter Norah. You've turned two, and it is for you and every little Indian girl like you around the world for who I write this book. May you always see what we see—a fierce and brilliant hero of your own life's story. You inspire me endlessly.

And lastly, but most devoutly, to my husband, Rohan Moradian, after whom I named 'Rohan Chettri.' This book would not be possible without your steadfast support, your willingness to bend work hours to fit in my writing time and your belief in me and this book. You are my pillar of strength, the sun breaking through the clouds, the light at the end of every tunnel. Thank you for listening to me go on and on about plot and story ideas and understanding my frustrations when the characters in my fictitious worlds don't cooperate with me. You are my everything, forever and always.

Writers dream of many things—putting that final period at the end of the last sentence of their manuscript, seeing their words in print, holding their book with their name in their hands. It has been a decade long journey and I feel blessed to have experienced what it feels like to have a dream come true. It's like a sprinkle of pari dust.

REA AND THE SORCERER OF SHADOWS

SEQUEL TO *REA AND THE BLOOD OF THE NECTAR*

S now fell thick and fast, pelting the waters of the Sea of Lilies. Sullen clouds blanketed the sky, casting a veil of gloom that matched Rea's mood. She looked outside; her head leaning against the carriage window, her palm propped under her chin. It was her first winter in Astranthia. The snow had come early, they told her, and the white and yellow lilies, cured of their serpent curse, bobbed over the waters, stubbornly weathering the onslaught of snow collecting within their petals.

Soon, they'll sink, thought Rea, knowing what that felt like. She remembered how she and Leela had been pulled under by the wretched serpent-lilies. More than a year had passed since that fateful night on the lake. Still, whenever the water rippled, try as she might, she couldn't forget the horrific sight of the serpent-lily bite on Leela's leg and how close she had come to losing her best friend.

With a shiver, Rea pushed the memories aside and turned her gaze back into the carriage, taking comfort in the company of her friends. Xeranther was sitting beside her, and Leela and Rohan sat across. They were on their way to have lunch at the

Royal Palace of Astranthia as they did every day after school.

"We've got to find out where Razya is," Rea said. She drew her pistachio-green school robes around her to keep the heat from escaping her body. "Oleandra is getting impatient. Every week during our Vossolalia training sessions, she grills me about when I'm going to make good on the bloodoath."

The idea of another potentially fatal quest made Rea queasy. The only reason she didn't regret taking the bloodoath to kill Razya was because it had saved Rohan. The problem now was that she had to put it into action.

"Has Thubian heard anything?" Xeranther asked, a flicker of reverence in his voice. Ever since she had introduced him to the cefflydwer a few months ago, Xeranther worshipped him.

"Just that Razya was spotted in a desert called the Desert of Perpetual Dusk."

"Where's that?" asked Rohan.

"I don't know. Astranthia is as foreign to me as it is to you," Rea said with a hint of irritation, and then immediately regretted it. A year didn't turn a place into a home. Most days, she felt as clueless and lost as she had the first time she portaled into Astranthia.

They all turned to Xeranther.

"The Desert of... what was that?" he asked. Breath misted from his nose.

"Of Perpetual Dusk," repeated Leela.

"Not a blossom of an idea."

"Are you sure?" asked Rea. She wanted to know what surprises lay in store for them if they decided to go there.

"You're all aware, I don't know *every* place in Astranthia, right? Although, if you want to go during exams week then count me in. It would be a better use of my time than failing a pile of tests."

"Oh, you'll be fine!" said Leela, slapping his knee tenderly. "I'll bring my notes and we'll study together, okay? Besides, it's multiple choice—those exams are much easier."

Rea sighed. "I feel you, Xee. Whenever I don't know the answer, I always check the second option. Probability says you'll luck out with at least a few."

Xeranther dropped his head. "Ugh, I hate exams."

The royal carriage, drawn by three silver horses, gave a low rattle as it trundled along a lilac-stone bridge.

Bajai's first order of business as Queen had been to build a bridge over the Sea of Lilies, connecting the palace to all Astranthians. It arched, long and wide, over the mammoth lake. Under Amma and Bajai's reign, the bridge became a symbol of the New Astranthia. Citizens from all over the realm gathered together and planted the most beautiful flowers along its railings in tribute to their true Queens returning to the throne.

Rea cracked open the carriage window as she always did when they reached the bridge. White, iridescent blossoms with glittery stamens wrapped the bridge's parapet from end to end like strings of mogra on a bride's hair. She breathed in their scent—dense and heady like summer flowers in an earthen pot. Amma had magicked the blossoms with her nectar so they smelled like tea leaves and tuberose, Rea's favorite flower. She had known Rea and Rohan were going to miss Darjeeling terribly.

"Anyway, it doesn't matter if we don't know where the Desert of Perpetual Dusk is," said Leela, rounding the conversation back to Razya. "Since it's in Oleandra's best interest that we find her, I'm sure she'll brew us more of the root-traveling wortel-motus potion that we used to get to the Village of the Dead."

"And how are we going to get to Oleandra?" asked Rohan. He loosened the stem-belt around his school robe. The cold hardly ever seemed to bother him. Rea, on the other hand, shivered and quickly closed the window. "Amma never lets us step out anywhere without *him*."

He eyed their chaperone, a man dressed in Astranthian winter casual—a russet-leaf-tunic, softbark trousers, a coat of feathers, and a jute-woolen hat—who doubled as a soldier and a caretaker. He was sitting in front with the coachman, out of earshot for once. "Besides even if we did figure out how to get to Oleandra and the desert, how do we find Razya?"

"Glad you asked," said Rea, grateful that Rohan wanted to help shoulder the burden of their bloodoath in spite of never signing the oath himself. There was a time when they couldn't count on each other. Thankfully, that time was in the past. "Leela and I had an idea."

Rohan traded a quizzical look with Xeranther, and Leela nodded for Rea to go on. They'd been discussing ways in which they could hunt down Razya, and it was only today in class that they stumbled upon something intriguing.

"We know that Shadow Magic is the darkest application of nectral magic and that its effects can linger a long time. Sometimes for days or even years," said Rea. The others nodded, encouraging her to continue. "Well, Leela and I were studying for ethics class, and we found this interesting passage in our *Civics of Nectral Magic* textbook." She dug around in her bag and presented the worn, leather-bound book. Beneath its title were the words: *Rights and Duties of the Bearers of the Nectar.* "There's a list of places mentioned in here that were destroyed or damaged by Shadow Magic. One of those places is the Reed Caves. It isn't too far away. A day's journey at most."

Xeranther leaned back. "I'm not so sure I like where this is going..."

Rea glanced at Leela and then out the window. They were barely halfway to the palace. The bridge stretched before them, seemingly without end.

"Wait a minute," said Rohan. "You both *actually* think we'll find Shadow Magic at the caves?"

"We can't be sure until we look, but if we're lucky, maybe we'll find some lingering residue..." Rea tried not to sound too hopeful.

"But would we know when we saw it?" asked Xeranther. "I don't know about you, but I could be standing right in the middle of a ring of Shadow Magic and not have the faintest idea."

"He's right," said Rohan. "Not to mention the last time someone might have used Shadow Magic there was probably years ago."

Xeranther nodded, unwrapping a yellow aam-fruti. He squeezed his eyes shut when the mango-flavored candy burst into a fizzy sherbet in his mouth and he licked his lips, relishing its sweet and tangy taste. A drop splattered on his lotus-pink school robes and he wiped it with his ungloved hand. Xeranther *never* felt cold. "If I remember correctly, Shadow Magic has no color or appearance that can be spotted easily. It changes with every bearer's intentions and motivations. I reckon we wouldn't know what to look for."

Leela turned towards him looking impressed.

"What? I pay attention in class sometimes," he grinned.

"I had to kick you awake in *History of Astranthia* today."

"On my orders!" Xeranther said, and Leela laughed, shaking her head.

"Rea, what do you think?" asked Rohan, raising an eyebrow. "Isn't it a problem, not knowing what to look for?"

"Not for now," she replied. "Leela and I considered it, and we think we might have found a way to identify Shadow Magic."

"Please, do expound," he urged with a regal gesture. Only Rohan could carry off using unnecessary fancy words and sounding pompous while not offending the people around him. It was no secret that one of his biggest pet peeves was not being in the know about something others knew about.

Some things never change, thought Rea, with an affectionate eye-roll specially reserved for him.

"Okay, so in your *Study of Manifestations* class, you're learning how to use your nectral powers to create manifestations, right?" Leela chimed in, waving her arms excitedly as she tried to demonstrate creating a nectral manifestation.

"Like when Razya turned into Mishti Daadi?" Rohan asked with a slight tilt of his head.

"Er, sort of."

"I'm not following the connection," said Rohan.

"Me neither." Xeranther shook his head.

"Well," Rea said, turning to Rohan, "Leela and I were wondering if there was any way you could create a manifestation that I could charm to sniff out Shadow Magic."

"Like a dog that can follow a trace..." explained Leela.

"...and lead us straight to Razya!" Rea finished.

"Let me get this straight," said Rohan. "Your plan is for me to manifest into a being whose nose you will charm into having super Shadow Magic sniffing abilities that will then lead us to Razya?" He glanced at them with such skepticism that Rea, on hearing their 'plan' being described like that, realized it was as stupid as licking an icicle. Just last week, she had licked one thinking it might taste like a popsicle but instead her tongue got glued to it!

"Don't look at me," Xeranther said, holding up his hands. "You're the one who has to turn into a dog."

Rea glared at Xeranther. But he was right. Rohan was the most crucial aspect of this far-fetched plan and she didn't want him to think it was ridiculous. Ever since she had saved him, he told anyone who listened how brave and smart she was to have found the portal and battled Razya. She didn't want to lose her newly acquired standing in his eyes. Or anyone else's for that matter. She had finally begun to shed the image of being the 'dumb twin.'

"What if you tried an *outward* manifestation instead of turning yourself into the manifestation? That way I can charm the object with a sniffing spell, and we can take it to the caves to pick up the scent of Shadow Magic," said Rea.

"Great idea!" exclaimed Leela. "It would also take away the pressure to get the charm spell right the first time. Incorrectly charming an inanimate object would be infinitely better than incorrectly charming Rohan's nose with super-sniffing abilities and causing potential irreversible damage."

Blasting buds, I hadn't even thought about that! Rea shuddered at the thought. She looked at Rohan, but he was biting the inside of his cheek like he always did when he was assessing a situation. If she had to guess, she'd bet he was trying to work out if she and Leela had lost their minds.

Snow sprinkled over the bridge like a dusting of flour on a dough-ball of roti. Rea waited for Rohan to say something, anything. Thirty seconds went by. *Thirty-one, thirty-two...* The only sound filling the silence was the clip-clopping of the horses' hooves.

"You know what, it could work," Rohan said, giving a definitive nod, and Rea squealed with delight. "I'll have to do some research, but I think I can create a manifestation that will do the trick."

"We knew we could count on you!" Leela said, high fiving him.

"I still don't understand how we're going to do this, but if everyone's on board then we're going during exams week," Xeranther stated, once and for all, as though exams were the scarier of the two options.

"Let's not get carried away," said Rea. "I don't know if the plan will work."

"Only one way to find out," said Rohan. "Let's get to the

palace and brainstorm on possible ideas. I already have a few I can think of."

He had automatically assumed the role of a leader even though it was Rea and Leela's idea. Things like that rarely bothered Leela, and for the first time Rea didn't mind that Rohan was taking charge. She could tell his mind was racing with their next steps. He looked beside himself with excitement even though he was the one who had had the worst experience with their last adventure. For a brief second, Rea felt as if she, Leela and Xeranther were the cool kids Rohan wanted to hang out with, and she smiled.

Suddenly, the carriage trembled, and a flash of billowing white robes flew past them. They peeked out.

An Asurai Master was galloping towards the palace on horseback.

Leela frowned. "Protocol suggests you cannot supersede a transporter of royalty unless permission is obtained. The Asurai Master had to know this was a royal carriage. The crest is hard to miss."

"The silver horses are pretty telling too," said Xeranther. Silver horses were exclusively bred in the palace stables and were only used by Astranthian royalty.

Rea didn't care about royal protocol. It didn't bother her that the Asurai Master had overtaken their carriage. Last time she checked there were no speed limits on horses in Astranthia.

"*Why* is he in such a hurry though? It has to be something serious." She opened the carriage window and stuck her head out. The galloping horse was already out of sight. An icy gust of air buffeted her face and she quickly drew the window shut.

Rea slumped in her seat as the carriage rolled along leisurely. At this rate, they would never catch up with the Asurai. They needed to go faster, but the coachman was under strict instructions by Amma not to drive recklessly.

Then, Rea's eyes glinted.

"Hold on tight, Baxflut Uncle!" she yelled to the coachman, who she felt uncomfortable calling by his first name alone. It was unthinkable to address an elder like that in India. "You, too, Sepai Sabir!" The steely chaperone turned towards her, his expression stoic.

Placing her palm on the door, Rea concocted a charm, weaving the right words with the right intentions. Her woolen-hemp gloves embellished with frozen dew glowed silvery-golden. As she cast forth her nectar, it flowed through her fingers, onto the window, and over the carriage wheels. Swift as wind, the carriage lifted above the ground, and flew towards the palace.

Xeranther, Leela, and Rohan lurched backwards but their shock quickly turned into knowing grins.

"Diddley dingleloppers!" yelped the coachman as the horses whinnied. He swiveled to face Rea, who winked at him, and he roared with laughter. "Fly, fly us, high into the sky!" he sang as Sepai Sabir rigidly held onto the carriage railing. He wasn't pleased, Rea could tell (although that was his general disposition anyway), but this time she made sure to give him a heads-up before wielding her nectar. She had learnt early on (after a spine-shuddering reproach) that he did not enjoy being surprised.

As soon as the carriage came to a halt, the four of them

jumped out and darted towards the palace. Rea glanced backwards to check if Sepai Sabir was furious at her, but he gave her the tiniest nod as he tucked away a lock of sun-golden hair that slipped out of place from under his hat. Rea grinned and ran to catch up with Rohan, Xeranther and Leela, who were almost through the ornate palace doors.

The last thing Bajai had done before handing over the reins of Queenship to Amma was restore the Royal Palace of Astranthia back to its former beauty. She had banished the macabre rot that Razya had infused into sconce, wall, and chandelier, and replaced it with warmth and welcome. The dark, grim façade had been painted over with hues of peach and mauve with sparkles of gold and pomegranate pink. The creepy, decayed flowers that once covered the walls were gone, and in their place, opulent and delicate blossoms rich with fragrance and song detailed door frames and vestibules. The bone-colored balconies with their gaping holes, which had once given Rea the shivers, were repaired and decorated with rainbow-colored ivy. The palace felt like a celestial garden in the heavens of Indra—fresh, airy, scented, and magical—as if new life had been breathed into it.

Rea, Leela, Xeranther, and Rohan dashed past the household staff polishing silverware in the Lunch Chamber and ran across the Grand Hall, the Reading Parlor, and the Court's Quarter until they spied the Asurai Master's white robes disappearing behind the doors of the Throne Room.

"An official meeting!" exclaimed Leela, who had studied *The Complete Guide to Royal Procedure, Protocol, and Etiquette* from start to finish and knew all the rules. If she were asked, she could explain in detail what rooms were used for which meetings and what type of food was served during feasts and banquets. Rea tried to keep track too, but etiquette failed to interest her. She had read four chapters and given up out of boredom.

"Please, might we enter?" Rohan asked the guards stationed outside the Throne Room.

They shook their heads.

"It's important!" said Rea.

The guards refused, blocking the door further. Defeated, they turned to leave when an exclamation of horror rang from within the Throne Room.

Rea grabbed Xeranther's arm.

"That was Bajai," she said, her eyes wide.

"If Amma asked for Bajai's presence at the meeting, something serious is afoot," said Rohan.

The three of them turned to Rea with a look she knew all too well. Rea shook her head. "This is exploitation, you know. I could get into serious trouble."

"Pleeeease," said Leela. "You're the best with charms."

"Fine," Rea said, giving in. Since their adventures last year, she had trouble saying no to Leela. Besides, she wanted to eavesdrop on the conversation as much as they did.

Ushering them around a corner, Rea concocted a simple spell to charm their ears so they could listen to what was being said inside the Throne Room. Her ears tingled with a buzz and when she looked at the others, their ears had grown considerably larger. Huddling together, they ran back to the Throne Room and pressed their heads against the wall.

"It's like we're back at the Whispering Walls!" Leela said, excitedly.

"Thankfully, I haven't been kidnapped again," Rohan said, and Leela's face fell. Xeranther looked away and Rea tried to think of something to say to defend Leela.

"I'm kidding," chuckled Rohan. "You don't have to take me so seriously!"

They sighed with relief.

"What are you lot up to?" asked a light, tinkling voice behind them.

"Flula, you're here!" Rea turned towards the Pillywiggin pari fluttering above their heads. Her paisley-shaped wings glimmered in gold. "Come hear this," she said, and charmed Flula's tiny ears.

"The S-Sorcerer of Shadows?" Bajai's voice quivered. The gang exchanged looks.

"Are you certain, Mitra Bhuma?" Amma's voice rang forth, her tone strong and clear. "If memory serves me, he's been dead for centuries."

A typical Amma response, grinned Rea. First to poke holes and get straight to the point.

"Yes, Your Greatness. The readers of the Som postulate that the Sorcerer of Shadows has indeed returned," Mitra Bhuma said, the fear palpable in his voice.

"Who's this Sorcerer?" Rohan asked Xeranther, who looked every bit as clueless as them.

He shrugged. "Never heard of him before. Floo?"

Flula shook her head.

"Shush!" said Leela. "We'll miss something."

"When my Zulgar was King, we heard rumors that the Sorcerer had mastered a Shadow Magic charm to make him immortal..." said Bajai.

"Even if that were true, why rise now?" asked Amma.

"We can't say for certain, Your Greatness." The Asurai Master cleared his throat nervously. "As you know, Queen Razya was his pupil. She learned to wield her Shadow Magic through his teachings. We fear that Razya's defeat might have enraged him. It might be why he has chosen to rise, wanting to reclaim the Kingdom of Astranthia that was once his."

Mitra Bhuma went silent and Rea heard Bajai take a sharp breath.

"The readers of the Som also believe that the Sorcerer has darker plans—plans to taint the Som's nectar so that every being with a living soul will be forever damned to live in sorrow. The Som fears that if a tainted blossom were to portal into other worlds like Earth, the curse of sadness will lay seed and spread there, too."

"How does one go about tainting the nectar of our sacred Som?" Amma asked in a tone Rea had grown up listening to. Cold, hard, and matter-of-fact. She couldn't see the Asurai Master's expression, but she could well imagine the nervousness Amma's stare was eliciting in him.

"I'm afraid we have not a seed of an idea," Mitra Bhuma said and Rea imagined his gaze lowering to the floor.

"Oh, Razya, what have you dragged us into now," Bajai whispered under her breath. The spell carried her saddened voice to each of their ears.

"It is imperative that you do everything in your power to

learn how the Som can be tainted, if such an occurrence is even possible," ordered Amma. "And I require more proof that the Sorcerer has returned. I won't have my people thrown into a panic simply because of a portent reading."

"Indeed, Your Greatness. I will see to it right away."

"Mitra Bhuma, your discretion is vital."

Rea was picturing the Asurai Master nodding his head when a bang threw her off-balance. She scrambled to her feet and noticed that the guards had been pushed aside and the Throne Room doors thrown open. Before anyone could stop her, Rea rushed into the chamber.

What she saw made her stop dead in her tracks.

A dwarf dressed in tattered robes embroidered with the royal crest of the House of Flur stood before Amma and Bajai, struggling for breath. His hair was disheveled and matted with dirt. His hat and coat were filthy. Bloody toes peeked out of the holes in his boots, and in his hand, he held a shapeshifting mace made from copezium. Shadows swirled from its spikes, sizzling like black steam, as the weapon settled into the shape of an axe.

Amma rose from her throne, towering before the intruder. Golden nectar thrummed from her palms like balls of fire threatening to be hurled.

Rea staggered back a step. She recognized the dwarf. It was Torgar: one of Razya's guards. He had saved Leela's life, but he had also betrayed Rohan and fled with Razya. She glared at him with fury and loathing.

Why was he back?